Copyright

Other novels by the same author

Closure

Jokerman

To Square the Circle

1

Lieutenant Art Gardiner and his partner, Detective Sergeant Gina Garcia, waved their badges and walked straight through customs at JFK airport before making a bee line for the coffee bar. It had been a long and tiring trip and they were both happy to be back on American soil after what had been an unexciting but necessary trip to Santiago. They had been called as material witnesses to provide evidence on a cold case involving the murder of a young teenage girl and her involvement with an employee at the American Embassy in Santiago. However, with that case put to bed they wanted nothing more than to get back to normal duty and the general chaos that comes with it.

Having finished their coffee they grabbed a taxi and headed straight for the 9th Precinct building on East Street, Manhattan where they are based, arriving there in time to witness their boss Captain Marcus Delgado giving a young newcomer a right earful about some evidence that appeared to have gone astray.

"I see you haven't lost any of your lovable charm during our absence, Captain." Suggested Art, somewhat cynically.

Delgado wheeled round at the sound of Art's voice. "Welcome back you two, it's good to see you back in harness. Go and get yourselves sorted out then you come and see me, Art, there are things we need to discuss." He turned away and headed for his office as Art turned to his partner with a raised eyebrow. "Nothing much has changed while we've been away." Gina shrugged it off. "Did you ever think it would?" she asked.

"Let's do as he says and get ourselves sorted out," suggested Art, "then we can find out what has our illustrious leader's knickers in a twist." With a casual shake of the head he wandered off in the direction of his own little office, while Gina went off in in search of a free workstation.

It didn't take Art long to rifle through the bundle of files that were gathering dust on his desk and once he'd sorted through them he went off in search of his boss and was waved straight in.

"Come on in, Art, it's good to have you back." Delgado almost sounded like he meant it. "There's something important we have to discuss so your arrival back here is well timed." Art grabbed a chair and planted himself in front of the desk, happy in the knowledge that he hadn't done anything for his boss to find fault with. "You sounded a bit rough on that young rookie earlier, is it something I should know about?"

"Forget it, Art, it's already sorted, and we have more important things to discuss." He pulled a file from his in-tray and waved it in front of Art's face. "This overrated piece of statistical jargon tells us we're in danger of having our budget cut." He slammed the file back down on his desk in disgust. "I have no idea exactly how big a reduction they have in mind, but you and I both know that the only way we can conform to anything drastic is to shed staff and we're not exactly over-staffed as it is."

"So what do you intend doing about it?" asked Art, looking justifiably concerned.

"Our friends up in the higher reaches of this fine establishment have been making noises about each unit giving up at least one Sergeant, and as you know we're not exactly overloaded in that category, and the one who falls into that exclusive category is your fiancé Gina, going on a last in first out basis." Art took a step back and folded his arms defiantly. "She's the best sergeant we've got, Marcus, you know that. Surely you're not seriously thinking of letting her go?"

"It might never come to that but since you're my next in line I feel duty bound to give you fair warning, and please do not mention it to anyone else yet, and definitely not to Gina."

Art looked resigned to the inevitable, knowing there was little he could do about it even if he was minded to. "Let's just keep our fingers crossed and hope for the best then," he suggested, "now what have we got on the go that I can get my teeth into?"

"Believe it or not it's all very quiet at the moment," explained Delgado, "in fact it's been that way since you and Gina went off to Santiago. Maybe I should send you away more often and keep the crime figures down."

"You should be so lucky, Chief, but are you seriously telling me you have nothing on the go that needs the attention of an experienced detective?"

"Nothing of a serious nature, Art, a few shop break-ins, a number of car thefts and a couple of out of luck homeless guys passing away in their sleep, most likely from an overdose; plus the usual run of petty larceny of course." He rubbed his hands together energetically "Apart from that there's no need for any overtime, thank heavens, but it's all very low-level for someone of your standing to get involved with."

"Did you say a *couple* of homeless guys?" asked Art. "That's right, but it's nothing to worry yourself over. Just a couple of crack addicts with nowhere to live I imagine they were probably hitting the happy sauce to help them cope with their situation. When you think about it you can't really blame them; who the hell wants to live rough on the streets of this messed up city?" Art wanted more information, and it showed on his handsomely rugged features. "Did they die in each other's company?" he asked.

"Yeah, it looks that way, but what's got you interested? It's not exactly the crime of the century for a couple of down-and-out's to kick the bucket."

"Probably not, Marcus, but you know me, anything out of the

ordinary needs a look. We don't get many homeless guys littering our streets, not around here, let alone two snuffing it together. When did this happen?"

Delgado shrugged his beefy shoulders. "They were discovered yesterday morning not very far from here by one of our own patrol guys and a young street cleaner."

"Well you're probably right, it doesn't sound like anything terribly exciting," conceded Art, "but if any more turn up I'd like to take a look, okay?

"What can I say? If you're so interested why don't you have a word with young Vince, he's the one following up on it. I'm sure if there's anything dodgy going on he'll welcome your input, but I don't recommend you get too excited."

Art got to his feet and made to leave but Delgado hadn't finished. "Remember what I said about these proposed budget cuts, Art. I don't want you telling Gina and have her worrying unnecessarily about something that might never happen."

Art gave him a thumbs up and disappeared through the door to wander round the main office, his mind preoccupied with thoughts of early retirement, at least it was until he spotted Vince heading his way.

"Hi, Lieutenant, good to have you back, how was Santiago?"

Art shrugged off-handedly. "Pretty boring, Vince, certainly nothing to write home about."

He reached out and wrapped his arm around the young detective's shoulder. "Why don't you and I head for my office, and you can bring me up to date with what's going on. The captain didn't have much to say on the subject when I met up with him."

Vince followed him round a couple of desks and into his office. "There's nothing in the pipeline that would interest you, Lieutenant, it's all very routine stuff." Art eased the door closed behind them. "These homeless guys who turned up dead, is there any connection between them? It sounds a bit unusual that both of them turn up so close together on our patch, and just a few blocks away from our station house?"

"We haven't found anything suspicious. The story goes that they were both members of a group of four who travelled from state to state together and ended upon our patch about a month ago?" He stopped to think for a moment, but Art could see there was something preying on his mind. "If I'm perfectly honest I'm not sure what to make of it, Lieutenant, but we'll know more when Boswell has finished his examination." Art slid into his chair and gave young Vince a steely look, aware that there was something bothering him. "Would I be right in suggesting you're not entirely happy with Delgado's take on the matter?"

Vince definitely looked slightly uncomfortable, in fact he cringed visibly at what was going on in his mind. "It's not for me to question our Captain's judgement on these matters, after all, he has a lot more experience than I do."

"Stuff his Goddamned experience, Vince, you're the guy out on the street so why don't you tell me what it is that's getting up your nose?"

Vince pointed to a vacant chair and Art waved him into it, and once he was comfortable he folded his arms and stared up at the ceiling like he was looking for heavenly inspiration on how best to explain himself. "I think we sometimes take things at face value round here just because it's the easy way out." He sounded annoyed.

"Easy way out, take things at face value, what the hell does that mean? What exactly is it that we're not following up on?"

Vince shifted uneasily on his chair, it was as if he had said more than he wanted to and regretted it.

"Come on, Vince, out with it, you've known me long enough now to know that I will always support you when you're in the right, no matter who it upsets."

He went round his desk and planted his ass on the edge of it right in front of the young detective. "So why don't you stop being so bloody shy and just get on with it. Tell me what's bugging you so we can

5

discuss it openly. I'm on your side remember."

Vince took a deep breath and let it out again through puffed cheeks. "I know I'm not the most experienced detective in the squad, but when I smell a rat I at least expect to be allowed to go hunting."

Art stroked an imaginary beard as he studied the young detective. He had a lot of respect for him as he had shown himself to be both canny and intuitive and ever-willing to go the extra mile to get the job done. Which was enough to suggest that if he smelt something nasty going on there was probably a good reason for it.

"Get on with it, Vince," prompted Art, "you have my full attention, so get it off your chest."

"Thanks, Lieutenant, I appreciate your support. I'm a bit put out that the captain is so quick to accept that these two homeless guys were just a couple of junkies who overdosed."

He stopped talking to gather his thoughts before carrying on. "I did a bit of checking once we realised there were *two* fatalities, and what I discovered makes me think that we might be barking up the wrong tree." Art prised himself away from the edge of his desk and went back to his seat. "What did you find to make you think that?" he asked, looking much more interested.

Vince shifted uneasily on his chair before answering. "You know as well as I do that we don't have many rough sleepers in this area, but these two fatalities were part of a group of four young people who had moved into the area within the last month. Their group comprises of two guys and two young ladies who met up somewhere along the line and have stuck together ever since. So much so that they genuinely care for each other and share their cash and their food equally amongst the group."

He paused for a breath. "Each one of them has sworn to me that none of their group ever touched drugs of any sort. They were very convincing about this, and they certainly convinced me that they're being truthful." He raised his hands palms open in a questioning manner. "If this turns out to be true, as I believe it will, then how the

6

hell did they die from a drugs overdose?"

A frown gathered on Art's face as he thought about what he'd been told, and it was quite a while before he got round to saying anything. "Who was it decided that these guys had died from a drugs overdose?" he asked.

"It was first muted by the paramedics who were the first responders, but it was also confirmed by our own medical examiner." Art could hardly believe what he was hearing. "I don't get it, Vince, if Boswell has confirmed the cause of death to be a drugs overdose then why the hell are you querying it? If anybody round here knows what they're doing, it's Boswell. Surely you're not arguing with his findings?"

"There's a bit more to it than that, Lieutenant. You can check the statements I took from the other group members. Every one of them maintain that they are very close knit and have stayed closely together every day since they arrived here. They're willing to swear that no one in their group had any opportunity to buy drugs without the others knowing about it. And they are absolutely adamant that drug taking has never been an issue within the group, in fact they told me that they discussed the matter quite openly and are all totally against the use of drugs." Art was even more confused by this. "That may well be so, Vince, but if the toxicology report tells us they died from a drugs overdose, that's factual forensic evidence that can't be disputed."

"I'm not disputing the evidence, Lieutenant, what I'm concerned about is how the drugs got into their system in the first place, when we're told that neither victim was a known user?"

The frown revisited Art's face as he considered the matter a little longer, leaving Vince sitting in silence with a concerned look on his face as he questioned in his own mind if he was doing the right thing.

"Are you suggesting they were murdered, Vince? Is that what this is all about?"

Vince screwed his face up and shook his head in denial. "No, not necessarily murdered, but there is the possibility, unlikely though it might be, that they somehow managed to take the drugs unknowingly, or by mistake, but yes, when I think about it I suppose I do see murder as a possibility."

Art stroked an imaginary beard again and gave it even more thought. "Where are the rest of this group right now?" he asked.

"I have them lodged in a nearby hostel on a temporary basis."

"Where you authorised to book them in there?"

Vince shook his head before answering. "No, I wasn't authorised, but I thought we might want to question them more formally, so it seemed the logical thing to do. Anyway, it's not costing us anything as I have an arrangement with the manager."

"Okay, Vince I'll take a look. Bring me the statements you took from the group, and the toxicology report, and let's talk our way through this in more detail."

Vince got to his feet and headed for the door, but before he got there, Art gave him a quiet word of warning. "Let's keep this between the two of us for now, Vince, okay?"

"If that's what you want, Lieutenant who am I to argue." He turned to leave, but Art still wasn't finished. "And ask Gina to pop in and see me on your way out, Vince."

Vince gave him a thumbs up and went off to find Gina.

It was only a matter of minutes before she stuck her head round Art's door. "What's up, lover? Vince says you want to see me?"

"Come in and grab a chair." Gina dropped into the chair Vince had just vacated. "Have you been updated on these two homeless guys who snuffed it on our patch?" asked Art.

"Well, not exactly undated, Vince mentioned it in passing, but why do you ask? Surely there's no need for you or me to get involved in something that Vince is already dealing with?"

Art screwed his face up. "I'm not committing myself to anything at the moment but I'm definitely going to have a look at what he's got and see where it takes us. Young Vince suspects there may be more to this than meets the eye and from what he has tole me I'm inclined to think

he's on to something, so I reckon it's worth a more in depth look."
Gina didn't seem to agree "From what I'm hearing on the shop floor
it's just a couple of homeless junkies overdosing, which isn't exactly a
crime wave."

"Be that as it may, but I want you to get on the blower to Boswell
and find out exactly how the drugs that killed them were administered
or ingested by the victims." He leaned forward in his chair. "I think
quite highly of Vince, as I imagine you do, and I don't see him as the
sort to go off at half-cock without cause." Gina got to her feet with a
cheeky grin on pretty her face. "You can't help yourself, can you, Art?
You'd make a bloody mystery out of a fairy tale if it got you out of this
building and back on the street." She made a move for the door, but
Art wasn't finished. "Before you go, Gina, make sure you keep this to
yourself for now and tell Bow to do the same as it's not exactly
official, if you get my drift." He winked and waved her away.
Gina was no sooner gone before Vince turned up again with the
statements and the toxicology report.

"Do you want me to sit in with you, or should I come back when
you've read it?" he asked.

"Give me fifteen minutes to look through it, Vince, and then pop
back." With Vince gone he sat back in his chair and started going
though the case folder, and quickly discovered that the statements
from each member of the group backed up the argument Vince had
put forward, and generated, with fierce conviction he noted, the same
high level of doubt over what had happened that Vince had voiced.
There was also a statement from the innocent street cleaner who had
found the bodies, and another from the patrol officer who was first on
the scene and had alerted the paramedics, but when neither of these
offered anything useful he switched his attention to the toxicology
report.
According to Boswell both victims died from a massive overdose of a
very powerful cocaine-heroin based drug thought to be Speedball, and

although that had yet to be confirmed it was undoubtedly a very potent drugs cocktail that was more than capable of being lethal. Having read the report he was about to go for a coffee when Gina walked in on him, he stopped reading and looked up, greeting her with a question. "Well? he asked, "What did Bow have to say?" She shrugged offhandedly. "Not an awful lot if I'm honest, well not to me anyway, but I get the feeling he's close to siding with Vince. I'm only guessing mind you as he didn't go into any detail. Which has me thinking that you should pay him a visit and find out for yourself."

"Have we managed to identify the victims yet?" he asked.

"Yes," confirmed Gina, "admin have come up with the goods. One of the victims is from Mississippi and the other is a British national, which is a bit odd as I can't figure out what a guy from dear old England is doing prowling our streets. No doubt we'll find out soon enough, and if it's any help, their possessions are being held downstairs in the evidence room." Art got to his feet. "A Brit you say. I hope to hell that doesn't go muddying the waters." Gina shuffled her feet impatiently. "I'm not trying to tell you what to do, Art, but I do think you need to have a chat with Boswell." Art sighed like he was already tired of the topic. "Okay, I will if you think it's necessary, but since you're so keen to side with Vince on this I want you with me in case you need to get involved if thing go downhill on us. There's a distinct possibility it could pan-out the way Vince sees it and we end up with a full scale investigation."

They left the office together and headed off to meet up with Boswell, with Art looking like he had other things on his mind, quite likely the threatened departmental cut-backs and they were still a big worry for him as he walked in on Boswell.

"Well, well, well," muttered the pathologist, "would you look what the cat dragged in." His comment was no less caustic than Art expected and was typical of frequent exchanges between the two men, who were actually close friends. "So how was Santiago?" he went on, "or is that too secret to discuss with us mere mortals about?"

"Santiago was fine, Bow," replied Art, "and I'm sure if there were any secrets you would know all about them by now, nothing much gets past you." Boswell sniggered quietly. "Kidding aside, Art, what brings you down to my lowly domain. Or is that a secret too?"

"I'm sure you already know what that is, Bow, since you were discussing it with Gina just a short while ago. Boswell turned away and wandered back behind the bench where he had been working. "Maybe you should tell me why you people upstairs are so interested in a couple of homeless stiffs? Is there something going on that I'm not aware of?"

"Just routine enquiries, Bow. We need to track down their relatives and pass on the sad news so any information you can grace us with will make that a little bit easier." Boswell crossed his arms over his burly chest. "I know you guys well enough to know when something's cooking, so let's have it, mister secrecy, what's going on?" Art shook his head. "It's nothing for you to get worked up about, Bow. Young Vince has a bee in his bonnet over the idea that these victims died from a self-inflicted overdose. I've listened to what he has to say, and I'm tempted to suggest we take a closer look. Better safe now than sorry later." Boswell raised an eyebrow. "And what has this, *closer look*, got to do with me?" he asked. Art shook his head. "Don't get your knickers in a twist over this, Bow, nobody is pointing fingers, let's just say it would be beneficial all round if you were to take a more in depth look at the cause of death and explain exactly how the fatal overdoses were administered. That's all I'm asking of you."

Boswell came out from behind the bench he'd been leaning against and dropped into a chair on the other side, well away from Art and out of reach. "One other thing you can do for me, Bow," suggested Art, "is to confirm, or rule out, any evidence of habitual drug use prior to the fatal overdoses being administered." Boswell got back to his feet again and folded his arms, looking quietly at ease with himself. "I can tell you right now that there are no track marks on either victim, and no other *obvious* signs of heavy or persistent drug use, and before you ask, Art, I have already sent both hair and blood samples off to the toxicology lab for further testing. I followed this through because I have enough experience to know what a persistent drug user looks like; and experience tells me that neither of these guys fit the profile." Art smiled readily. "Well done, Bow, I knew we could rely on you to be one step ahead of the game. How soon before you get the results?"

"Later on today, I hope but I can't guarantee it."

"Give me a bell as soon as soon as it comes through," said Art, "I know this isn't an official investigation yet, but young Vince is very reliable and if he suspects there could be more to this than just two homeless guys overdosing I'm obliged to support him, and it goes without saying that I would appreciate your help as well."

"I'm behind you all the way, Art, just keep me up to date with developments." Art gave him a cursory thumbs up and ushered Gina ahead of him out through the door.

"We seem to have Bow on side, and I'm certain if there's anything to help clear this mess up then he'll find it. It's really interesting that he already has doubts over the manner of these two deaths, and without any prompting from you or me. So why would he even be bothered if they were previous users or not unless something got his dander up?" They continued on their way to Art's office where they found Vince already in attendance. "Sorry to keep you waiting, Vince, but I thought it would be useful to have a quick word with Boswell before we met up again." He brushed past the young detective, leaving him and Gina following behind. "Grab a seat you two, I think we need to talk this through and get some sort of action plan in place in case it gets more serious." He dropped into his chair and put his feet up on the desk "I'm siding with you on this, Vince, in so much as I can see there is more that needs looking into."

He thumbed through the file Vince had left him before passing it to Gina. "Read up on this and find out who is tracking down the victims' relatives. I want to know where we are with that. Then take Vince and head over to the hostel where he has the rest of this group bedded down and do in-depth interviews with all concerned. Vince has indicated that they are all very open and eager to help so it shouldn't take long. Most of all I want to you to probe their inner feeling about what has happen and gather as much personal background as you can on the whole group." He got back on his feet. "I'm off to convince our illustrious Captain that this is the proper course of action, and although I don't for one-minute think he'll agree I intend to have my way so he will just have to accept that we three are all in agreement on the matter." He glanced down at his watch. "It's eleven-thirty now so try and be back here by around three or four o'clock so we can see what we've got before the end of play. Okay?" Gina gave him the thumbs up and led the way out with Art heading off to see his boss.

Delgado looked up when he saw him at the door. "Come on in, Art, but please don't take too long as I'm up to my eyes in paperwork right now and I need to get on with it?"

"Got that, Marcus, but we need to talk about these two guys who died on our patch. I've already had a quick look at it and discussed it with Gina, Vince, and Bow, and we all suspect that there's more to it

13

than just a couple of druggies overdosing" Delgado leaned back in his chair with his hands clasped behind his head. "I don't remember asking you to look into it, but setting that aside it seemed straight forward enough to me so what tweaked your nostrils?"

"It just doesn't smell right, Marcus. Gina and Vince are interviewing the rest of their little group as we speak, and if nothing comes to light then we'll walk away, but I would like your blessing to give it another forty-eight hours and see what we come up with. Things are fairly quiet around here anyway so we're not neglecting anything important, and we don't want City Hall finding us with our fingers up our bums with nothing to do. That might convince them to cut our budget even more."

Delgado didn't like what he'd heard. "Using the budget as an excuse is a bit of a low blow, Art, even if I do accept your argument that we need to keep busy." He got out of his chair and rounded the desk, standing over Art. "Are you sure you're not just eager to get back in harness after being away, or is there sufficient evidence to warrant an investigation?" "Something doesn't smell right, Marcus. It's likely nothing for us to worry about but I would like the forty-eight hours to prove it one way or the other." Delgado went back behind his desk and waved Art away. "You've got twenty-four hours, so get your ass out of here and start looking." Art raised his six foot one inch frame to its full height and nurturing a sense of achievement was gone before his boss was back in his chair.

2

Gina and Vince arrived back at the station house much later than they had hoped and found Art behind his desk grinning like he'd won the numbers. Gina got straight to the point. "We have a young lady downstairs who I think you need to listen to, Art, and I think it's much better you hear what she has to say first-hand. She's one of the four from the group we interviewed, and I think you should listen to what she has to say."

"Who is this young lady?" asked Art. "Her name is Claire Mathews," explained Gina, "she's twenty-three years of age and comes from Toronto in Canada, and from what she has told us she was in a relationship with the British guy who died, a guy by the name of Roger Bentley, and she stressed the fact that it was a close and serious relationship. A point that is strongly supported by the other group member, but that said our main interest comes from the fact that she strenuously rejects any claim that her man was ever a drug user. A rebuttal that is vehemently supported by the other group member in similar robust fashion." Art closed his eyes and ran his fingers through his hair,, When he opened them again it was to scrutinise the expressions on the faces in front of him. "Judging by the expressions your two faces you're obviously accepting what she told you as the truth. Or Am I misreading the situation?" It was Vince who took up the challenge. "The way I see it she's far too convincing for us to do anything but believe her." he prompted.

Art shrugged his shoulders in acceptance "Okay. Bring her up and let me hear what she has to say." Gina nodded to Vince, who took off and headed downstairs.

"I hope we're not being duped by this lot, Gina." muttered Art. "I don't see it that way," countered Gina,. "this young lady is very articulate and bright as a brass button, so I think you need to listen to what she tells you. She's far too forceful with her argument that her boyfriend was ever a drug user to be play-acting. Vince and I both rate her as the genuine article." Art gave a wry smile. "You know I trust your judgement, Gina, and you have Boswell on your side since he's casting doubts as well, so I guess I'd better listen to her since you've already brought her in."

Two minutes later Vince walked in with a rather striking looking young lady in tow. A young lady who did not have the appearance of someone who was homeless and living rough. "This is Claire Mathews, Lieutenant." Offered Vince, by way of an introduction. "Thank you, Vince. I think you and Gina can be getting on with something more important for now." The two of them shot off leaving the young lady in front of Art's desk.

"Please take a seat, Miss -- Miss, sorry, is it okay if I call you Claire?" he stammered. She nodded in agreement. "I'm Lieutenant Art Gardiner, Claire, and I'm very sorry to hear about your sad loss. It must be very distressing for you losing your boyfriend in such a sudden and unexpected manner so I will try not to add to your distress. My detectives have indicated that you have reservations about the manner of your boyfriend's death, which compels me to try and understand your reasons for doing so. You should be aware that this conversation is entirely of the record, so you have absolutely nothing to be concerned about. Are you okay with that?

16

"Thank you, Lieutenant, I do understand, and I'm very grateful to you for taking my grievances seriously. I'm no fool, Lieutenant, and I know how Roger's death must appear to others, but you didn't know him like I did or you would be as eager as I am to clear his name of the accusation that he was a drug user."

"You're quite right, Claire, I didn't know Roger, and it would be a great help if you were to introduce me to him in a way that gives me some knowledge of him as a person and his background. Can you do that for me?"

She moved to the edge of her seat in her eagerness to get started. "Of course, but I think I should explain what our group is all about first so that you have an insight into the relationship between us as a unit before I get round to Roger, if that's okay?" Art nodded and settled back in his chair. "In your own time, Claire."

She pursed her lips before getting started, but it looked like she knew exactly what she wanted to say. "We met up as a group just over two years ago at a rally for underprivileged stricken children. It turned out that we all had similar views on the issue which was what brought us together. As a result of this group agreement we decided to travel the country to assess how serious the situation is for young children. Our aim was to highlight those areas where we found child neglect to be most prevalent and uncover what we considered to be the main issues involved. We would then hold a series of rallies to highlight the issue and raise local support to put pressure on the authorities to take action. Roger was the main driving force behind our group, and I'm not sure we will carry on now that he's no longer with us."

Tears welled up in her eyes and she fumbled in her pocket for a tissue. "I'm sorry," she sobbed, "but I find this very distressing."

"Can I get you something, Claire?" offered Art, "a glass of water, or a coffee, or would you like to take a break?" he asked.

"No, but thank you, Lieutenant, I'll be fine in a moment, I promise. I need to get round to the subject of Roger." She wiped her eyes and settled back in her chair. "I found Roger to be a quite remarkable person." She had a far-away look on her face as she reminisced over this. "He was extremely intelligent, very well educated and beautifully spoken with what I can only describe as an upper crust English accent. Having said that he was no sort of snob, quite the opposite in fact, he was the most down to earth human being I have ever been fortunate enough to meet." She paused to gather her thoughts. "I'm afraid I can't tell you anything about his life prior to us meeting up as for reasons known only to himself he was very private about his family background and his life prior to joining up with us. I must admit that I always had a feeling deep down that he wasn't on the road out of necessity, that just didn't seem to fit, not to me anyway. I believe he was doing so with a definite sense of purpose."

Listening to her Art became absorbed by her, and her general attitude, but he wanted to know more. "Would you say he was being *secretive* about his personal life?" His guest shook her head. "No, I don't think secretive is the right word, I would say he was just being a bit private, for while he was a very open person in many ways, I sensed that deep down he had some kind of hang-up with his family. I didn't see it as anything more serious than that, and as I'm sure you know, Lieutenant, we can all suffer from family hang-ups." Art nodded in agreement. "Yes, I understand all that, but this detailed description you've just given me of Roger has me wondering why he was on the road in the first place? He doesn't come across as the kind of guy who needs to bum his way around the country." His visitor almost choked on his last comment. "None of our group, *bum their way around*, as you so crudely put it, Lieutenant, we each have a definite purpose in life and we always ensure that we find enough casual employment to pay our way and maintain a reasonable standard of living. We have enough skills within the group to secure casual work for at least one of us wherever we are, and as we share everything equally amongst the group we don't suffer from any serious issues." Art screwed his face up at the rebuke. "I'm sorry, Claire, I didn't mean to be offensive, believe me, I'm just a little confused as to why Roger found it necessary to be on the road when it appears from your very elegant description of him that he was more than capable of finding employment. But you will be pleased to know that we are in the process of tracing his relatives and should be able to tell you more about his family background when our search is concluded."

"Thank you, Lieutenant, I would be very grateful any information you can give me as there are a few blanks in our relationship that need filling in." Art smiled readily. "I must ask you and your friends to remain at the hostel until we have concluded our early investigation. If we do decided there is a case to investigate you will be informed, and I promise to keep you informed regarding any of Roger's family connections that come to light. So unless there is something else that you feel might be helpful I see no reason to detain you further, but thank you for your assistance, Claire, and once again I am very sorry for your loss. We'll be in touch again as things progress."

Mathews made to get out of her chair but hesitated momentarily with a thoughtful frown on her face. "There is one other thing, Lieutenant, although it might not have any bearing on what happened, but I think you should know that Roger and our friend Sam were both away from the rest of us on the night they died. They had been working some distance away at a burger bar and must have decided to spend the night where they were found rather than travel back to join us. Although I have to say that was definitely a first as we always planned to stay together as a group whatever the circumstances."

This last piece of information had a profound effect on Art and brought a deepening frown to his handsome features. "How unusual would this have been?" he asked.

"It was a one off, Lieutenant, a first, we definitely expected them to come back and join us." She was very adamant and forceful with her response.

Art found this last piece of information extremely valuable, if somewhat concerning as well. "I would like you to discuss the matter of this temporary separation with my detectives before you go and give them as much detail as you can about where they were working and when and where they were expected to re-join you on that night. Can you do that for me before you leave please?" Mathews nodded her agreement. "Certainly, Lieutenant, I'll be only too pleased to help."

Art picked up the phone and rang Gina who wasted no time getting back to his office, arriving there just as he was ushering his young visitor through the door. "Claire has some valuable information on where Roger and his friend were working on the night they died. So get all the details of that, and when you've finished check out the burger bar and the area where they were found to see if there is any CCTV coverage we can use. If you find any get them back here asap. I'm heading for the evidence room to go through our victims belongings, so you can drop Claire off back at the hostel when you've finished with her." Gina was eager to get down to business. "I'm on my way, Art, but you need to know that Bow was looking for you earlier, but he didn't want to disturb you while you had a visitor so you need to give him a bell." She was on her way through the door with Claire in tow before he had time to reply.

3

As soon as Gina left Art grabbed his phone and hit Boswell's number, drumming his fingers impatiently on the desk top while waiting for him to pick up.

"Hi, Art, thanks for getting back to me." He sounded unusually cheerful. "I've just received confirmation from toxicology that the hair follicles from both victims show no evidence of persistent drug abuse, I can also confirm my own findings that the drugs that killed both men were administered orally and were digested along with their last meal, namely a beef burger. It seems like you get good value for your money with a Big Mac these days."

Art wasn't amused. "I'm not in the mood for your jokes, Bow, although I do find this confirmation from toxicology really interesting, especially as it clears the air on any frequent drugs use by the victims. I mean, come on, Bow, do we honestly believe these guys were stupid enough to deliberately shove drugs down their throat while they're enjoying their evening meal? It just doesn't make any kind of sense. Something stinks and I intend to find out what it is. Vince was spot on to raise the hare over this and while I enjoy our little chat I have to go, but I will keep you informed as things progress and thanks again for your help."

He replaced the phone and headed off to the evidence lock-up, where he found Sergeant Norwell safely hiding behind his glass kiosk. "Hi, Lieutenant, what can I do for you on this fine day?"

what can I do for you this fine day?"

"I'm after the belongings of our latest two street deaths, a Roger Bentley and a Sam somebody or other."

"Sam Blackwell is the name you're looking for, Lieutenant, but I'll go and get their things right away." He was hardly gone a couple of minutes before reappearing with his arms wrapped round a couple of back packs, sleeping bags and other belongings. "If you intend taking them away you'll have to sign, time, and date the register, Lieutenant, I'm required to retain the witnessed contents list from inside the bags until you either return them or they go to court as evidence. I know you're aware of the procedure, but I'm obliged to remind you by law, sorry."

"Yeah, I know all about that and you're just doing your duty, Sergeant."

When they'd finished the paperwork Art headed back to his office with two large bundles filling both arms and draped over his shoulders as well. Once inside he dropped them on his desk, poured a coffee from his flask, and settled down to the task in hand.

Picking up the bag labelled Bentley he undid the security tag and shook its contents out on the desk. The first thing to grab his attention, and it really did grab it, was a Chubb key ring with a key attached. He was rather puzzled over what a down-and-out who was living rough wanted with a Chubb key. His attention was further roused by the identity tag attached to the keyring and he stared at it long and hard, deep in thought with all manner of questions running through his head. The cause of this intensity was the identity tag attached to the key ring that indicated it was for a storage locker at JFK airport.

Taking the key ring with him he headed off to his boss's office at a rapid rate of knots

When he got there Delgado looked up and shooed him away. "I'm too busy right now, Art. You'll have to come back later." Art waved his comment aside. "You're not too busy to hear what I have to say, Captain." he insisted. Delgado looked up from what he was doing. "I beg your pardon! Are you hard of hearing or something?" Art waved his rebuke aside yet again and sat down in front of him. "We may have a homicide on our hands, Marcus, and from what I'm looking at it could well get complicated." Delgado downed-tools and looked at him over the top of his glasses. "Get on with it then, but this had better be good." Art gave him a quick run-down and when he'd finished Delgado put his hand over his mouth in a thoughtful pose and shook his head slowly from side to side. "What in the name of all that's Christian is a street bum doing with a storage locker at JFK?"

"My sentiments exactly, Captain. I need to get over there and check it out." He tossed the key ring up and down in his hand for a moment or two as he thought things over. "Are we making any headway finding their relatives?

Delgado shook his head. "Not that I know of, Art, so get your ass out there and chase things up for me, just do what you need to do to get things moving. I'm getting all the wrong vibes about this bloody thing." Art got to his feet and headed for the door, leaving Delgado nursing his rumbling ulcer. He headed back to his own office to contact the admin manager, who promptly told him they were having difficulty chasing down anyone in the UK called Roger Bentley that wasn't accounted for. This little set-back prompted him to go back and take another look at the victims personal effects, and after a bit of eager searching he uncovered a small black plastic bag sewn into the

24

lining of Bentley's sleeping bag. The mystery deepened even more when he opened it up and discovered a passport in the name of someone called Benjamin Silverman, plus a platinum credit card in the same name issued by the National Bank of Switzerland. He immediately booted up his laptop Googled the name and came up with a couple of likely candidates. The one that stood out like a sore thumb was a sixty-five-year-old man of Jewish descent who had an address in an up-market area of England called Seven Oaks. According to his lengthy and very detailed biography he was the father of one son and was a person of considerable wealth as the Chairman of several high-profile companies dealing in precious stones, plus other assets with overseas connections in both oils and precious minerals.

Thankfully, the bio also contained a recent photograph of the individual, a photograph that looked like an older version of the face on the passport in Art's hand, convincing him, without having to think too much about it, that both men must be related. If this was right, and the victim had this vast wealth behind him then why on earth was he hiding behind a false identity and bumming his way from state to state? He was unable to conjure up an acceptable answer, but being convinced that the two men were related he decided to dig a bit deeper and eventually came up with the name of older man's legal advisors. A company listed as Mendelson and Ackermann who had offices all over Europe and America.

Further searches through the dead man's belongings turned up a little piece of paper bearing what he believed was a British national health number, an invaluable piece of information that would prove the guys true identity when they had it checked out. All they needed to do was contact the proper authorities to get their answer, which wasn't something he wasn't willing to do; that was a job for someone further up the ladder and it needed doing with some urgency. Shoving the documents back into their little bag he headed off to interrupt Delgado one more time, but he was waved straight in this time by a boss who looked suitably expectant. "What's the buzz, Art, you look like trouble is brewing."

"You're not wrong, Marcus, trouble could well be brewing. I think we need to get in touch with the British Embassy about this dead Brit because from what I've uncovered without even digging too deeply, he appears to have serious family connections. When I googled him I came up with a guy I believe to be his father, judging by the fact that they share the same name and an uncanny facial likeness, more importantly the guy is a serious highflyer and extremely wealthy into the bargain. He's the chairman of a sizeable corporation that deals in everything from diamonds to oil and precious minerals. If he proves to be our young victim's father, and I'm convinced he is, we need to tread a bit warily and stick rigidly to protocol."

He stopped to think for a moment. "The old boys legal representatives are a company called Mendelson and Ackermann with their headquarters in London, so I guess you had better make contact with them as well as the family to confirm that he *is* the young victims father." He stretched his shoulders to ease the building tension. "I have the victim's passport and credit card, plus what I believe to be a British nation health number to back this up. So now you're in the picture what do you reckon our next move should be?"

"No harm to you, Art, but I wish to hell you'd stayed in Santiago, every time you come through my bloody door you bring me a load crap to deal with." He ran his fingers through his hair. "But you're right about one thing, if these two guys are connected we will need to tread a bit warily. We don't want to cause any sort of rift with our

British friends, we've already had one international incident recently when one of our thoughtless citizens killed a young British lad by driving on the wrong side of the road. We sure as hell don't need another incident of that magnitude." He rubbed a hand over his brow. "You'll have to leave this with me for a while, Art, I need to get the commissioner involved and get him to have someone contact the British Embassy, but you were right to bring this to me as the whole thing was almost swept under the carpet as just another couple of homeless guys suffering an overdose. It has the potential to be a lot more than that now by the looks of it." He ended with a loud sigh.

"It sure looks that way, Marcus," agreed Art, "I have Gina and Vince interviewing the victim's pals as we speak. They seem to be a harmless bunch of do-gooders who have been travelling state to state as a team for a couple of years. They'll also be interviewing the staff at the burger bar where both victims were working on the night they died and check for any CCTV coverage in the area. I hope they come back with something useful." He rubbed the back of his neck before going on. "Bye the way, Marcus, I don't intend going over to JFK just yet, I'll leave it until I hear from Gina in case she turns something up." Delgado nodded affirmatively. "Good thinking, Art. I'll get straight on to these legal guys and see what the buzz is with them. Come back to me for an update after you've been to JFK." Art gave him the thumbs up and headed off.

It was well into late afternoon before Gina and Vince put in an appearance. Art met up with them at the tech lab to view a couple of CCTV recordings they had uncovered. The first of these showed both victims walking along the street and was timed at eleven-thirty-two on the night they died. While the second video showed them being joined by two other guys who were carrying what looked like a couple of take-away food cartons, both of them were wearing baseball caps

27

pulled down over their brow and scarves up over the lower part of their faces. The recording showed all four men engaging in a brief conversation with the victims accepting the food cartons offered by the other two men. Both of these charitable benefactors were much taller than the average male at over six foot and were dressed in a manner that left their faces almost completely hidden from view, making it obvious to Art that the face coverings were an intentional disguise.

Art suddenly jerked upright on his chair over something that grabbed his attention. He immediately rewound the video and got the tech guy to enlarge the image, he then got out of his seat and went over to the monitor for a closer look. "If I'm right, that guy on the left has a bit of dark beard sticking out from under his face scarf." Gina moved up beside him and peered over his shoulder at the image. "Looks like it to me too, Art, and if what they handed our victims were the burgers that killed them then we have our culprits on video." Art turned away from the monitor. "This is timed just after eleven-thirty-five, so if what they gave our victims *was* what eventually killed them, and I think that's highly likely, then we know exactly where it came from." He looked at Gina first, then Vince, before asking the obvious question. "Did either of you interview anyone at that Burger Bar sporting a bushy beard?" Vince responded right away. "Yes, Lieutenant, I did. In fact it was a guy who was on the late shift that night and the same person who closed up after our victims had finished their nights work and left."

"Find out where he is and bring him in, Gina. I want a word with him." Having said that he started walking away, until Gina reached out and stopped him. "It's getting a bit late, Art. Are you sure you want him in tonight?" "Bring him in." He repeated, before heading back to his office without comment. Gina took Vince by the arm and they headed through the door after him, but there was no trace of a smile on either face as they both knew it was going to be a very long day.

Art didn't go straight back to his office as planned but paid another visit to his boss, eager to know how he'd got on with Silverman's legal people. He also needed to bring him up to date with the fact that they now had two likely suspects, albeit unidentified. He saw this as a big step forward and was keen to get to grips with the burger bar employee.

He ran his fingers through his greying blonde hair. "Is that a glimmer of light I see at the end of the tunnel?" he asked himself.

4

After listening to Art's update his boss didn't look overly excited. "So we now have two suspects, neither of whom can be identified. I can't say that gives me a big thrill, Art, have you any good news to cheer me up?"

Art wasn't best pleased either, so he gave things a little thought before saying anything else. "We have some good news, Marcus. We know for sure that both suspects are above average height and one has a bushy beard. Coincidently, one of the burger bar employees who just happened to be on the late shift that night has a similar beard. Gina is on her way now to bring him in for questioning. He could well be one of the guys handing out freebies to the victims since he was in a prime position to do so." He suddenly switched to another subject. "But what about your chat with Silverman's legal people, how did that go?"

"It didn't." snapped Delgado angrily. "The bastards stonewalled me. Just kept repeating that they were not at liberty to divulge any information about their client. Thankfully, we had more joy from the Embassy staff." Art's eyes lit up. "Are you going to tell me about it or is it to be kept secret?" Delgado smiled for the first time that day. "Not secret, Art, but important nevertheless. It turns out that Silverman, and this has been confirmed, *is* the father of our victim, or perhaps I should say *was* the father as it's also confirmed that he passed away two weeks ago, quite unexpectedly by all accounts but from natural causes. Our contact at the embassy advised us that the people responsible for old boy's corporate and personal finances is a London based company called Johnston, Johnston, and Jacobs. I tried to contact their head man, a guy by the name of Charles Matheson, but he was tied up with a series of meetings for most of the day. Although they have assured me that he will contact me just as soon as he's free. I must confess that I found their general attitude much more polite and welcoming, but only time will tell if that turns out to be the case." Art was about to say something when the mobile in his pocket buzzed. It turned out to be Gina texting him with a warning him that they were on their way back with the suspect. He got to his feet. "I have to go, Marcus, one of our suspects is on is way in and I want to do the interview myself. I'll keep you up to date after I've interviewed him." Delgado waved him away and wished him luck as he headed off to reception to meet up with Gina and Vince.

It was only a matter of minutes before they got together allowing Art the chance to get his first look at the guy, and he wasted no time in deciding that he couldn't be a suspect as he was far too small. "Never mind taking him to the interview room, Vince, my office will do fine." He motioned Vince to take the guy on ahead while he lingered behind with Gina. "Did you get anything out of him?" he asked, expectantly. Gina shrugged her shoulders non-committedly. "He's the supervisor at the burger bar and appears to be very cooperative and willing, although he does deny having any connection with what happened. To be honest I didn't press him too much, Art, as he doesn't look tall enough to be one of the guys in the video, but you seemed determined to have him brought in, so here he is." Art gave her a knowing wink. "I spotted that as well, Gina, now do me a favour and organise a couple of coffees. It might help to get him relaxed, bearing in mind that while he may not be a suspect he is definitely a witness as he was the last person on duty at the burger bar and likely the last person to have seen our victims alive He might know something we don't." Gina veered off to go for the coffee while Art chased after Vince. When he caught up with him and had another look at the suspect he judged him to be a man in his early thirties, who might have reached five-foot-seven standing on tiptoes, alone cleared him as a suspect. Vince introduced him as Andreas Sanchez and got him seated before leaving. Art brought out his mobile and switched it to record before greeting his witness. "Thank you for agreeing to assist us with our enquiries, Andreas. I'm Lieutenant Gardiner and I'm sure you are already briefed on what this is interview is all about. I'd appreciate it if you would tell me what you remember from the night our two victims died. Are you okay with that?"

The young man wriggled upright on his chair. "I'll be only too glad to help, Lieutenant, what happened to those guys is absolutely disgraceful, especially as we had them working for us for most of that evening, and I have to say they were very industrious and really switched on." Art moved to the edge of his chair to pay closer attention. "What time did you close up that night?" he asked. Andreas came straight back at him. "Same time as usual, eleven-thirty. I was getting ready to do just that when I had two late customers walk in on me." Art edged a little closer. "Can you describe what they looked like?" he asked.

"They were both really tall, well-built guys with baseball caps and scarves pulled up over their lower faces. They ordered a couple of burgers with all the trimmings and just turned their backs on me and stayed like that until I served them, which I found little threatening. In fact I was genuinely worried that they were about to mug me, but the slightly smaller of the two paid me without any hassle and they took their burgers and left." Art was quietly impressed by how composed and articulate his witness was. He appeared to have a good sense of recall which was a useful skill that few witnesses possess. "You seem to have a very clear memory of them considering you never saw them before. Was there something about them that generated this interest, something that made them stick in your mind perhaps? Even the smallest detail can make a big difference to our investigation."

The witness closed his eyes and concentrated on searching his memory banks. He then shuffled upright in his seat again. "I don't know that it will help much but I did notice that the guy who paid me was wearing a gold Rolex watch. We don't see many of our customers wearing those round here."

Art leaned away from the desk. "Everything you tell us is helpful, Andreas, it all helps to paint a picture. Now I want you to think really hard while things are still fresh in your mind and try to recall anything else about these two guys. Even the smallest detail might help us to identify them."

Andreas rubbed his face vigorously with both hands and sat thinking for a few moments. "Oh my God yes, there is one other thing that comes back to me now that I think about it. Just as they were about to leave the bigger of the two pushed the other guy towards the door and told him to get a move on." He stopped talking for a moment to gather his thoughts. "I remember exactly what he said now, he said '*get a bloody move on Joe or we'll be too late to do anything.*' Yes, that's what he said, I remember it quite clearly as he seemed a bit worked up about it, he looked to be in a big hurry to go somewhere."

"You're absolutely sure he called him Joe?" asked Art, who was now on the edge of his seat. His witness shook his head. "Yes, I'm

33

certain of it, he definitely called him Joe just as they went through the door and out of sight"

Art had his eyes fixed rigidly on his witness and knew straight away that the guy was telling it exactly as it was. "That's a really useful piece of information, Andreas, and if you're certain there's nothing else you can tell me that might be useful I'll have someone take you back to wherever it is you want to go. But before you do that I want to thank you for coming forward and helping us like this and should you remember anything else that might help feel free to get back in touch. It would help a lot if you would give a description of what these two suspects were wearing to our detective before you leave, and thanks again for your help."

He walked him out to the main office and left him with Vince to note the details and see him home before heading over to give Gina something else to think about. "Some very interesting developments from Andreas about our two suspects that was enough to convince me this was a planned attack and that has me thinking that the culprits must have had a car somewhere close by. It would be useful if you and Vince get on the go early tomorrow and follow the trail from the crime scene all the way to the nearest car park to check the route for any CCTV coverage. Things are beginning to take shape so let's stay on top of it while it's hot. I'm off to see Delgado again so you get Vince to take you home and I'll see you later." He kissed her on the cheek, then wheeled away, eager to catch up with his boss.

Delgado looked to be really pleased with himself when Art walked in on him. "How are things progressing at you end, Art? Are we making progress?" Art pulled up a chair and sat down. "Some headway, although the guy we had down as a suspect turned out to be nothing more than a witness, albeit a very useful one. I'm convinced from what we have to date that this was a planned killing, and you know as well as I do, Marcus, that planned killings usually have to do with money, drugs, or sex. I'm already convinced we can rule out the latter in this case."

Delgado nodded his agreement, but he backed it up with words. "I totally agree, Art, but just to keep you in the picture, I got a very useful call from Charles Matheson at JJ and J's in London, and I can tell you there is a *serious* amount of money floating about. He reckons old boy Silverman's empire could be worth something in the region of two and a half billion pounds Sterling, and he went on to explain that there's a long way to go before they can pull everything together. Although he did say that the old boys personal fortune would be somewhere in excess of one and a half billion. He reckons there's a huge chunk of real estate involved as well as company shares. He even explained why our young victim left home and went walk-abouts, and from what he told me I don't blame the guy for bailing out." He reached into his drawer and came out with a bottle of Irish, pouring two small measures as he continued talking. "Have a quick one for the road, Art, it's well past time we were out of here and I'm sure Gina is waiting for you. The story about young Silverman can wait until tomorrow as it's a long story."

He knocked his drink back in one swallow, as did Art, and they left the office together to head home, with Marcus having the longer journey to look forward to.

Gina had picked up a carry-out on the way home and was delighted when Art arrived in so soon after her. They got through their meal without much conversation as both were feeling the pangs of hunger after such a long day, but as was usually the case they couldn't leave the job behind them for long, and once they were settled down with a drink in hand Art switched the conversation back to their investigation. "I know I'm in danger of repeating myself, Gina, but I want you and Vince to pay close attention on your hunt for video coverage tomorrow." Gina didn't even question the fact that he was repeating himself as there was always something that needed attention where her man was concerned. "I'm more convinced than ever that this was a professional hit," Art went explained, "which means our killers didn't arrive at the scene unexpectedly, they must have planned to be there, so it's almost certain they had a car nearby. With that in mind I want the two of you to follow the route we discussed for any witnesses. You need to check the whole route on both sides for any CCTV coverage, right up to and including the carpark and check if the staff there can tell us anything. It could well be a bum-steer, sweetheart, I accept that, but what have we got to lose?" He ran his fingers through his hair. "We have to find these bloody killers in case they're on some evil campaign aimed at homeless guys on a planned killing spree."

Gina moved her head ever so slowly from side to side and grinned at him in a mischievous way. "You never leave the job behind, do you, Art? You can't just walk away from a case and ease down, not even over an evening meal." He grinned at her. "Easing down is for dead beats, sweetheart, and I'm not quite there yet. Anyway, we're two of a kind you and me and you know it." Gina kept her thoughts to herself. "What do you really think is behind these murders? Is it just about money or is it possible there's something more sinister going on?"

"I can't see any motive other than money with what we know up to now, but it's likely that even if we catch the perpetrators it won't necessarily mean there isn't someone else loitering behind the scenes pulling the strings. There can be lots of issues involved to muddy the waters, it's my experience that where big money is involved there are always complications. This won't be an easy case to solve, I can guarantee it." He raised the glass to his lips and knocked back what was left. "I'm in with Marcus first thing tomorrow so you can give me a buzz if you find anything useful, anything at all. I want to know straight away." Gina kissed him on the cheek. "Let's find another topic to talk about, Art, the bloody job will still be here when we're not." She knew from experience how easily her man could become over-involved and obsessive, especially with murder cases; and she didn't want it happening with this investigation, although she had a feeling he was already heading in that direction, leaving her incapable of doing anything to change it.

5

The following day started with Art's scheduled meeting with his boss, and Delgado was really eager to get things under way so kicked off as soon as Art was seated. "Some of the things I'm hearing from this guy Matheson are pretty mind boggling to say the least, but I reckon he's a genuine, up-front sort of guy, who even took the trouble to warn me that he would only divulge or discuss information about his client that was already in the public domain. Although he gave me a fairly detailed explanation as to why young Silverman left the family circle and hit the road. An upsetting tale it is too, and one that pointed the finger of blame firmly at the father. It turns out the old boy, quite publicly and unforgivably, declared fierce opposition to his son's relationship with a young lady he was going out with. She was a nurse at a hospital in London, with an English mother and a Nigerian father, the father being a senior surgical consultant at another hospital in London. It turns out that this mixed bloodline caused the old boy to interfere and go public with his feelings. But he did so openly during a live television interview, during which he aired a suggestion that he intended to include a codicil to his Will that would ensure his son would only remain a benefactor if he chose someone of a known Jewish or English bloodline for a wife in the event that he ever got married, or if he could be declared single at the time the Will was executed."

He eased back in his chair and shook his head in despair, but he gave the matter a lot more thought before continuing. "This cantankerous old git must have been a real control freak, but back to the explanation. The outcome of the old boys public rebuke was that his son's lady friend was so driven to despair that she committed suicide. A most regretful event that had a disastrous effect on the young man, as you can imagine, and one that prompted him to sever all ties with his father and desert the family home, heading over here to seek his own fame and fortune." Delgado, who looked genuinely saddened by the sorry tale, folded his arms and flopped back in his chair with a look of genuine revulsion on his swarthy features?

"What kind of a selfish cretin was this old boy? Does he have any other siblings who *haven't* walked out on him?" asked Art. "It appears not," replied Delgado, "young Benjamin is his only off-spring, although he does have a step-son who was once a director in one of his companies prior to a mysterious parting of the ways. The stepson now runs a business out in Brazil somewhere that trades in Palm Oil, although he also has an office over here in Detroit, plus one in London. So it would appear that Palm Oil is a very lucrative commodity."

"I know it's a change of subject, Marcus," said Art, butting in, "but what about that other poor soul who was killed? We seem to be concentrating all of our efforts on one victim."

Delgado pulled a file in front of him and opened it up. "Young Blackwell's parents are arriving here tomorrow for a positive ID, but with everything we know about the Silverman family and taking everything in the round I'm accepting that he was an innocent by-stander. If we solve the Silverman murder I'm convinced the other will follow in its wake. Young Blackwell was probably taken out just because he was there and could identifying the killers. He comes from a middle-class background and there doesn't appear to be any reason for someone wanting to kill him. On the other hand, I can see lots of reasons for Silverman's son being a target."

Art screwed his face up at this. "Just collateral damage I guess."

Delgado nodded affirmatively. "That about sums it up, Art, sad though it is." He was about to say more when Art's phone buzzed in his pocket, and when he saw it was Gina he turned the volume up. "Hi, Art, just calling to let you know that we've uncovered some useful CCTV recording showing both of our suspects making their way down the street after their meeting with our victims. There's a managed car park about five hundred yards or so further up the road so we're checking it out for any other coverage, after that we'll hit the car park staff and see what develops. It's my guess they were heading for the car park just like you thought they were. Anyway, we should be back at base within the hour." She finished without waiting for an answer.

Delgado gave Art the thumbs up. "That was a good move, Art. If our suspects went into the car park we should be able to get their car registration. I know that car park quite well and there's only one way in and one way out, so its fingers crossed. You said you were hoping to head over to JFK this morning but I suggest you wait until we see what Gina turns up; she reckons she'll be back soon enough." Art nodded agreeably. "Am I needed when young Blackwell's parents get here?" he asked.

"No, I have that organised, you just stick with the investigation. I think it would be useful if we have a debrief at the end of play each day until this case begins to make sense." Art voiced his agreement and headed off, casting a little dig at his boss as he went. "With the hours we're putting in it might mean upsetting your sweet wife again with more late suppers." He giggled quietly to himself as he hurried through the door.

It was almost two hours before Gina and Vince arrived back, and after collecting Art along the way they all headed to the tech lab to view the CCTV recordings. The first one showed both suspects hurrying along East 11th Street, while the next showed them entering the car park at exactly eleven-fifty-nine on the night in question. The same recording later showed a black limousine leaving the car park exactly six minutes later., its number plate clearly visible. "Well done you two, that car registration will help nail these two murdering scumbags." Art looked like he'd just hit a home run. Gina gave him a loving smile in return. "Better than that, I've already checked the car out and it belongs to the Hertz car hire company over at JFK. It was booked by a London company for one of their employees and was collected the day before our two victims died."

"Well, well," mused Art, "it's very convenient that I'm heading there as soon as we're finished here so it couldn't have worked out better if we'd planned it. We might have our suspects within easy reach." He jotted down the car make and number and stuck it in his pocket, then he patted Gina and Vince on the shoulder. "That was a good mornings work, so off you go and I'll see you whenever I get back, Gina."

He hurried from the room and sprinted down to his car.

The drive over to JFK was uneventful, apart from the heavy rain, and when he got there he went straight to the security office where he was greeted by the manager who turned out to be an ex-cop. "Grab a seat, Lieutenant, and tell me how I can help." Art pulled out his little notebook. "I need to check your CCTV for a male passenger over six foot tall, possibly with a thick, bushy beard who arrived here from London on that date. He handed the manager his open notebook and the guy left his seat. "We'll need to go to the video storage facility just along the corridor."

Art tailed along behind expecting a long wait, but and it only took a few minutes to find the videos and head back to the office.

"The best place to start looking is always the baggage collection area," the manager explained, "all arrivals from London have to go through it as it's their only way out." They sat down together to watch the video that showed the time to be exactly twelve-thirty-two when the arrivals from London started pouring into view, and it only took a matter of seconds to zero in on an obvious candidate who was so much taller than those around him that he stood out like a sore thumb. "I reckon that's your man." The manager was quite excited as he hit the pause button. Art moved even closer at the monitor. "I'd say your right, can we see where he goes after he leaves the baggage area?"

The security manager rummaged amongst the videos and stuck another one into the machine, and sure enough there was the same guy following the crowd out of the baggage area and heading across the concourse where the camera suddenly lost sight of him.

"Wherever he's going, he's not heading for the exit, he's more likely heading for the coffee kiosk so just hang on a minute." He pulled another video from its slot and loaded it up, and right on cue there was the same guy in the middle of a thinning crowd heading for the coffee kiosk, but as he got closer to the kiosk he was met by another man who was an inch or two smaller. The fact that they dived straight into a deep conversation told the viewers that the meeting must have been prearranged. They were picked up again leaving the kiosk and heading over to the Hertz car hire stand at the other side of the concourse. The security manager looked to be enjoying himself. "I reckon you should pay a visit to that Hertz stand, Lieutenant, they have their own CCTV on site so they might be able to give you a better look at those guys."

Art had his fingers crossed behind his back. "That's exactly what I aim to do, but I need copies of those videos so I can pick them up on my way back."

"Only too happy to oblige," replied security guy, "and the best of luck with the Hertz people." Art gave him a friendly wave and headed down the escalator and across the concourse to the Hertz stand where he was greeted by a very pleasant young lady in company uniform. He flashed his warrant and explained the purpose of his visit. "You spoke with one of my colleagues earlier today about a car that was hired by a London company for one of its employees." The young lady's eyes lit up. "Oh yes, your very nice associate asked me to search my videos for him."

"Did you manage to find him?" asked Art. "Indeed I did," she replied, "and although our camera only covers the area directly in front of the stand, exactly where you're standing in fact, we have the customer and his friend on record as clear as day. They only came here to ask where the car collection point was, but I've already made a copy of the video just like your detective requested. I even have a copy of his driver's licence as is required by state law." Art gave her his Sunday best smile. "I would like the name of the individual who picked up the car, the name of the company who booked it, the time and date it was collected, and a copy of the driver's licence. If you can manage all that for me."

The young lady went straight to her computer and printed out the information and handed it to him. Having got what he was after Art thanked her and left the Hertz stand to head back to the security office to pick up the video copies. He then persuaded the security manager to accompany him to the storage lockers as it was necessary to have a witness on hand when he hadn't a clue what they might find in the locker.

As soon as they had the locker opened Art pulled out his phone and handed it to the security manager to record what he was doing, and got quite excited when he realised it contained a medium sized, brown leather suitcase. Having decided to check its contents back at the station house he got the security manager to seal it with security tape and sign over the tape to prove it hadn't been tampered with.

He was on his way again much sooner than he had ever thought possible feeling quietly satisfied with the way things were progressing and mad keen to get back to base and share the news with his boss.

6

When he got back in front of Delgado he dropped the suitcase on his desk with an exaggerated flourish and an expression that told his boss he was well pleased with himself. Delgado lowered his head and peered at him over the top of his glasses. "Shouldn't that be in the evidence lock up?" he asked. Art shrugged off his remark. "I think we should see what's inside it first, don't you?" He was really keen to see what secrets it held, if any?

"For God's sake get on with it, Art, maybe then we can get down to the more important business." Art sliced through the tape and opened it up. The first thing they saw was a neatly folded Saville Row suit, several classy shirts, some underwear, and a few up-market toiletries. All that plus a few other personal items that looked to be of little value, but tucked into a back pocket almost out of sight was a large wad of hundred-dollar bills that Art estimated to be around ten grand, plus an up to date driving licence and a photograph of a very pretty young lady in a silver frame. "It looks like our poor street bum wasn't so poor after all." he muttered, cynically.

"Don't be a total cynic, Art," cautioned Delgado, "the poor guy never did us any harm." Art took the collection of airport video's from his pocket and set them down in front of his boss. "A little present just for you, Marcus. These videos identify both of our suspects, so we have now tracked them all the way from the murder scene to the carpark on CCTV and their car registration as they drove away. Gina was quick to identify that it was a hire car from Hertz up at JFK, and they very kindly gave me the name of the company involved, plus the name of the guy driving it, and a copy of his licence that you have there on your desk, and guess what, Marcus, it's the very same damned company that handle Silverman's legal requirements, Mendelson and Ackermann. The guy who drove the car is called Joseph Hardwick and I suggest we get on to the Brit police asap and have him lifted; we need to check out his position within the company." Delgado rubbed his hands together excitedly. "Well done, Art, what a scoop. I'm tempted to phone his damned company right now and find out what the hell is going on but having already spoken with them I know they won't open up, it's not in their nature. I think we can leave that to the Brit police." Art edged forward on his chair. "Why don't you try your friend Charles Matheson? You said he was a decent sort who you thought was trustworthy, maybe he knows something that can help." Delgado's face perked up. "It's worth a try, Art, that's for sure." He already had Matheson's number on his phone contacts, so he ran down the list and hit the call button, followed by the speaker button.

"Charles Matheson, how may I help?" The voice was both cultured and friendly and Delgado got straight to the point by explaining what he was after, catching Matheson by surprise. "Did I hear you right, did you say Joe Hardwick?" he quired, forcing Marcus to repeat the name. "I can tell you exactly who *he* is. Joe Hardwick is the head of security at Mendelson and Ackermann. He is a well-known individual among some of the more dubious institutions. In fact, he once worked for the old boys step-son in exactly the same role out in Brazil. I would say he's been with M and A about three years now. Rumour has it he's quite a hard nut, ex Australian special forces. Everyone who has any connection with M and A know him, but can I ask why you're interested in him?"

Delgado screwed his face up as he considered how much he should divulge. "Let's just say his name has cropped up in our investigation into young Silverman's death."

There was a lengthy pause before Matheson came back, but when he did he sounded genuinely concerned. "I got the worrying impression after our last conversation that you believed young Benjamin was murdered, is that still your belief?"

Delgado had to decide whether or not to trust Matheson. "My gut instinct tells me you can be trusted to keep a confidence, Charles, am I right?"

"You may confide in me without fear of anything you say being repeated, Captain Delgado, and I can assure you that I will assist you in any way I can to uncover the truth about what happened to young Benjamin. If you believe I can help with your investigation you only need ask. With regards to Mendelson and Ackermann, I have no particular axe to grind with them, nor do I have any favours to put their way."

Delgado inched forward in his chair. "I'm glad to hear that, Charles, but please call me Marcus, especially as we may have reason to keep in touch while this case remains open. But in answer to your last question, we have irrefutable evidence that young Silverman *was* murdered, along with a friend of his who happened to be in his company at the time. We also have video and photographic evidence of Hardwick's participation in both murders, so the more I can get to know about him the better." He paused for a moment, "On a separate topic altogether, Charles, it would help me a lot to know more about old boy Silverman's step-son, Joshua, more about his character than his business attributes if you get my drift."

"I can't tell you very much on that score I'm afraid, except to say that he and my client shared a very distant relationship. arms-length if you know what I mean; no love lost is the expression I would use. Nobody knows why they parted company, in business terms I mean, but something must have rocked their boat. One thing you should bear in mind is that old boy Silverman was a very diligent, honest, and disciplined person for such a successful businessman. Most powerful businessmen have their less disciplined moments in life, Marcus, but not Benjamin, he was as straight as a dye. If he did have a problem it would probably be that he was too outspoken and too traditionally Jewish conservative, although I have to say he wasn't quite so before his wife died. I think he was grieving ever since."

Delgado picked up the conversation. "Everything you're telling me is extremely useful, Charles, as it allows me to form a background picture of the individuals involved. We still have to track down Hardwicks accomplice, but we have plenty to go on and I'm really hopeful we will have him under lock and key before long." He stopped talking for a few moments to gather his thoughts, then picked up the thread again. "I know you can't divulge anything to do with the old boys finances, Charles, but I'd like to know if everything is on a sound footing within the business?" There was a momentary pause before Matheson came back to him. "I don't see why not, it's public knowledge anyway. Everything is fine within the whole group, Marcus, they are very successful and there are no irregularities or issues on the go that I'm aware of, if that's any help."

"Thank you, Charles," replied Delgado, "I won't bother you any more for the moment, and I appreciate your candour, so thank again."

"I'm always willing to help in any way I can, Marcus. I just hope you get the people responsible and bring them to justice, young Benjamin was a lovely, decent young man and did not deserve such a dreadful fate. I'll wish you goodbye for now and have a good day."

Art had been pacing about the office while listening in on their conversation and he was pleased with what he heard. "That was a very useful conversation, Marcus. This guy Hardwick is the one we need to focus on. I take it you're going to have Scotland Yard lift the bastard and charge him with murder?"

"No, I'm not, not yet anyway, Art, I want to keep a lid on things for now, we don't want Hardwick raising the alarm with his accomplice and sending him on the move before we can reel him in. We already have his facial image so we can run that through our computer first and see what comes up. If he's not on there then we'll have to try something else." Art leaned across the desk. "One thing I should have done back at JFK was check with airport security to see which direction Hardwick went when he left the airport. It might be a good idea for me to do that now as most of the routes out of JFK have CCTV coverage ever since nine-eleven, so there's a good chance we can track his journey at least part of the way. It would help if find out where Mendelson and Ackermann have their offices over here, that would most likely be where they were heading."

"We already know where it is, Art," Delgado admitted, "they're based at Newark, which is only thirty odd miles up the road so it will be easy to pay them a visit when the mood take us."

"In which case that has to be where they were heading," suggested Art, "we should make arrangements to see them asap and have a look at their employee profiles, see what we can turn up. We already know that one guy from that bunch is involved but we need to know if anyone else is." Delgado shook his head negatively. "I'm not arranging a damned thing with them, Art. We go in unannounced, cold and call the bastards to catch them off guard."

"Still the same canny old bastard as ever, Marcus," muttered Art, before adding in a louder voice, "but I couldn't agree more." Delgado cocked an eyebrow. "Glad you agree, but let's have less of the old, eh!" he grinned as he said it, "we'll leave first in the morning unless you have something on that's more important on the go?"

"Nothing that can't wait, this is much more important. Anything I've got on the go can be handled by Gina." He was about to leave when the desk phone rang. "Delgado." He announced, raising a hand to stop Art from leaving.

"Hello, Marcus, it's Charles Matheson, I'm sorry to bother you again like this so soon after our last but there's a news bulletin on TV over here that I believe might interest you, especially as you were asking me about Joe Hardwick."

"Really, anything to do with him sounds interesting. What has he been up to?"

"He's not up to anything, Marcus, he's dead. It appears his body was found in the car park at Heathrow airport late yesterday evening."

A long silence ensued with Delgado sitting behind his desk staring at his opposite number, a stunned look on his swarthy face. "Is there any indication as to how it happened?" he asked.

"No mention of cause, or suspects, or anything like that I'm afraid, just a brief bulletin that I thought you should know about." Marcus wriggled upright in his seat. "Thank you for letting me know,

Charles, if you hear any more I'd appreciate being kept up to date."

"Take it as read, Marcus, but one little tit-bit before I go, the money markets over here are a bit jittery over the delay in appointing a new Chairman to the Silverman Corporation, caused mostly by your investigation I'm afraid." He hung up straight after saying his piece..

"Well, what are we to make of that?" asked Delgado, aiming his question at Art. "At a guess, I'd say someone is doing a bit of early spring cleaning."

"They're bloody quick of the mark, Art, and you know as well as I do that it takes big money to pay that sort of cleaning bill." He ran his fingers through his hair. "We need to find out who has access to old boy Silverman's finances, his accountants or his solicitors? It's always wise in a case like this to follow the money." Art scratched his head. "His legal people are sure to have possession of the old boys Will, but nobody knows who benefits from it until it's opened u and its content made known, although I guess the main benefactor must be his son, and since he is now dead we need to know who is next in line for the big bonus? Seems to me that's where we concentrate our efforts."

"I couldn't agree more, Art. I think it's time I got the commissioner to contact Scotland Yard and inform them of our interest in Hardwick, his death is obviously another murder and making contact might keep us abreast of things as their investigation progresses. There's always the possibility that his step-son might be involved. I assume he will be next line for the big pay-day since he appears to be the only other relative?"

"That would be my reading of things," agreed Art, "but what are we going to do about it. We don't even know where the guy is, but I do think we need to take a tougher line with Mendelson and Ackermann. They have serious questions to answer now that one of their employees is involved in a murder over here before heading back to England to get himself creamed. They can't duck the issue this time by giving us the cold shoulder, otherwise we go in with a team and tear their offices apart."

"When are you planning to hit them, Marcus? I think it would be wise to allow us plenty of time in case they spring some kind of legal stunt to wriggle out of answering our questions."

"Tomorrow morning, Art, we hit them first thing tomorrow morning." snapped Delgado, "you and I will leave here around eight o'clock, which should get us there just as they open up and hopefully before their big guns get too settled. We need to check this lot out on the internet before we go in so that we have the names of responsible individuals in the company. Can I leave that to you, Art?"

"No problem, Marcus, I'll get on to it right away, and if I don't see you before the end of play then I'll see you first thing in the morning." He gave his boss a mock salute and vanished through the door.

7

It was a little after nine the following morning when they arrived at Mendelson and Ackermann's offices in Newark, thanks to the morning rush hour, but they were early enough to catch the staff before they got too well organised, as some of them were still shoulder rubbing and chatting in the company car park when they drove in.

Art headed straight for the nearest group and broke in on their conversation. "Excuse me folks, is there anyone here by the name of James Magee?" The guy nearest to him, who was dressed in a thousand-dollar suit looked him up and down before stonewalling. "Who's asking?" He smirked at the others in the group as he said it.

Art pulled out his warrant card and waved it under the guys nose. "The New York police are asking, and if you don't answer me when I ask you a question I'll probably arrest you for loitering in a public place." The smirk vanished in a flash to be instantly replaced by a look of dismissive arrogance. "Maybe you should go and find him then, I'm nobody's paid sniffer dog." Art was a good inch or two taller than the guy he was addressing so he moved in on him and forced him back against the wall. "Don't get cocky with me, pal. I've got a hangover and I'm not very nice when I'm hung over. Now answer the fucking question before you find out how nasty I can be."

"Okay, okay, no need to get your knickers in a twist." Snapped the man in the suit. Art wasn't at all pleased, as the suit was about to find out. "Maybe you wear knickers, pal, you certainly come across as the sort who would, but just so you know, I don't," he warned, "and if you don't answer properly when I ask you a question it will be your neck that gets twisted, not your knickers. Now I'm going to ask you one last time, is there anyone present here by the name of James Magee?"

The mouthy guy slid along the wall away from his attacker and dusted himself down. "I don't know that it's any interest of yours but I happen to be James Magee." He looked a lot less ambitious with this admission. Art looked him up and down with a sneer. "Yeah, I thought you might be, I can smell your wife's perfume, I hope she knows you're using it." He reached out and smoothed the guys lapels down." What's going to happen now is that you're going to invite my Captain and me into your office for a cosy little chat and a cup of coffee, my hangover needs a caffeine fix." He didn't have a hangover, but what did that matter among friends.

Magee turned away and began walking, muttering over his shoulder as he went. "You had better follow me then, hadn't you?" The rest of his little group followed in their wake, sniggering behind his back. Art joined in with them, while his boss, who had been watching all of this from their car, got out and chased after them. "Nice day for a visit, don't you think so, Art?" He said this loud enough for everyone to hear. Art turned and gave him a smile; he didn't need to say anything, Delgado knew exactly what had taken place and he was enjoying it every bit as much as his Lieutenant.

The offices proved to be well furnished and cheerfully decorated with lots of space between workstations. Magee's own office overlooked the main work area from the top of a set of metal stairs, and as they went inside he motioned to his secretary that he wanted coffee, mindful of Art's request and now eager to comply. "Well, gentlemen, what is it you think I can do for you." he asked. Marcus decided to take a chance by pretending to know more than he actually did. "What was the purpose of Joseph Hardwick's recent visit to your offices?"

Magee looked genuinely confused and had to think for a moment or two before daring to answer. "Why would you be interested in Joe Hardwick for God's sake? Joe is our company security director and visits us quite frequently to ensure we are complying with company policy. Don't tell me being employed has suddenly become a crime?" Marcus moved in on him and stared him down. "We're interested in him because he's a prime suspect in a double murder." He allowed the message to sink in before going on. "Now stop asking stupid questions and start answering ours. Which of your staff met Hardwick at the airport when he arrived?" Magee appeared to have no understanding of what was being asked of him as he couldn't see any purpose to the question, but he eventually found his voice and spoke up. "That would have been our local security manager, Rodney Sharpe, he always meets Joe when he comes to visit, but why in the name of God are you interested in him?"

Marcus backed off to give Magee some space. "We have evidence, both forensic and photographic, that proves he was complicit in this double murder, and we intend to bring him to book. Now cut the crap and tell me where Sharpe is right now, right at this very moment?"

Magee looked totally bewildered. "I'm sorry, gentlemen, but you must have made some awful mistake, Rodney would never be involved in anything of a criminal nature. It's preposterous to even think so." Marcus moved in on him again forcing him to take a backward step. "If you continue to avoid answering my questions I will march you out of here in handcuffs. Is that what you want?"

Magee shuffled backwards. "I'm sorry, I'm truly sorry, gentlemen, I'm not being deliberately awkward, I just can't believe what you are telling me so please make allowance for that." He shook his head in despair. "But in answer to your question, Rodney does not appear to be in just yet, but I will go and check his desk diary and see what he has planned for today. Please wait here until I return, I should only be a few moments." He disappeared through the door and down the metal steps with a loud clatter of feet. Once he was gone his young lady came in with the coffee, greeted them very politely and left again, but it was much longer than expected before Magee reappeared, and when he did he was quite flustered and a little breathless. "I must apologise for taking so long gentlemen, but I had to ask our staff if anyone knew why Rodney hasn't turned in yet. I'm sorry to say I do not have an answer to that, unless of course he has some domestic issue that has held him back as he is normally very punctual."

Marcus set his cup down on a nearby desk and he had a seriously concerned look on his face when he next addressed Magee. "You are not the one at fault here, Mister Magee, and I appreciate your efforts in trying to help us, but we need to track Sharpe down with the utmost urgency, so with that in mind I need you to give me his home address, his home phone number, his cell phone number, and details of the car he is currently driving."

Magee nodded vigorously. "Of course, of course, just give me a moment to look up his details." He dived over to his computer and jotted down the information, then handed it to Marcus. "That's everything you asked me for, and I took the liberty of adding the address of the hotel where Rodney is currently lodged. There is an ongoing domestic issue between him and his wife lately that has led to her laying claim to possession of the family home until the matter is resolved. I'm sure you understand."

Marcus took the note and thanked him, but he had other words of warning to offer before leaving. "Should your Mister Sharpe turn up here again or contact you or any of your staff in any way, shape, or form, you must contact me immediately. Is that understood?"

Magee nodded frantically "Of course, it goes without saying." Marcus handed over his calling card. "Now tell me how we get to this bloody hotel." Magee gave him directions and sent them on their way, looking for all the world like someone whose world had just fallen apart.

Marcus wasn't best pleased; he was concerned that Sharpe was still running free and as a consequence their journey to the hotel was much quieter than it might otherwise have been.

When they got there the young man manning reception explained that their guest was not currently in residence and had not been since the previous evening. He further explained that there had been a couple of phone calls for Sharpe while he wasn't in residence that had needed to be recorded. He ducked down under the counter and retrieved the phone logbook. "Here we are, according to this there were two international calls, neither of his callers left a call-back number. He closed the logbook before offering further help. "If it helps, I can check with our car park attendant to find out exactly when Mister Sharpe collected his car and left the car park." Art took him up on his offer and the young reached out and picked up the phone, and after a quick conversation, he hurried straight back. "It appears our guest picked his car keys up at ten-thirty-two precisely yesterday evening before driving out of the car park and has not been seen since." Marcus looked distraught. "Would you take us to his room please." The young man grabbed a key card from a rack and led them to an empty first-floor room, exactly as Marcus expected, and it was noted by both detectives that the emptiness included the wardrobes and cupboards, making it obvious that Sharpe had flown the nest. When they got back to reception Marcus checked Sharpe's car details in case he had hired a different one, after which he left his calling card with the young receptionist and instructions that he was to be informed if and when Sharpe returned. He thanked the young man again for his help and they got on the road back to Manhattan.

"It looks to me as if Sharpe has been warned off, what's your take on it, Marcus?" Delgado muttered something indiscernible under his breath and pulled the car over to the side of the road before turning to face Art. "We need an all units call out on Sharpe right away, Art. We have his image on file so that will help uniform to keep an eye out for him, and we also need to cover the airports and ferries as well. Get on to Gina and have her organise it and let her know we're on our way back." He fired the car up and got back on the road while Art made the call.

When they got back to the station house Marcus found a note stuck to his monitor telling him the Commissioner had called. Having read it he muttered a stream of expletives under his breath and tossed the offending note into a nearby bin. "What in blue blazes does he want this time?" He had never been keen on unexpected calls from those higher up the ladder, he just didn't like surprises. "You're asking the wrong person, Marcus," countered Art. "so why don't you just ring his lordship and find out, you never know, he might even have something useful to say." Marcus just grunted. "That'll be a first, but you're right of course." He grunted noisily as he reached for the phone. As it turned out his conversation with the commissioner was much briefer than expected and dropping the phone back on its cradle he flopped back in his chair. "You were spot on, Art, there was some good news.

The British police have recognised our interest in Hardwick's death and are detailing someone to liaise with us. We can expect a call from whoever it is later today." He rubbed his hands together excitedly.

"Well done the good old Brit's." said Art, hoisting his fist in the air like some triumphant athlete. Marcus still looked a bit anxious. "To be honest, Art, I've always admired the British police and the relationship they have with the public, I just hope they don't land us some off-beat pen-pusher."

"Let's wait and see what happens before condemning them." Said Art. Marcus still looked anxious about something. "I'm worried that Sharpe might get the same treatment as Hardwick. We need to have at least one living suspect to interview if we're going to get anywhere with this case."

Art screwed his face up. "I think the answers lie with that shower Mendelson and Ackermann; they have two guys in their employment who are known killers, yet they don't even want to cooperate with us."

"I think the British police will get their measure soon enough. I can't wait for them to link up. At the very least it will give us an insight into what happened to Hardwick and anything else he was involved in that we don't know about, and that can only help with our case." The desk phone rang, and Marcus could see from the warning light on the panel that it was Lisa in admin. "What is it, Lisa, I'm very busy right now."

"A call came in for you a few minutes ago, Captain, from a Mister Magee, but your line was engaged, and he couldn't hold on. He didn't leave his number, but he did say he would ring you back shortly." Marcus thanked her and set the phone down looking very thoughtful.

Dropping back in his chair he folded his arms and engaged Art with a quizzical expression. "Well now," he muttered, "that's a turn up for the books. While I was on to the commissioner our friend Magee was on the phone looking for me, and it sounded urgent too? I'm not sure what to make of it but we'll find out later as he intends to call back."

Art cocked an eyebrow at the news and was about to make a comment when the desk phone rang again. Delgado squeezed his brow between finger and thumb. "That bloody thing never stops, I think I'll have it decommissioned." He snatched it up angrily. "Delgado." He had the sense to speak calmly this time, turning his temper down a notch in case it was the commissioner back online. "It's James Magee, Captain Delgado." There was an unmissable urgency in his voice, which was little more than a whisper, implying to Marcus that he had no wish to be overheard. "We need to talk, Lieutenant, but not over the phone please, walls have ears and as I do not want you coming to my office again it will have to be a meeting at your place, and it will have to be tomorrow morning. Are you okay with that?" Delgado's head jerked back in surprise. "That would suit me fine, Mister Magee. When would you like us to meet?" There was hardly a pause before his reply came back. "As early as possible. I need to be seen by others to be sticking to my normal work routine, if you get my drift, and that means I must be back at my office by nine o'clock. So I suggest five-thirty tomorrow morning or is that too early for you?"

"That will be fine by me, Mister Magee. I look forward to seeing you then." Magee hung up without further comment, while Art, who had been listening in on the conversation allowed a big grin to take over his face. "Well, well, well, there's a *real* turn up for the books, mind you, he did sound very guarded, almost as if he was under threat, what about you, Marcus, what's your take on it?"

He had to wait for Delgado's answer as he was deep in thought. "Yes, it sounds like he suspects he's being watched, or under threat even, but who does he think is watching him or threatening him? Could it be Sharpe? I for one can't wait for tomorrow morning to get here, and you can take that smile off your face, Art, because it means an early start for you too." Art gave him an even bigger smile. "That suits me fine, Marcus, I wouldn't miss it for the world, but it means an early call for Gina too because we're sharing a car at the moment." It was Delgado's turn to smile. "I bet she'll just love you for that, better you than me, but joking aside, Art, this might be the break we're looking for if it turns out that Magee has some inside information to offer. Anyway, we'll know soon enough, but for now it's time to get on with something else."

Art made to leave when Delgado's phone rang again. He took a deep breath and held his hand up to stop Art from leaving. "Hang on, Art, let's see who this is before you go." He took another deep breath as he glared at the flashing light that told him it was Lisa. He snatched up the offending handset. "Yes, Lisa, what is it?"

"I have a call holding for you from a Detective Inspector Ian Stewart."

"Thank you, Lisa, put him through please." He had a smile on his face as he turned and gave Art the thumbs up. "Good afternoon, Captain Delgado, this is Inspector Ian Stewart from the Met police. I've been detailed to be your liaison officer over this Hardwick case that we both have an interest in. So please tell me how I may help?" Delgado closed his eyes for a moment's thought before replying. "It's good to meet you, Ian, my name is Marcus so let's not stand on formalities. I'm sure our commissioner will have briefed you guys, but to put it briefly we have Hardwick listed as an accomplice in a double murder. I can assure you that this is irrefutable as we have video and forensic evidence to back it up. We don't know much about what has happened to him but I'm assuming the worst knowing his recent record and we will appreciate any information you can give us"

"Quite simple, Marcus, he was shot in the back of the head with a thirty-eight dum-dum in the car park at Heathrow airport while attempting to leave the country. It was a very messy hit; his face and brains were sprayed all over his luggage in the car boot. It appears he was about to retrieve his luggage when somebody came up behind him and took him out." Marcus jumped straight in again. "What makes you think that he was fleeing the country?" he asked. "It wasn't any great detective work on our behalf if I'm honest, Marcus. The guy had a flight ticket in his pocket for a one-way trip to Brazil, but I don't think he'll be getting a refund as he has no known relatives that we can trace. He was identified by the documentation on his person and by his employer who turned out to be very helpful, bearing in mind the circumstances. On top of that there was the rest of his personal belongings in the car and a gold watch he was wearing with his name engraved on it. It was an absolute mess if I'm honest, his brains were scattered everywhere."

"It sounds like a messy one, Ian, and I know what they can be like, but I find it interesting that he was heading for Brazil. Are you aware that he worked for a company out there before he took up his latest position?"

"Yes, Marcus, we got that from his current employer." Marcus decided to update him further. "We tried to speak with the top man at Mendelson and Ackermann's but got the brush off, how did you find them, Ian?" he asked. "Well, they helped with a messy identification so I'm not knocking them, but I'm sure you know how secretive these legal eagles can be so I'm not reading too much into the fact that they cold shouldered you. They had a lot to deal with at the time having just lost a senior member of staff, but is there anything happening at your end?" Delgado told him about Magee coming forward and promised to update him after their meeting. "That sounds promising, but is there anything else we need to discuss right now?" Delgado glanced over at Art, who shook his head negatively? "I don't think so, Ian, but I'm really glad to have you on board. I'm certain that between us we can come up with a satisfactory outcome and I promise to keep in touch, I already have you saved on my contacts list."

"That about raps it up for me then," replied the inspector, I'm sure that working together we can get it sorted, whatever *it* is. Bye for now." He ended the call, leaving Marcus looking at Art in a way that asked a question. Art knew what that question was. "He sounds like the sort of guy we can work with, and more importantly he seems eager to help."

"My sentiments as well, Art. I think we're on a winner with him, he sounds switched on. Now then, if you've nothing else right now you can be on your way as well since we're both here early tomorrow. I'll see you just before five so we're both switched on with our caffeine intake up to scratch before Magee gets here." Art didn't say anything, he just got up, gave his boss a farewell wave and disappeared from view.

8

Marcus was already behind his desk looking fresh and ready for action when Art and Gina joined him. "You look like someone who enjoyed a good night's sleep, Chief." Gina smiled when she said it. "And before you bother asking, why don't I go and get us some coffee and let you two get yourselves sorted?" Her offer got an immediate thumbs up from Delgado. "You say the nicest things, Gina, especially at this early hour." Gina just smiled and wandered off to fulfil her promise, leaving Art with Delgado, who looked really buoyed-up and full of expectation.

"We don't usually see you up and buzzing at this early hour, Marcus," said Art, a bit tongue in cheek, "I just hope Magee comes up with the goods when we get down to business." He gave Marcus a cautioning look. "Surely he wouldn't set up a meet like this unless he has something important to offer." He gave Delgado another meaningful look. "I agree, he wouldn't be going to all this trouble unless there was good reason. I think he's bright enough not to go wasting police time." Art shrugged off-handedly. "There's always the possibility that he's involved in what's going on and is looking to bail out now that the heat is on."

"You could be right about that," agreed Delgado, "we'll know soon enough because it's almost time he was here." Gina arrived back with the coffee's and handed them round. "I'll go and catch up with my paperwork now while you two meet up with your visitor." She wandered off with her coffee in hand.

By the time Marcus and Art had topped up their caffeine levels it was nearing five thirty and the air of expectation between them was almost palpable, but it had gone noticeably quiet as they dwelt on what lay ahead, and when five-thirty came and went with no sign of Magee, Delgado started to get restless. He was on his feet and pacing about aimlessly, before returning to his seat and fidgeting with anything that was close at hand. Art took note of it. "Calm down, Marcus, if he comes, he comes, if not we'll just have to pay him another visit."

"I want this meeting here on our patch and on our terms rather than his place." He grimaced at the thought. "If I'm honest, Art, I'm concerned that he's not here yet, it's well past our agreed time." Before he even finished talking he was back on his feet and pacing around the office again, and it went on like this for another few minutes before both men admitted defeat, and it was Marcus who conceded first. "The bastard isn't coming, Art. If he had a genuine reason for running late surely he would have made contact to explain himself. We have to ask ourselves if he's giving us two fingers, or does he have some sort of unscheduled issue that cropped up?"

"Only time will tell, Marcus. I think we should give it up as a bad job and phone the guy, but we have to bear in mind that people do have genuine reasons for missing appointments." Art's comments did nothing to console his boss who snatched up his desk phone. "I know he doesn't want us to contact him at work, but what the hell, I'm not sitting on my ass waiting for him to get off his." He dug out Magee's number and dialled, nodding at Art when his call was answered almost immediately by a young female voice. "James Magee's office. I'm afraid Mister Magee is not available right now; may I take a message."

"Good morning, Miss," greeted Marcus, "I need to contact Mister Magee rather urgently, can you tell me when you expect him back?"

There was a brief silence before she answered. "I'm dreadfully sorry, Sir," came her reply, "but I am not aware of his movements at this time, however, if you leave your number I can have him call you back as soon as he becomes available." Delgado grimaced. "No I'm afraid that won't do, can you let me have his cell-phone number and I'll try him on that." There was another slight pause before she answered. "I'm terribly sorry, Sir, but I am not at liberty to release such information." Marcus cursed under his breath feeling seriously frustrated. "That's not at all helpful, Miss, but I do understand. Please tell him Captain Delgado called and ask him to get in touch as soon as possible. Thank you for your help." He dropped the handset back on its cradle and turned to face Art. "What now? he asked.

"Why don't we let things rest for a while and see if he gets in touch?" suggested Art, rather tamely. "We don' seem to have much choice," snarled Marcus, "but I want you over at his place first thing tomorrow morning, collar him as soon as he gets there and bring him back here for questioning. If he has something to tell us and let's find out what it is the hard way."

Art left his seat and made ready to leave, but Delgado waved him back into it. "Stay where you are, Art, we need to decide on a way forward with this case. We need get a strategy in place so that we all know what we're each meant to be doing." He had just finished talking when his phone rang, causing him to swear under his breath again "I'm gonna disconnect that that bloody machine before it drives me crazy." He snatched it up angrily. "Delgado." He snapped, too pissed-off to say anything else.

"I have a call for you on line one, Captain, from a young lady at Mendelson and Ackermann's in Newark." It was Lisa at reception. Delgado hit the flashing key on his phone unit. "Captain Delgado." He announced wearily. A very down-beat female voice greeted him. "This is Miss Greenlaw again, Captain, Mister Magee's secretary, I hope you don't mind me calling but I traced your number from your earlier call and as you seemed so eager to get in touch with James I thought it was the right thing to do."

There was a moments pause before she explained the reason for her call "I have just been informed by the local police that James was found dead in his garage early this morning. I'm afraid I have no information as to how he died but I thought it only proper to inform you." There was a much longer pause this time, with the hint of sobbing in the background. "It's such devasting news I can hardly take it in." she sobbed.

Delgado sagged into his chair, but he knew he must respond. "I'm very sorry to hear such awful news, Miss Greenlaw and I know how devasting it must be for you. I can only offer my deepest sympathy to you, and all concerned. I won't detain you unnecessarily, Miss Greenlaw, as I'm sure you have enough to deal with, but thank you for letting me know, and please feel free to call me again if you think I can be of assistance." Dropping the phone on it cradle he clasped his hands on the desk in front of him, looking totally devastated. Unfortunately, Art had only heard one side of the conversation and was curious as to why his boss was looking so glum. "What's up, Marcus, is it something serious?" he asked.

"Well, one thing is for sure," he replied, with a shake of his head, "we now know why Magee didn't tun up for our meeting, and I'm afraid we won't be dragging him in for questioning either, the poor bastard is dead." Art's eye's widened with shock. "Bloody hell, Marcus, the bodies are beginning to pile up with this case." Marcus wasn't listening, he was thinking. "We don't know the cause of death yet, but get yourself over there right away, Art, and see what's going on. Magee looked far too spritely to be dying on his feet this soon after our little visit. I'll phone the Newark boys and tell them of our interest and his connection with these latest murders and let them know you're on your way. If this is what we suspect it to be then it's something we should be handling and not the Newark guys. I'll ring you as you go and give you Magee's address, just give me a bell as soon as you're in the picture."

Art almost bolted from the room in his eagerness to get away, he was convinced in his own mind that it was another murder. He thought back to Magee's warning about walls having ears and wondered if it wasn't more of a prediction than a warning. Either way, he was in too much of a hurry to dwell on it and only stopped to pick up Gina before heading off.

They were already on the outskirts of Newark before Marcus came through with the address, forcing Art to reset his Satnav as he hadn't a clue where he was going, but they got there easily enough in the end and found the driveway leading up to the house sealed off with police tape, although they were quickly ushered through thanks to a vigilant young patrolman. As they cruised up the driveway Art noted that it was an expensive, up-market property in a high-end area; the long gravel driveway festooned with flowering plants and bushes surrounding a pair of beautifully maintained lawns.

There was a fair amount of frantic police activity still in progress, although most of it appeared to be concentrated on the right-hand portion of a large double garage to the left of the house. On approaching the garage Art waved his warrant at another uniformed patrolman and was waved straight through, and once inside they were met by a plain clothed detective who greeted Art with a friendly smile.

"Hi, Art, good to see you again. I'm told your guys have an interest in the dead guy." Art carried on past without comment, he was more interested in the body that was dangling from a metal beam at the far end of the garage. Three or four strides took them there with the other detective following in his wake. "That's the pathologist with his back to us, Art," the other detective told him in a hushed voice, "you can have a word with him when he's finished, although to be honest I'm not sure why you're even here, it appears to be a straight-forward suicide from what I can see, but I've been told to bow to your greater knowledge so I'm about to get offside, unless you need me for something?" Art shook his head. "I've got my partner here, Jake, so I'm sure we can cope, but thanks anyway. You can take off and leave us to it."

Having said his piece, Art moved up behind the pathologist who he was also familiar with. "I'm told you're treating this as a suicide, Ted, is that right?" The pathologist wheeled round to face him. "Preliminary findings, Art, we won't know for sure until the medical examiner carries out his post-mortem."

Art rubbed his face and peered over the pathologist's shoulder at the body swaying gently on the end of the rope. "Do you not think it a bit odd that the body hanging there is fully dressed in a bloody pin stripe suit and wearing a collar and tie? How many suicides have you known to be dressed like that?" Ted stepped back from the dangling corpse. "Not many, if I'm honest, Art, white collar jobs normally use a gun or fill themselves full of tablets. Having said that, this guy smells strongly of shower gel, like he has just had a shower, that certainly is a first, for me anyway, I've not come across many suicides who go to all that trouble, but we are talking about people who have reached the end of their tether, and there's no accounting for their actions when they reach that stage." Art dwelt on the pathologist's comment for a while before saying anything else, but he really he wanted to know more. "Have you come across anything that doesn't fit the storyline, Ted." The pathologist shook his head. "Nothing so far, but we're not finished yet, I only got here ten minutes before you."

"Fair enough, Ted, I'll check with you again before I leave if that's okay? But tell me how do we get into the main house?" Ted pointed to a door at the far end of the garage. "I'm reliably informed that leads to a back hallway of the house, but if you intend going inside you'll need to boot up and the normal restrictions apply of course." He pointed to a satchel on the floor. "Gloves, shoe covers and shower caps in there, help yourselves."

Gina went to the satchel and got what was needed while Art had a whispered conversation with the pathologist. "That corpse needs to be sent over to our man, Boswell, Ted. Between you and me, the guy you have dangling from that beam was supposed to meet up with Marcus and me this morning to assist us with an investigation into a double murder, and both of our suspects work for his company."

The pathologist took a step backwards. "Oh dear, I wasn't aware of that; it sure puts a different slant on things. Clearly your guys are already on top of things, so I feel obliged to do as you ask. Just leave it with me, Art." Art patted him on the shoulder and turned back to Gina who was beginning to wonder if she had suddenly become invisible. "Let's go see what pandora's box has to offer."

As soon as they were kitted out Art led the way into the rear of the house which was well maintained and laid out in a modern, open plan Design. Art headed straight for the main lounge where a number of cupboards and wall units invited attention. "We're looking for a lap-top or a desk diary, Gina, anything that will give us an insight into his recent activities." They each took a side of the room and began their search, but when nothing of importance came to light Art decided to move on. "Let's try that other room down the hall." he suggested. The other room turned out to be a well-furnished gentleman's study, giving Art's enthusiasm a boost. "This looks more like it." he said, rubbing his hands in anticipation.

The centrepiece of the room was a large oak desk with shelved wall units immediately behind that were lined with books of all ages and descriptions, as was the wall to the left of that. Art made a bee-line for the desk and was disappointed to find no sign of a computer or a desk diary anywhere in sight.

"What sort of businessman doesn't have a computer or a desk diary in his bloody study?" he asked. Gina gave a little snigger. "One who has something to hide I imagine," she muttered, "but let's keep searching and see what turns up." She was already on her knees searching a low-level unit while. By now Art had shuffled round to the side of the desk and spotted a computer cable laying on the carpet. The fact that it was still plugged into a wall socket that was still switched on told him all he needed to know. "There's no sign of computer in here that I can see, Gina, but there's a cable for one behind the desk here that's still plugged into a live wall socket, which probably means it was taken by someone in too big a hurry to even switch it off before snatching it." He scratched the back of his neck. "Someone was either looking for something important that was on the computer or was trying to get rid of something that was on it. I'm heading back to the lounge, but you carry on searching those cupboards and see if there's a diary anywhere." Turning away he left Gina on her knees rummaging inside the cupboards, and contrary to what she was thinking, he wasn't going back to the lounge on a whim, he was going there because he recalled having seen a landline phone on a side table that they hadn't checked.

On snatching it up the messaging service told him there were two new messages, and on pressing the connect button he learned that the first message, which was recorded the previous day, was from Magee's wife and was just a call about her visit to her mother and when she would be back. The second call though was the one that really grabbed his attention, it too was dated the previous day but was of much more interest.

"I know we were meant to meet in person to discuss the outstanding issue that you raised, James, but you are a long way off and I have no intention of traveling with things as they are. However, I do take heed of your concerns, as I always do, and I will take immediate action to fulfil and conclude my end of the bargain. The package that we recently agreed will be delivered to you at your home this very evening, James, but it's a requirement with this delivery that your lovely wife should not be in attendance when my man arrives, for reasons that I know you will understand." There was a short pause, then the message continued. *"I believe this will bring the outstanding matter of our mutual concern to an agreeable and acceptable conclusion. Take care, James, from you know who."* Art kept hold of the handset for longer than necessary, staring at it like it owed him something, he was deep in thought over the message he was trying to de-cypher. When he'd finished thinking it through he set the handset down rather gingerly and dropped into a nearby armchair to gather his thoughts.

"Sounds very like a pay-off to me," he told himself, but if that were true then what was Magee being paid for, and who the hell was paying him? It wasn't very helpful that the person who had made the call had deliberately withheld his identity." These were the questions rattling round in his brain, and he had at least stopped talking to himself when Gina came to re-join him. "You look in a bit of a stew, Art, so what's up, why are you looking so pensive?"

Art ruffled his hair with both hands before telling her about the weird message. "Certainly sounds a bit strange, in fact it sounds more than a little of the beam. Who the hell makes a phone call and doesn't say who is calling?" She was as puzzled as Art was and gave him an uncustomary grunt to back it up. "Clearly it's someone who doesn't want anyone, other than the recipient, knowing who made the call." She was answering her own question and looking seriously thoughtful. Art on the other hand wanted action, not words. "We need a trace on that call and find out where it came from. Can I leave that with you?"

"Of course you can, it might even stop me feeling like a spare prick at a wedding."

"Don't be like that, sweetheart," he moaned, "you know how much I rely on you when the going gets tough. Believe me when I tell you that we have a long way to go with this case, a very long way indeed I shouldn't wonder." He got up and grabbed her round the waist. "Let's get the hell out of here and see what our pathologist has turned up."

When they got there they found Ted packing his kit and about to wind things up. "I'm done here, Art, but you might ask Bow to let me have the results of his post-mortem, and I wish you luck tracking down your killers, it sounds like you're going to have your work cut out."

Art gave him a pat on the shoulder. "We're off as well, Ted. See you again sometime, but not like this I hope." He led Gina from the gloom of the garage into the brightness of the day outside. "Let's get back to the ranch and see what's cooking."

They went straight to their car and headed off.

9

When they got back to Manhattan Art's first port of call was to link up with Boswell the medical examiner. He found him peering into a microscope, but true to form when he looked up and saw who it was he was clearly more interested in Gina than Art, although there was nothing new in that. "To what do I owe this unforeseen pleasure?" he asked. Art winked at Gina. "Hi, Bow, nothing much really, I only popped in to warn you that you'll be having a visitor very shortly." Boswell lowered his head and peered at him over the top of his glasses. "I'm not expecting any callers, so who the hell thinks they have an appointment with me that I don't know about?" Art gave Gina another crafty wink. "Doesn't matter who he is, Bow, you won't get much of a conversation out of him, he's dead already."

Boswell gave him a two fingered salute. "Okay, so who the hell have you managed to bore to death this time?" he asked, smirking at Gina. Art smiled in appreciation. "Okay, Bow, joking aside, a guy by the name of James Magee is going to be occupying your gurney very shortly, and you need to know that he's the same guy who had arranged to meet up with Marcus and me at half-five this morning but didn't turn up. We believe he had information to offer on our double murder, but he was found dangling from a beam in his garage this morning dressed like he was heading for a business conference. We're both convinced he was murdered, so we're looking to you to prove it, just give it your best shot and keep us all happy."

Boswell chuckled quietly and shook his head from side to side. "When you need me, you need me, Art, and I'm always here to oblige, you know that, but I can only find what's there, I can't make it up just to please you." Art draped an arm round his shoulder. "I would never ask you to do that, Bow, you should know that by now. I'm only asking you to be your usual diligent self, as I'm sure you will be." He turned away and took Gina by the arm. "We have to go and brief Marcus, but do me a favour, Bow, and let me know as soon as you've completed your post-mortem and send a copy of your report over to Ted over at Newark please." Boswell gave him the thumbs up and carried on with what he'd been doing before he was interrupted.

Delgado was in a jovial mood when they got to him, laughing, and giggling with somebody on the other end of his phone; he deliberately ignored their presence until he'd finished the call. "Well? he asked Art, "how did you get on at Magee's?" Art gave him a frosty look, proving that he didn't appreciate being ignored. "The local pathologist believes Magee committed suicide."

Delgado grunted noisily. "Stuff what *he* thinks, what do you think?" he snapped. Art pulled up a chair and dropped into it, leaving Gina languishing by the door. "Boswell will be able to tell us for sure, but I have never seen anyone hang themselves in a bloody pin-stripe suit and tie before, not to mention smelling like a freekin' beauty queen. It's my call he was murdered." Delgado screwed his face up. "Jesus, Art, we already have three dead bodies stacked up in the morgue and not a single living suspect under lock and key. My money is on our fugitive Sharpe, we don't have to prove he's a killer, we already have proof of it, and Magee's murder, if that's what it is, convinces me it was Sharpe who got the cleaning contract. What's your take on it?"

Art gave it some thought before making his feelings known. "The way

I see it, we need to go through Mendelson and Ackermann's business with a fine-tooth comb, including a forensic audit of their accounts. There is something not right about that lot, Marcus, and we need to find out what it is. We already know they've had two killers on their company books, with both involved in company security, albeit at different levels, maybe we need to look further up the chain and not at the rank and file. Someone higher up than Sharpe is running this, whatever *this* turns out to be. We haven't even decided on a motive yet, but if they are involved in these murders it will almost certainly be directed from their London HQ and not from Newark." He stopped talking to gauge the reaction from the other two, but it was slow to come, and when it did it was Gina who took the lead. "Have we turned up anything more on Silverman's wayward step-son? He seems to be keeping himself well under the radar since the old boy died, even though it's highly likely he's the main beneficiary now that young Benjamin has left the scene, and if that turns out to be the case he has good reason to protect his inheritance and not let it slip from his grasp." Art was quick to back her up. "She makes a valid point, Marcus."

"I know she does," countered Marcus, perhaps a bit too sharply, "I've been chasing it up as best I can and I'm advised that he's bedded down at his Detroit office since his step-father died, although he does visit New York on a regular basis for business reasons. So I think we should interview him the next time he's in our neck of the woods. What I want you to do, Art, is to link up with Inspector Stewart and keep in regular touch with him, and I mean on a daily basis if possible, I'm interested to know if the Met police are looking into Mendelson and Ackermann's affairs. Bring him up to date with the Magee saga and explain our interest in that grubby little lot." Having finished with Art he turned his attention to Gina. "Somebody should update young

76

Benjamin's lady friend with what we've found out about his family, and I can think of no one better suited to the task than you. From what I know of her she seems to be a very nice young lady and I did promise to keep her updated. Can I drop that in your lap?" Gina nodded positively. "Happy to do it, Captain. Is that us finished here?"

"I'm finished with *you*, Gina, but I need another word with Art about what went on at Magee's." Gina was out the door in the blink of an eye, leaving Art wondering what his boss had in store for him.

"Don't look so glum, Art, just tell me what went down at Magee's." Art delved into a lengthy explanation about the phone message and his slant on it. "Whoever made that call went to a lot of trouble to keep a low profile. It's my guess that the so-called package the caller was meant to deliver to Magee was his death sentence." He paused to think of what to say next. "Magee's wife is due back from her mother's later today and I want to interview her as soon as she gets home, but just so you know my take on it, Marcus, I have to believe that Magee's killer is none other than our man on the run Rodney Sharpe."

Delgado didn't argue. "I agree, Art, you're right on the button listing him as our number one suspect, so for now I want you to treat Magee's murder as a top priority. Get to grips with his wife and see what she has to say. We've had no positive feed-back from our all-unit's alarm on Sharpe's movements. I can't believe how quickly that bastard flew the nest, but at least we know he wasn't in London when Hardwick was murdered, so there has to be another killer on the loose over there, but that's a job for Ian Stewart's team, not ours. You do whatever you have to over the next few days to get on top of the Magee case. I see that as our main priority, and there's no need to keep updating me unless you have a breakthrough, okay?"

Art got up to leave. "I'm happy with that, Marcus, but what about this stepson in Detroit? Should we not be making inroads there too?" Delgado waved him away. "You concentrate on Magee and leave the rest to me." Art turned on his heel and made for the door, throwing a parting suggestion over his shoulder as he left. "I think you should get Gina to follow up on the stepson before he flees the country and heads back to Brazil." He didn't wait for a reply, just pulled the door shut behind him and headed off to Newark to catch up with Magee's wife.

There were tattered remnants of the police visit from the previous day fluttering in the breeze when he got there, and the garage doors were also decorated with torn remnants of tape, as was the front and side doors to the house, but Art wasn't much interested in any of that as he sat in his car outside. He looked bored to tears as he waited for Debra Magee to get back from visiting her mother, and it was well into the afternoon before she turned into the driveway in her natty little sports car.

Art got out when he saw her approaching and greeted her sympathetically. "Good afternoon, Missus Magee," he said, sounding almost apologetic, "I'm Lieutenant Gardiner from the New York Police Department and I'd like to express my sincere condolences on your sad loss. I know this must be a very difficult and trying time for you, but I would like to join you indoors for a little chat, if you feel up to it?" Debra Magee was an attractive woman in her late thirties, with auburn hair and a lightly tanned complexion. She carried her slender frame with a noticeable air of confidence without looking overbearing or arrogant, and appeared, at first glance anyway, to be well composed in the circumstances. She even attempted a timid smile in response to Art's greeting, but it got lost somewhere among the worry lines.

"Good afternoon, Lieutenant," she said, returning his greeting, "do you mind if I ask why you're interested in my husband's death?" Art wrung his hands together while deciding how to answer. "I would prefer not to discuss such personal matters out here, Missus Magee. I think it would be much more appropriate if we were to go inside."

She turned away without thinking and ducked under the police tape to get to her door. "Please come in, Lieutenant." she invited.

Art followed her into the lounge, making a mental note that there were no visible signs of his or Gina's earlier visit. "Can I get you something to drink, a coffee or a cold tea perhaps?" she asked. Art declined the offer as he was keen to get down to business. "You asked me why I was interested in your husband's death, Missus Magee." She raised a hand in protest. "There is no need for such formalities, Lieutenant, please call me Debra." Art smiled in reply, he had already taken a liking to the lady. "Thank you, Debra, I'm here to try to help and support you at this difficult time, and it will be useful if we *can* be less formal with each other. My name is Art, short for Arthur." He held his hand out and it was readily accepted. "Pleased to meet you, Arthur, but do take a seat and tell me why you are here as I'm a bit confused by all this."

Art slid into a nearby chair and got himself settled before explaining about the murders and the ensuing events, including the none-event of the planned meeting with her husband. He finished by expressing his own feelings on this latest turn of events. "Before I offer you my personal feeling on what has taken place may I ask if you know of any reason why your husband would want to commit suicide?" Debra Magee looked horrified at the thought, and strongly defended her husband. "There is absolutely no reason on God's earth why James should want to do such a thing. I couldn't believe it when the police

79

phoned me with that awful news, and I still can't believe it, even now." She was getting worked up and stopped talking to compose herself. "Look around you, Lieutenant." She quickly corrected herself. "Sorry, Arthur, of course, but to get back to James, I can assure you that we were perfectly happy as a couple and totally committed to each other and our way of life here in Newark, and I know James absolutely loved working here. So I'm finding it really difficult to understand what could have happened to drive him to even think of doing such a thing. It's so out of character and so contrary to everything he believed in that it's not even conceivable."

Art knew he was about to move into dangerous territory with what he was minded to say next, especially as the results of Magee's post-mortem hadn't yet come through to back it up, but he was confident enough in his own assessment of the situation to take the plunge. "What I am about to say is unsubstantiated, Debra, as it's not yet supported by our medical examination or the post-mortem, which is currently taking place, but it comes from my many years' of experience as a homicide detective." He waited a few moments to gauge her reaction. When she showed no adverse reaction he carried on. "I take no pleasure in telling you this, but it's my belief, and the belief of my other detectives, that your husband did *not* commit suicide. All the available evidence we have gathered convinces us that your husband was most likely the victim of an outrageous and callus murder." He waited for this dreadful revelation to take effect before asking the obvious question. "Having said that, Debra, can you thinks of anyone who might have any reason to kill your husband, or anyone who would benefit from your husband's death?" Debra Magee was sitting with her head buried in her hands, sobbing her heart out. Art waited for her to regain control of her emotions before pressing her for an answer, but he didn't wait very long before kicking off again. "It's vitally important that I have an answer to that question, Debra, because if James was murdered, as we suspect, then we have to get an urgent investigation under way to find his killer before he flees the country and finds a hiding place." A very distraught and shocked Debra Magee raised her head and looked up at him with tears in her eyes. "I'm very sorry," she sobbed, "but it's painful enough to be told that James is dead after committing suicide, but you're now asking me to believe that he was murdered? It's all too much to take in." She went into another bout of uncontrolled sobbing.

Art could see it was futile to try getting through to her in her present state. "Let me get you a cup of coffee." he offered, but Debra jumped up and hurried past him. "It's quite alright, I can manage thank you." She got quickly on her feet and headed for the coffee machine.

Once they were seated again with their coffee in hand Art approached the topic a second time. "I'm sorry to keep on about this, Debra, but it's terribly important that I know if there is anyone you can think of who would want to harm your husband." Debra closed her eyes in response, as if to shut herself away from the world she was facing. "I'm sorry, but I find that the most preposterous suggestion I have ever heard. Surely you're not considering murder as a serious possibility?" Art shrugged his shoulders in defeat. "You have already said that you your husband's suicide was too unbelieve for you to even contemplate, so why then is murder any harder to accept?" She wiped away her tears before answering. "No, it's not, but I don't know of anyone in this world who would want to harm James or think to murder him." Art was having none of it and kept forcing the issue. "We are convinced that someone did, and if you check the voice mail on your landline you will find that it holds a very cryptic message from someone who went out of his way to remain anonymous. More importantly, I'm convinced the message was planned to ensure James was here alone at a prearranged time when someone came to murder him. Go and listen to it please, Debra, and tell me if you recognise the voice."

She got up from her seat and went to the phone, and after listening to the message she looked seriously confused by she'd heard. "I haven't a clue who that is, but I can see why you find it puzzling as it is a very strange message and no mistake." She stared at the floor for a little while looking like she was searching for answers. "I can understand why you might suspect something underhand with that phone message as it sounds very odd indeed, but I'm asking myself, why, why would anyone want to murder my husband?" Art couldn't think of an answer, so he didn't bother offering one. "Did your husband keep a laptop or a desktop here at home?" he asked. Debra looked a little confused by the change of topic. "Yes, of course he does, he keeps a desktop in his study. James runs a sizeable company for God's sake and has to keep in regular touch with what's going on, there are always lots of e-mails flying about, but surely there's nothing sinister in that, is there?"

"Nothing sinister at all," agreed Art, "but there was no computer in his study when we were here earlier today, and I have to say that we would have expected James to have left a note of some sort to explain himself if he was minded to commit suicide. Would you not have expect that too, Debra?"

She eased back into her chair with a sad, far-away look on her pretty face. Art wondered if she might be thinking of happier times. "James was a brilliant communicator, and we always discussed our problems quite openly, so why would he not speak to me if he had something really serious preying on his mind, something serious enough that it drove him to take his own life?" She curled up on her chair with her arms wrapped around her body. "I find it *very* odd that his computer is missing." She sounded really confused. "I can't explain how it vanished. His computer was a very important part of his life and was always kept in his study." She left her chair and began pacing about the room with her arms still wrapped around herself. "I'm beginning to make sense of your theory, Lieutenant. I'm beginning to believe that James might have been murdered, but only because I can find no other rational explanation for his death." Art got to his feet as well. "I'm treating your husband's death as murder, and our medical examiner will soon give us a definitive answer with the result of his post-mortem." He quickly changed the subject. "I have to be leaving now, Debra, but before I do I need to know that you have someone nearby to turn to. Someone to help you through the next few days."

"Please don't concern yourself, Lieutenant, I have plenty of friends close at hand if I need them, but I'm a very capable person anyway, and my mother is coming to stay with me in a few days, so you have no need to worry, but thank you for your concern."

He edged closer to the door. "We'll keep you informed as things progress, Debra, and we will appoint a family liaison officer to keep you up to date and to help you with any issues you have regarding our investigation, but should you remember anything that you consider might be useful to our investigation, or if you feel in need of our assistance, please feel free to get in touch. I'll see myself out and thank you for the coffee"

He handed her his calling card and began walking away as she dropped into her chair again looking very lost and lonely.

The first thing Art did when he was outside was phone Gina to find out what she was doing, and to let her know he way on his way home.

They hadn't been in touch since earlier in the day and he wasn't sure what time she would be finished. With that sorted he drove off with Debra Magee very much on his mind, not in any personal way, but because he was worried that she was on her own at a very vulnerable time. However, by the time he got home all thought of that had taken a back seat as he had other things to occupy him. Like where their case was heading rather than what was for dinner?

10

The following morning offered a cold and overcast start to the day as Art and Gina headed off to work. There was only one thing of importance on Art's mind during their drive in, which was a worrisome concern over the results of Boswell's post-mortem, because if Magee's death was to be listed as suicide he would have to rethink where Sharpe fitted into his investigation and renew his approach to the whole case. A thought that filled him with absolute dread, as did the lack of progress in their hunt for their fugitive. That was another worry bearing down on him as there had not been a single sighting of Sharpe since he'd left his hotel in Newark., nor any leads as to his whereabouts that were deemed strong enough to follow up on.

Gina on the other hand, who had also been quiet during breakfast, and since, was aware from a previous conversation that Art was seriously stressed out over the lack of progress in finding Sharpe. She had listened to him pacing about the floor late into the night after she had gone to bed and knowing he would be heading straight in to see Marcus she was hoping their meeting would be constructive and not destructive. Although she suspected, from his inability to hold a conversation, that he was still feeling a bit tetchy. A thought that bolstered her concern that the two men might end up locking horns as they were both quite capable of making a mountain out of a mole hill. More so when the case they were working stalled, as this one was in danger of doing if they didn't catch up with their only living suspect. She decided to try and pre-empt such an event from happening.

"How do you feel about getting Marcus to consider me as family liaison for Debra Magee?" she asked, believing any conversation was better than none. "I'm way ahead of you on that one, Gina," replied Art, "I've been thinking along the same lines. You're better suited than anyone else in the department for that role and I don't see Delgado raising any objection, unless of course he has something more important in mind for you. I'll tackle him with it when I get in to see him."

Gina was surprised that he had agreed so readily, it made her think his mood was beginning to lighten up, so she pressed on. "I'd like to come in with you when you go to see him if that's alright, it might help to force the issue a bit."

"Why not?" he agreed. Without giving the matter further thought.

Twenty minutes later they were parked up and heading indoors, but as they made their way past reception the duty sergeant called Art over. "Good morning, Lieutenant. I have a message here for you to contact a Missus Magee?" He handed Art a stick-it note with the telephone number scrawled on it. Art took the note and went on through to the main office.

"I wonder what she wants to talk to you about, Art?" asked Gina, "It was only last evening when you were with her for God's sake." Art looked just as puzzled. "I haven't a clue, but we'll find out soon enough because I'm going to phone her before I go in to see Marcus." Gina peeled off to her workstation as Art headed for his office phone.

Having dialled her number he was rewarded an immediate connection. "Good morning, Debra Magee." she said in greeting. "It's Lieutenant Gardiner, Debra. I'm returning your call."

"It's good of you to get back to me, Lieutenant. After you left me yesterday I got round to thinking about my husband's missing computer and it came back to me that there was an occasion quite recently when it was giving him a few problems and he borrowed mine until he had it checked out. It was only for a couple of days, well, three actually, but I thought there might be something on it that could help you with your investigation as I haven't deleted any e-mails or anything like that. I know I'm clutching at straws, but you gave me the impression you were eager to investigate the content of his computer. So if you think it might help I'm very willing to let you have access to it." She gave a loud sigh. "I will do anything in my power to help you find out why my dear husband lost his life."

Art didn't even need to think about it. "How recently was it that James borrowed your computer, Debra?"

"It was only for three days last week." she explained, without realising the effect her answer had on Art. "I really would like to check it out, and I'm about to have someone appointed as your Liaison officer, a detective sergeant Gina Garcia. She will be in touch with you later today. It would be helpful if you could let her have it and we keep hold of it for a day of two?"

"That will be fine, Lieutenant, it's like I said earlier, anything I can do to help, and I look forward to hearing from your sergeant later. Goodbye for now." She disconnected without further comment. Art replaced the phone and rubbed his hands together excitedly; his whole mood had suddenly gone up a notch as he charged out through the door and along to Delgado's office.

"Did we have a meeting scheduled for this morning?" Asked his boss, questioning his own memory in the process. "I don't think so,

Marcus," confessed Art, "but I need to clear a few things with you." Delgado gave him a surly look. "You had better get on with it then as I'm busy." Art wasn't pleased with his greeting but decided to leave it be. "We need a case liaison officer for Magee's wife, and I would like Gina to take it on. I think the female touch might be what's needed, especially as the lady in question is being very helpful." When he'd finished he went on to explain about the missing computer and Debra's offer. Delgado stopped him saying anything else with a raised hand. "Before you go on, Art, our friend Boswell has completed his post-mortem, so I suggest you go see him and catch up with me again whenever he's finished with you." Art didn't even bother answering but took off like his pants were on fire.

When he got to Boswell he was greeted with a knowing smile. "I don't need to ask why you're here," he said with a smile, "and in good time too as I'm heading out shortly." Art was stood with both hands prayer like under his chin. "I hope you've got some good news for me, Bow?" Boswell looked nonplussed. "Depends on what you call good news. I would never describe murder as good news."

Art had to stop himself from rushing over and hugging his friend. "So, I was right, he was murdered. You had better explain, Bow, I need the details."

"You friend Magee was strangled with a ligature before that rope was put around his neck and he was hung up from that beam in his garage. I have to admit it's a bit weird that there's absolutely no evidence of a struggle of any kind, and you know as well as I do that our victim wasn't a small man, not by any measure, just an inch or so shorter than you in fact, and he was fairly well built too, so why didn't he put up a fight? It's an issue that baffles me, and before you ask, yes, there was alcohol in his blood, but nowhere near enough to incapacitate him. So why did he allow himself to be strangled without fighting back? That's a proper mystery if ever there was one. Do you not think so?"

Art was on a different plane altogether; hyped-up and elated but he still gave thought to Boswell's question. "Could he have been drugged?" he asked, "that would account for a lack of resistance, wouldn't it?"

Boswell's shake of the head gave him his answer, but he confirmed it verbally as well. "No drugs of any kind in his system so you had better try something else." Art looked around Boswell's office as if he was searching for something. "I don't suppose you have any coffee on the go, I'm dying for one and I could do with a sit down and a chat if you can spare the time." Boswell sighed wearily. "I did say I was going out, Art, so make it quick, and no time for coffee I'm afraid."

"Okay, Bow, but tell me something before you bale out, is there any other way we can account for Magee not defending himself from his attacker, might it be that he trusted whoever killed him and was caught napping?" Boswell shrugged. "That's a possibility, in fact it's a distinct possibility, but don't ask me to prove it, that's your job."

Art put his hand up to his mouth and stayed like that for some little while wondering where to go next. "Did you find any other marks or scars on his body that were unaccounted for?" Boswell nodded affirmatively. "There were some light fingernail type scratches on his back and shoulders, nothing serious and they looked to be a few days old. It could just be that his wife was enjoying herself during their last bedroom encounter." He sniggered quietly at his own salacious remark.

"That's a possibility," muttered Art, "but I don't think I'll be questioning her on it." He was ready to be on the move again. "I guess if there's nothing else I might as well head off." He gave his friend a farewell wave and headed for the door, reminding himself that he had to revisit to his boss.

When he got to him Delgado was on the phone, but when Art walked in unannounced he offered his apologies to whoever was on the other end and handed the phone over to him. "It's Ian Stewart from the Met, Art," he explained, "so it's over to you now." He was acting like a man in a hurry to be somewhere else and Art was happy enough to take over from him. "Good morning, Ian, it's Art Gardiner here, I'm to be your liaison at this end so tell me, have you been brought up to date with what's going on over here regarding our man Magee?"

"Good to meet up, Art, and yes, Marcus has just finished updating me. I believe you visited the victim's wife earlier, did anything come from it or is the situation still as it was?"

"Well," said Art, drawing the word out, "our family liaison officer is with her later on today and she'll be picking up her computer in the vain hope that it will give us something, but until we get to see it we're none the wiser." There was a lengthy silence before Stewart came back to him. "We've been having a tough time with this Mendelson and Ackermann bunch. They know how to pull a legal rabbit out of the bag to keep themselves protected. We.ve been blocked at every turn so I've decided to go in with a warrant later today to have a closer look at them, although I don't believe they knew anything about what Hardwick was involved with, nor do I believe they had anything to do with his murder. When you think about it, why would one of the top legal firms in the country get involved in something as serious as homicide? Having said that, I'm minded to check out their e-mails to see who has said what to who, especially the people at the top."

He let that sink in for a while before going back to their original topic. "What has you so interested in his wife's computer; how does it tie in with your investigation?" Art was unsure how to answer, but he did his best. "It's simple really, we know Magee's own computer was stolen from his study, most likely by his killer, but he had cause to use his wife's computer for a few days prior to his murder so we need to check it to see there is anything of interest there that might open a new line of enquiry. We're clutching at straws really, Ian, nothing more than that. I doubt if it will lead us anywhere, it's just part of the process."

There was a quiet little snigger at the other end. "Isn't that what we're all about, Art, clutching at straws? We never know the outcome of anything until we follow through on our hunches. Anyway, if there's nothing else I'll be off, I just wanted to touch base with you guys and keep in touch."

"I appreciate your call, Ian, and I'll let you know how we get on. Take care my friend, and good luck with M and A." He ended the call without waiting for a reply, and as Marcus still hadn't returned he went back to his own office to work out what to do next.

His thoughts were focussed on Rodney Sharpe as he sipped his coffee, and in particular how he had managed to evade capture for so long. Although he suspected, without having any evidence to support his hunch, that working for such a high-profile company probably meant he was well connected. That said, he couldn't imagine anyone in their right mind willingly assisting a fugitive who was on the run from a murder rap. In fact he could only come up with one possibility and that was old boy Silverman's step-son, but that was because he had been Sharpe's previous employer. Thinking along these lines tempted him to get off his ass and go to Detroit to check him out rather than

91

wait for the unlikely event of him coming to New York.

The more he dwelt on the problem, and he dwelt on it for longer than he should, the more convinced he was that the short-term answer was to get the Detroit police involved and put a surveillance team on him to cover his home and his business premises in case Sharpe turned up at either location. In the end he settled on that as a short term remedy, but he still had the job of selling the idea to Marcus, and that would be no simple matter.

When he caught up with him and ran his idea past him he was quietly impressed at how quickly Delgado had agreed to contact the Detroit police and set it up. He was also impressed by his sudden show of enthusiasm in getting it done.

Having had a long chat with the Detroit police Delgado sounded quite chirpy and up-beat when he hung up. "It shouldn't take them long to find out if Sharpe is holed up there and if he is we'll soon have him under lock and key." Art's dismissive expression warned his boss that he had other things on his mind. "I can't wait to get hold of Debra Magee's computer, bearing in mind that her husband used it so close to his untimely death. There might be something there that will lead us to the maniac behind all this bloody mayhem."

Delgado earlier enthusiasm took a bit of a nose-dive. "I hope you're right, Art, because the D A has ants in his pants over this case. He wants it wrapped up and put to bed, and quickly too." Art suddenly remembered something he should have mentioned earlier. "I forgot to tell you, Marcus, Ian Stewart's team are going into Mendelson's and Ackermann's later today with a warrant. Like us, he's interested in going through their e-mails, so let's hope they turn up something useful." Marcus gave a wry smile. "I hope you're right, Art, just let me know if anything comes of it. Now if we've got nothing else to discuss I have things to do." Art was more than happy to be on his way, he was chomping at the bit to get to grips with Debra Magee's computer, and as it was now late afternoon with no sign of Gina, or the computer, he wouldn't be able to settle until she got back, and he took possession of it. Sitting behind his desk he was toying with the idea of phoning her when she walked in unexpectedly and caught him off guard.

"Sorry I took so long, Art, but Debra Magee is such a lovely lady that I may have overstayed my welcome a little, the poor girl is absolutely devastated by the loss of her husband. Especially so as she can't figure out why anyone would want to harm him, let alone murder him." Art was in no mood for girly talk. "Did you get the computer?" he asked dryly.

"Of course I did," she snapped, feeling a bit put out by his surly attitude, "but you might let me get through the bloody door before kicking-off with an inquisition." Art gave her an up and down look. "Just get me the computer please, Gina." She wheeled away and headed for her workstation wearing a disgruntled expression, although she returned in record time with the object of Art's concern under her arm. It proved to be a modern, blue tooth design with the computer and monitor all in one. She plunked it down noisily on his desk without saying a word. Art stared at it like it was a visiting alien. "Thank you," he said quietly, "now let's see if we can get the bloody thing rigged up and working." It only needed to be plugged it into a wall socket to bring it to life, and Gina looked on with a knowing smirk as he booted it up, "You won't get very far without this." She warned, handing him a piece of paper with Debra's password scribbled on it. Art reached out and looped his arm round her waist. "Thanks,

Gina, I'm glad you're on hand." He sounded a touch more respectful this time, so Gina decided to give way help him out. "Maybe you should let me do that?" she offered, "I know my way round these things better than you do." Art ended up with a silly grin on his face. "Just get me into the e-mails, honey, that's all I want for now."

Gina opened up the e-mails and stepped aside to let him at it. "There you go big man, fill your boots."

Art started working his way through the mail file looking for any addressed to Debra's husband, it turned out that over the three days he'd had access to it he'd received more than fifty e-mails. He kicked things off with the earliest date and began working his way through them from there, only stopping to read those that looked inviting, and it wasn't long before he found one that looked seriously inviting, in fact it glared up at him like a laser beam.

It had been sent on the day Magee was murdered and was from none other than his security manager, Rod Sharpe. Art's eyebrows shot up as he tried to make sense of what he was reading, and understandably so because having read it through for a second time he was still wearing the same inquisitive frown. The e-mail in question was typed in a free-hand style font and was phrased in such a way as to be open to interpretation, although Art believed he knew exactly what it meant.

"Hi James, thank you for the invitation, I do hope it's certain that Debra will be staying at her mother's, and we won't be disturbed? I have just bought some very interesting equipment that I want to share with you, I'm told it achieves the ultimate. Much better than last time I promise" There was a reply from Magee that was every bit as cryptic. *"I can't wait to see it, and you Rod. Do we set it up indoors or in the garage? (Lots of laughter). I'll leave that up to you. I look forward to seeing you and your equipment, but don't forget to bring a bottle."*

Art leaned back in his chair with a knowing smile on his face. "If that means what I think it means, Gina, then it tells me exactly why Magee didn't put up a struggle when he was murdered." He stopped to towel his face with both hands before going on to explain. "I can hardly believe what I'm reading here. The only interpretation I can put on it is that Magee was having a sordid love affair with his security manager, and it was so sordid that there was equipment involved. The guy was a freekin' pervert for God's sake, and I'm beginning to think it was his security manager who killed him because he was given an ideal opportunity to do so."

Gina gasped at the suggestion. "For God's sake, Art, you can't go accusing people of things like that without any evidence to back it up." Art pointed at the e-mail he'd just read. "You read it then, and tell me you don't feel the same way?"

Gina peered over his shoulder, and when she'd finished reading she was also aware of what it meant, although she wasn't ready to admit it. "Well," she said, drawing the word out, "I can see why you might interpret it that way, but it stretches the imagination to come up with such the assumption that Sharpe killed him." Art tapped a finger against the side of his nose and winked at her in a knowing way. "Go and see if Marcus is available to come and have a look. I need his take on this because for me this is solid proof that it *was* Sharpe who killed Magee, and that makes him a *triple* killer. It might also link Sharpe to that weird telephone message."

Gina hurried away while Art continued going through the e-mails without finding anything else of interest. Most of them were just routine business stuff and nothing to get excited about so he scrolled back up to the important one ready for Marcus to see it.

95

Marcus got to him in record time and Art dutifully gave up his seat before directing his attention to the e-mail in question.

Once he had read it a second time he nodded positively? "Well done, Art, I'm in absolute accord with you on this, to me it's meaning is as clear as day. All we have to do now is catch Sharpe and see how he explains this little love note and how conveniently it set Magee up to be taken out."

Gina grunted her objection and Art twisted round in his seat to face her. "What's up? Can you not see from that e-mail what Magee has been up to behind his wife's back?"

She hesitated slightly before answering, but after a bit of mental anguish she got round to making her point. "Well, one of you two can break that wonderful news to Debra Magee because I'm definitely not doing it." She sounded seriously determined as Art scratched the back of his neck as he stared at her. "I think the poor woman deserves to know, maybe not yet, but pretty soon, and we would only use information of that nature during a trial if we were forced to do so, and we would only do so if it were absolutely necessary."

The concerned expression slipped away from Gina's face just as quickly as it got there. "Okay, I can see where you're going with this, but changing the subject for a moment, if it was Sharpe who murdered Magee then what on earth was his motive, especially as you two are already convinced that they were secret lover's?"

Art scratched the back of his neck a bit longer this time while he thought about it. "That's an interesting question, Gina, and I don't have an answer to it yet. Maybe he didn't have a motive, or didn't need one, maybe he was just following orders." Marcus piped in unexpectedly.

"So who gave him his bloody orders? That's the big question that needs answering," said Art, spreading his feet and folding his arms in a more aggressive manner. "No one can convince me that Joshua Silverman isn't mixed up in this. He's the only person left to gain from young Benjamin's death, and we are talking about a legacy worth mega bucks here, not pocket money."

Marcus gave a disapproving grunt. "That's motive, Art, not intent. Give me some evidence to put before the judiciary, that's what's needed if we're to get that theory past the District Attorney." Art wasn't letting go of it, he was convinced he was right and determined to prove it. "We need to sort out who it is that each one of us considers to be the guilty party, that will allow us to concentrate our efforts." He swung round to face Marcus. "I freely admit it could be someone else from Mendelson and Ackermann behind what is going on, I'm not disputing that scenario, but I'm asking myself what have they got to gain? Unless they can fiddle the old boys final instructions they have absolutely nothing to gain apart from their usual professional fee as executors. The same goes for Johnston, Johnston and Jacobs, so who the hell are we left with if not Joshua Silverman?"

Delgado still wasn't buying into it "We don't know for sure what the old boy's final instructions are or who is legally entitled to his legacy." He pointed an index finger at Art. "The next time you're on with Ian Stewart ask him to get us the answer to that. We're only guessing that the step-son is next in line for the inheritance so let's get some proof, only then can we know for sure where we stand."

Art headed for the door muttering over his shoulder. "I'm sure he's clever enough to have that in mind already, but I'll raise it with him anyway." He swung round to face Gina. "I suggest you get a hard copy of those e-mails before we hand Debra's computer back and when you do return it, Gina, ask her not to delete any of them just in case the originals are needed later." Gina gave him the thumbs up, a parting gesture that brought their little get together to an end as Delgado squeezed past her and headed off, while Art got on the phone to Ian Stewart.

Art could very easily become over- obsessed when grappling with things that were outside of his control, and that was very much the case when he and Gina drove home that evening. She could tell by the way he was driving, and the stern look on his face that he wasn't going to leave the job back at the station house, so she decided to pre-empt the oncoming situation. "Can we leave the job behind us tonight, Art, and have an evening meal in peace and quiet for a change. We don't get paid extra for working from home, and I can tell from the stubborn look on your face that you're still on the job." Art threw his head back and laughed fit to bust. "You truly are something else, sweetheart, I think I'll have to wear a mask to stop you reading my mind."

She joined in with his laughter and considered the matter put to bed.

11

Gina arrived at Debra Magee's house very early the next morning, in fact her host was still in her night attire when she opened the door and looked genuinely surprised to see who was ringing her bell. "Are you always on the go this early?" she asked. Gina donned her Sunday best smile. "Not normally, Debra, but I wanted to get your computer back to you without delay."

She sniffed the air and was rewarded with the smell of fresh coffee. "If that's fresh coffee I smell I could kill for a cup, my caffeine levels are seriously depleted." She smiled at the thought.

Debra returned her smile. "I know how you feel, if you can spare the time for a cup come on in, there's plenty to go round." Gina followed her into the kitchen and set the computer on the table before planting herself in front of it.

"You must be very proud of your lovely home, Debra, it's so modern and functional that it makes me envious." Debra had her back turned to Gina as she poured the coffee, but when she turned round again there were tears in her eyes, causing Gina to wonder if she was the cause of her distress. "I'm so sorry if I've upset you, Debra. I really didn't mean to, that's the last thing I would ever want to do." Debra placed the coffee in front of Gina and sat down at the opposite side of the table. "It wasn't anything you said or did, Gina, I can assure you of that. I was just having an off moment when you got here. I was wondering how I will ever manage to hold onto our lovely home now that James is gone and left me on my own. I will have to go through his papers and see what insurance he has, if any?" Her sad admission gave Gina a bit of an off moment too, but she quickly covered it up. "I'm sure James will have done the right thing by you, Debra, so don't go worrying yourself unduly. At least you don't have any children to cope with like some who have lost their husbands." She suddenly realised that she might have said the wrong thing by mentioning children and wished she could swallow her tongue. "You're absolutely right in what you say, Gina, although I always wanted children." She sounded sad when she said this and even hesitated a little before saying anything else. "Am I being a bit forward calling you by your first name?" she asked. "Good gracious no," replied Gina, "I should have made that clear from the start, but tell me, Debra, was it a joint decision not to have children?"

"Oh my God, no," she said, with a shake of her head, "to be perfectly blunt about it, after years of trying it turned out that James's little swimmers could only manage the breast-stroke." Gina almost burst out laughing, and in order to contain herself she got up rather hurriedly and pushed her chair back under the table. "I think it's about time I was making tracks." Debra couldn't hide her disappointment. "Can you not stay a little longer?" she pleaded, "I could do with some company right now as I'm terribly confused and upset over what happened to James, even more so now that it looks like he was murdered." Gina slid her chair back a little. "If you want to talk about it, Debra,. I'm a good listener." Debra looked terribly frail and emotional at that particular moment. "I don't know what to say, I don't even know where to start, I'm beginning to feel as if my whole life has been turned upside down and I can do nothing to right it again." Gina saw an opportunity to delve into her husband's past and she had no intention of letting it slip by. "I can see that you and James were a very happy couple, and it must be a very trying time for you now that he's gone. That's only natural, Debra, but sooner or later need to plan for your own future, and I suggest the sooner you do it the better you will be for it."

Debra wiped her eyes with the back of her hand. "We were always happy together," she admitted, "although maybe a little less in recent months. James had become distracted and less attentive over the past four or five months, you know the sort of thing I mean, a bit snappy and uncommunicative. I thought perhaps things at work weren't going as well as he hoped, and maybe he was getting a little stressed out over it, but he had changed quite rapidly from the smiling, contented, and happy go lucky husband he always had been, to being much more distant and solitary."

"Did you challenge him about this sudden change?" Gina was really interested to find out more.

"I didn't see any point. I knew it wasn't another woman as he has never shown any interest in that respect. To be perfectly honest I sometimes wonder why he married me as he's not exactly known as a woman lover. I suppose in a way it was me who did the loving in our relationship, James was always very reserved about that sort of thing. But don't get me wrong, he was very good to me, and my mother, and what else can a girl ask for?" She gave another weary sigh.

Her defeatist attitude took Gina by surprise; she expected a lot more from someone of her standing and she made a point of telling her. "In my opinion women like us have every right to ask for what we think we deserve, Debra, and quite often that's much more than we dare believe."

She got to her feet again. "I really have to be going now, Debra, as

I have a lot on today."

They both got to their feet and Debra walked her to the front door. "Thank you for giving me of your time, Gina, I'm feeling a much better now thanks to our little chat." Gina stepped out onto the driveway and waved goodbye. She was eager to get back and tell Art that what Debra had told her more or less confirmed his take on her husband sexual appetite. Although deep down she felt it something of a betrayal to do so.

She was back at the station house within the hour and went off in search of Art, who wasn't where she expected him to be, and it took her a while to catch up with him.

He smiled readily when he saw her approaching. "Hi, honey, how did things go?" Gina was in no hurry to answer, but she did. "Well enough to give credence to your theory about her husband's underhand activities." Art moved in on her. "Really? Well now, that does sound interesting, so tell me all about it." He made no attempt to hide his eagerness, and Gina didn't keep him waiting "Debra was very open with me today, in fact she almost pleaded with me to keep her company. She obviously needed someone to talk to just to unburden herself." She felt a like she was betraying a confidence by going on but accepted that she needed to finish what she had started. "I have to admit that I felt really sorry for her, Art, but she spoke to me quite openly and in some detail about their lives together. She stressed the point that James had become unusually distant and snappy over recent months, a change in attitude that she assured me was totally out of character. She also stressed that this was unlikely to have been because of another woman as he wasn't terribly interested in the opposite sex. She even explained why they had no children, and I quote, 'James's little swimmers can only do the breaststroke.'"

Art burst out laughing and was joined in the moment by Boswell who had been listening-in. "Well, well, well, what more is there to say," he mumbled, "it's pretty obvious from what you've just told us that her husband was as gay as a bloody badger. It must have been a very weird marriage to be tied into." He swung round to face Boswell. "All this helps to tie up some of the loose ends, Bow. We were confused as to why Magee hadn't put up a struggle when he was killed, now we know he was playing party games with ropes and things along with his lover Sharpe, who would have been able to get behind him and strangle him with one of their toys. We even know that he arranged a convenient time and place in order to be there and do it, all very neat, tidy, and well executed, but that's three murders now that are down to Sharpe, probably maybe more if we dig deep enough, who knows? We need to get our hands on that callous bastard before he kills somebody else."

He turned back to Gina. "Well done, sweetheart, you did a great job with Debra. Now let's go and brief the boss. He tells me he's getting some flak from the DA so maybe this will ease the pressure." They gave Boswell a pat on the back before leaving.

Delgado greeted them in his usual abrupt manner. "Come in and sit down." He turned to face Art. "Well what have we got that's new?" Art gave him a telling smile. "You're gonna love this one, Marcus." He chuckled quietly at the thought as Delgado eased back in his chair. "Just get on with it, Art." he moaned, "I'm extremely busy right now." Art couldn't wait to get started and charged straight in.

He started off by telling Marcus about Gina's experience with Debra Magee and when he'd finished his boss slammed his fist down on the desk, looking quite excited.

"I'd say that does away with any doubts we might have had over

Sharpe's involvement, not only did he have the perfect opportunity, but he was very conveniently invited into Magee's home along with everything he needed to carry out the damned murder, right there in Magee's own bloody home."

He stopped talking rather abruptly before putting a downer on the moment. "But where's the motive, Art? What was his reason for killing Magee?"

"Give me ten minutes alone with him and I'll give you his motive." Delgado snorted at the idea. "Yeah, I imagine you would, but more to the point, maybe I should give the lads in Detroit a bell and see if they've turned anything up yet."

Art didn't see any sense in phoning them. "Wouldn't they have been in touch if they had something to report?" Delgado shrugged his suggestion aside. "I'll ring them anyway. It's something we need to keep on top of." Art and Gina sat in silence while he made what turned out to be a lengthy phone call, but when he'd finished and replaced his phone he shook his head negatively. "Nothing happening there, although they did say that Silverman is someone they are aware of, so they are more than happy to continue keeping an eye on him."

"Did they say what their interest in him was about?" asked Art. "Nothing specific," replied Delgado, "just mentioned he was on their radar, but they didn't offer any detail as their investigation is still on going, although they made it clear that no charges had ever been brought so I guess it's probably something and nothing." Art wasn't best pleased; he couldn't see any reason for the Detroit police to even consider withholding information from another force. "Do we know why they're holding back on us, Marcus? I can see any justifiable reason for them doing so."

"If I knew why I would have told you, Art. You know as well as I do what some police departments are like, they're trained to keep everything close to their chest and away from the eyes of the media and their paid snitches, so let's just accept it for what it is." Art gave him cursory look. "To my reckoning I should be in Detroit right now questioning Silverman. I rate him as a high level suspect who needs to be brought in and treated as such."

Delgado didn't seem interested, and he let it show on his swarthy features. "Forget it, Art, it's not going to happen, not with our over stretched budget. My intention is to leave it up to the guys in Detroit to keep a watch on him. They'll wave the flag if Sharpe goes anywhere near their patch and that's good enough for me, for the time being anyway."

Art took hold of Gina's arm and walked her out of Delgado's office. "I might as well talk to the goddamned wall," he hissed, "he's not listening to a word I say, and he's completely missing the point. I can't understand why he won't treat Silverman as a suspect, the guy stands out like a sore bloody thumb to the rest of us." He was in one of his rebellious moods and Gina knew from past experience that he wasn't going to drop his theory just to please his boss.

Neither of them were in very good spirits when they left the station house.

12

Joshua Silverman arrived at his business premises in Detroit and ran straight upstairs to his office without so much as a greeting to his receptionist as he passed her by. Once upstairs he removed his jacket and tossed it over the back of a chair and went straight across the room to the front window where he remained for some time staring down at the busy street below. He had no interest in the passing traffic, or the gaggles of busy workers scurrying off to earn a crust, he was only interested in one thing, and that was a dark blue Sedan that was parked in a disabled bay some thirty yards from his premises on the opposite side of the road. His interest stemmed from the fact that he had seen that very same vehicle, parked in exactly that same spot, with the same two male occupants for a third day running! Being a suspicious character by nature and being aware of the turmoil surrounding his step-father's death, he was very much on his guard and more security minded than he would normally have been.

So unnerving was this little incident that it sent him straight to his desk to check that his personal weapon was still safely stored in its locked drawer. The solid feel of it in his hand gave his morale enough of a boost to have him decide to wait another day before doing anything serious about it.

Inside the blue Sedan the aging detective sergeant in charge of the surveillance unit had just reported that Silverman had entered his business premises unaccompanied at his usual time. The same guy was quick to let it be known that he considered his current duty to be a complete waste of his investigative skills. "This guy we're watching comes in to work, puts in a day's graft, then toddles off home to his cosy little out of town life while you and I sit on our asses all day long listening to a load of crap on that goddamned radio. Where the hell is the job satisfaction in that, and how long are we going to be stuck here twiddling our thumbs?"

His partner was no decision maker either and didn't see anything worth getting excited about, so he didn't have a lot to say on the matter, but he said it anyway. "Maybe there's something going on that we don't know about." His throw-away remark was ignored by the sergeant whose attention was focussed on the image of Sharpe's beefy face on his computer screen. "We haven't seen hide nor hair of this jerk since we started this detail. Not here, nor at our targets home either, so what's the use in sitting on our asses wearing out the seat of our pants when there are serious crimes to be solved?" He didn't get an answer, but then he didn't deserve one.

While this little gripe was going on the object of their surveillance was on the phone to his step-father's legal advisors, Mendelson, and Ackermann. "It's Joshua here, I need to know when my step-father's final instructions are to be made public, I can see no justifiable excuse for this long delay in fulfilling his wishes."

"If you hold for one second, Mister Silverman, I will transfer you to the person responsible." The voice left him in the company of the Berlin Pheromonic Orchestra until Mendelson came to the phone.

"Alexander here, Joshua," greeted Mendelson, "and before you go off on one, my hands are tied by this damned police investigation, as you already know. They have given me a warning not to acquaint myself with the content of your step-father's Will or divulge its content to anyone until their investigation is completed." There was a gentle clearing of his throat. "You should remember that we each have a vested interest in completing your step-father's instructions, and the moment I'm free to do so you will be the first to hear of it."

Silverman was so enraged that he slammed the phone down without even saying goodbye. "Fuckin interfering cops." he snarled; his face contorted with rage. Fortunately, there was no one else within earshot to bear witness to his rant, but this angry little episode, brief though it was, highlighted the fact that his quota of patience was noticeably underwhelming. He wanted the matter of his step-father's Will over and done with so he could get back to the safety of Brazil where he planned to spend the rest of his life in solitary isolation as a very rich man. He dropped into his chair and buried his head in his hands.

It might well have been the sheer boredom of the job, or perhaps the fact that both detectives on the surveillance team lacked the discipline required for the job, but something tempted them into assuming it was time for breakfast, and without so much as a glance at their targets premises they drove off in search of the nearest eating house. A decision that was fatalistic in its timing because no sooner had they left their post than a car with Rodney Sharpe's registration number turned into the car park right beside the premises they were watching. More importantly, it was being driven by the very fugitive they were after, and his body language when he got out of the car told anyone watching that he was in a confrontational mood as he ducked into the building through the rear emergency exit, his broad, heavy shoulder's hunched up like a prize fighter.

Silverman had spotted the blue Sedan driving away and ended his on-off vigil at the window, which wasn't very well timed as it allowed

Sharpe to enter the building unseen, and Silverman with no prior warning of the serious confrontation that lay ahead when he walked in on him. In fact he was horror stricken at the sight of Sharpe right there in his office. "What the hell are you doing here?" he demanded angrily.

Sharpe crossed the room and shoved a ham-like fist under Silverman's nose. "I should shove this down your skinny throat, you bastard. You were meant to meet me and get me out of the country after I did that last job for you, but you didn't even turn up, did you? You really are one useless piece of crap." He stepped back a couple of paces while glaring at Silverman. "I'm not sure what to do with you. I know what I should do but I left my gun in the car. Maybe I should kick your useless butt down the stairs and up the street"

He moved in on Silverman again, punching his open palm with a clenched fist, sending tremors of fear through Silverman's feeble body. "It couldn't be helped, Rod," Silverman stammered, "I haven't got my inheritance yet to pay you, and my plane was grounded for servicing by some dozy inspector, so what the hell was I meant to do? I couldn't fly you out of the country without a bloody plane, and we both agreed not to contact each other in case our calls were traced. I have stuck rigidly to that arrangement to help keep us safe."

Sharpe backed off and drifted over to the window and earned himself another angry response from Silverman. "Get the hell away from that window you bloody idiot," he yelled, "I've got a couple of guys watching me, and I'm convinced it's not me they're after, but you." Sharpe instinctively ducked behind the curtain, looking a lot more cautious, but Silverman wasn't finished. "The cops must know by now that you once worked for me, so I guess they're watching to see if we make contact." He ran his fingers through his thinning hair. "I thought you had more goddamned sense than to come here in broad daylight."

Some of Sharpe's aggression had eased off a touch, but only because of his reliance on Silverman to ferry him out of the country, and he couldn't risk damaging his chances by threatening him. "So what do we do now?" he asked.

"We have a mug of coffee while I think things through." explained Silverman. Who then went and filled two mugs with the steaming liquid and after passing one to Sharpe dropped into a chair behind his desk. "The first thing we do is get you out of here and away to somewhere safe. I think I know how to sort that out." He went back to the window. "There's no sign of those two nosy bastards at the moment so nip down and make sure your car can't be seen from the road." Sharpe shook his head. "There's no need for that," he explained, "I'm not stupid, I've already tucked it away." Silverman nodded agreeably. "Whoever is watching here will also be watching my house as well, so we need to be very careful." He buried his face in his hands while he considered their options, and there weren't many, although one thing was blatantly obvious, as he told Sharpe. "I need to stick to my normal routine for going home, that should draw our watchers away and give you a chance to get out of here without being seen, but it means you staying here until after dark." There was something else he needed to check out. "Did anyone see you when you arrived?" Sharpe shook his head. "I made sure no one saw me, that's why I came in through the fire door and up the back stairs."

Silverman gave a sigh of relief and grabbed his desk phone. When he'd finished his call he definitely looked more at ease with himself. "That was an old acquaintance of mine who lives a little way out of town. He

110

has an apartment not too far from here that he uses for occasional stop-overs when he has business visitors. The important thing is that he's agreed to let you use it for the next two nights, so let's keep our fingers crossed that my plane is back in service by then. I've been told they'll have it ready by tomorrow so things could work out very well, but you need to remember that you and I can have absolutely no contact of any sort from here on in. When you leave for my friends place you must keep your head down until I phone you to confirm your flight out." Sharpe reacted well to the news, so much so that his hunched-up shoulders were no longer evident. "Yeah, okay, I understand all that crap," he stammered, "but you can believe me when I tell you that I can't wait to get the hell out of here, but what about this big windfall you're meant to get? When is that going to happen? I need my cut like yesterday, I'm out of work now and I can't live of fresh air." Silverman waved his concerns aside. "It won't be long now until everything is settled and we're enjoying a much fuller lifestyle back in Brazil. Believe me, Rod, I'm every bit as eager as you are to get there, but this police investigation is holding everything up."

Sharpe turned away to refill his mug, but it didn't stop him from continuing to gripe. "I haven't had a single thing to eat for the last two days, what with being on the run and all that, so you need to nip out and get me something?" Silverman didn't relish the idea. "It's not that easy, Rod. I don't normally go out for lunch so it might look like a break in routine if I do so now. Don't forget these premises are being watched." Sharpe crouched over and covered his face with his hands, and when he looked up again it was to scowl angrily. "For Christ sake, do you intend to starve me as well as holding me a fuckin' prisoner?" Silverman's face opened up in a smile. "Come on now, Rod, surely an old soldier like you can go without food for a couple of days. I thought all you special forces guys were as tough as old boots."

"Old boots?" snarled Sharpe, "if I had a pair right now I would eat the damned things." Silverman couldn't help but laugh, he could do nothing else, but he conceded the point. "Okay, I'll get you something, but it will have to be something that fits into my briefcase. You stay here and don't make any noise, try to remember that I have a girl down in reception, so if you hear someone coming up the stairs hide yourself away in the toilet. He pointed to a door at the back of the office. "I'll find some excuse to give her the day off and not take any chances." He grabbed his briefcase and emptied its contents out on his desk before walking out of the office and down the stairs. When he got back, some twenty minutes later, he found his unwelcome visitor fast asleep in the chair and taking a sandwich pack from his briefcase he nudged Sharpe awake and dropped it on his lap, along with a can of coke. Sharpe jolted upright, but he was still very dozy and took some time to regain his senses. "Eat, drink, and be merry, Rod." Silverman said jokingly, quietly relieved that he had managed to get back to his office before his observers were back on site.

Sharpe ripped the wrapping off a chicken sandwich like he hadn't seen food before and began filling his mouth. "It's been so long since I've had a meal that even something as uninspiring as this bloody sandwich tastes like heaven." He didn't bother checking what the filling was, he just set about shoving it into his mouth.

When he'd finished eating and was feeling more refreshed he decided to fire a shot across Silverman's bows with another dire warning. "It wouldn't be advisable to try to double-cross me, Josh. I've fulfilled my end of the bargain as you required so don't try welching on our deal." "Why on earth would I do that? demanded Silverman, "there will be so much money coming my way that paying you off won't even make a dent in it."

"Won't make a dent in you say," challenged Sharpe, "if that's true then maybe I should be getting a bigger cut since I'm the one taking all the risks." Silverman gave him a menacing look. "Don't go getting too big for your boots, Rodney. You're not the only paid killer I know." He pointed a warning finger at his co-conspirator. "You'll get exactly what we agreed and not a red cent more, understood?" The threat of another hired killer trimmed Sharpe's ambitions a little. "Okay. Okay, I get the message. I'm only looking after my interests so don't go making threats, it doesn't suit you." The atmosphere in the room had gone down-hill a couple of notches with both men looking edgy and wary of each other. Sharpe had already admitted that he didn't have his gun on his person, but Silverman was also aware that it was downstairs in his car, should he need it.

"Why don't you settle up with me here and now, today? You're not exactly on your uppers, are you? You need to bear in mind that I never agreed to any deferment of payment once the job was done, or any delay to my payment because you're waiting to make good on your inheritance."

Silverman shifted uneasily on his chair. He didn't have the money to pay Sharpe, not until his legacy came through, which was why he was in his current position. On top of that Sharpe was getting on his nerves with his constant badgering. He inched his chair forward a little and glared at across the desk at Sharpe. "Don't go too far, Rodney, I don't take kindly to being harassed." Sharpe leapt to his feet. "And what are you going to do about it?" he demanded. Silverman eased his desk drawer open and reaching inside pulled out his Browning automatic, and holding it in both hands he leaned over his desk and aimed it straight at Sharpe. "Is this really what you want?" he asked, "or are you going to be sensible and wait for your money?" It wasn't meant as a question and Sharpe knew it, but he had already made sure he was covered before turning up at Silverman's office. What he did next warned Silverman that the threat he had just issued was as empty as his briefcase.

Sharpe got to his feet and laughed in his face before telling him why he was laughing. "If I don't contact my solicitor, by voice, before the end of play each day, he will hand my letter to the authorities detailing your involvement in all three murders that were carried out upon your instructions. Is that what *you* want?"

He went back to his seat, sat down, and crossed his legs casually. "Now why don't you put that silly gun back where it came from and act your age."

Silverman didn't know what to say; Sharpe had him over a barrel. "You've covered all the angles, haven't you, Rod, so we need to stop playing stupid games and get serious. I'm mindful of our agreement to head back to Brazil, and that will happen as soon as my inheritance comes through, and you get your money. Isn't that what we both agreed to do?"

Sharpe's eyes narrowed into accusing slits. "There's something I want answers too before I accept any new agreement this late in the day. You've been living in Brazil for a lot of years now, Josh, so tell me, have you been granted Brazilian citizenship?" Silverman shrugged it off. "Of course I have, I was made a citizen a number of year back, but what has that to do with anything?"

His reply had a strange effect on Sharpe. "It's got everything to do with our arrangement because although Brazil has an extradition arrangement with the United States that arrangement does not include Brazilian citizens. Which means your ass is well and truly covered while mine could be hung out to dry." All he got in response was a surly sneer from Silverman, who had a good idea where Sharpe's argument was heading.

"God's sake, Rod what do you want me to do? Denounce my citizenship? He smoothed his thinning hair back from his forehead. "You need to get real my friend and if you're no longer interested in going back to Brazil then you need to tell me where the hell you do want to go? I'm not a bloody mind reader, but wherever it is, I will get you there and that's a promise."

Sharpe rubbed his chin as he thought his options through. "I'm beginning to think Cuba would suit me better, they don't have an extradition treaty with America, and I do like the Cuban ladies. On top of that I find the Cuban lifestyle much more to my liking, relaxed and easy going comes to mind and my money will go further there."

Silverman cocked his eyebrows knowingly. "I can't argue with you on that. I've been there a few times myself and enjoyed every minute of it, so if that's your decision then so be it. I can arrange to get you there easily enough, but let's park that thought for now, at least until we get you safely out of here tonight and I can arrange a more permanent solution regarding your accommodation, should we need it. How does that sound? Sharpe crossed his legs again and eased back in his seat. "That sounds a bit more like it but bear in mind what I said earlier and don't get any more ideas about hit-men or welching on our deal."

Silverman gave a sigh of relief. He knew he had just escaped a sticky situation; he also knew that he would have to live up to what he had promised this time. "Now that we have this new arrangement, Rod, let's not allow things to get ugly between us again. We've known each other far too long for that. I know we're both a bit anxious right now, but things will work out for the best, believe me."

That was to be the last serious or sensible piece of conversation they would have because Silverman pulled out a bottle of whiskey and two glasses from his desk drawer and began pouring.

13

Gina was up and about long before Art had even opened his eyes, he'd been struggling with his conscience all night and she sensed it was likely she would be greeted by one of his stroppy moods when he decided to surface. The idea of going to Detroit and having a face to face with Silverman's step-son had him so fired up he was chomping at the bit to get there and make good on his theory. An attitude that convinced him that he needed to force the issue with his boss. He was incandescent at the time being wasted, and nothing anyone would say or do was going to change his mind. The fly in the ointment was Delgado who had bluntly refused to even give consideration to his idea when they had discussed it, and Delgado's stubbornness was a huge problem for Gina who suspected her man was getting close to going off the rails if he continued to be blocked. Even more so as his theory had been turned down on the grounds of cost and not for any operational or evidential reasons, which she guessed was what was really bugging Art. She wished he had opened up and discussed his worries with her the previous evening as she wouldn't be feeling so anxious now if he had. She knew he was bottling everything up inside his head where it would remain a constant irritant.

Her thoughts were suddenly interrupted by the sound of Art moving about upstairs urging her to give her attention to breakfast, and when he eventually put in an appearance he was already showered, shaved, and dressed, although he didn't look any more approachable with his down in the mouth expression.

They greeted each other with their customary peck on the cheek before settling down to eat, although the meal offered a strained interlude that was lacking in conversation, thanks to Art's self-imposed silence.

"I was thinking, just before you came down, how it might help if we could prove who left that cryptic message on Magee's phone?" Gina had her mind set on drawing her man into a conversation. "Especially now that we each accept it was part of a set up to have Magee murdered. Surely with all the modern technology that's available today it must be possible to voice match that call against each of our known suspects, or anyone else for that matter. Especially as it was a very cultured voice that should be relatively easy to find a match for. What do you think, Art?"

Art was in a little world of his own and didn't pick up right away, although when he got round to it he at least sounded genuinely encouraging. "It's worth looking into, sweetheart. Why don't you visit the tech boys and see what they say, just get something organised and stay with it. Right now I'm more interested in getting to Detroit before Silverman heads to Brazil." He stopped for a much needed caffeine top-up. "I need to push Ian Stewart on this damned inheritance business too because if Silverman *is* the sole benefactor it offers strong motivation for him to get rid of his step-brother, and if that turns out to be the case then he's almost certainly involved in the other murders as well." He crossed his arms aggressively. "Marcus is in for a right earful when I tangle with him later."

Having no wish to get involved Gina left the table. "It's time we were making tracks, Art, you know what the traffic is like on a Friday." Art took the hint, finished his coffee, and got up. "I'm ready when you are, sweetheart." He was already heading for the door as he said it. Gina grabbed her bits and pieces and hurried along behind him.

It turned out that she was right about the traffic as it forced Art to resort to his flashing blue light to get them to work on time, although it didn't earn him any bonus points from his boss when he got to him. "I shouldn't have to come looking for you when we have a meeting scheduled, Art. The bed get stuck to your back did it?" Art was in no mood for sarcasm, and he wasn't backward in letting his boss know it. "You're lucky I'm here at all. I was almost on my way to Detroit." Delgado stuck his burly chest out. "You've still got a bee in your bonnet about that have you? I thought we agreed to wait until we get definite proof about who the real benefactor is before going down that road." Art gave him a surly look. "Maybe we should give Silverman a call and ask him to stay where he is until we're ready to arrest him."

Delgado slammed his big fist down on the desk. "That's enough of the attitude, Lieutenant. You're here to do what I tell you and that's exactly what I expect from now on. I'm in charge here and don't you ever forget it." Art unfolded his arms and stuck his hands deep into his pockets out of the way. "As if I ever could." he snarled, his body language backing up his comment.

Gina, who had been eavesdropping their conversation got off-side once she knew their meeting was over and seeing Vince at his workstation she made a beeline for him. "A quiet word of warning, Vince, before my significant other half gets near you, he's not in the best of moods so just try to humour him please." Vince flashed his gleaming white teeth at her. "Whatever you say, Gina, I'll do what I can to keep him at arm's length." They enjoyed a little chuckle together before Gina headed off to see the tech boys. She's known the guy in charge of the unit for a couple of years and had a feeling he

Would be keen to help out and he greeted her warmly enough when she got there. "Well now, what brings the best-looking girl in this miserable place down to see me?"

"How can a girl stay away from the best-looking *guy* in this miserable place?" Her little tease got them both grinning, but it was short lived. "Seriously though, Mark, it's to do that weird message on our latest victim Magee's phone." Mark nodded. "Okay, I'm with you, so what about it?" Gina explained what she was after with a little twinkle in her eye, a successful ploy that worked a treat on Mark. "It's possible to voice match if you get me samples from your suspects to match with the evidential sample." Gina screwed her face up. "That's the problem, Mark, *I* can't, but a request from your department would get a much more favourable response." She gave him another little girl look. Mark grinned mischievously. "Do I get a kiss if I do?" he teased. "If you give me a proven match it will get you a hug as well, how's that?" Mark treated her to an even bigger smile. "That'll do for me, something to look forward to at last." He waved a finger at her like she was a naughty schoolgirl. "But I'll hold you to it, so don't forget."

Gina moved away with a casual wave and a slightly pink complexion spreading over her pretty face.

It was much later in the day when she met up with Art again and to her surprise his mood had lightened considerably. "Hi, Gina, I'm glad I bumped into you because there's something I want you to do for me." He moved in closer and slid his arm round her waist. "I want you to see Debra Magee again. I've been thinking a lot about that revealing e-mail her husband got from Sharpe, and I'm not sure she has ever read it, so I'd like you to have her read it while you're with her and check out her reaction. Just find out if she was aware of their illicit little romance."

Gina screwed her face up; the thought of having to pry into the woman's sex life so soon after her husband's death didn't rest easy with her. "Is this really necessary, Art? The poor girl is already suffering without me putting her through the ringer all over again?" Art squeezed her waist a little harder. "I'm not asking you to interrogate her, Gina, just broach the subject indirectly so to speak, not head on, okay?"

Gina didn't look happy. "Okay, I'll go see her, and if she opens up enough to allow me to broach the subject I'll do my best, but you had better understand that I have no intention of getting under her skin." Art gave her another little squeeze. "That's my girl, I know you'll get her talking, and by the way, I had another set-to with Marcus earlier over this bloody step-son. I swear to God if he keeps blocking me from going to interview him I'll ignore what he says and go there anyway. What are people going to say if he turns out to be responsible for all this mayhem and takes to his heels back to Brazil without even being interviewed as a suspect?"

She gave him a warning look. "You can't go interrogating an innocent member of the public without authority, you'll only land yourself in trouble and you know it. Silverman must be arrested and cautioned properly before you can go anywhere near him." She gave him a peck on the cheek. "I agree with your theory though, as does Vince. Silverman must be someone of interest, but it will be more tactful if we approach Marcus as a group and show him the error of his ways." Art's face brightened up. "I'm pleased you and Vince are in agreement; I'll try to arrange a meeting with Marcus to clear the air." Gina nodded in agreement. "I'll leave you to set it up, Art, I'm off to see Debra Magee, so wish me luck." He ruffled her hair as she turned away. "You'll be fine, I know you will. I'll catch you later." Gina took off with her mobile phone in hand, she was eager to check that the lady in question was available to see her before setting off.

While all this was going on Inspector Ian Stewart and his team had just arrived at the premises of Mendelson and Ackermann. Having shown their credentials at reception they warned the staff to remain at their workstations while waiting to be interviewed, he then made a beeline for Hardwick's office and his computer, looking for any correspondence linked to anyone else involved in the case. The inspector took it upon himself to tackle Mendelson about recent events leading up to the death of his security manager. It turned out Mendelson was rather vague and maybe even a little secretive on the matter, although he couldn't be accused of being deliberately obstructive. With that in mind Inspector Stewart didn't miss the chance to shake him up a bit. "I have a warrant authorising me and my team to search every inch of these premises, so you need to understand that it could take me all day to carry this out or it could take all week, which will keep this place under lock and key until I decide that my search is completed. I hope you're getting the message." Mendelson was certainly getting the message; he knew exactly what it meant, and he didn't like it one bit. "I cannot afford to have my premises blocked from my clients for that length of time, so what is it you are so eager to know that I haven't already told you?" Inspector Stewart smiled in response. "I'm sure you're a reasonable man, Mister Mendelson. All I want is the name of the main benefactor to Benjamin Silverman's legacy now that his son Benjamin can no longer lay claim to it?" Mendelson looked genuinely perplexed and unable to conjure up an answer, but he didn't look like someone who was trying to withhold information, in fact he looked more like someone who was frightened of saying the wrong thing. "I find that a rather difficult question to answer at this particular time, there are serious ongoing difficulties in asserting who is to be the beneficiary."

The Inspector looked shocked. "I don't get it. You are Silverman's legal representative and you're telling me that you don't know who is the legal claimant to his estate?" Mendelson folded his arms with a defeatist sigh. "Believe me Inspector, I'm every bit as confused as you are, especially so when we recently received notification from a solicitor somewhere in Nevada, informing us of young Benjamin Silverman visit to their premises on a pre-arranged appointment to have them draw up a Will on *his* behalf. They allege that the Will was witnessed by a local Rabi plus two members of his congregation, with one other unnamed witness in attendance." Mendelson was lost for anything more to say. "So where the hell does that leave our investigation?" demanded the Inspector. "Up bloody queer street," snapped Mendelson angrily, "I don't know any more about the authenticity of this claim than you do, nor do I know the identity of the claimant." Inspector Stewart gave him a surly look. "So when will you know?" he asked. Mendelson shook his head. "You can't expect me to answer that when I haven't seen any documentation in support of the blasted claim."

"Well when you do, and I suggest you do it quickly, I want to know all about it, and I mean right away. You need to bear in mind that the identity of this person could, and probably will, have a serious bearing on our ongoing murder investigation. I hope you're getting the message." Mendelson looked like a man under extreme pressure. "Yes, Inspector," he stuttered, "I get the message, but you will have to wait for that to happen like the rest of us I'm afraid."

"In that case you had better give me the details of this bunch out in Nevada. I might have more persuasive ways of getting the answer to this little mystery than you do." Mendelson went back to his desk and got him what he wanted, but Inspector Stewart got up close and personal with him yet again. "I'm taking my team away now, but you mark my words, and mark them well, I'll be back, and should anything to do with Hardwick's murder come to light around here you had better get it to me asap. Understood?" Mendelson could only nod; he was already talked out.

14

Gina was greeted like a long-lost friend by Debra Magee, even though the same lady was displaying all the symptoms of being over-burdened with grief and lack of sleep. "How are you feeling now, Debra?" asked Gina, as she was led indoors. "Lost, is the only way I can describe my feelings. I can't believe what has happened and I don't think I ever will." She wrapped her arms round herself as she walked into the kitchen ahead of her visitor. "I feel like my whole body is in pain and I can do nothing to ease it." She dropped into a chair by the kitchen table. "Please sit down and tell me why you're here? Have you some news for me?"

Gina could see she was in no state to answer questions and decided to play the sympathy role for a while to get things rolling. "I'm only here to see how you're coping, Debra. I can't begin to imagine what you're going through, and I must say that you don't look like you've had much sleep." Magee managed a smile, albeit a timid one. "I must admit that sleep and I have become distant strangers, but I guess that's par for the course when your world falls apart without warning."

Gina decided on another approach. "Can I get you a coffee or something?" She was already heading for the percolator, so Debra didn't bother stopping her.

"Can I ask you something on a more personal note, Debra?" Debra swung round swung round on her chair to face her, but she waited until Gina poured the coffee and returned to her seat before answering. "How personal?" she asked, sounding a bit cautious. Gina decided to bite the bullet and get on with it. "It's to do with an e-mail on your computer that was sent by Rodney Sharpe to your husband James." Debra stared at her with tears running down her cheeks. "I believe I know exactly which e-mail you're referring to. You need to know that I took the liberty of going through all of the mail addressed to my husband on my computer, and I found one that was extremely painful and disturbing to read. She covered her face with both hands and remained like that for maybe twenty seconds or so. When she remover her hands from her face she appeared to be much more determined. "Before I say any more about it, Gina, I need you to tell me how that e-mail was interpreted by your own people?" Gina hesitated; she was fearful of causing Debra further distress. "Do you really want to know the answer to that?" she asked. Debra nodded firmly "I have to know; surely you can see that." Gina stood up and paced around the table before stopping directly in front of her host. "I believe you already know my answer, Debra."

Debra got up and left the kitchen without explanation, leaving Gina staring at an empty chair. When she came back, and she did so quite quickly, she had a bundle of letters in her right hand and looked like someone whose life had no further purpose as she handed them to Gina. "I forced open one of the locked drawers on my husband's desk and found these letters all neatly tied together with ribbon, and although I only read one letter it was enough to absolutely disgust me as it was an extremely explicit love letter from that sick deviant Sharpe, and as I imagined the rest of the collection would be much the same I couldn't face reading them." She stopped to take a breath. "I've always known James had no great fondness for the fairer sex, but I never suspected him of anything as cruel as this. I was so shocked and upset when I read that disgusting rubbish that I spent the whole night crying

126

over it, but I'm crying no more, it's no use hiding from what I know or making excuses for it, I just have to accept that I have been married to a deviant homosexual for all these years, and the pity of it is that I can't even confront him about it, or that deviant bastard Sharpe. He escaped any revenge I might enjoy by dying on me, more's the pity." She raised her chin as far as it would go in an unconscious act of defiance. "I *will* rise above this shameful discovery, given time, and I will take pleasure in telling his friends and his family all about his guilty little secret." Her emotions were in turmoil, leaving her seeking relief from her pain by seeking revenge. Gina could see she was hurting like she had never hurt before, the very core of her being was burning with shame and horror at the painful legacy her husband had left her to deal with. It was even more painful to have to admit it in front of a total stranger. "Is there anything I can do to help?" asked Gina, but only because didn't know what else to say. "Yes, I believe there is," replied Debra, as she paused to work up a spiteful enough reply to justify her burning anger, "you can catch that bastard Sharpe and hang him up by the balls, if he's got any that is."

Gina burst out laughing, with Debra joining in, it was one of those moments when they could do nothing else, a painful moment that needed release. For Debra it was either laugh or cry and she had done enough crying to last a lifetime, so she laughed. Gina admired her for it. "That's the way to go, Debra, give as good as you get and enjoy your revenge. The good news I have for you is that we have a good idea who is hiding Sharpe. We have his location under close surveillance as we speak in case Sharpe turns up there, and when we do catch up with him he will never see the light of day again."

Without any warning she burst into tears again, the pain of her suffering was too much, and she simply lost control. Gina wrapped her arms around her and drew her close. "Come on, girl," she soothed, as tenderly as she could, "don't give you up on me now, you've been doing brilliantly. You can't allow your husband and that twisted bastard Sharpe to upset you like this. You need to show everyone that you're better than they are."

Her sobbing stopped almost immediately as she wiped her eyes on her sleeve. "You're right of course. I don't know what I would have done if you hadn't called with me this morning, but I'm all right now so if you have to go, I will understand." Gina gave her another hug and explained that she did have to go. "But I will be visiting from time to time, so you haven't got rid of me just yet. Are you okay on your own now?"

"Yes. I'm fine now, thanks to your support, and please feel free to call anytime." Gina got up and headed for the door with Debra close behind. They exchanged another farewell hug before she got into her car and drove off, but she was very subdued on the way back to base, blaming herself for Debra's distress, and her mind was already made up to tell Art in no uncertain manner exactly how she felt for being sent on such an unpleasant mission.

But that was for later.

15

Delgado was having a real old fashioned, ding-dong of an argument with Art over his fixation with Joshua Silverman, and it had become so heated that Gina and Vince, who were also involved in the meeting, refused to stay and listen to the two most senior detectives in the department openly balling each other out. They simply made their excuses and got off-side.

"Why are you so damned insistent on going after Silverman's step-son when I have made it perfectly clear that we leave him to the Detroit police?" Art looked at him like he'd lost all sense of reason. "Because I'm absolutely convinced he is responsible for our three murders and possibly the one in London as well. Maybe he didn't carry them out himself but I'm certain he's involved. For God sake, Captain, if you're so sure he's not involved then stop being so bloody bashful and tell me who is."

Delgado leaned across his desk. "We have no evidence to even suggest he's ear-marked to inherit his step-father's fortune, which is what you're basing your assumption on. So why don't you show a bit more patience for a change and wait until we know for sure who the legal claimant is?"

Art nearly had a fit. "It doesn't matter a damn who the hell is going to get the inheritance, can you not see that? What matters is that Silverman *expects* it to come his way as he's the only living relative, and with the amount of money and assets that's waiting to fill someone's pockets who wouldn't resort to murder to lay claim to it. Especially if there was the slightest chance it might slip through their fingers. Once young Benjamin was taken out the others were just collateral damage, a simple clean up job as I see it."

Delgado's patience was wearing thin. "Are you willing to drive to Detroit to get your way on this? Because we do not have the funds to authorise a flight." Art scowled across the desk at him. "I'll crawl there on my belly if it gets me what I want." Delgado couldn't quell his laughter. "You might need to if the Commissioner gets to hear of it." Art's eyes widened in expectation. "Does that mean you're sanctioning my trip?" he asked. Delgado leaned closer to him. "You had better give this idea a bit more thought, my friend, because I reckon it's an eight-or-nine-hour drive to Detroit and I can only spare you for three days at most."

He moved back from his desk with a satisfied smirk. "Are you still keen to go to here?" he asked.

The thought of a nine-hour drive wasn't very inviting, but Art didn't give up that easily. "I can get a cheap flight to Detroit for under a hundred and fifty dollars. I'll pay for the flight myself if you agree to reimburse when we get round to charging Silverman. How's that for a deal?"

Delgado folded his arms and shook his head. "You really are a determined bastard, but that sounds like a fair deal to me, just tell me when you're going so I can warn the Detroit police. Now get the hell out of here and let me get some work done."

Art couldn't believe his luck and made a bee-line for the door before Delgado changed his mind.

Gina was in deep in conversation with Vince when Art caught sight of them, but seeing him heading their way, and knowing where he had just been, she offered up a muted prayer that his mood had changed for the better. She sensed that might be the case as he drew closer, and she saw the big smile on his face.

"It looks like I'm off for a short break to Detroit." He boasted, with no small measure of self-appreciation. There was a look of astonishment on the other two faces. "How the hell did you manage to wangle that?" asked Gina. "That's immaterial, sweetheart, but I need you to do me a favour and find me a cheap flight for a two-day return trip. I need to contact Ian Stewart and see how he got on yesterday as I want to be fully briefed before I head to Detroit." He turned on his heel and headed off, but it took him longer than expected to get through to Inspector Stewart, and when he did he dispensed with the usual formal greeting and got straight down to business. "Hi, Ian. I'm just looking for a quick run-down on how you got on yesterday?"

"What can I say, Art, the honest answer is that the whole exercise was a total waste of time, a bit of expert stone-walling going on, if you get my drift. We didn't find a single shred of evidence linking any of the staff with the case we're investigating, which was a real downer. Although there was one little gem that came to light that I found intriguing. It would appear that another party, as yet unidentified, has crawled out of the woodwork to lay claim to the old boys vast empire. The news completely gob-smacked me coming out of the blue like it did, although I believe Mendelson was every bit as shocked over it as I was. It turns out he was notified of this claim by some legal firm based in Nevada. The guy who raised the hare is called Jack Benson and the company name is Benson and Benson. You can Google them if you're interested."

Art nearly fell from his chair; this latest hiccup about a new claimant had the potential to undermine his theory on Silverman. "Christ almighty, Ian," he moaned, "that's a real downer that doesn't do anything to back up my theory. You weren't to know it but I'm about to go to Detroit to interview Silverman's step-son in the belief that he is the only one with a genuine claim to the inheritance and a prime suspect. I'm working on the theory that he orchestrated this whole bloody shindig just to claim the money. Where the hell do I go now?"

Ian Stewart thought about it before offering some advice. "If it were down to me, Art, I would stick to my original plan. After all, from the evidence you know you can trust nothing has changed. This step-son won't know anything more than we do about this new claimant. Mendelson doesn't even have a clue who it is and he's the one who should be holding all the aces as he's entrusted to release the old boy's final instructions. It's confusing that he is no more aware of its content than we are, the legacy details and the names of claimant's were apparently handed to him in a sealed portfolio. Which leaves us all double guessing until he opens pandora's box and spills the beans. However, we do know he can't do that while there's an ongoing murder investigation in progress that's so closely linked to the inheritance." Art valued Ian's input more than most, and he made a point of saying so. "Thanks for that, Ian, I'm inclined to agree with you, I reckon I'll go to Detroit as planned and see where it takes me. The way I see it this step-son has to be up to his eyes in it, so I'll just stick with my original plan."

"I would say that's the right decision, Art," agreed Ian, "we have to go where the evidence takes us, but if you have nothing else that we need to discuss right now I have a host of things to do that need my urgent attention."

132

"I don't have anything else, Ian, except to say thanks for keeping me up to date and for the free advice. I'll let you know how I get on in Detroit." When they had finished the call Art sat back in his chair chewing over the conversation he'd just had. He had to concede that Silverman was unlikely to know anything about the new claimant when Mendelson didn't even know who it was, but he had gained a little leverage by knowing who was representing the new claimant, maybe that would open a closed door.

Having decided to stick to his original plan he was keen to find out if Gina had got him a cheap flight, and after a quick phone call she told him he was booked on an early flight with Delta Airlines the following morning. He couldn't have been happier, even though he expected some serious flak from his lover when she found out she would have to drive him to the airport!

16

Art's flight touched down about twenty minutes later than scheduled, which was of little concern because as soon as he disembarked he made a beeline for the nearest taxi stand and collared the first cab in the line. He got himself a cheerful cabby as well, and one who turned out to be a willing asset to the Detroit tourist industry. "Welcome to Detroit, my friend," he said with a smile, "is this your first visit to our wonderful city?" Art returned his smile in the rear-view mirror. "Yes, I'm sorry to say it is." The cabby passed him a card. "If you ever need showing around I'm always happy to oblige." Art took the card and muttered his thanks. "Do you know of any cheap lodgings where a guy could book in for a couple of nights." The driver pulled over to the side of the road and turned round in his seat. "This must be your lucky day, my wife and I run a B and B, and we have a room free if you're interested?" Art couldn't believe his luck and took him up on the offer without even asking the price. All he wanted was a place to lay his head.

"Can I dump my overnight bag at your place," he asked, "I need to get to an address in the centre of town. Can you help me with that?" The cabby grinned happily. "Consider it done, will you need me to hang around for you?"

"It would help if you can, although I don't know how long I'm going be, but I do need to get there before four o'clock to make sure I catch the guy. The way it goes I could be there for a couple of hours or a couple of minutes, I've no way of knowing how it will turn out."

"It doesn't matter how long it takes," the cabby agreed, "but can I ask you a personal question?"

"Be my guest." invited Art. The cabby smiled. "I reckon I can spot a cop a mile off, am I guessing right?" he asked. Art had to smile. "I didn't know it was that obvious?" he conceded.

"It probably isn't to most people," explained the cabby," but I'm an ex-cop myself, twenty odd years on the force before I hung up my shield. But tell me, is this a duty run you're on?. I only ask because you don't look much like a sightseer to me." Art grinned and patted him on the shoulder as he drove off again. "It looks like I picked the right cab. I'm Art Gardiner, Lieutenant with NYPD and it's good to meet another career guy." The cabby angled round in his seat. "Good to meet you, Art, I'm Jack Davis." He reached a hand over his shoulder. Art gave it a slap and the connection was made.

Jack's place turned out to be a neat little two storey building in a quiet part of town, and after meeting his wife Art got settled into what was a comfortable bedroom before re-joining his hosts. "If you're ready to go, Jack, I'd like to get under way," he told the cabby, "I want to catch my man in case he decided to shuts up shop early, he has an address at some place called Woodward Avenue, if you know where that is." The cabby laughed. "If I don't I need my bloody head testing, I had late fare from Woodward last night, another stranger in town like yourself who needed taking to an up-town apartment block. I thought it was a bit odd as he looked a bit scruffy and haggard, like he hadn't washed in days, but exactly where is it you want to go?" Art passed him a piece of paper with the address on. The cabby cocked an eyebrow. "Jeez, man, it really is a small world, that's the same address where I picked up my fare last night, a sullen bastard he was too, and big with it."

135

Art had a strange look on his face as he dropped into a nearby chair and rifled through his inside pocket, pulling out a sheet of paper with Sharpe's image on it. "I know it's a shot in the dark, Jack, but that wouldn't be the fare you picked up last night, would it?" He handed it to the cabby who gave it a quick once over. "I don't need to look twice at that ugly mug, that's the same guy I picked up, I'm certain of it." Art couldn't believe his luck. "Bloody hell, Jack, that's the fugitive I'm looking for in connection with three murders over here and possibly one in England, but how the bloody hell did you manage to pick the guy up when we have the Detroit police on permanent surveillance at those premises just watching for him?"

Art had to concentrate really hard to work out what had taken place, but that's what he did. "Of course," he muttered, "I can see exactly what must have happened. Your fare had to be picked up after dark to allow his buddy who owns the place to lead the surveillance team away from the premises when he headed home. That would have left the place unguarded for him to be picked up. It's easy to see how the surveillance team where hood-winked." He got up on his feet and patted the cabby on the shoulder.

"You're right about one thing, Jack, it really is a small world and I'm so glad I picked you out from the rest of its inhabitants." The cabby responded with a big grin. "That was just pot-luck my friend, but seriously, I think you need to make your mind up about which of those premises you want to hit first? If it's any help the apartment block I took that guy to is much closer than the other address, but it's up to you, I'm only the driver."

Art didn't need to think about it, of the two Sharpe was already a known killer, therefore he came first by a country mile. "I'd like to hit

136

the apartment block first, Jack, but the problem is that I don't know which apartment my suspect is using when we get there?" The cabby came to his aid again. "That place is an up-market apartment block my friend, so you only have to get hold of the janitor. He'll know who moved in last night, that's his job, but I can do that for you while you stay in the cab and not expose yourself too soon, I'm always happy to help out." Art gave him a no nonsense look. "The guy you picked up last night is a vicious killer, Jack. I wouldn't ask you or any other member of the public to take the kind of risk that would involve, but thanks anyway. Just get me there and leave the rest to me."

His cabby nodded in return. "Whatever you say, Art, and I'm ready to go when you are." They left the house in a hurry and were soon under way.

It only took about ten minutes to get to the apartment block, where the cabby pulled up at the side of the building where there were no windows, a tactic that told Art he still retained some of his old policing skills.

"You be careful in there my friend," the cabby warned as Art exited the cab, "I'll be waiting right here when you come back, no matter how long it takes, so don't rushing the job on my behalf, just be careful how you go." Art left the cab and made his way to the front entrance and pressed the button labelled janitor looking relaxed and at ease, even though his stomach had other thoughts on the matter.

It was only a matter seconds before an elderly Hispanic looking guy came to his aid and buzzed the door open for him. Art flashed his badge and raised a finger up to his lips as a warning for him to keep quiet. The old guy nodded in response and stepped aside to let him into the hallway where Art drew him into a corner. "You have a resident who moved in late last night and I need to know which apartment he's in and if he's still in residence, and I'll need a key to his apartment. The janitor moved away motioning Art to follow and led him into a tiny little office where he handed him a key card, he then pointed at the stairs and whispered. "He's in apartment nineteen on the second floor, third door on the left, and as far as I know he hasn't left the building since he arrived last night." Art wrapped an arm round the old guys shoulder and drew him into the corner again. "You keep yourself well out of sight and keep your office door locked. I don't want you getting in my way, okay." The janitor gave him the thumbs-up and Art took off up the stairs on tiptoes and found the apartment easily enough and sidling up to the door he stopped and listened for any sound or movement from within. When he sensed all was quiet he slipped the key card into the reader and eased the door open a few inches and peered through the gap. With no sign of danger he eased it open a little further and squeezed through the gap, easing it closed behind him. It took a few moments for him to get his bearing as the apartment had a large, open plan layout, and from where he was standing he could see straight into an empty kitchen, which was of little concern as his attention was firmly focussed on the only door in sight that was still closed. The law of averages told him it had to be the bedroom and pulling out his phone he switched it to record before crossing the room on tiptoes to the bedroom door where he stopped and listened for any sounds from inside. Convinced all in order he drew his weapon and threw the door open, leaping into the room with the gun held in both hands.

Sharpe, who was curled up facing away from Art, came to his senses almost immediately on hearing the door open and leapt to his feet on the opposite side of the bed, putting the bed between himself and his intruder.

"Who the fuck are you?" he demanded; his voice slurred with sleep, "and what the hell are you doing in my goddamned bedroom?" Standing by his bed in only a pair of blue boxer shorts he was very exposed and vulnerable. Art pointed his gun at a nearby chair. "Get your hands behind your neck and plant you ass in that chair, and don't shift an inch until I tell you to." Sharpe moved across the room really cautiously and squatted down on the chair, while Art reached under his jacket for a set of cable ties and passed them to him. "Cuff your right wrist to that radiator pipe beside you and don't try any heroics. I'm just looking for any excuse to do away with your wedding tackle." Sharpe made no move to comply, although it was obvious from his facial expression that he hadn't a clue who Art was or what was going on. His instincts had him believing that his intruder must be one of the hired killers Silverman had bragged about during their row the previous day. He could think of no one else who knew who he was or where he was, or anyone who would dare to threaten him in this way. "I don't know who the hell you are pal, but you need to know you're not going to get away with whatever it is you're planning. And you can tell that snivelling bastard Silverman that he needs to remember what I told him yesterday about my solicitor. I suggest you phone him now and remind him of it."

Art hadn't a clue what he was rabbiting on about, but he soon got the drift and decided it was too good an opportunity to miss, a situation that brought to mind an old adage passed to him by an ex-army buddy: *Never interrupt your enemy when he's making a mistake, just take advantage of it.*

"It doesn't matter who I am, all you need to know is that

Silverman doesn't need you anymore, you've past your sell by date; your time is up. Now do what I told you and cuff your wrist to that radiator or this will end right here and now." Sharpe decided to do as he was told, but he had paled noticeably and was no longer the aggressive animal he had been at the start. In his confused state of mind his thoughts drifted back again to the argument he'd had with Silverman, and he blamed that for his current predicament, but only because he couldn't think of anything or anyone else to blame. He cursed his own stupidity for having gone too far with his threats and inuendo's and believed he was now paying the price for that aggressiveness, but he wasn't the sort to give in easily either, and seeing a possible escape route he decided to give it a go. "It would be a wise move if you phoned your boss and told him he has nothing to fear from me. I'll just fade away into his distant past if he calls off this nonsense. I'm not out to cause him trouble, I was just after the money he owes me for services rendered."

Art sat down on the end of the bed with his gun levelled at Sharpe's forehead, looking really threatening. "You can't have fulfilled your contract very well or Silverman wouldn't want rid of you so soon." Sharpe jerked hard against his cuffed wrist in an effort to break free from the radiator, but it was a wasted effort as he wasn't going anywhere, and to Art's relief he had just admitted that Silverman *was* behind what was going on. "Why is Silverman doing this to me?" he shook his head angrily, "I don't understand what he's up to. I did a really professional job for him, just like I was contracted to. All three people he wanted dead, are dead, what more did he want from me?" Art lowered his weapon but decided to keep up the charade and see how much more he could learn. "Speaking as one professional to another how much was your contract worth, was it worth the payback you're getting now?"

Sharpe looked more confused than ever, he never expect to be asked such a question, and it raised his suspicions. "What the hell has that got to do with anything, just who the hell are you anyway." Art sighted his weapon on Sharpe's forehead again. "Just answer the damned question." Sharpe gave a noisy grunt. "It wasn't enough, I can tell you that. It was four hundred g's if you must know, he wouldn't go for the half mill, the tight bastard." Art did his best to look impressed. "Easy money though for a simple job that only cost you the price of a couple of burgers." Sharpe's mouth dropped open; he was absolutely gobsmacked as he struggled to work out how this total stranger knew anything about what he had done. Art chose to enlightened him. "I wish to God I got paid that sort of money, but us poor policeman don't get it that good." Sharpe almost died on the spot; his heart was pounding like mad in his chest with the realisation that he had just confessed to murder in front of a police officer. How the hell had he managed to stumble into such a simple trap? All too soon he realised that nothing of what was happening might have nothing at all to do with Silverman, he couldn't believe he had been duped so easily, but it didn't stop him from trying to worm his way out of his situation. "If you really are a cop then you must know that what I said can't be used as evidence without a witness, nor can it be used for a conviction in court as it's only hearsay." He smirked knowingly at Art. "Thought you were being clever, didn't you, but you've been too clever for your own good. Now take this fuckin tie off and I'll go away from here and forget this ever happened."

Art reached behind him and picked up his phone with its red recording light still glowing. He showed it to Sharpe with a flourish. "I think you've just been on candid camera." Sharpe sat in silence as Art read him his rights. When he had finished he switched his phone to call and dialled the emergency police number to report the arrest and seek assistance, then he went downstairs to find his cabby friend leaving Sharpe well secured.

Art joined his cabby outside and sat chatting about whatever came to minds while waiting for the police to arrive, mostly about the cabby's former time in the force, but also with stories of his lovely wife thrown in for good measure. It took a lot longer than expected for the local boys to turn up, but when they did the team consisted of a sergeant and a younger officer, and when they met up Art got a real shock when the sergeant hailed his cabby like an old friend. "Good, God, Jack, don't tell me it was you who made this arrest." The cabby laughed fit to bust. "Lord no! I'm not guilty this time, Jess, that's down to my new-found friend here, Lieutenant Gardiner, from the NYPD."

The sergeant came forward with his hand outstretched "Sergeant Jess Wilson, Lieutenant, pleased to meet you." Art took his big hand in his own and gave it a warm shake. "What's the score with your angry friend here? Has he been stealing lollipops from the sweet shop again?" He nodded in Sharpe's direction. "Multiple murder; two in Manhattan and one in Newark, but watch him, he's a canny bastard."

Sergeant Wilson moved forward and crowded in on Sharpe, staring at him with a forced intensity. "You're gonna stand up like a good little boy while I undo your cuff from that radiator, then you're gonna put both hands behind your back so I can cuff you properly. If you don't do as I say I'll hit you so fuckin' hard you'll be shitting teeth for a week. Understood?" Art was quietly impressed with Wilson's gifted vocabulary, and he watched with interest as Sharpe got to his feet and was cuffed. Once he was under control the sergeant switched his attention to Art. "We'll need you down at the station to file your charge sheet and make a statement, Lieutenant, if that's okay?" Art gave him the thumbs up as Sharpe was shoved through the door and down the stairs.

Art had things to do that needed urgent attention before Silverman got to know his paid killer was under lock and key and decided to take off for distant shores. "Are you okay to run me to the station house, Jack?" The cabby agreed right away, but there was something else Art wanted to know. "You seem to be well in with these local boys so maybe you can tell me who runs their homicide team?"

"That would be Pat Delany." The cabby told him. "A real good guy by all accounts and a tough Irishman to boot, but unlike most of his peers he carries a good reputation with the powers that be, and the foot soldiers." Art needed to see Delany without delay. "Can we get under way, Jack?" he asked, "I really need to see him asap." The cabby was already heading for the door before Art had finished, and twenty minutes later he delivered him to the station house where he was invited into Delany's office without any fuss. Once the formalities were dispensed with they got straight down to the business at hand. "What's the buzz with this guy Sharpe?" asked Delany. Art gave him a quick run-down but soon changed the subject to Silverman. "This guy Silverman that your boys have been keeping an eye on, can they go in now and make the arrest? We need him locked up before he gets a chance to disappear?"

"If you have the evidence to make the charge stick I'll be only too happy to oblige." Art pulled his phone out. "I have Sharpe's confession on record plus a voluntary admission that Silverman paid him to carry out three murders." Delany got up from his seat. "That'll do for me, Art, be back in a minute. He shot out of the room like a scalded cat, but he wasn't gone more than a couple of minutes and looked well pleased when he got back. "My boys are going in as we speak so we'll have your man under lock and key and back here within twenty minutes. Let's have a coffee, then we can make the necessary arrangements to have your prisoners transported back to Manhattan." Art felt a surge of relief and it might have been more intense but for the fact that there was still the unsolved murder of Hardwick lurking at the back of his mind. He knew Sharpe wasn't responsible because they had sound evidence that he wasn't in the UK at the time of the murder. So who did kill Hardwick? He knew their case wasn't over just because they had arrested Silverman and Sharpe. They needed *everyone* involved under lock and key before that became a reality.

"I'd like to interview Silverman as soon as you have him booked in, Pat. We have another homicide that doesn't have a suspect yet, but it's indelibly linked to the case we're investigating with Silverman in the firing line for masterminding everything, so I need to find out what he knows about it."

"Why don't you interview him when they bring him in? That would tell you exactly what to charge him with before we book him in." Art could hardly believe how helpful Delany was being and he made it known. "Sounds like a plan to me, Pat, and I can't thank you guys enough for your help." His body language highlighted just how eager he was to get to grips with Silverman before the guy got his wits about him and the shock of his arrest wore off. Added to that was the other issue of his return flight back to New York that was booked for early the following morning. An annoying little issue that made everything that little bit more urgent, especially as he needed to know how he stood with Silverman before heading back to Manhattan and the inquisition that would ensue once the D A heard of his exploits.

Especially so as their current D A being a real stickler for protocol and box-ticking legalities.

It was a full three quarters of an hour before they got Silverman into the interview room and when Art joined him he didn't look in the least bit intimidated by his situation. Art dropped into a seat in front of him and laying his hands on top of the table he asked Silverman if he would like a coffee or a cold drink. His reply was not meant for less delicate ear. "Never mind the fuckin' coffee, just tell me what the hell do you jumped up bunch of clowns think you're doing dragging me away from my place of business like this, and who the hell are you anyway?" Art flashed his badge and warrant card. "Lieutenant Gardiner from NYPD and you're here to be questioned about complicity in the murders of Sam Blackwell, Benjamin Silverman and James Magee."

He paused to let his accusation sink in. "I arrested an accomplice of yours this morning by the name of Rodney Sharpe, who is currently being charged with carrying out all three murders on your orders." Silverman folded his arms angrily over his skinny chest and smirked at his accuser. "You must be off your tiny rocker if you think I had anything to do with murder, I'm a businessman not a goddamned murderer. What on earth has you thinking I could ever kill someone?"

Art pulled out his phone and set it down very purposively in front of Silverman. "I didn't accuse you of murdering anyone, Mister Silverman, I accused you of complicity to murder, now pin your ears back and listen to what your accomplice Sharpe has to say on the subject. He switched the phone to play-back and allowed the sound of Sharpe's confession to fill the room, but the expression on Silverman's face remained deadpan, his only physical reaction was a narrowing of his eyes as he scrutinised Art's face. When the recording had run its course Art returned the phone to his inside pocket. "I think you should choose your friends more carefully, Joshua, because Sharpe has given me all I need to charge you with soliciting him to murder three innocent people for the sole purpose of financial gain. You will be taken back to New York where the murders took place and face these charges. Now what have you got to say for yourself?" Silverman didn't look in the slightest intimidated by the gravity of the charges, in fact he looked quite relaxed, even a little bit arrogant, but he clearly felt the need to offer an explanation.

"Thank you for that, Lieutenant, I can now see why you made this awful error of judgement, but I can assure you that I am most certainly not an accomplice of Sharpe's. He must be playing some sort of game with you to have made up such a ludicrous accusation." He stopped briefly, taking his time to think carefully about what to say next.

Art let him get on with it, he just wanted him to keep talking. "It's a known fact that Sharpe and I go back a long way, Lieutenant, not as friends I must stress but as a former employer and employee. You see he once worked for me in Brazil and to my misfortune, at least that's how it would appear now. He came to me looking for help, but only because he knows I have a business back there and frequently travel between here and there," He stopped for a moment or two to decide what to say next. "He contacted me in the hope of getting a lift back to Brazil in my plane the next time I go home. A journey that he deemed to be very urgent and for personal reasons."

He leaned closer to Art. "I can assure you, Lieutenant, that there is no other reason why he contacted me and the sole reason why I got a friend to put him up for a couple of nights while my plane is serviced."

Art leaned back in his seat and smiled at his prisoner; it was a smile that disguised his concern that Silverman had been so quick to come up with such a plausible explanation. "You don't expect me to buy that schoolboy excuse do you? You're up to your eyes in all three homicides and we both know it. The lure of big money was too much for you to ignore, Silverman. I know you think you have a big inheritance lined up now that you have young Benjamin out of the way, but I have news for you, there is another claimant on the scene who is reputed to have a stronger claim to that inheritance than you do." Silverman's face took on an angry red hue, but it was only temporary, and Art was shocked at how quickly he had recovered his poise. "What inheritance is that? I don't know of any inheritance. Who on earth is going to leave me anything?" Art was shocked by his rapid dismissal of the inheritance, even more so at his ability to look genuinely horrified at what he'd been told. "Don't play the innocent with me, Silverman. You know all about your step-father's death and you certainly know about his son's death as well, so you can stop messing about and admit your involvement in his murder."

Silverman threw his hands up to his face, his body shaking with the muted sound of sobbing that lasted longer than it should have. When he finally dropped his hands away his eyes were wet with tears. "Is this some sort of cruel trick you're using to try to confuse me? Do you seriously expect me to fall for such an underhand attempt to have me believe my step-father *and* my step-brother are both dead without me knowing about it?" He paused to calm himself down. "You have a lot to answer for when my solicitor gets here."

Silverman's performance was so intense and realistic that Art found himself questioning his own beliefs. He was overcome with a heart-stopping feeling that this painful display of grief might be genuine. He stopped talking to consider the performance he'd just witnessed but having done so decided to stick with what he knew to be fact and not concede to Silverman's play-acting display. The evidence was too strong to do otherwise. "Are you asking me to believe that Mendelson and Ackermann have failed to inform you of your step-brother's death? Is that what you're trying to do? I believe they must have made contact with you as you are now your step-father's only living relative, and from what I hear he has one mighty big legacy to pass on to someone."

"I'm well aware of the value of my step-father's estate, Lieutenant. I do not need you to tell me about it, and yes, you are right, I would expect that I have a legal right to a share of any legacy since I am the only living relative, if my other relatives is deceased as you say then I feel safe in saying that as there are no other relatives in existence." Art cocked an eyebrow at him. "So, are you now admitting that you do expect to inherit your step-father's estate?"

"I don't see how it can be otherwise if both he and my step-brother are deceased like you say, that would leave me to be the last surviving relative." Art leaned across the table and peered into Silverman's eyes. "Who said anything about a relative being the beneficiary?" He said it quietly for effect. Silverman's jaw dropped and some of the colour drained from his face. He hadn't expected this slap in the face, and it took him quite a while to regain enough composure to challenge it. "You seem intent on playing these silly games, Lieutenant. Firstly, you accuse me of murdering my step-brother. A charge based on an outrageous accusations by someone you freely admit is a multiple killer. You then tell me that young Benjamin is dead and there is now someone else laying claim to my step-father's legacy." He sat upright in his chair and stuck his skinny chest out before continuing. "You haven't a single shred of evidence to support these accusations, and I demand an apology and immediate release." Art was feeling less sure of himself now, even though his every instinct told him Silverman was responsible for orchestrating at least three murders, the evidence provided by his hired killer wasn't enough on its own to put him before the judiciary.

The door behind him opened unexpectedly and Pat Delany stuck his head in and motioned Art to come out and join him. Art stood up and pointed a finger at Silverman. "You stay right there; you're going nowhere until I say so." He turned away leaving Silverman staring at his back as he went to see what was bothering Delany, who he knew had been watching the interview through the observation window. "I can see where you're going with this, Art." he explained, "and I completely sympathise with you, but Silverman has to walk. He is absolutely right, your evidence is unacceptable as it's an unsupported accusation made by a known felon, and we cannot hold him on it without something more substantial. I'm sorry my friend, but we have to release him." Art could only nod in reply. He was feeling fit to burst and almost incapable of speech, which was just as well because Delany wasn't finished. "Your other suspect, Sharpe, is a completely different kettle of fish. He's been stupid enough to openly confess to murder and from what you tell me you have video and forensic evidence to support the charges, so we will transport him back to New York as agreed. I just wish we could do the same with Silverman as we know from Sharpe's confession that he's as guilty as hell, but we also know what the law requires of us." Art placed a hand on Delany's shoulder. "It's okay, Pat, no hard feelings, I knew I was on thin ice with Silverman. I just wanted to have a go at him and shake him up a bit, maybe force him into making a mistake and admit something by accident. I'll get him in the end though, I can promise you that. Now are you going to tell him, or do you want me to do it?"

Delany draped an arm round Art's shoulder and walked him away. "You come up to mine and have a quick drink to take the bad taste out of your mouth, Art. We can let that mouthy bastard stew for a while longer before we let him go."

Once they were sat down with a glass of Irish Delany brought up the subject of Sharpe again. Art was quick to put him at ease by explaining that they had sufficient evidence to guarantee him three life sentences, and although he enjoyed Pat's company he couldn't afford to waste any more time as he still had his Cabby waiting outside. It was a case of a quick goodbye and another few words of thanks before he headed off.

Tomorrow was another day, and one that would let him see Gina again, which was the only thing he had to look forward to.

17

Art had been held captive long into the night by his new-found cabby friend as he reminisced about bygone days, and enjoyable though it was he was paying a heavy price for their late night revelry by the time he got off the plane at JFK.

Thankfully, Gina was waiting for him at the airport pick-up point to whisk him back to the station house, although he wasn't looking forward to meeting up with his boss, believing it would be an uneasy meeting having to explain the Silverman debacle, but he hoped Sharpe's arrest would help ease the pain.

When he walked in on him an hour later Delgado wasn anything but complimentary. "You look like you've just come off a bar-cruise. I hope you weren't hitting the bottle up in Detroit?" Art rubbed the tiredness from his eyes. "I should be so lucky. I happened to meet up with a very exuberant ex-cop who turned out to be my cabby, but I can't knock the guy as he looked after me very well, including lodgings for the night at no cost, but he likes to reminisce about old times to any friendly ear in attendance. I guess it goes with the territory."

Delgado cocked both eyebrows in response and nodded his head to indicate his acceptance. "Okay, so let's get down to business, Art. I've already had a call from Pat Delany who gave me a quick run-down, but I'd much rather hear it from you." Art fumbled in his overnight bag for his phone. "Why don't you hear it from Sharpe himself, he's very eloquent, so listen closely." He messed about with his phone and

Marcus and Gina were soon concentrating on Sharpe's angry protestations, grabbing everyone's attention with his very detailed, if unwittingly offered confession.

"What can I say, Art, self-confession by a murderer is a wonderful stick to beat him with, sadly not too many felons subscribe to the idea, and I don't think Sharpe will be recommending it to his cell mates any time soon. It's as word perfect an example of self-betrayal that you and I are ever likely to come across."

He smoothed his hair away from his forehead. "I don't know how you managed to get him to confess and implicate Silverman as well, but you always were a canny old fox so I guess I shouldn't be too surprised. Well done anyway, now tell me about Silverman, I hear he got off the hook?"

Art grimaced at the thought of Silverman running free. "That bastard has it coming, and I intend to bring him to book one way or the other, even if I have to go to Brazil to do it, and without wanting to rock Delany's boat I believe there was sufficient evidence for a District Attorney to put him in front of a Judge, but I can see why Delany played it safe and released him. What really got up my nose was the fact that he denied even knowing his step-father had died or his step-brother had been murdered? Even if he wasn't involved in the homicides his solicitors must have contacted him to chase up his inheritance and they would surely have told him." Delgado wasn't interested. "Don't get all worked up about it, Art, I have a feeling when the judge gets Sharpe in front of him, and the DA opens him up he'll want to know why Silverman isn't in the court room alongside him." Art was in the mood for false promises. "Can we restrict his movements somehow to stop him fleeing the country. He has a private plane revving up somewhere ready for a trip back to Brazil, and it would be a serious failure on our part to let him get away without being properly investigated." He paused for a moment's thought. "Something else that needs taking into account is the fact that Silverman has Brazilian citizenship, and the Brazilian government do not extradite their own citizens to America, or anywhere else for that matter."

Delgado fingered an imaginary beard. "I'll take it to the D A tomorrow and see what he says, maybe he'll issue a holding order of some sort, but don't you go worrying about it, Art, we'll catch him in the long grass, I know we will, we'll outsmart the bastard or my names not Delgado."

Art was already thinking of something else entirely. "We still have that unsolved murder of Hardwick to contend with and while it took place outside our authority it's undoubtedly linked to our three homicides. I haven't been in touch with Ian Stewart for a couple of days, but I intend catching up with him later. We need to keep on top of things with him, especially so as we know for sure that neither Silverman nor Sharpe were directly responsible for Hardwick's murder. Neither of them were anywhere near England when that took place. So who *is* this other killer who is still running free, and what the hell is his motive?"

Delgado pinched his upper lip between finger and thumb looking seriously thoughtful. "You're right to raise that point because I find it bloody strange as well, a real challenge for all of us. We know why Silverman got involved in these killings and the same goes for Sharpe, but a third person with no known motive, that's a real puzzle. Why don't you chase up Ian Stewart and see if he has anybody in his sights yet. It's imperative we find out who killed Hardwick, it's too closely connected to our case not to."

Gina had been listening intently during this exchange, and while her tongue wasn't active her brain certainly was. "Maybe it's time we put some effort into tracking down this other claimant. They're keeping a very low profile, and we must ask ourselves why are they doing that? Could it be they're involved in what's going on?"

Art gave her a sly wink and turned back to Delgado. "Do we have the name of the company representing this claimant?" There was an unnecessarily long silence before Delgado reacted. "I agree with you, Gina, but to answer your last, Art, the solicitor involved is a guy called Jack Benson from Nevada, you can look him up on Google or something. Out main focus for now is Sharpe, when he gets here I want him taken straight up to Rikers Island holding facility, so you will have to interview him up there I'm afraid." Art didn't argue the point, just held his tongue. "Did Delany say when we can expect him here?" he asked. "Tomorrow evening is what I'm told, but you know what airlines are like, some are more temperamental than the wife." Realising his lack of judgement with Gina present he quickly back-tracked. "Sorry, Gina, just an expression, no offence meant."

Gina raised both eyebrows at him. "Why should I be offended, I'm not a wife, not yet anyway." She swung round to face Art with her arms folded over her chest. "Although I sincerely hope someone not too far away is thinking to change that." Art didn't know where to put himself, his face had taken on a pinkish hue, and he found it hard to look Gina in the eye. Luckily for him, Delgado offered him an escape route. "Don't go jumping the gun, Gina, you never know what that old fox is planning. We know how he likes to play that sort of thing close to his chest." Gina headed for the door with an overstated sway of her hips. "He had better be planning something soon, weddings are much more expensive in the summer."

She disappeared from sight leaving Art with his beady eye on Delgado. "Thanks a bunch, Marcus, you walked me right into that, and I know exactly what the conversation is going to be over dinner." Marcus just laughed it off and waved him away. "Make yourself scarce, I've got calls to make."

As soon as he was gone Delgado grabbed his phone and dialled Mendelson's number and he was surprised when he got an immediate response. "Good morning, Alexander Mendelson." Delgado took a deep breath. "It's Captain Delgado here, Mister Mendelson. sorry to bother you again but I'm enquiring into this latest claimant to the Silverman estate that you spoke of when interviewed by Inspector Stewart. I understand you were informed about this claimant quite recently by a solicitor from Nevada, but I need to know if there are any further developments?"

"I'm afraid not, Captain Delgado, it would appear that Jack Benson, who is the solicitor involved, has been advised by his mystery client not to release any personal information until given leave to do so. A situation that leaves me unable to offer any advice on the matter, as I have no way of knowing the identity of the person involved. I should perhaps make it clear that I am unaware as to the identity of *any* benefactor, *or* benefactors who may be named in Mister Silverman's Last Will and Testimony, and the situation will remain that way until such time as the police investigation is concluded and his final instructions may be made public. You should understand that this is no more helpful to me than it is to your good self, Captain Delgado."

There was an uneasy silence before Delgado decided to continue the conversation as he was trying to work out a way to overcome the current hold up. "Surely you legal guys are capable of conjuring up

155

some magical excuse to force this guy Benson to name his client. I can only assume that whoever the claimant is they would have been made aware of our ongoing investigation, so why haven't they come forward to assist us. I find that rather strange; would you not agree?"

"Well, I can't disagree," conceded Mendelson, "but as things stand right now it's highly likely that whoever this claimant turns out to be, they may not have any interest in your investigation. How are we to know?" Delgado wished he had his hands round Mendelson's throat. "That's easy for you to say, Mister Mendelson, but I'm responsible for sorting this mess out and I can promise you that I will judge events in any way that I see fit." His next comment was deliberately snappy. "Since there is nothing else for us to discuss, I can only say that this whole episode seems to have turned into a battle of wills, in more ways than one I might add, but I see no purpose in continuing this conversation, so thank you for your time." Mendelson hung up without reply. While this was going on Art was having his own conversation with Inspector Stewart. He'd been hoping for some good news on the Hardwick murder, but he was to be sorely disappointed.

"The only thing I can tell you that offers even the smallest glimmer of hope is that we have a security video showing a car entering the airport carpark a matter of minutes before Hardwick arrived there. This is confirmed by the time clocked on Hardwick's parking ticket, but what has us interested in this other car is that it drove out of the car park within ten minutes of arriving. Now why would it drive away so quickly when it was parked in the *long stay* carpark where the murder took place. We are currently following up on the car as all the evidence we have points to it being involved, and you know a well as I do that number plates can easily be replaced.

The good news is that we know the make, model and colour of the car so we expect to make good headway in tracking it's owner."

While this news wasn't anything to cheer about it gave Art some hope that things were at least moving in the right direction. "Thanks for that, Ian, I know you guys will pull out all the stops to find the culprit, and I wish you luck. I know you're already aware of the connection between Hardwick and our ongoing investigation into a double homicide, so with that in mind it's vitally important we get this killer quickly so we can determine whether or not he is linked to both cases. I think I've used-up enough of your time, Ian, so I'll leave you to it. Thanks again for your help."

He was deeply thoughtful when he replaced the phone. Mostly because Hardwick's killing was a really tantalising mystery, more so because of where it took place and the fact that the NYPD would have no part in the investigation. He was toying with the possibility that there could be a connection between Hardwick's killer and the mysterious new claimant who was laying claim to the Silverman fortune. But he couldn't determine if such a connection was viable at this early stage, and without an answer to that little conundrum all it succeeded in doing was to cloud the issue even more, an issue that was already clouded by the unlikely possibility that Hardwick's murder might have no connection at all with the other murders. There was always the possibility that somebody just didn't like the guy or had a personal grudge to settle with him. They needed to determine where Silverman had been when all this was going on, and how many paid killers he had access to, but being unable to make any headway with it he switched his thoughts to Gina and her follow-up visit to Debra Magee, it had completely slipped his mind with everything else that was going on. He was eager to know if Debra had been aware of her husband's romantic transgressions. Although his interest in the matter stemmed more from curiosity than necessity as he didn't believe it had a direct influence on their case. He would catch up with her later and find out how things went.

Unlike her man, Gina was already at home enjoying a few quiet moments just lounging about with nothing else for company but a nice glass of wine. It wasn't something that happened very often, in fact it was so rare that she'd almost forgot what it was like to have nothing more important to deal with than which wine to drink.

Sadly, her enjoyment was short lived as she was soon back on her feet refilling her glass and checking how dinner was progressing. Satisfied that all was well she wandered over to the window and peered out through the rain drenched glass, praying that her man would be home in time for a hot meal and not one that had to be reheated.

She had just turned away from the window when she heard his car turn into the driveway and rushed to top up another glass.

"Hi, honey, your dearly beloved is home." He sounded quite cheerful as he headed up the stairs to get changed before joining his lover in the kitchen. "I hope that tastes as good as it smells because I could eat a horse." Gina smiled at the thought as he sneaked up behind her and wrapped his arms round her waist. "How did your day end up?" he asked.

Gina twisted round to face him. "Pretty bloody awful thanks to you, that poor woman was at her wits end when I got to her, but she had enough wit about her to go through her husband's e-mails, just like we did, and she wasn't long in uncovering the truth about what had been going on. She was completely shell-shocked by it of course, and rightly so, but thankfully she's a good deal tougher than she looks and wasted no time in deciding that revenge is a sweeter pill to swallow than grief. I wish her the best of luck with, as she deserves her revenge. Art squeezed he a little tighter. "Sorry I caused you to have such a miserable day, sweetheart, but if it's any consolation I happen to like that young lady as much as you do, which is why I thought a visit from you might help her get over her misery. I'm sure she felt all the better for your company."

Gina passed him his wine. "You can have whiskey next time if you learn to behave yourself." They both had a little chuckle before she decided it was time to eat.

As soon as their meal was over Gina darted from the kitchen in a frantic hurry and headed for the lounge, causing Art to wonder what she was up to? As it turned out she wasn't gone very long and when she came back she was clutching a little package in her hand like it was something important, and after giving Art an inviting look she held the bundle out to him. "I have a little present for you, lover, and knowing how you enjoy a good read this lot should keep you busy for a while."

Art's brow gathered inquisitively. "Don't know what I've done to deserve a present?" he said, "and I'm not sure what that is, it looks a bit too light to be a book." Gina flicked her eyebrows at him. "Open the bloody thing and find out." Art tore at the wrapping excitedly but was seriously disappointed when he saw that all he had for his troubles was a bundle of letters, but on closer inspection when he saw the address on the top envelope a shiver of excitement ran through him. "Where the hell did you get these." he asked. Gina raised her eyebrows invitingly. "What you have there is the beginning of Debra Magee's revenge mission, from what she told me it's a bundle of very explicit and sordid love letters from Sharpe to James Magee that she

159

found tucked away in a locked drawer in her husband's study. She admitted that after reading the first letter she was too disgusted to read the rest and was about to burn them but thank God she had the good sense not to. I took her word about the content as I have no bloody interest in their sordid little fantasies, but you need to go through them with a fine toothed comb and see if they contain anything to help our case. I don't want anything more to do with them."

Art had the bundle letters clutched tightly in both hands like they were something precious. "Are all of these letters from Sharpe to Magee?" he asked.

Gina nodded. "I think so, Art. Debra assumed them to be, but she wasn't entirely sure as she didn't have the stomach to go through them all to find out. All she's determined to do now is damage her husband's *holier than thou* reputation by handing them over to us. She has her mind set on revenge, and although she didn't say so in as many words, I get the impression she would be very happy to have them used as evidence in open court where they will do the most damage."

Art was tossing the little bundle up and down in his hand. "God only knows what I'll find in here if neither of you have been through them yet."

His excitement was gathering pace and it showed on his rugged features. "I'll need to tackle this with an open mind," he muttered, "but I might need a glass of whiskey to keep me company. I have a feeling I'll need something stronger than wine to wash the bad taste away if I'm going to read about their sordid little love life."

He went over and gave Gina a big hug. "I don't know what to say, sweetheart, you must have won Debra over big-time for her to trust you with something as personal as this." He stopped to count how many were in the bundle. "Twenty-seven romantic outpourings for me to read, how absolutely thrilling!" Having said his piece he wandered off into the lounge with his whiskey in one hand and his precious little bundle in the other.

Gina watched him go with a winning smile on her face, she had nothing else to do for the moment but put her feet up again and relax.

The first thing Art did was to sort the letters into chronological order according to the post dates on the envelopes, where possible, and it turned out to be a wise decision because he quickly pounced on an envelope that had a Brazilian post stamp and was franked a few weeks earlier. He opened it up with a heightening sense of expectation and found the very first paragraph to be a real eye opener that got him excited beyond measure.

The first line began with an apology from Sharpe for his sudden absence, he then went on to reveal a lot more by explaining how he had been forced to visit a former employer in Brazil on some rather urgent business, he then rambled on with all sorts of promises before explaining, in disgusting detail, how he intended to make up for lost time when he got back.

Art almost leapt from his chair with excitement, he could hardly believe what he was reading. That very first sentence contradicted everything Silverman had said during his interview with Art. While under caution he had blatantly denied having seen or heard from Sharpe after he left his employment three years earlier and had strenuously denied having any contact with his former employee until he came to visit his business premises in Detroit to hitch a ride back to Brazil.

Art's heart was thumping as he leapt from his seat and darted back to the kitchen.

Gina couldn't miss the excited look on his face when he charged in on her. "Don't tell me Sharpe's sick little fantasies got you this worked up?" Art threw both arms round the waist and swung her round. "If you only knew what you were doing when you got hold of those letters. We have that lying bastard Silverman right where we want him and no mistake." Unaware of Art's discovery Gina couldn't understand what caused him to be so excited. "I think you need to explain yourself, lover, because I haven't a clue what you're going on about."

Art guided her back to her seat before explaining why he was so excited, gushing his words excitedly in the process, and when he'd finished explaining he shot off to get another bottle of wine. "Come on, sweetheart," he gushed excitedly, "this calls for a real celebration, let's get plastered." He popped the cork and filled their glasses. "I can't wait to see Delgado's face when he hears about this." Gina wasn't so excited. "I suggest you calm down a bit, Art, I'm as excited as you are at the thought of seeing Marcus's face when we break the news, but there's heck of a long way to go before we get Silverman locked up. We need to keep our feet on the ground and not get too worked up about this; the time to celebrate is when we have Silverman locked up."

Her words were wasted on Art, he was as high as a kite with his discovery and had every intention of remaining that way. "Roll on tomorrow morning, sweetheart, I can't wait to get in front of Marcus, but let's enjoy the rest of this wine before the bloody stuff goes off." Gina gave him a warning look. "Would it not be wiser to check out the rest of those letters and see what other little secrets they hold?" Art gave her a mischievous smile. "There are times when you can be a right little spoil sport, but you're right of course and I guess I'd better go and finish what I started."

He got up and wandered back to the lounge looking like he'd just won the lottery.

18

They arrived at the Station House early next morning with Art bouncing around like a two year old, he was mad keen to get in front of Delgado and brighten his day. He knew Sharpe's letter from Brazil was sufficiently damning to counter Silverman's denial that there had been any contact between the two men in recent years. Sadly things didn't go as planned, because the District Attorney having beaten him to it and was already in deep conversation with Delgado when he got there. He was about to turn away and leave them to it when Delgado spotted him and waved him in. "You're the very the man we need to see, Art. Come in and sit down."

Art's euphoria took a sudden nose-dive when he heard that they *both* had a need to see him. Something didn't smell right. "Now why would you both have a need to see me?" he asked, but before Delgado could explain the DA dived in. "You probably don't know it yet, Lieutenant, but the Commissioner has been made aware of a complaint by a highly reputable businessman in Detroit who claims to be the victim of a wrongful arrest. Since you are listed as the arresting officer I think you need to explain exactly what you were up to in Detroit."

Art felt like he'd been punched in the gut, and he was deeply angered. "The Commissioner can go suck eggs from a duck's ass, and you had better explain why you are interfering in this case, District Attorney? It's the responsibility of *this* department to investigate crime and gather the evidence to bring offenders to court, in this case for three murders on our patch, with a fourth connected murder being investigated by our counterparts in England. Maybe I'm missing something but it's my understanding that *your* role is the presentation of that evidence to the court, which has absolutely sod all to do with solving the goddamned crime." He wrung his hands together. "And while I'm on the subject, I am answerable to the man sat in front of you and I'm certainly not answerable to you, or the Commissioner for that matter. So if you don't mind I'm off now to do some crime detection and I'll come back see my chief when you've completed your business with him."

He turned on his heel and walked out without giving either man a chance to challenge him, but it was little more than a second before he stuck his head back round the door. "And so you both have something worthwhile to discuss, I have uncovered proof that Silverman deliberately lied to me under caution when he denied having any contact with Sharpe until three days ago. I have definite proof that Sharpe visited him in Brazil quite recently." He didn't wait for a reply, just slammed the door shut and walked off, leaving the other two looking at each other like they had just wallowed a wasp.

Delgado was the first to get his wits about him. "If my Lieutenant has proof to support his claim then the Commissioner needs to wind his goddamned neck in and stop taking things at face value before they're fully investigated." The DA just got to his feet and walked out, shaking his head in despair.

Art of course heard none of this, he was absolutely livid with his boss for not listening to him before siding with the DA, that, and his lack of support over what he had uncovered had him really wound up. Delgado would need to do some serious grovelling the next time they met. With nothing else on hand now that his meeting with Delgado had fallen through he wandered off in search of his partner, and when he couldn't find her he headed back to his own office and snatched up the phone and keyed in Delany's number.

Delany could see who was calling. "Hi, Art, what's happening?" he asked. "Hi, Pat, I know this is not something you want to hear, but I would be eternally grateful if your guys would go back and take Silverman into custody again." Their conversation didn't end there as Art went on to explain about the letter, although there was much more to it than that. "I'm worried that he'll take off back to Brazil, especially as that damned country doesn't extradite its citizens, regardless of the severity of their crimes. More importantly, he has a private plane tucked away somewhere, so he doesn't even need to worry about booking flights with commercial airlines to slip the net, he can go anytime he feels like it without us knowing about it." Art could almost hear Delany's mind rattling though his options.

"That's a mighty big ask, Art, and I'm not sure I can deliver on it. We've already had the guy in custody and released him without charge." He stopped talking to conjure up something that would help his fellow lawman. "I tell you what I'll do, Art, I'll find out where his plane is laid up and have a word with the operating authority to put a hold on any flight plans he submits. I think that's the best I can offer as things currently stand, and if I'm honest I'm not even sure I can deliver on that, but I'll certainly give it a go. Sorry I can't be more helpful, but on a more positive note, Sharpe will be back with you by mid-afternoon today, subject to flights being on time."

Art had to chew his gums for a while before he was fit to respond. What Delany was offering wasn't even close to what he wanted, but he understood the difficulty involved if they arrested Silverman again so soon after releasing him. An action like that could quite easily lead to accusations of police harassment, and that was the last thing anybody wanted.

"I knew I was asking an awful lot of you, Pat, but if you can stop him from heading off in that bloody plane it will be a big help. All I'm after is a little time to convince the powers that be at this end that we have enough evidence for a conviction, and I'd appreciate it if you would let me know how you get on as I'm not exactly in my boss's good books at the moment. I had a bit of a bust up with him *and* the DA a short while ago, and I think I can hear them sharpening their knives for a head hunting safari." He laughed at the thought. "But thank God I've got a harder neck than they seem to realise."

Delany joined in with his laughter, but he had no time to waste. "I'll see what I can do for you, Art, but I have to go as I'm up in court in twenty, but I'll let you know how I get on." Art wished him well and hung up. It was time for a large mug of coffee with plenty of cream to sooth his rumbling ulcer.

While Art was soothing his ulcer Gina was being offered some words of advice by her irate boss, who did nothing to cheer her up by telling her about his run-in with her partner.

"You need to have a word with that man of yours and tell him to wind his neck in. He can't continue to speak to his seniors the way he does and expect to come out of it unscathed. There will be a price to pay if I ever get a repeat of that performance, and I will definitely be having words with him later when he has cooled down and comes to his senses, but take my advice, Gina, because you need to follow my lead if we are to protect him from himself." Gina gave his advice a few moments thought before daring to say anything, and when she did it wasn't exactly what Delgado expected to hear. "Art is, without any

any shadow of doubt, the best detective in this whole department bar none, and you know that as well as I do, Captain. He isn't having a go at you or authority in the way you see it, he's just so bloody enthusiastic about getting the results our public want from their police that he gets irritated and frustrated when others block his efforts. Okay, so maybe he did go over the top a bit this morning, but perhaps you and that dick-head of a DA should have checked your facts before making a big issue over some fucked-up suspect making complaints about wrongful arrest. Art uncovered new and important evidence in some letters I gave him from Debra Magee that got him really hyped-up and eager to tell you about it. Yet that all he got for his troubles was a senseless put-down for his troubles."

She pulled herself up to her full height and stuck out her considerable chest. "I will have words with him as you ask, but it won't be to undermine his efforts, it will be to congratulate him on coming up with a new piece of evidence that proves Silverman lied under caution. I know this isn't what you want to hear from me but maybe the DA should stop interfering in our investigations, he's a prosecutor not an investigator and I think you both need to remember that."

Delgado was absolutely speechless, he couldn't believe she was being so aggressive, disparaging even, it was so unlike her that he was totally lost for words, and it left him to come out with the only reply that came to mind. "I suggest you get back to work before you say something we both regret." He waved her away dismissively. Gina turned on her heel and left Delgado chewing his gums.

While she'd been having her little tete-a-tete with Delgado, some six hundred miles away in Detroit Pat Delany was in conversation with the flight controller at the private airfield where Silverman's plane was hangered. The outcome of this conversation was a somewhat cautious agreement to ground the aircraft indefinitely, but with the sworn agreement that the Detroit police accepted full responsibility for any legal action that might ensue. Having got what he wanted Delany got on to Art to let him know, which was why Art was sitting with a satisfied grin on his face when Gina walked in looking very business-like. "You're in danger of taking early retirement if you don't curb your temper, Delgado is absolutely incensed with your performance in front of the DA, and he intends to have some harsh words with you about it the next time he sees you." She flung her arms in up the air out of despair. "Why the hell can't you be a little more prudent in your approach to your seniors?" Art shrugged her comment aside like it didn't matter, he was too elated by Delany grounding Silverman's plane to get riled up over Delgado.

"Delgado doesn't know it yet but he's going to see me pretty soon and I can tell you and he'll be even more upset when he hears that I've arranged for Silverman's plane to be grounded indefinitely. That should stop the bastard slipping away on us, and I intend to have Delgado organise a warrant for his arrest, so we get him under lock and key. That should give him and The D A something to think about.. Happy days, eh, sweetheart? Now I'm off to see his highness again, and I suggest you keep a low profile for a while as there's bound to be a blast or two of hot air flying around this place very soon."

He breezed off humming a catchy little tune to himself. While Gina stood shaking her head in wonderment at his ability overcome the insurmountable so damned easily.

Delgado was in no mood to see anyone let alone the cause of his misery, but he couldn't refuse to speak with Art when he walked in and planted himself right in front of him. "We need a serious talk about Silverman, Captain, and it can't wait."

Delgado looked like something nasty was stuck in his throat. "Talk?" he spluttered, struggling to control his anger. "You want me to listen to what you have to say after this morning's damaging performance, and I really do mean damaging. Damaging to the standing of this department in the eyes of our District Attorney. If I weren't your friend I would kick your ass back out through that fuckin' door and have you writing parking tickets until you retire. You seriously embarrassed me and our department in front of our D A this morning and you have the temerity to come into my office again demanding to discuss the very cause of your outrageous performance."

There was a lot more he wanted to get off his chest, but Art cut in on him. "I approached you this morning in good faith, Captain, but before I even got to open my mouth to explain why I wanted to see you, the District Attorney issued me with a warning that a so-called high flying member of the public had levelled a complaint against me for wrongful arrest. Well, I'm here to tell you that I need an arrest warrant for that very same member of the public, Joshua Silverman, and I want it just as soon as it can be typed up."

Delgado's brow was glistening with sweat and his face was so flushed he might have been bordering on a heart attack. For his part, Art waited patiently like a well-behaved little schoolboy for what came next.

Delgado managed to find his voice before blowing a gasket. "I'm at an absolute loss to know how your mind works, I really am, but setting that aside for now, what in the name of God would possess me to even consider doing such a monumentally crazy thing? Do you seriously believe the D A would dare to even consider such a stupid idea after what happened earlier today? Have you lost all sense of reason, or have you been hitting the bottle already?"

Art pulled a seat up in front of his desk and dropped into it. "I'm about to take you through a sequence of events that have convinced me Silverman isn't just up to his eyes in these murders but is probably controlling the whole bloody show. Now are you willing to give me a proper hearing or do I hand my badge in?"

Delgado closed his eyes to shut out the image in front of him. He was forced to concentrate on finding a way out the situation facing him, but in the end he simply gave in. "You have five minutes, so start talking." He wiped his damp brow with the back of his hand.

Art had already thought through everything he intended to say and was all set to go. He dived straight into what was a long and detailed evaluation of the situation as he knew it to be, and he hardly stopped for a breath as he very cleverly linked all the pieces of evidence he had unearthed to paint a vivid picture that even Delgado found compelling, and he could do little else but admit it. "Okay, so maybe we should have listened to you earlier, but you need to listen-up and modify your approach and not get people's back up so bloody easily. We've known each other for a long time now, Art, and I like to think we're friends below all this professional hassle and its outside influences, so can we please try to see each other's point of view calmly and thoughtfully without making such a big issue of it every time? Can we agree to try and do that please?"

Art got to his feet and stuck his hand out, which his boss accepted eagerly, and when they had dispensed with the handshake Delgado pulled a bottle of from his drawer and shared what was left in it between two glasses. "There's just enough left to help put this ruckus behind us." It had to be a quickie as Art was in a hurry to get away. "I have things to do in preparation for interviewing Sharpe when he gets here later, but it's crucial that I get to know about Silverman's arrest warrant before he has a chance to slip away," he gave a little snigger, "although that might not be so easy for him now that I have his plane grounded." He tipped his brow and headed off before his last comment even registered with Delgado, almost tripping over Gina who had been eavesdropping their conversation.

"Well done, Art," she whispered, not to be overheard by their boss, "that was a bit more diplomatic. It's not right that you two are constantly at loggerheads, you're supposed to be friends for God's sake. Now why don't we go and get a sandwich or something, I'm absolutely starving." Art wrapped his arm round her waist and led her away, but she wasn't finished giving off to him. "I don't want to hear a single word about this blasted case tonight when we get home tonight, do you understood?"

Art gave her a mock innocent look. "I don't know why you should even think to mention that, but I'll do my best, sweetheart, I promise, although the sandwich is out of the question I'm afraid, I have to get ready to interview Sharpe, he's due here any time soon. Delgado wants him shipped straight up to Rikers, but I intend to interview him here before he goes. You head off and get something and I'll catch up with you later when we interview Sharpe."

They split up and went their separate ways.

19

Sharpe arrived pretty much on schedule and went through the booking in procedure while chained at his wrists and ankles.

Art had been a bit restless while waiting for his arrival, but after his meeting with his boss he was primed and ready to deal with something different. "Well, well, fancy seeing you here. Mister Sharpe isn't it?" He was being deliberately obtuse.

After this little exchange he turned to the desk Sergeant with a scowl on his face. "Get this murdering scumbag whatever he's entitled to, drinks, food, the crapper, whatever. Then take him down to interview room one and let me know when you have him there."

He turned to their prisoner again. "I'll be seeing you later, Sharpe, and a little word of advice before I go. You had better get your story straight because I intend to have some fun." He left the desk Sergeant to get on with his booking him in and headed off for some refreshment, he was expecting a lengthy session ahead and needed to be ready for it.

Twenty minutes later he was peering through the one-way observation window at his prisoner, who appeared to be having an issue coping with his security chains.

Gina had caught up with him and was enjoying the sight of Sharpe's unease every bit as much as Art was. What's the plan of attack, Art?" she asked. "Well," he said, drawing the word out, "we already have everything we need to prosecute him for multiple homicide, but what I'm after right now is convincing proof that Silverman is the brains behind their murderous campaign. We now have evidence of contact between both men that is verified by that letter Debra Magee gave us, plus Sharpe's own very detailed accusation of Silverman's involvement, but we might need stronger evidence than that to get Silverman past the D A. We simply can't afford to have the bastard slip through our fingers again on some trumped up legal technicality. Between you and me, Gina, I'm not convinced there isn't someone else involved as well. Someone we haven't identified yet, someone working behind the scenes who is pulling the strings. That's the challenge that I see in front of us, and it's a big challenge too, make no mistake."

"Do you want me in with you on the interview?" she asked. Art looked her up and down with obvious surprise. "Good God girl, I'm banking on it. Have you forgotten that this guy is as queer as a badger, so I don't think women are exactly top of his fantasy list? I can't wait to see his face when he's confronted with a gorgeous looking female like you, a female who has more power than he has."

Gina gave a mischievous smile. "You really are a devious old so and so, you never miss a trick, do you?" Art gave a little chuckle. "Would you still love me if I did?"

She closed one eye and looked him up and down. "I might have to think about it." She confessed, jokingly. They giggled their way out of the conversation and headed inside to confront their prisoner. Sharpe was studying his manacled wrists on the tabletop, but he looked up with a scowl when they walked in, giving Art an excuse to offer him a slightly caustic greeting. "How nice of you to call and see us again, Mister Sharpe. Have you nothing better to do on this fine day." He raised a hand to his mouth. "Oops! How remiss of me, you're under arrest aren't you, I almost forgot."

He dragged a metal chair from under the table noisily and planted his ass on it. Gina did the same and when they were both settled with the recorder switched on and advised of what it needed to know he gave Sharpe a glimpse of what lay ahead. "Let's get one thing straight before we begin, Rodney." Leaning his elbows on the table brought him a bit closer to his quarry. "We're very lucky in that we don't have to prove you're a killer as you have very kindly done that for us, so we can dispense with the normal legalities for the moment and get down to a much more important issue, which is really very simple, so you won't have to think very hard to keep up. I want you to tell me who the top man is behind this killing spree that you and your friend have been on, and if you decide not to tell me then things are going to get really nasty around here, and I'm sure you know what that means."

Sharpe wriggled upright on his chair and planted his manacled wrists on the metal tabletop again with a rattle. "I'm saying nothing until you take these bloody manacles off. I can't even reach for a cup of water while my hands are chained to my waist?" Gina gave him a cheesy grin. "You shouldn't complain, Rodney, at least you can still reach your little play-thing, or has that already been decommissioned?" If Sharpe had been capable of doing so he would have leapt across the table at her, but all he could do was swear and confront her. "Jumped-up stupid bitch, you'll get nothing out of me with that attitude," he switched his attention to Art, "you'd better get that catty bitch beside you out of here or *you* get nothing out of me either."

Art wrung his hands together. "Settle down, Rodney, you and I both know what's going to happen. You're going to take a little trip up to Riker's Island Correction Facility until you enter your plea before a

175

judge and it can get very claustrophobic up there, and that's being nice about it, even I know that. So why don't you sit back and tell me what I want to know and let's see how easy we can go on you. We're willing to go softly, softly if you give us what we want"

Sharpe attempted to scratch his face, but his chains stopped him. "For God's sake take these bloody chains off my wrists. I'm not even going to acknowledge your presence until you do." He dropped back into his chair and closed his eyes with his jaw set stubbornly.

Art winked at Gina. "If I have your chains removed, Rodney, are you willing to talk?" he asked; "you need to remember that no matter what happens from here on in you're going down for a very long time, but as you know, things can be made a little easier if you co-operate. There are a couple of pieces of information I want from you. Firstly, I want the name of the person who killed your buddy Hardwick, and secondly, the name of the top man running this little shindig."

He shrugged his shoulders. "There has to be someone a bit more tuned in than Silverman directing you people and I want to know who it is?" He observed Sharpe closely while waiting for his answer. When none was forthcoming he got up and whispered something to the police officer on the door, then returned to his seat with a smile. "Tea, coffee, or a cold drink, Rodney, what's it to be?"

Sharpe opened his eyes. "Coffee." he said, before closing his eyes again., having decided to remain disengaged from his inquisitors.

Art motioned to the police officer on the door who left the room, allowing the interview to lapse into silent mode until he returned with the coffees, and having set them on the table he went round to Sharpe and undid his manacles.

Sharpe opened his eyes in surprise and immediately set about massaging his wrists. "Thank you, Lieutenant, those things were unnecessary you know, it's not as if I'm going to make a break for it. Where the hell would I go if I did?" Art cocked an eyebrow at him. "Brazil sounds attractive," he joked, "those chains were just a reminder of just how difficult life can get if you don't co-operate, and you better remember that they can go back on again just as quickly as they came off." He took a sip of coffee from his plastic cup. "Now, are we ready to get down to some serious conversation?" Sharpe also had his cup up to his mouth, but he set it down very slowly and deliberately before answering. "I can't help you with Hardwick, I wish I could as Joe was a very close friend. If I could help bring his killer to book I would do it without a second thought. That said, I have absolutely no idea who did for him, although I can tell you that I would never have let it happen if I'd been in a position to stop it."

Art was watching him much more closely now, looking for any facial tics or signs that he was lying or covering something up. He was also watching his body language for any indication that he was being defensive or evasive, but there were no signs of either. The outcome of this little study was that he tended to believe what he was being told.

"Okay, I'm willing to go along with that for now," he conceded, "but what about the brains behind this whole thing, I need you to tell me who that is?" Sharpe looked genuinely puzzled. "I wish to God I knew because that's the bastard who put me where I am now, neck deep in bog-shit." He rubbed his face vigorously, as if to waken himself up. "Joe and I got all our instructions from Silverman, so we both assumed he was in charge, we didn't have a clue what the whole deal was about at the start. I still don't know the whole picture. We

177

just did what we were paid to do and nothing more. Before he died old boy Silverman hired a private detective to track down his son to try and convince him to come home, but it also meant that we knew where to find him. Once we knew that I just tailed the group for a couple of days to get their routine before Joe came over to join me. Then we simply went ahead and set it up." He stopped to think for a moment. "To be perfectly honest I wasn't all that keen on the job as I'd never done anything like it before, but the money was far too tempting to miss out on. Where else would somebody like me get their hands on four hundred grand? I know you probably won't believe this, but I freely admit that I'm genuinely sorry for what I did. I don't know what got into me to be tempted into doing such a thing. Those poor guys never caused us any harm and they didn't deserve to die the way they did." Art had his arms crossed over his chest with one hand up to his mouth listening intently to Sharpe's explanation. He was in two minds whether to believe him or not, although he was leaning towards doing so, but if he believed Sharpe *was* telling the truth then it presented him with a much bigger problem because he would have to accept that he had nothing more to offer. Which meant he would learn nothing about his supposed mister big and any further probing would only be a waste of time.

"I'm almost ready to believe you, Rodney, but it's very challenging to reconcile your story with your background. You're a top-class security manager for Christ sake, not some naive little schoolboy, so how come you didn't know who you were working for and why didn't you try to find out?"

Sharpe did his best to look guilty. "I just lost sight of reality with all the money that was on offer. It was plain bloody stupid, and I admit that, but I can't change anything now even if I want to, can I?"

Art unfolded his arms and leaned across the table to get closer to his prisoner. "No, you can't, but you can help me find out who is running this murderous campaign. You need to think hard on what you know about Silverman's connection and try to put a finger on the person I'm after. You must know enough to point me in the right direction." Sharpe shuffled his feet under the table, without saying say anything.

Gina, who had been observing all this in voluntary silence decided it was time to get involved. She didn't believe a single word Sharpe was spouting, she reckoned it was a practiced performance by a confirmed out and out liar, and not being so easily side-tracked by his performance as she thought Art was, she decided it was time to cut in and let Sharpe know she had his measure. "I read some of the sweet little ramblings you sent James Magee," she lied, "so I guess you must be quite a practiced lover on the side. I'm only guessing but I imagine there must be a lot of the sexually deprived lifers up in Sing-Sing who will welcome you into their midst with open arms. You'll be quite an attraction for them once they get their hands on you. At least that's something you can look forward to?"

Sharpe almost bust a gut. His face turned crimson and the veins on his neck swelled up like tram lines. "Get that stupid bitch outta my face before I do her a serious injury." He yelled threateningly.

For the first time since his arrest Sharpe had resorted to his true character. He showed that he *was* a seriously violent individual and not the repentant, mixed up individual he claimed to be.

Gina watched his performance with an immense feeling of satisfaction. She had succeeded in what she had set out to do and exposed his malevolent character for Art to see. She had been quietly nursing a very serious concern that he was being hoodwinked by Sharpe's

179

performance and wanted to end it. Art reached out and grabbed Sharpe by the shirt front and dragged him half-way over the table. "You ever dare threaten an officer of the law in my presence again and I'll knock your teeth so far down your throat that you'll be eating through your ass." He shoved Sharpe back into his seat with such violence that he toppled over the chair and landed on his back on the concrete floor. There was a loud clatter from the chair tumbling over and a mouthful of obscenities from Sharpe who was struggling to get to his feet. "I'm reporting you for assaulting a prisoner, I'll have your fuckin' badge for this." Art cocked his eyebrows at him in a questioning way. "I take it you have a witness to this alleged assault because no one here has a clue what you're rambling about. You need to join the rest of us in the real world, Sharpe, this is the NYPD you're dealing with now not some village cop shop, now plant your ass back in that chair and don't you dare move it again until I give you permission." The door behind Art opened unexpectedly and Delgado walked in without warning. "It's time to feed the beast," he told Art, "it's an unfortunate act of human kindness that his civil rights forces upon us."

Sharpe climbed to his feet and pointed an accusing finger at Art. "If you're the one in charge here, I want to report this thug for assaulting me while in police custody." He glared across the table at Delgado.

Delgado looked at him like he'd lost all sense of reason. "Let's not delve into the realms of fantasy, Sharpe, you should focus on the fact that you're a prisoner on a homicide charge and not visiting some Sunday church convention. Now plant your ass and don't say another word until you're spoken to." Delgado was mindful that he owed Art a bit of back-up after wrongly putting him down over the Silverman incident, he saw this as a way of repaying him. "It's time our prisoner was fed and locked up until we can get him some legal aid. I have a feeling it might take a day or two, but when you have him organised, Art, just pop in and see me. I need a quick word." He disappeared through the door leaving Art to get on with it, a task he dealt with in a hurry as he had other things that needed attention. In any case it was a done deal as far as Sharpe was concerned, they had more than enough evidence to send him down for at least three life sentences, and since he appeared to have nothing to offer in return for leniency he was sent back to his cell. Then Art and Gina headed off together, Gina back to her workstation and Art away to see what his boss had in mind.

"You have something to tell me, Marcus." He was standing just outside the door as he wanted the meeting over with quickly. He was more interested in getting in touch with Pat Delany.

"I won't keep you long, Art, but first things first. I have your arrest warrant for Silverman so you can get on to the Detroit police and have them pick him up. Dare I say well done?" He shifted his reading glasses to the end of his nose and looked at Art over the top of them. "Now then, I'm minded to give more attention to this idea you have that there's someone big hiding in the shadows, someone that we haven't caught up with yet. Is this a definite line of investigation we're on or are you just on a fishing expedition?"

Art was caught unawares and had to think on his feet. "If I'm honest, Marcus, it's no more than a suspicion right now, but my gut instinct tells me that with the vast amounts of money, real estate, and company holdings involved in this dammed legacy we should be looking higher up the ladder, but I admit it's no more than a hunch just now."

Marcus scratched his head and screwed his face up like he'd just sucked on a lemon. "I'm beginning to fall in line with your theory, so how do we go about proving it when we haven't got a serious suspect in the frame? If your theory is right I would suggest it's more likely to be someone from across the pond, likely from London, and we don't have any authority over there. The only thing we can do is convince Inspector Stewart to take a closer look at Mendelson and Ackerman. It would make sense to check them all out since they're the ones at the business end of things." Art stared at the wall behind Delgado's head, deep in thought. "That would require us to do exactly the same with Johnston, Johnston and Jacobs as they could have as much to gain as anyone else. A forensic audit of their accounts might tell us something. You see, Marcus, this might not even be about financial gain, not in the straight sense of the word."

Delgado looked puzzled. "If it's not about financial gain then what the hell is it about?" Art looked like he had something new to offer. "It's possible that someone has *already* been syphoning off company funds or is fiddling the books somehow, and after the death of Silverman senior they might be worried about being exposed when the company assets are audited for hand over to the beneficiary of the Will. Okay. I admit I'm clutching at straws with this idea as I have nothing concrete to support it, but it has to be another possible motive."

Delgado rubbed his forehead with his fingertips before saying anything, but when he did it wasn't to undermine Art's theory. "It is a possible scenario and no mistake, Art, and not one I had thought about so it's something new to think about, but where does Silverman's step-son fit into the grand scheme of things? He doesn't have to do a damn thing now that his only other relative is out of the way, except maybe show a little patience while our case rumbles on." Art's cheeks puffed up as he blew up an imaginary balloon. "I haven't a clue, Marcus, we're kind of groping in the dark with this, and I don't

182

believe there's anything new to be had from Sharpe. He was nothing more than a paid stooge who hasn't even been paid for the job yet, and never will." He pushed himself away from the door post. "Do you mind if I head off, Marcus, I have things that need doing before the end of play, like arranging a flight to Detroit and giving Pat Delany a bit of warning that I'll be dropping in on him again." Delgado waved him away. "On your bike, Art, there's nothing that can't wait."

Art headed off with a spring in his step, although he needn't have hurried too much as Delany was tied up with other business and wasn't contactable, so with that idea kicked into touch he decided to phone him before boarding the plane the following morning. All he had in mind was to let him know he was heading his way and when he would be arriving.

20

Having started the day full of pent up enthusiasm Art was all set to board the plane when he decided to phone Delany and let him know he was on his way with a warrant for Silverman, a piece of news that went down very well with Delany. "Well done, Art, I'm with you all the way on this. You and I both know that skinny bastard is guilty as hell, and I'm looking forward to seeing you again anyway, but if I'm not available when you get here feel free to make yourself at home in my den until I get back." Once Delany had disconnected Art phoned his indispensable cabby and arranged to meet up with him at the airport pick-up point, and with everything in hand he joined the rest of the crowd bustling forward to get on board.

Four boring hours later he was climbing into the front passenger seat beside his cabby friend and belting up. "Where to this time, Art? I take it you're still after that skinny guy. You sure don't look the type to give up?" Art didn't have to think about it. "You got that right, Jack, but I need to see Pat Delany before I do go charging in as I want an update on our suspects movements. I'm hoping it will only be a case of moving in and making the arrest, all very straight forward."

The cabby gave a slightly muffled snigger. "Isn't that what they all say, Art, but we both know that things rarely pan out that way." Art ignored the remark, he had his fingers crossed that the cabby prediction wasn't an accurate one. Although his remark offered serious food for thought, and rightly so because the first thing Delany told him when they met

184

up was that Silverman had changed his routine for the day and had failed to go into his office as usual. According to the latest surveillance report he hadn't left his home yet and Delany's team were still in attendance.

Art didn't have a clue where Silverman lived, which meant he would have to rely on others to get him there, and as the arrest was to be executed in Detroit it would be up to the local police to officiate. The last thing anyone wanted were any last minute cock-ups, or legal irregularities fogging the issue, but even with that annoying little doubt in mind Art was feeling fairly relaxed and laid back. More so when he learned that the same team that had helped him on his last visit were to support him once again. Apparently they'd volunteered for the detail, which was comforting to know as they had worked well together on his last visit.

While they were waiting to get organised Delany got called out on an urgent job leaving Art hanging about and straining at the leash to get under way. There was further frustration ahead with everything happening far too slowly for his liking, he wanted action, and he wanted it now, yet here he was stuck in Delany's cramped little office waiting for Sergeant Wilson to put in an appearance. That turned out to be another nightmare as he'd been despatched on the same detail as Delany. Sadly, it would be another hour and twenty minutes before they got back, and things got organised.

"Are we going to make the charges stick this time, Lieutenant?" asked Sergeant Wilson as they headed away from the compound. Art gave a quiet little chuckle. "You can bet your bottom dollar on it. That's if we ever manage to catch up with him of course. I'm worried that he hasn't put in an appearance at his business premisses today, a break from his normal routine and any break in routine with a suspect is always a concern, but how long before we get there?" he asked. Sergeant Wilson pointed to his satnav. "We're only two miles away according to that stupid gismo, so it won't be long."

Art was primed and ready for action, but he was concerned over the endless delays and would remain that way until Silverman was safely in custody, regardless of what the bloody Satnav said.

They suddenly took a sharp right into a smart, tree lined estate and drove straight up the first driveway. The house in front of them was quite respectable, with wood clad frontage and a small garden either side of a short gravel drive that went all the way round to the back of the house. The minute they were out of the car Sergeant Wilson pointed to the rear of the house and sent his patrolman off to investigate. "We need to cover the rear of the house as well." He warned Art, who gave him a thumbs-up as they headed straight for the front door where he banged hard on its wooden panel, ignoring the doorbell that was right in front of him. When there was no response, or any sign of movement inside he banged more heavily on the door panel a second time, but it was another futile effort that brought no response. "Let's have a nosy around." He suggested, feeling a little uneasy as he peered through the nearest window, but with no sign of life inside they went round to the side of the building checking every available window en route. When they met up with him the younger officer was peering intently through a glass panel on the back door, even though there wasn't much to see with the view shielded by a heavy net curtain. "It doesn't look like anyone's home," he confirmed, "but there's a car in the garage so he can't be far away." Art needed to get inside the house, but he didn't have a search warrant and he wasn't sure if an arrest warrant authorised him to force an entry. The sergeant answered the problem for him. "In this state, Lieutenant, an arrest warrant authorises you to search for and retain the person named on the warrant, wherever he or she is detected, so let's get in there and search for him, but before we do why don't we check with the surveillance team in case they have eyes on him."

He led Art back to the car to make the call, and to their horror they discovered that the surveillance team were sitting a mere fifty yards further up the estate and were totally unaware of the ongoing situation. Art was horrified at the lack of professionalism shown by the local police and without giving it another thought he decided to take matters into his own hands. "We have to get inside, Sergeant, for all we know Silverman could be sat on his skinny ass in there having a good laugh at us. This is no time to hang about out here, I have to know one way or the other, so leave your buddy here to watch the front entrance and you come round the back with me."

When they got there Sergeant Wilson pulled out his night stick and smashed one of the smaller glass panels on the door and eased his hand inside. Within seconds they were safely inside with weapons drawn. Their search of the ground floor was unsuccessful, but when Art checked the kitchen he had the foresight to check the coffee percolator and found it to be still warm to the touch, an indication that Silverman, or someone, was either still inside the house or had very recently bolted. But if, as he suspected, his quarry had taken to his heels then there was every possibility that he could still be in the local area since he was more than likely on foot. With this in mind they completed the remainder of their search at a faster pace with Art as eager as hell to get the surveillance team on the move cruising the local area for any sight of their quarry.

Once that was organised he was left with more time to search the property for any clues to Silverman's whereabouts.

While the house didn't have a study, one corner of the lounge held a neat little computer desk although no computer was anywhere to be seen. There was however a small filing cabinet nearby that Art plundered excitedly, but most of its contents were just old business e-mails and brochures and nothing of interest.

With no clues coming to light he decided to head over to Silverman's business property and see what it had to offer. Thankfully Sergeant Wilson had already been to the premises on his last visit and got them there in record time. Where the young lady manning reception was very pleasant and welcoming, as one would expect, but when Art waved his badge under her nose she became a bit more subdued.

"We're here to interview your boss, Joshua Silverman, if he's available to see us?" The receptionist shook her head. "I'm afraid Mister Silverman is not here today; he has a number of business meetings in New York and won't be available for at least two or possibly three days." Art pinched his nose, disappointed that everything seemed to be going wrong for him. "I need to know how your boss is getting to New York and who he is meeting. I also need to know where these meetings are taking place and the phone number of the person he is meeting so that we can contact him, and while you're at it I would like his mobile phone number and car registration as well."

The young lady reached for her desk diary and having browsed through its pages she looked none the wiser. "I'm afraid, Mister Silverman has not availed me of the details for his meetings, so I'm not at liberty to help you on that score. I can let you have you with his personal phone and car number." She wrote the details on a piece of paper and handed it to Art, who made a note of her name from the name tag pinned to her breast. "Thank you for that, Sylvia, you've been really helpful, but tell me, does your boss normally go off on meeting without making you aware of who he's meeting or where he will be?" She gave him a disapproving look. "As a matter of fact, no, he doesn't. Mister Silverman usually keeps me very well informed, but I will forgive him his absent-mindedness on this occasion as he has been very busy lately." Art could see she was simply being loyal and protective of her boss and nothing underhand, so her attitude didn't cause him any ill feeling, but she wasn't about to get off the hook too easily. "I would like you to do something for me, Sylvia." She looked a little uneasy about what might be asked of her but agreed without argument. "If I can help in any way then of course I'll be happy to do so, but what is it you want me to do?"

Art leaned both elbows on the counter. "Nothing too difficult. I just want you to phone your boss and ask him where he is and when he intends returning to Detroit." Sylvia reached for the phone, but all she got for her trouble was an unavailable signal. She looked at Art and shrugged her shoulders. "There doesn't appear to be a signal where he is, I'm afraid I can't do anything about that." Art pointed to the stairs. "I'll just pop up upstairs and see if he has left any clues that might help. We really need to contact him urgently, Sylvia, you see I have a warrant for his arrest and his absence means that he is now a fugitive from the law" The young lady stared at him like he'd gone mad. "I've never heard anything so ridiculous. There must be some mistake, my employer would never do anything to break the law." Art gave her a curt look. "We're not here to charge your boss with some traffic violation, Sylvia, we're here to arrest him for involvement in three murders, so you can see how important it is that I find out exactly where he is, and quickly too." He gave her a few moments to come to terms with the situation before giving her another much gentler warning. "It would be unwise to cover for your boss, Sylvia, if you know where he is, or where we may contact him, you should tell me now."

The poor girl looked totally bewildered, she was on the verge of bursting into tears, an issue that Art had no desire to deal with. "You haven't done anything wrong, Sylvia, so don't get yourself all worked-up for no reason. I'm only asking you to help us if you can and to warn you that if Silverman gets in touch it is vitally important that you tell us right away. Can you do that?" She wiped her eyes before answering. "Of course I will. I'm not a criminal, and if Mister Silverman is guilty of the crime you accuse him off then I want nothing more to do with him. I will most certainly inform you if he gets in touch. Why would I not?" Art gave her his Sunday best smile. "I know you will, Sylvia, and that's all I'm asking. Now I'm going to pop up stairs to see if he has left any clues, but I suggest you get yourself a strong cup of coffee while I'm away." He turned away and motioned Sergeant Wilson to follow him as he raced up the stairs two at a time. The upstairs office could only be described as utility, with limited furnishings and precious little evidence that it had ever been occupied. They began their search by rifling the drawers on Silverman's desk, there were four in all, although only one had any contents and that was only reams of blank paper and a few stick-it pads. The top of the desk was partially covered by a large, leather backed blotting paper with lots of scribbled notes and doodles all over it, none of which made any sense, but when Art turned it over he found a stick-it note on the reverse side bearing a scribbled reminder that read, '*meet Ali Tuesday 1800 JFK*' He felt a sudden tingle of excitement, which was a bit odd as he had no idea which Tuesday the note referred to, but one thing he did know, it was Tuesday when he got out of bed this morning and when he married that up with Silverman's trip to New York he was forced to a hurried and rather rash decision. Pulling his phone out he dialled Gina's number in the vane hope she'd be available.

"Hi, Art, what happening?" She sounded surprised to hear from him. "Don't say anything, Gina, just listen. I need a few uniforms over to JFK and the place closed down tight. Silverman has given us the slip at this end, but I believe he's meeting someone called Ali at the airport at six o'clock this evening. We need to get our hands on him before he flees the country. Can you organise that for me?"

Gina didn't stop to think. "Consider it done, Art but I hope Delgado doesn't get wind of it until it's all over. See you soon, lover." Sensing his urgency she was about to hang up. "Wait up, Gina, I haven't finished. There's a photograph of Silverman in the top left drawer in my office desk. Make copies of it and circulate them among your team, good girl, bye for now, honey."

Sergeant Wilson hadn't a clue what Art was up to as he'd only heard one side of the conversation. "Did I hear you mention JFK?" he asked. Art took the time to explain to explain what he had found. "I'm taking a massive risk in case this meeting is planned for today. If it's not then I'll get some serious trouble when I get back to Manhattan."

Wilson almost brought the house down with his boisterous laughter. "That's a career hazard for us sewer rats as I see it?" Art joined in with his laughter, he couldn't do anything else, but it was a nervous laugh not a joyous one. He knew he was walking on thin ice with what he'd organised, but he was determined to see it through, even if it meant breaking a few rules. With these worries weighing down on him he went back downstairs for another chat with the receptionist.

"Tell me something, Sylvia," he began, "have you ever heard your boss mention someone called Ali?" She didn't hesitate for a moment. "Oh yes, that will be Ali Imran, he's a very good friend of Mister Silverman. They've known each other for a number of years now and they keep in contact quite regularly." Art's eyes lit up. "Have you any idea what he does for a living, Silvia?"

"Of course I do, he's a financer," she replied, "he works for a Dubai based company, but he spends a lot of time over here and in London." Art could hardly believe what he was hearing but he knew what needing asking next. "Would he ever have worked works for a company called Mendelson and Ackermann?" he asked. She looked totally confused. "I'm sorry but I have no way of knowing anything about that."

Art accepted her reply without question. "Never mind, Sylvia, we need to be leaving you now, but I want you to remember what I said earlier, and a little bit of friendly advice before I go, if you value your future you should be looking for alternative employment as I can assure you that your current boss of Silverman Palm Oils will be out of circulation in the very near future."

He walked away with Sergeant Wilson shadowing him.

21

Vince strode into the main concourse at JFK airport looking very purposeful with Gina trailing some way behind. She had the unenviable task of ensuring there was a police officer posted at every entrance and exit, each of them armed with a photocopy of Silverman's gaunt features. When she caught up with Vince they headed for the security managers office, eager to get set up in the control room in front of the viewing monitors. It was almost five-thirty before they were fully briefed and organised with a copy of Silverman's ugly image in front of each monitor. The security manager was the same guy who had dealt with Art on *his* visit and was eager to help, which made life a lot easier than it might otherwise have been.

"What's the buzz with this guy you're looking for? Is he likely to get violent when we approach him?" The manager enquired. "I'm afraid there's no *we* about it, friend," warned Vince, "but just so you know, the guy we're after is wanted for involvement in three homicides." The security manager threw his hands in the air and backed off. "You're damn right there's no *we*, I definitely want no part in any of that." With that little issue put aside they each got back to studying their monitors. They had only been doing so about ten minutes when Vince got suddenly got excited. "Over here, Gina." he yelled. Gina rushed over to his monitor. "Top left, by the book shop, isn't that our man?" Gina leaned over his shoulder for a closer look. "You're spot on Vince that's definitely him. Well spotted young man, just give the guys outside a buzz and warn them we're on the move and tell them to keep a low profile we don't want them spooking Silverman. He doesn't know either of us, so we won't stand out in the crowd." She stopped to think how best to make their approach. "When we get downstairs, Vince, just slip an arm casually round my waist like a couple of lovers or something." She cocked an eyebrow at him as a warning. "But only until we get within striking range." Vince was still staring at his monitor. "Shouldn't we wait until he meets up with his friend and lift them both together?" Gina grabbed him by the arm. "Come on, it will be a lot easier to watch them from down below so we can work our way gradually in their direction."

Their final position allowed them to watch their target peering into the crowd in search of his pal, and he was soon scurrying across the concourse in the direction of the escalator where Gina and Vince were sited. When he got about a third of the way over he suddenly stopped, raised his arm in the air and began waving at someone in the crowd. Gina spotted the guy he was waving at easily enough as the two of them were desperately trying to force their way through the crowd in each other's direction, which was difficult enough with the crowd milling about the way it was.

Gina has seen enough. "Let's go, Vince," she said, "you take the guy he's meeting up with and I'll tackle Silverman, but no guns please, it's far too crowded in here, fists, feet and threats only, a kick in the nuts won't go amiss if he gets too cocky, okay?" Vince gave her the thumbs up, and they set off across fifteen yards or so that was separating them from their target.

As they headed in his direction Silverman had already made contact with his friend and had him wrapped in a friendly embrace, but Gina

194

was aware that he was still scanning the crowd and appeared very alert. Indeed when he caught sight of Gina and Vince heading in his direction he knew straight away from the purposeful look on their faces exactly what was happening. But he was too slow in making his move to get away, and with Gina's sudden spurt he suddenly found himself with a gun jammed into his back.

"One wrong move and you'll spend the rest of your life in a wheelchair. Now be a good little boy and put both your hands behind your back, and no nonsense or you might not live long enough to regret it." Silverman was wise enough to know there was no escape and did as he was told, with his friend doing the same when Vince pounced on him. Together they forced S up against the nearest wall, frisked them, and read them their rights. Then with both men securely handcuffed they marched them out of the airport to a waiting police van and handed them over to the uniform officers for transporting back to Manhattan. "That was easier than I thought it might be," complained Gina, "I was hoping he'd put up a struggle, it makes me feel a little bit cheated that he didn't give me an excuse to slap him, but let's get back to the precinct and tell the boss what we've been up." She was on a high with their success and as they made their way out of the airport and with everything completed she phoned Art to him the good news.

"I knew there was nobody better suited than you two to get the job done, sweetheart, I can't tell you how relieved I am, but I'll catch up with you when I get back. You can give Marcus the good news, no doubt he'll blow a gasket and froth at the mouth a bit when he finds out what I got you to do, but he'll just have get over it. The way I see it he has little option since we have our hands on Silverman. Get him and his buddy booked in and locked away out of sight, we'll let them

195

stew in their cells overnight and tackle them first thing in the morning before they go to Rikers. If you have nothing important on the go tomorrow I'd like you in with me. But before I go, Gina, you need Marcus to sort out a holding charge for Silverman's pal, aiding and abetting a fugitive or something like that should be enough for us to offer him free lodgings until I interview him. I don't want him released until I have a word with him, we need to find out if he has anything to answer for. Maybe he's the mister big we're looking for or maybe he's just an innocent bystander? Bye for now, honey, see you tonight." He didn't give her time to answer, just ended the call.

When she got back to the base Gina went straight in to see Delgado and feeling justifiably pleased with how things had panned out she made the point of telling him so with a notable sense of pride. "Art was very lucky to find a little note that Silverman had left behind or we might never have caught up with him, and he wasn't at the airport to buy a book, he was heading off to God knows where."

Delgado wasn't best pleased. "Who the hell is this guy Ali Imran who has suddenly come on the scene, and what the hell are we supposed to charge him with?" Gina just repeated what Art had told her. "Art wants him held with Silverman, and he did stress that he shouldn't be released until he interviews him, although he did mention that you could use a holding charge of aiding and abetting a known felon to keep him here until he has a chance to deal with him." Delgado sighed with frustration. "We can't just hold someone we've never heard of because he knows Silverman, he must know lots of people and we can't arrest all of them. So why the hell did Art have him arrested in the first place?" Gina shook her head "That's a question for him, Captain, not me. Vince and I were only following orders." Delgado gave a loud sigh. "Okay," he gave another weary sigh, "I guess I had better find something to keep him locked up, but I'm not happy with this. I've no issue with you or Vince, Gina, you did exactly what you were told, and you did it pro-quo, so well done. I'll take it from here." He was about to send her on her way when he suddenly remembered something else. "Did that man of yours say when he's due back?"

"I'm expecting him back tonight if all goes to plan." Delgado nodded. "Okay you can go now, but tell him to see me first thing tomorrow, okay." With their conversation over Gina decided to warn Art of the possible flak that was lying in wait for him. She didn't think for one moment Delgado wanted to see him just to wish him good morning!"

It was close to nine o'clock that evening when Art arrived home, and he looked pretty worn out when he got there, especially as he'd had to wait for ages for a taxi at the airport. But apart from feeling worn out he was really buoyed-up with the knowledge that they had Silverman behind bars where he belonged.

Gina gave him her usual warm welcome and stuck a glass of Whiskey in his fist before he even got his jacket off. "Thanks, sweetheart, but don't put that bottle away yet, I'm going to need another of to help me wind down, it's been a really long and tiresome day." He dropped into a chair and put his feet up, looking for all the world like he was ready for bed, which he wasn't. "Now tell me how you got on with Marcus after your JFK ordeal?" he asked. Mindful of what probably lay in store when they met up in the morning. Gina stopped what she was doing and swung round to face him. "I can't say he was best pleased that we arrested this other guy, Imran, and for what it's worth I can see his point. The more I think about it the more convinced I am that we don't have anything to hold the guy on. Marcus reckons he can claim for false arrest, although he didn't stop us from booking him in, so I guess he wasn't too worked up about it." Art emptied his glass and handed it back to her for a refill, then poured herself one and sat down beside him. "You must have had a lucky shamrock in your pocket when you found that note about Silverman's meeting." She sounded really chirpy when she said it. "You've no idea just how lucky I was, Gina," he admitted, "I took a wild punt that the meeting would be today without a shred of evidence to back it up. It was nothing more than a wild guess, but it paid off for lucky old me, and it sure needed to work out because it wasn't a cheap operation sealing off the airport."

Gina fell quiet for a moment, then changed the subject for no particular reason. "Do you still think Silverman is responsible for everything that's going on?" Art shook his head. "I wouldn't bet on it anymore, but don't ask me why, I just have this uneasy feeling that someone else is pulling the strings. We need to list everyone and anyone who has even a remote possibility of gaining from old boy Silverman's death, including all the professional as well, then we do a deep search on each of them, and I really do mean a deep search, Gina.. There are too many people employed by the companies involved for us not to take a closer look at them all. Although getting agreement from Marcus and getting it started means a round table meeting with input from London as well." Gina frowned at the suggestion. The seriousness of what he was proposing, in terms of cost and international cooperation took their case to a totally different level, and she didn't see Delgado agreeing to such a wide-spread investigation when there was no guarantee of a successful outcome. "Good luck with that, buddy. Personally, I think you've a better chance of getting to the moon on a scooter than getting Delgado's blessing." Art gave a little chuckle. "Oh ye of little faith." He muttered, although it was directed more at himself than his partner, even though he was still grinning from ear to ear at the time. "Our immediate priority is to interview Silverman and Imran first thing tomorrow, and if Imran turns out to be innocent then we'll release him right away. We have all the evidence we need to put Silverman away, that's a given, so it's just a case of having him admit that he's the scumbag who's running the show, or if he denies it, which I believe he will, forcing him to tell us who is running it. He must know by now that he's going down for a very long spell so he should be focusing his energy on earning a few brownie points."

Gina stood up and yawned, she was ready for bed. "It's time we stopped talking shop and went up the wooden hill to see the Panda. I don't know about you, lover, but I'm done in."

Art got up and joined her, wrapping his arms around her waist as he whispered in her ear. "Is it just a Panda you want to see or have you something else in mind?" She slapped his backside and slinked across the room with him in tow; her finger curled under his trouser belt as she literally dragged him up to the bedroom.

22

Going past the reception desk on their way into the precinct building Art directed the duty Sergeant to have Silverman taken to an interview room and having no need for Gina to be involved in the early part of the interview he dispatched her to get the coffees and meet him in his office. He then went off to ensure that everything was as it should be for the interview, checking the recording equipment was in workable order and had a fresh tape loaded. When he was satisfied everything was as it should be he went back to his office in search of his caffeine fix, but he got a bit of a shock when he found Delgado already there and waiting for him, and not Gina as he expected. The sight of his boss installed in his office first thing in the morning did nothing to lift his spirits. "Good morning, Art," greeted Delgado, "I know you're busy this morning, but I need a few words?" Art's shoulders slumped noticeably. "Do I really have to, Captain, I'm about to interview Silverman, and I have his buddy to do straight after that, so my time isn't my own right now." Delgado raised his hand in a stopping motion. "I know all about that, but none of us know anything about this guy Imran that you foisted on us. What the hell has he done to get himself arrested?" Art was in no mood to cross swords with his boss, so he gave him a hurried explanation. "He might have been involved in shielding a fugitive, which means he ould have something to hide that we need to know about. But it's only precautionary and I'll be able to tell you more after I've questioned him. I do need to go now, Marcus. I have two prisoners waiting for me. I'll catch up with you later, I promise." He headed off without waiting for Delgado's blessing and passing Gina as she came in he grabbed a coffee from her tray. "I'll need you in interview room one in about ten minutes." He told her, without even breaking his stride.

Art didn't expect Silverman's to look relaxed and laid-back when he walked in on him, although he noticed right away that he hadn't shaved. He sat down and greeted him with a cold, hard look. "You need to stand a bit closer to your razor in the mornings if you're hoping to impress people." Silverman shifted uneasily on his chair, although there was nothing to suggest he was at all bothered. "Why should I have any desire to impress someone like you?" he asked, "Someone not just guilty of one, but two false arrests, albeit one that you will undoubtedly pay for when my legal team get here from London." Art's right eyelids twitched excitedly. "From London you say, now that is interesting. Mendelson and Ackermann have a place just up the road in Newark so why don't you use them? Or are they too low down the corruption ladder for your needs?" Silverman just crossed his arms and eased back in his chair.

"But I don't need to tell you how corrupt they are since you're a big part of that corruption. I find it very strange the effect money can have on some less educated individuals like yourself, but I guess that's all down to ones upbringing, or lack of it." Silverman looked fit to bust, his face reddened considerably and the veins on his temples became much more prominent, even his eyes narrowed and became more piercing. He obviously didn't take kindly to being put down and Art made note of it as a weakness to be explored. "What's the matter Joshua, is the truth had to swallow?" Silverman gathered himself together and wriggled upright on his chair and scowled at Art with a hate filled intensity. "Go to hell where you belong, Gardiner, I'm saying nothing more until my lawyer gets here."

Art held his hand up and counted, one, two, three on his fingers. "Triple murder means three life sentences without parole. You'll die in prison unless you sort yourself out and do some sort of a deal to lessen the burden. I know you didn't actually murder anyone yourself, Joshua, but you were a prime mover in having three innocent people put to death." He leaned on the table to get closer to his prisoner. "It's time to start talking and tell me who the top dog is that's running this show, maybe then we can talk about the possibility of minimising your sentence, but be warned, Joshua, if you decide not to cooperate I will take it all the way and have you incarcerated for the rest of your corrupt and meaningless little life." Silverman smiled for the first time. "You might think you hold all the aces, Detective, but I will have the best legal brains in Britain in my corner. Who do you have in your corner, some washed-up D A? Believe me, it's a no contest." Art stretched his legs under the table. "Really, Joshua, and who exactly is this brains of Britain that you think is going to save you from a life in prison?" he goaded, "he'll need to be a bloody magician to have any impact on your future."

"You'll find that out soon enough," snapped Silverman, "and he will prove that this fictitious fantasy of yours is just that, a fantasy, nothing more, nothing less. By the time he's finished he'll have you regretting you ever heard of me."

Art was bored listening to this meaningless rhetoric and decided to let him stew back in his cell for a while. He called in the guard. "Get this piece of crap back in its cell, I'm fed up looking at it." He spun round to face Silverman again before leaving. "Maybe your little friend Imran will have something to say that's more interesting, I think he probably has more to lose than you, or maybe he's another gay snowflake like your friend Sharpe?" He turned on his heel and left him for the guard to deal with.

When Art got his first look at Ali Imran he saw a short, stocky little man of middle eastern appearance, who looked very nervous and alarmed over what to expect when Art marched in and planted himself on a chair in front of him. After introducing himself he switched on the recorder and turned to his prisoner. "You look surprised to be here, Mister Imran, why is that?" Imran was sat prayer like with both hands clasped together under his chin. "I don't know why I'm here, I'm very confused about what's happening, can somebody please explain to me what is going on?" Art could see he was genuinely confused and nervous. "It's not very complicated, Mister Imran, you have been arrested on a provisional charge of aiding and abetting a criminal fugitive, namely your friend, Joshua Silverman." A horrified expression spread over Imran's face. "I'm only a business acquaintance of Joshua's and I haven't the slightest idea what you're talking about. Joshua asked me to meet him at the airport and put him up for the night which was all I agreed to do. As I would for any business acquaintance. I don't know anything about him being a fugitive. Surely there must be some mistake. You must believe me when I tell you that I'm a very law-abiding citizen."

Art did believe him. He had enough experience to know when someone was telling the truth, the guy was definitely blameless, he was just unfortunate to have been caught up in the situation that was nothing to do with him. Art decided it was time to tell him so. "Of course I believe you, Mister Imran, I don't for one minute believe you are in any way complicit in any of this. I consider you to be an honest individual and I'm terribly sorry that you somehow managed to caught up in all this, but your so-called acquaintance is under arrest for involvement in three, possibly even four murders, so you can see why we had to bring you in for questioning."

Imran slumped back in his chair looking lost and helpless. "I have absolutely no knowledge of any of this, I'm shocked to the very core to hear that Joshua is a criminal. I've only known him for a few years, but he has always acted like a perfect gentleman in my company." Art was more interested in what this little man knew of Silverman's plans. "Did Silverman mention where he was going or what he was planning to do when you spoke with him?" Imran thought for a moment before answering. "All he did was ask me for a bed for the night as he was booked on an early flight to London the following morning. He did say he was meeting up with some business acquaintance or other, but I don't know anything more than that. I would tell you if I did."

"Did he make any mention of who he was meeting up with?" Imran appeared to be thinking quite hard as he tried to recall their conversations. "When he phoned me about meeting him at the airport he mentioned a company he was visiting, but I wasn't really interested and didn't pay much attention. It was one of those double-barrelled names, if you know what I mean." Art decided to prompt him a little. "Could it have been a company called Mendelson and Ackermann?" He was only probing but felt it was worth a try. Imran's face lit up. "That's it, yes, that's definitely the name he mentioned." Art rubbed his hands together excitedly. "Thank you, Mister Imran, you have just given me is a very useful piece of information. Now I must apologise once again for detaining you, but I'm sure you will accept that circumstances alone dictated our actions. You will of course be released immediately, and I will arrange to have you taken home or wherever it is you wish to go." He reached his hand across the table and Ali Imran took it willingly.

"Now that you have explained the situation to me, and I am more than happy to have been of help. I would appreciate it if you could have me taken home. I thank God this is over as it has been a very trying time for me." Art led him out to reception and got him documented and on his way, then he had Silverman bought back to the interview room; he wanted another go at him now that he knew about his planned trip to London.

Silverman looked even more drawn and unkept than he had earlier, although he had the same arrogant and surly look on his skinny face. "We meet again, Joshua," said Art casually," what a pity you weren't here when your friend Ali was sat in that chair. He's a delightful young man, and very talkative too." Art studied his prisoner's facial expression in search of any-give signals but there were no indicators that he was particularly nervous or harassed.

"He was telling me all about your proposed trip to London, it's such a pity we interrupted your journey, but London is far too busy at this time of the year for the likes of you. You would be much happier back in Brazil forcing the underprivileged indigenous people to work punishing hours so they can afford a loaf of bread, while you live in the lap of luxury on the back of their labours." Silverman refused to be drawn, he maintained the same passive expression that he had earlier. Art decided it to try a little shock treatment. "Your friend Mendelson will be disappointed he didn't get to see you, he's another of your pals who can be quite talkative, at least he was the last time I spoke with him." Silverman's left cheek developed a nervous twitch, and he shifted a little uneasily on his chair. "Alexander is my family solicitor, and he is bound by his code of practice and ethical responsibilities not to divulge any of our private conversations. So you won't get any information out of him that I haven't authorised. A nice try, Lieutenant but a wasted effort, just like your other feeble effort to try and convict me on the say-so of a known criminal who you have already charged with the same murders you accuse me of."

Art leaned his elbows on the table and stared into Silverman's eyes. "You are not charged with murder, Joshua, but you are charged as an accomplice to those three murders, and that's enough to lock you away for the rest of your life." He cocked a questioning eyebrow at Silverman. "How old are you now Joshua? forty-four, forty-five? You'll be the oldest prisoner in Sing-Sing before you come up for parole." Silverman's brow was gleaming with sweat, and he was less composed than he had been. "What is it you want from me?" he yelled, why are you bothering to question me like this when I have nothing to tell you." Art got up and wandered round the table and back again. "I want you to tell me who it is that's running this murderous campaign, and you need to tell me very quickly because you're running out of time for any favours."

Silverman folded his arms tightly across his chest and leaned back in his chair. "Go to hell, Gardiner, I'm finished talking with you." Art left his chair and knocked on the door to bring the guard in. "Take this piece of crap back to his cell." He turned his back on Silverman and went to walk away, but Silverman was determined to have the last say. "I will sue your ass big-time when I get out of here, your career with NYPD will be finished when my people get you in court, that's a promise." Art gave him a two fingered salute and carried on walking, he already had his mind made up to see his boss and he was pretty buoyed-up and looking forward to their meeting now that he had both suspects under lock and key and awaiting trial.

Delgado was on the phone when he got to him, but he waved him in with some urgency and ended his call almost immediately. "We seem to be making good headway now, Art, but tell me about your interview with Silverman, how did it go?" Art shook his head. "He didn't give me anything I wanted, except to let me know that Mendelson will be representing him when he goes to trial, and that has to be of interest, although as he's the family lawyer I imagine it was always on the cards. It makes little difference to us who defends him as we both know he's going down for a very long spell no matter who wears the robes."

"Do you still think it's Silverman who's running this unholy mess?" asked Delgado. Art leaned back against the door jam. "That's how it looks at the minute, contrary to my earlier suspicions, the trouble is there isn't anyone else in the picture to support my theory."

"All that does is tell me you're still tied to the theory that someone other than Silverman is pulling the strings?" Delgado looked genuinely puzzled.

"I don't deny it, Marcus, the problem is I haven't found anyone else to fit the bill, but I do question Silverman's ability to run what's going on. I don't think he could run me some water." Marcus smiled at the remark before offering some advice. "Maybe you're not looking in the right place, Art, bearing in mind that we haven't a clue what the hell is going on across the pond. Come to mention it, have you been in touch with Inspector Stewart lately?" Art screwed his face up, looking a little guilty. "I'm sorry Marcus, my trip to Detroit kept me on the go but I'll catch up with him later. It's important that I do because he doesn't know we've got Silverman and Sharpe in custody, which is sure to cheer him up with one of the victims being old boy Silverman's son. I guess we can add Hardwick to that list as well since they all seem indelibly linked to this bloody inheritance."

He suddenly had a weird mental image that brought a smile to his face.

"Wouldn't it be some sweet justice if old boy Silverman left the whole damn lot to charity." The thought that it might happen brought a huge smile to both faces. Art was the first to get serious again. "To get back to where we were, Marcus, no, I haven't given up on the possibility that someone other than Silverman is running the show. And just in case I'm right, I'm listing all the prime movers in this case and get Gina to go through their background with a fine-tooth comb. Maybe something useful will come to light, something, or someone we might be overlooking. What do you think?" Delgado looked a little blasé about it. "It's your hunch, Art, not mine, just do what you have to do to get it out of your system, but please don't complain to me if it turns out to be a bum steer."

Art came away from propping the door up. "What about this new claimant, Marcus, have we identified who it is yet? Seems to me they're well practised at keeping out of the limelight and away from public scrutiny." He cocked his head to one side. "Might that be an indication they have something to hide? Surely it would make more sense if they made their claim official and went public. If you or I had that sort of money heading our way we'd be shouting it from the roof tops." Marcus had nothing more to say on the matter, but he said it anyway. "What can I say, Art. If their solicitor refuses to identify his client our hands are tied. There's nothing we can do about that except wait it out like everyone else." Art didn't like what he was hearing, and it showed on his tightly drawn features. "I'd better get busy, Marcus."

Ten minutes later he was back in front of his computer rummaging through his memory banks for the names of everyone his digital device had told him was connected with the Silverman corporation, no matter how vague the connection. He began his search by checking out the executives in each of the companies that the old boy took a leading role with, and heading the list were those who handled his legal and financial affairs. He googled the organisation of each company and listed its executive officers, and there were a lot of companies involved, with everything from diamond dealers to high-end jewellery outlets, plus a large number of five-star hotels and holiday resorts dotted around the globe. To shorten his list he concentrated his effort on European based companies, but even that proved to be a time consuming exercise. Mendelson and Ackermann got his closest attention, and he was soon going through their organisation in search of anyone with a criminal background but was disappointed to find no one who fitted the bill.

It was close to knocking off time before he had everyone on his list checked out and finding nothing in need of further scrutiny he packed his search in for the day. He wasn't too disappointed as he knew it was nothing more than a sudden impulse that got him started in the first place, and although his idea had taken a bit of a hit he still intended following through with it but having done most of the preliminary work himself he would hand it over to Gina or Vince to carry on the search. Having finished for the day he decided to contact Ian Stewart, making Hardwick's murder the main topic of conversation. He knew for certain that neither Silverman nor Sharpe could have been involved in that killing, which made the outcome of the Met's investigation all the more important as it might help to identify the top man he was searching for. He was convinced the whole murderous campaign was being controlled from London, if only because it was the nerve centre of the Silverman Corporation and where the final answer to the legacy issues would be unveiled. When he pressed Inspector Stewart on the matter he was quite open with him. "We're making good headway with Hardwick's murder, Art, and I know that will help brighten your day. We've traced the car we suspected was involved and found it partially burnt out near a disused industrial estate, and we were able to lift some prints and DNA from what was left, and after going through our records we have a suspect in custody. His attempt to set fire to the car wasn't completely successful, which gave us the clues we needed. The culprit has a record a mile long, mostly for GBH and larceny, although he has done time for possessing a weapon with intent. The good news is that we arrested him yesterday afternoon and will have him in front of a judge tomorrow." Art sensed a breakthrough was on the cards "Has he told you anything about who hired him or why he murdered Hardwick?"

"No, he hasn't owned up to anything yet, but he will, unless he wants to take all the blame for himself. Experience tells me that most of his kind try to spread the blame, and usually try to get a deal of some sort once they know they're going down."

"I'm sure you'll get him to cough up, Ian, and I know you'll keep me informed, but tell me, do you think there could be someone higher up the ladder directing all this mayhem, say someone at Mendelson and Ackermann's for instance?"

Ian had to think for a moment. "That would make sense, after all, everything is being controlled from there in terms of the old boys business empire, not to mention his legacy as well. So yes, I could see that as a possibility, but no more than that if I'm honest. The reason I'm hedging my bet is that we don't have any evidence to support it, nor any candidate in the frame, but that doesn't mean there isn't a more secretive and controlling figure involved. Experience with cases like this tells us there always has to be *someone* running the show, especially when there is serious money involved." Ian Stewart's open minded approach on the matter was a real confidence booster for Art. "I couldn't agree more, Ian. It would be a massive help if the guy you have in custody was to open up about who contracted him to take out Hardwick. That could be the lead we're looking for in terms of our mysterious mister big."

"I'll bear that in mind, Art, as things progress, so leave it with me and I'll get back to you as soon as anything turns up. Bye for now."

Art was feeling more than a little pleased with himself, especially as he was more convinced than ever that he could trust Ian to produce the name he was looking for. The guy smelt like a good detective, and good detectives always get the job done. All he needed was the name of the person who hired Hardwick's killer, if he had that he believed he could quickly wrap up the whole investigation. With nothing better to do he went off in search of Gina, but his luck was out when he discovered she'd been roped in as squad member for a drugs bust. It was beginning to look like dinner was a long way off, and while his mind was on dinner Delgado was in his office with his feet up on his desk. He too was delighted with the way the investigation was going, even though he had reservations about Art's theory on a mister big who wasn't among their already known suspects. But like Art, he was nursing a lingering doubt over Hardwick's murder as that killer yet to be identified, although it was a bit of red herring since it took place outside of their jurisdiction, absolving them from any responsibility.

While Delgado was reminiscing Art was waiting for Gina to get back from the drugs bust. He had already tried phoning her in the hope that she might pick up, but when he failed to link up he was left with not knowing when she would be back. An issue that was a bit unsettling as they were still sharing a car and he couldn't just head off without organising transport to get her home. In the end he rang Delgado out of sheer frustration to explain the situation and was pleasantly surprised by his reaction. "Just leave it with me, Art. I'll make sure someone on that squad does the necessary when they get back. To be honest though it might be a while yet, sorry to tell you that, but this drugs bust was foisted on us at the last minute, but don't you go worrying about Gina, I'll make sure we get her home safe and sound."

Art thanked him and headed off on his lonesome.

Much later, while enjoying his third glass of Irish he heard Gina being dropped off at the bottom of the driveway and being quick on his feet he was at the door before she even got her keys out. He had enough experience to know how quickly drugs busts could turn nasty and he had been genuinely worried for her safety, but as soon as she had her coat of and was sat down he poured her a glass of wine, having already decided to let her get settled before bothering with supper.

When they had finished their meal Gina did the one thing she regularly accused Art of doing and began talking shop. "You know something, Art, it's almost uncanny, but I've been plagued all day with thoughts of this bloody mystery claimant in Nevada. I can't get it out of my head no matter how hard I try. I don't know about you, but I think it's time we found out who it is. I have an idea in mind that might work, so I intend to get on to it first thing tomorrow." Art looked ready for a bit of mischief. "I do wish you wouldn't bring your work home with you, sweetheart. We don't get paid overtime for working from home you know." Gina whirled round ready to retaliate, but when she saw the impish look on his face she burst out laughing. "Kettle and pot, Art, kettle and pot." They had another drink before waltzing up the stairs arm in arm.

23

Even though she'd enjoyed a good night's sleep Gina was still mentally harassed by the thought of the new claimant from Nevada. It was bugging her no end as she worked her way back through her notes to find out when she first heard mention of it. Having done that she googled the solicitor involved and brought their premises up on the google map, with the image showing they were situated in Nevada's central business area.

As soon as she had a close up of the site she magnified it to see if there were any businesses with CCTV cameras in the surrounding area. Having found a couple of likely candidates she noted the company names, jotted down their phone numbers, and sat back to think about what to do next, coffee immediately came to mind.

On her way back from the vending machine she bumped into Art who gave her an enquiring, almost challenging look. "How are you getting on with that big idea you mentioned last night?" he asked," you know, that other claimant thing?" She hadn't told him what she was planning and intended to keep it that way, at least until she got it under way. It was all part of her drive to make her mark within the department, and she had no intention of letting anyone undermine her efforts. "Not as well as I had hoped," she admitted, "but it's early days." Art gave her a more penetrating look that said he didn't believe her, but it left her quietly satisfied because it told her that he hadn't a clue what she was up to, for now anyway. For his part, Art knew he wasn't getting the full story and was quietly amused. "Don't go wasting valuable time if your idea is going nowhere, sweetheart." he warned.

Gina threw her head back and carried on with what she was doing, leaving him with a cheeky grin on his face as he disappear round the corner, but the grin was short-lived as his suspicious mind was now fully aroused. "That girl is up to something," he told himself, "I can smell it." He smiled at her attempt to keep it secret and headed off in the opposite direction, inwardly wishing her well with whatever sit was she was up to.

Gina, meanwhile, finished the last of her coffee and picked up the phone, aware that the only thing she knew about the company she was phoning was their lack-lustre company name, *The Shoe Shop*, plus of course their telephone number, but she also knew they were located directly opposite Benson and Benson's solicitors in Nevada, and that was enough for what she had in mind.

After the normal greetings were dispensed with she asked the lady at the other end if they had a security camera on their premises. The lady concerned introduced herself as Jill and sounded a bit confused by the question. "Everyone in this area has a security camera, they would have to be mad not to. We have so many young thugs running amok in gangs and out of control in the area that security of our premises is an absolute necessity, but why are you asking such a daft question anyway?"

Gina knew she'd struck lucky. "Well it's rather important in connection with a current investigation I'm involved with and it's also important to know how long you retain your video recordings for. Now I know that's an odd question as well, but I can assure you that it's a necessary one in this particular instance."

The lady at the other end placed her hand over the mouthpiece while she conferred with someone, but she wasn't long coming up with an answer an answer. "We have an arrangement with the company directly opposite us on the other side of the road. They very kindly direct their security camera at our frontage and we do the same for them in return, working together this way gives much better coverage. It's an arrangement that works really well for both companies, and since you asked, we normally retain our recordings for at least twenty-one days."

"I'm glad to hear that as it sounds like a well thought out security system, in fact it could be very helpful with my investigation; an investigation that involves a number of very callous murders. To put it bluntly, Jill, I could do with your help in identifying an individual we have an interest in who is known to have visited your neighbours premises sometime between two and three weeks ago. If I let you have the dates involved would you e-mail me copies of your recordings that cover the frontage of Benson and Benson's premises during that period. You can rest assured that your neighbour is not involved in anything illegal, this is not about them or their staff, but it's crucial to our investigation that we review your CCTV coverage for the period involved. Can you do that for me please?"

There was a lengthy pause that told Gina she was seeking advice from a colleague before agreeing to anything.. "Am I permitted to discuss this with my neighbour before agreeing to your request?" she asked. Gina cringed at the thought. "I would rather you didn't do that, Jill. This is a very serious investigation that we wish to keep under wraps for now."

There was another delayed response, and much longer this time while Jill sought further advice, when she came back she was anything but helpful. "I have to be careful in terms of data protection   " Gina cut her off in no uncertain manner. "You can stop right there young lady, and listen up, I don't want to hit your premises with a warrant so please don't force me to do that. You need to understand that we *will* access your security recordings one way or the other, so make it easy on yourself and cough up now and let's not make a big issue out of it." The young lady on the other end must have been pushed aside as it was a male voice that took up the challenge. "Okay, Detective, I'm the owner of the company and I get the message, so just give me the dates you're interested in, and your e-mail address and I'll have copies of the recordings with you later today." Gina gave him what he needed, and their call was brought to an end rather abruptly. She guessed he had the makings of a rather unpleasant person to work for, but she had what she wanted and couldn't be happier. Although there was no guarantee that the video's would give her what she was after, but the upside was that it would cost her nothing to find out.

With her call ended she went off in search of Art to bring him up to date, and when she didn't find him she tackled Vince as to his whereabouts. "Last I heard he was having another go at Sharpe, but I don't know if that's where he ended up. You know what he's like, Gina, here one minute and gone the next." The poor guy made it sound like an apology, but it turned out that he was spot as Art was where he'd said he was, locked in another verbal set-to with Sharpe and it looked like he had something specific in mind. It was certainly interesting enough to keep her glued to the security window.

"Do yourself a favour, Sharpe, don't hang all this round your own neck while Silverman gets an easy ride. He's taking you for a fool, but setting that aside, you and I both know there's someone higher up the ladder than him pulling the strings, so open up and tell me who it is and get yourself a few brownie points when you go to court." Sharpe's hands were laying on his lap, but he dropped them down by his side and leaned across the table. "You need to believe me when I tell you that if I knew who got me into this bloody mess I would tell you right now, if only to spite the bastard. I've never been involved in anything like this before, I just got in over my head because that bastard Silverman kept waving a big fat pay-cheque under my nose. Stupid I know, but I can't change that, I've shot my bolt and that's all there is to it."

Art leaned back and studied Sharpe intently, trying to figure out if the guy was showing genuine remorse, although in truth he couldn't care less about Sharpe's miserable self-reproach. He wanted him chomping at the bit for revenge, wanted him angry and spiteful enough to strike out at those responsible for ruining his life and keen to get the top man running the show sat beside him in front of a judge. "You're right on that score, Rodney," agreed Art, "you can't do anything to keep yourself out of prison, but you can have some influence on which prison you end up in and who you are bedded down with if you get a little help from someone like me and the DA. It's time to trade-up, Rodney, and do a deal for yourself." He stopped to think. "Why don't you just give me the name I'm after and stuff the people you're shielding. They can't do anything for you now, but maybe I can."

Sharpe planted his elbows on his knees and buried his face in his hands. It was a long time before he resurfaced, but when he did Art pounced on him like a hungry bear. "You need to waken up and realise that I'm trying to help you, Rodney, but you need to know that this is your last chance so don't go giving it the cold shoulder or I'll forget all about it too, then what?" Sharpe looked lost, drained and pathetic. His inability to do anything about his situation was written all over his face. A loud sigh cleared his throat before he found his voice again. "I wish to God I could give you what you're after, Lieutenant, I really do, but I can't. As far as I'm concerned Silverman is the only one who gave me orders, and I think you're wrong to go chasing ghosts because I'm certain you won't find any under his bed covers." Art ran his hand over his brow, it was hard to admit it, even to himself, but he was beginning to accept that he had nowhere to go with his theory, it was almost dead on its feet, and if it wasn't dead it was certainly in need of surgery. But he was no defeatist; if he even spotted a glimmer of light at the end of the tunnel he would keep going in that direction. He suddenly thought of a possible new approach. "Okay, Rodney, I take what you say with a pinch of salt, but I need some answers that I know you *can* give me. When you and Hardwick murdered young Silverman and his buddy, which of you decided what to put in that fatal overdose?"

Sharpe looked a bit wary at first, but he replied in the end. "It was Hardwick's idea, he's a heavy social user and knows all about these things. I don't know one drug from another as I've never had any inclination to touch the damned stuff." Art nodded his acceptance. "Okay, I accept that, but I have one more question before we wind this session up but before I ask it I want to assure you that I accept your belief that Silverman is the man running this conspiracy. Now this next question is very important so I want you to take your time and think very carefully before you give me your answer, and you can take as long as you like to think about it, but I want a well thought out answer when I do get it, okay?"

He raised his eyebrows in a questioning manner, and when there was no response from his prisoner he carried on. "I want you to imagine that Silverman is not the top man you make him out to be, and using your knowledge of all the other likely contenders who might fill the picture I want you to tell me who would come top of your list of suspects to replace him?" Having explained what he wanted from Sharpe he pulled the tape from the recorder and switched it off before getting to his feet and heading for the door. "I'm off for some refreshment now, Rodney, but I advise you to do yourself a favour and give some serious thought to what I'm asking of you, and bear in mind that you no longer owe allegiance to any of your previous employers because none of them or any of your fellow conspirators can help you now. It's time to start looking out for yourself."

He turned away, leaving Sharpe to think things over in the hope that a ten-minute break would do the trick. If Sharpe didn't have someone in mind by then he never would.

After a quick word with the guard he went next door to watch his prisoner through the viewing window, and when his ten minutes had passed he went back inside to find Sharpe sitting with both elbows on the table and his head buried in his hands. He didn't acknowledge Art's presence right away with his head buried out of sight, but if he was trying to hide from his situation he was seriously misjudging things. Art wasted no time bringing him out of his self-imposed isolation. "Don't bury your head in the sand like a fuckin' Ostrich, Rodney, there's no hiding from reality and you know it." He waited until Sharpe took his hands away and faced him before continuing. "You've had more than enough time to think things over. All I want from you now is the name of the person you believe could be responsible for your predicament. The person you feel is pulling Silverman's strings."

Sharpe reached out for the cold cup of coffee that was sitting in front of him and took a couple of gulps, and although it wasn't very refreshing it was enough to wash the dryness from his mouth. "I don't know what to tell you," he confessed tamely, "I only ever got instructions from Silverman, no one else, and you have to believe me when I tell you that I've thought long and hard to try and finger the possible substitute you're looking for." He gave a big sigh. "Having taken everything into account I can only think of one person who is powerful enough to fit the bill, although apart from his powerful position and his involvement in Silverman's business it feels incredibly stupid to even think of him in that way. But you did ask me to put someone forward, so I'll tell you, the only person I see capable of controlling Silverman is Mendelson."

Art felt a twinge of excitement, but he kept a straight face, he was looking for something to justify what he was feeling. "That's a very interesting choice, Rodney, now why don't you explain how you came to that conclusion?"

Sharpe shrugged his heavy shoulders and reached for his coffee again, but this time it never reached his lips, the temptation for another drink of cold coffee wasn't strong enough to tempt him and he decided to give Art his answer instead. "Mendelson is the one at the heart of this whole inheritance business, he has been from the start, and to my way of thinking that's what this whole thing is about, at least that's how I have always felt about it. I don't know if Mendelson is capable of twisting things for his own financial gain, but I do know he will do anything for money. Big money and social status are big motivators for the likes of him, and I should know; look what happened to me over the damned stuff."

The thought process Sharpe had used in reaching his decision wasn't totally convincing, but it did at least give it a ring of credibility to his decision. Naming Mendelson as the top man would be more acceptable if he or his company were found to have serious financial irregularities or other matters that were deemed serious enough to invite homicide as a final reckoning. A forensic examination of the company books would unravel anything that needed unravelling, but the way things currently stood with their budget restraints and Delgado's tight grip on finances, an operation of that magnitude could only be handled by Ian Stewart's team, prompting Art to contact him as soon as he was finished with Sharpe, and he wasn't finished with him just yet as Sharpe still had questions to answer, especially about Magee's murder. "Strange as it might seem, Rodney, I can understand why Silverman wanted his step-brother out of the way and of course his close friend was nothing more than collateral damage, we've accepted that, but why was Magee murdered? Surely he wasn't involved in what you lot were up to?"

Sharpe stretched his neck into his collar and rolled his head from side to side to ease the tension. "Believe it or not, killing him was the last thing I wanted, we were close friends after all, really close in fact, but while he wasn't involved in what I was up to he became a source of irritation with his constant questioning about what I was doing. I was convinced he suspected me of something and when I stupidly let it be known to Silverman he told me to get rid of him, so that's what I did." Art sat for a while studying Sharpe's surly expression, he was trying to figure out if he was sincere about being remorseful or just play acting? In the end he wasn't sure one way or the other and parked the thought for later, but as things stood he was ready to wrap the session up and getting to his feet he addressed Sharpe one last time. "Your idea about Mendelson being a suspect doesn't sound as far-fetched as you make it out to be, Rodney, in fact it has a lot going for it because it falls in line with my own suspicions, and if it has a positive outcome then I'll do my level best to make the court aware of your co-operation. For now though I'm afraid it's back to your cell to await your court visit, and since you have no other option but to plead guilty it should be a very quick appearance in front of the judge. Having said that, you need to know that we haven't heard from your solicitor yet, so we don't know when he or she will be arriving here from England." Sharpe didn't look particularly worried and just shrugged and allowed the guard to lead him away. "

With Sharpe gone Art considered the possibility of Mendelson being involved, and the more he thought about it the more plausible it became. He was in a prime position to control things, that was a God given fact, but was it a bit too much to suggest that the chief executive of such a high profile legal company would put his reputation on the line by working an illegal scam to rip-off a client.? Especially one of old boy Silverman's high standing. It was an enticing thought that kept his mind busy while he waited for Ian Stewart to answer his phone.

When he eventually picked up their conversation was brief and to the point, although it was sufficient for Art to get his message across and for his counterpart to respond every bit as readily. In fact he wasted no time in reassuring Art that the Met police had already carried out a forensic examination of Mendelson's company accounts. He further explained that the final report from the auditors had afforded the company's accounting methods, and their financial controls, a clean bill of health. Although there was one potentially serious little issue that remained outstanding in the form of a law-suit raised by a dissatisfied client, and while that had absolutely no known connection with the criminal case under investigation it was still worthy of consideration when set alongside everything else that was going on. But it took a huge leap of faith to consider implementing Mendelson without any creditable evidence to support a charge of criminality. It was with these tantalising thoughts rattling around in his head that he decided it was time to head off.

24

Gina was sitting in front of her computer munching her way through a ham sandwich while waiting for the e-mail from The Shoe Shop in Nevada to get to her. Sadly, it took full hour and a half before it arrived, although she had nothing to moan about when it did and she saw there were three separate attachments involved, however her excitement was tempered a little by a concern over the possible quality of the video's. As it turned out her concern was quickly dispensed with when she opened the first attachment and found the quality to be much better than she had expected, but when she ran it through without finding what she was looking for she suffered a touch of the jitters. She was about to press play on the second attachment when Art turned up. "I hope that's not a blue movie you're watching young lady." He was obviously in a frivolous mood, but his luck was out as Gina was feeling anything but frivolous. "I should bloody hope it's a lot more important than that." She pointed to a nearby chair. "Plant your ass down there and don't move a muscle until I'm finished with what I'm working on." He gave her a suspicious once over. "What are you up to that's so secret?" he asked. She raised a finger to her lips in a silencing motion. "Just wait and see." she told him, before hitting play on the second attachment with her eyes glued to the screen scrutinising it like her life depended on it, and after viewing a number of people going in and out of Benson's premises her patience reaped its reward when the one person she had hoped to see entering the building turned up and confirmed her suspicions. But it was still a big shock to recognise that person as none other than young Benjamin

Silverman's girlfriend, Claire Mathews!

Art could tell from the expression on her face that there was something of interest on Gina's screen, so he got up and went round behind her to look over her shoulder, but he wasn't quick enough as the recording had moved on and Claire Mathews had disappeared from view, leaving him with a bemused expression. He prodded Gina in the back. "Why have you got that superior, satisfied look on your face when what you're staring at is of absolutely no interest to anyone? Are you really that easily amused?"

Gina hit the pause button while struggling to stifle her laughter. "I'm beginning to think you need your eyes testing young man, or have you forgotten how to read?"

She swung round in her seat to look up at him. "For God's sake, Art, read the name of the company above the door." Art peered over her shoulder again. "Yes. I see can see that, it's Benson and Benson's, but why the hell are you eyeing them up?" He still hadn't cottoned on to what she was up to, so Gina gave him another little tease. "Let me play the last attachment through again and maybe you'll see something that's a lot more interesting." She refreshed the attachment and hit the play button with Art peering over her shoulder. "What am I supposed to be looking for?" he asked, "all I see is a load of people going in and out of some yuppy office block." Gina couldn't contain herself. "For God's sake, Art, wise up and look at the name of the company above the door." Art leaned further over her shoulder to get a closer look. "Okay, I've got that it's Benson and Benson's, so what?" Gina moved her cursor across the screen. "Now keep your eyes on their visitors and see if you can spot anyone we know entering the building."

Art narrowed his eyes just as Claire Mathews came into view. "Bloody hell," he yelled, "isn't that the young lady who was going out with young Silverman, the lady I interviewed?" Gina rubbed her hands together excitedly. "That's exactly who it is, and she's a lot more than that now, Art, because this proves to me that she's the mystery claimant who's chasing the big money. I don't think there can be any doubt about it when she's staring us in the face in full colour."

Art had his eyes glued to the monitor until the scene changed, then he spun Gina round in her seat to face him. "Christ, Gina, we know young Benjamin drew up a Will before he was murdered, so it's as clear as day from what's on that video who he appointed to be his benefactor." An interesting thought popped into his head. "So how does this tie in with the crazy codicils the old boy promised to add to his Will on that television interview? His intentions were made very public and restrict his son's claim to any inheritance unless his claim fulfils certain criteria?"

Gina shook her head. "I haven't a clue about all that, Art, but Claire Mathews will not be laying claim to old boy Silverman's legacy, no way, she'll be laying claim to his *son's* estate, so if the son is in line to inherit from the father then she is going to be one very rich young lady." Art slid his arms round Gina's shoulder. "You know something, Miss Garcia, you can be very secretive at times, but I have to admit that this is one occasion when I'm very glad I didn't interfere, and I congratulate you on a job well done, and since it was you who uncovered the identify of this secret claimant I think you should be the one to break the good news to Marcus."

When they got to him they found Delgado deep in conversation with the one person Art did not want to cross swords with, not so soon after their last little set-to, but Delgado looked really pleased to see them and waved them in like long old friends. "Brilliant timing, Art, come on in," he gushed excitedly, "you're the very man the D A and I hoped to see." The D A twisted round in his seat and got up with his hand held out at arm's length. "I owe you and apology, Lieutenant. You were absolutely right about Silverman, and you were also right to tell me to keep my nose out of your investigation. I should not have interfered, and I apologise wholeheartedly for doing so."

Art joined hands with him but cocked a wary eyebrow at him. "Apology accepted, Sir, and returned by me if I said anything out of place. I hope we can both put it behind us and move on." The D.A was still pumping Art's hand up and down like he was drawing water. "I hope that brings an end to the matter, Lieutenant, and please keep up the good work and keep me fully employed." He turned on his heel with a wave to Delgado and went on his way.

Art turned to his boss. "He's becoming very magnanimous in his old age." Delgado laughed lightly and gave a shake of his head. "I guess you're right, it's a pity he's younger than you." Art accepted the joke for what it was and dropped into a nearby seat. "Gina has something really important to tell you, Marcus, and I think you'll find it seriously interesting; I know I did." Marcus jerked upright and stared at Gina over the rim of his glasses. "You'd better get on with it then, hadn't you."

Gina pulled a chair round from behind the door. "I take it that's also an invitation to sit down?" she said. Delgado dropped his head into his hands. "Sorry, girl, I thought you were old enough to know how to sit without an invitation." They all had a little chuckle before Gina got started. "This mystery claimant to the Silverman empire, Captain, everyone here is on edge wondering who it can be, would it help move things along if you found out who it is?." Delgado's cocked an inquisitive eyebrow at her. "We would all like to know the answer to that, Gina, but if Benson won't tell us there's nothing we can do except wait until he feels fit to open his damned mouth." Gina gave Art a little wink and got up from her chair, determined to make the most of her moment in the limelight. "I know it's a well-kept secret, Captain, so keep it to yourself for now, but I can tell you that our mystery claimant is none other than Claire Mathews, young Ben Silverman's girlfriend. But I suggest you don't spread it around or everyone will get to know." She gave a little giggle to back it up.

Delgado didn't look terribly excited. "How the hell do you work that out?" he asked. Gina leaned forward in her chair. "I know it because I watched her go into Bensons solicitors on the day she lodged her claim." Delgado jerked upright on his chair. "You did what?" Art waved a hand at him. "Calm down, Marcus, we both saw Claire Mathews go into Bensons office, Gina has a CCTV recording that shows her doing just that, and you can see it for yourself if you're minded to." Delgado dropped back into his chair with both hands clenched in front of him and his eyes shut tight, and it was some time before he opened them again.

Gina was seriously disappointed with his less than enthusiastic reaction and told him so. "I had hoped you would show a bit more enthusiasm, Captain, but it appears I was wrong." Delgado reacted with a wry smile. "I fully appreciate that you've solved that little mystery, Gina. The reason why I'm not over excited is because I'm trying to figure out what it has to do with our case?" Gina was caught short and didn't know how to react, but her expression soon changed to one of outright disappointment. "Maybe I'm missing something, but it's my belief that preventing crime is as every bit important as solving it. Young Ben Silverman lost his life because he had a legal claim to his father's legacy, and if he has handed that inheritance over to Claire

Mathews, as appears to be the case, then it puts her in exactly the same situation that ended her boyfriend's life. More so if Art's theory about a Mister Big lurking in the shadows tuns out to be correct. We have to accept that it's incumbent upon us to do all we can to protect Claire Mathews from meeting a similar fate. Don't you agree?" She folder her arms over her ample chest and waited for an answer.

"Jesus, Gina, give me a break." Delgado was struggling with what he wanted to say. "We don't know anything about this so called mister big, it's all pie in the sky until we find proof that identifies one. I know Art is sold on the idea but I'm not buying it, not yet, not without conclusive evidence. I still believe Silverman is the top dog and we already have him safely locked away."

Art was keen to support Gina, indeed he welcomed the fact that she had raised the issue of the young lady's safety, but right then he had other things on his mind, things like Alexander Mendelson who was now an ever present irritant. "You know something, Marcus, if young Claire Mathews turns up dead it will be too late to protect her, but let's set that aside for the moment, we should start a separate investigation with our English buddies into Mendelson's background and find out who it is that's taking him to court and why."

Delgado slid forward on his seat. "I know nothing about Mendelson being taken to court. Where the hell did that suddenly come from?"

Art looked a bit guilty. "I got it from Ian Stewart when I asked him if a forensic audit had ever been carried out on Mendelson's company. Which indeed it has, and the auditors reckoned the books were all in order and the only thing outstanding was a lawsuit raised by a dissatisfied client. I would dearly love to know who that client is and what they're suing him for."

Delgado slumped back into his chair looking confused. "Am I to believe he didn't tell you who it is?" he asked. Art shifted uncomfortably. "To be honest, Marcus, I can't even remember if I asked him, but I'll give him a bell later on and see what he has to say." He got a withering look for his troubles. "Yeah, I suggest you do that, and make sure I get to know what he says this time." The surly tone of his voice was hard to miss, and Art wasn't about to let it go unchallenged. "It's not as if I slip up very often, Marcus," he claimed, "I'm usually well ahead of the game, as you know, so I could do without the veiled criticism." Delgado nodded. "You've got me this time, Art," he admitted, "things are just a bit fraught right now, so I'm sorry, alright?" Art shrugged it off. "Apology accepted, Marcus, but I'm serious about this guy Mendelson. He's in the perfect position to control what's going on, although I admit that I have no idea why someone like him would want to grab a slice of the action, but surely we need to have a close look at him. He stands out like a sore thumb in my book."

Delgado pinched his nose. "What do our two prisoners have to say about your theory? Especially about Silverman?" Art grinned cheerfully. "It's funny you should ask that, Marcus, because I'm about to arrange another session with him. He's a stubborn individual who doesn't give much away, and there seems to be a very cosy relationship between him and Mendelson that I hope to exploit. He certainly puts a lot of faith in Mendelson who he describes as his family lawyer, which in itself is a bit odd since he doesn't appear to have any family. It could be that's where his weakness lies. We'll know soon enough when I have another go at him."

"Yeah," conceded Marcus, "he is a bit of an odd-ball right enough, been divorced three time with no children, so it's quite likely he's paying heavily for maintenance, which might be why he would want to get his hands on the old boys legacy, if his ex-wives screwing him for maintenance".

"That's a good point, Marcus. Maybe I should challenge him about his ex-wives, it might get him riled enough to let something slip, he's the one person who can tell us if someone else is pulling the strings." He rubbed his hands together enthusiastically. "I think it's time to take the gloves off. Time to wind Silverman up a bit and see if he trips over himself."

"Let me know how you get on, now off you go and let me get on with some work, and well done again, Gina. I appreciate your efforts and it was a clever piece of work and no mistake. Art guided Gina away with a protective arm on her shoulder. "I wish Marcus would listen to what I'm telling him about Mendelson."

He stopped mid-stride and turned to face her. "You can do it for me, Gina, get on that computer of yours and see what you can dig up. Go really deep into Mendelson and Silverman's background and those of their relatives as well; let's see what their families are made of. I want to know what they have for breakfast, Gina. By the time you've finished I want to know everything that's worth knowing about both families."

Gina screwed her face up at the thought. "Christ, Art, do I have to? I seem to be strapped to that bloody computer these days, I want some street time, time out on the job and not stuck in a bloody office all day." Art gave her a peck on the cheek. "I need something juicy to help me upset Silverman, sweetheart, something really hurtful to make him open up, see if you can find it. Just do it for your old husband to be, that's my girl." Gina gave him a sideways look. "I'll bloody hold you to that husband to be bit, Gardiner, and don't you forget it."

230

With that thought in mind they headed off in different directions; Gina being the happier of the two, but only because she was already hearing the gentle toll of wedding bells!

25

Art was eyeing Silverman through the viewing window like a hungry Vulture watching its prey, although he seemed to be in no great hurry to go and join him. His had his mind made up to let him stew in his own juices for a while longer before having another go at him.

When enough time had lapsed he left the viewing window and approached the guard. "How long has he been in there?" The guard looked at his watch. "Twelve minutes to be exact." Art gave him a knowing wink. "I want you to take him back to his cell and leave him there for five minutes, then bring him back to the interview room and keep him here until I get back. Can you do that for me?"

The guard kept looking straight ahead. "I'm here to carry out your instructions, Lieutenant, so consider it done." Art gave him a pat on the back and wandered off in search of a quiet place to spend ten or fifteen minutes in preparation for his next confrontation. He had to find a way to damage Silverman's close relationship with Mendelson, or if that failed, make him confess to being the one who is running the show. It wasn't going to be easy as Silverman had already displayed an ability to dig his heels in when it suited him, but Art was more than ready for the challenge. Strangely, when Silverman was brought back to the interview room Art remained at the viewing window to study him a while longer, but this time he was more interested in his prisoner's facial expressions than anything else. And he undoubtedly looked more drawn and a good deal paler than when they last parted, more pleasingly for Art he looked nervous and uncomfortable, constantly wringing his hands and rolling his shoulders like someone suffering extreme discomfort. Having seen all he needed to Art decided it was time to get down to business and went inside. "Here we are again, Joshua," he said on entering the room, "you and I joined in conversation until I decide to end it. Isn't that nice?"

Silverman had his eyes fixed on the wall above Art's head and appeared in no mood for conversation, not that it mattered to Art as he had already decided on how the interview would go. "I apologise for having you shuttled backwards and forwards from your cell, Joshua, but I had an urgent phone call that I couldn't afford to miss. I'm sure you'll understand how important it was when I tell you it was from our mutual acquaintance Alexander Mendelson, and I must say he was very eager to talk. I wish you were as good a conversationalist as he is. The guy is so skilled at keeping a conversation rolling, and very open to answering questions, although I did find it strange that he was more interested in talking about you than anything I wanted to talk about. I think you should be a bit wary of him as he wasn't very complimentary about you. You two haven't fallen out have you?" He smirked at this last remark.

Silverman's eyes widened with shock; Art could almost hear his heart racing as he watched panic take its hold. "You don't look too well, Joshua, you've gone a strange colour, are you sure you're okay? Can I get you a glass of water or something?" Silverman wasn't up for friendly banter. "You can cut the crap, Gardiner, I know Alex is far too well versed for you to try and con me into thinking he would discuss anything of importance with the likes of you." Art folded his arms and shook his head. "You *would* think that, wouldn't you, Joshua, but I definitely got the impression from our conversation that he's more interested in this new claimant who has come on the scene than anything you have to offer. The way he went on about it I think he knows more than he's letting on about this scam. He displays all the attributes of a very clever and devious individual to me. You need to watch your back Joshua."

Silverman's confidence looked to have gone out the window, boosting Art's incentive to push him a little harder. "Is there something you want to tell me, Joshua? Something you need to get off your chest. You must see that Mendelson is not supporting you in your hour of need." Silverman was about to say something but stopped himself at the last minute. "Why would I converse with the likes of you, Gardiner? I have someone in my pocket who will be more use to me than your kind will ever be. Now get me back to my cell because I've had enough of this crap." This unexpected renewal of Silverman's defence was a huge disappointment to Art, he'd been convinced Silverman's faith in Mendelson was waning. It had been a very close call, but something had renewed his confidence at the last moment, demonstrating that he had a lot more will-power than Art had given him credit for. Although he was very interested in the *someone* Silverman had mentioned. Was that little outburst a threat against the other claimant, or could it have been a threat against Mendelson? He hadn't a clue, but he wasn't finished with Silverman yet, definitely not, there was a long way to go before that would happen. Maybe he just needed another change of tactic.

"I don't believe you fully understand the seriousness of your position, Joshua. You are going down for three, possibly four murders, unless you convince me that you are not the person responsible for running this outrageous fuck-up. You need to give some serious thought to the charges levelled against you because they aren't going away, and unless you change your tune you are about to spend the remainder of your life behind bars. So don't dismiss this opportunity lightly, because you need to convince me you are not the person controlling this shindig or life as you know it is finished. Is that what you want for yourself? To be locked away without any chance of ever being considered for parole?" Silverman looked to be in some sort of trance, his eyes were glazed and fixed on the wall above Art's head and his lips were firmly clamped together. Art decided to have one more go before bringing the interview to an end. "Being aware that your first court appearance is overdue, I took the liberty of asking Mendelson when he was coming here to afford you the legal advice you're entitled to, but he wouldn't commit himself. In fact he just brushed my question aside like it was unimportant. Surely that must concern *you* as much as it does me." Silverman stopped counting the bricks above Art's head and looked him straight in the eye. "I don't think Alex would be so dismissive of his duty, nor would he let me down in the way you suggest."

He was being brash now, but Art sensed a definite weakness in his presentation. "You just said you don't *think* he will let you down? For God's sake man if I were in your position I would want to be absolutely *certain* that I had someone totally reliable in my corner, I would not want to just *think* I had." He sensed a weaking in Silverman's body language, his shoulders had become more rounded, drooping slightly, and his eyes looked watery, and his left leg was jerking up and down like a fiddlers elbow. He saw this as an invitation to press on. "I reckon Mendelson doesn't see you as a valuable asset anymore, not now that he knows he will be forced to deal with this new claimant. We both know Mendelson holds your step-father's last instruction under lock and key, and we know that he is the only one who can release its content to public scrutiny. I'm being totally honest when I tell you that I don't believe he sees your involvement as essential to his plans anymore. You're past your sell by date, Joshua, in fact I'd say you're a spent force as far as Mendelson is concerned."

Silverman's looked fit to burst, he threw his hands up in the air and slammed them down on the table. "Fuck Mendelson if he lets me down he knows he will pay dearly for it. I'm holding all the trump cards, not him; he only thinks he has the upper hand."

This outburst of uncontrolled rage from was almost palpable, it was so fierce that Art could almost smell it. He had never seen him so fired up, and it couldn't have come at a better time because Art felt he was very close to saying things he didn't want to say, and he was keen to help him on his way. "Why are you protecting Mendelson when he treats you so shabbily by leaving you languishing in a cell while he supports someone else to lay claim to your inheritance. If it were me, Joshua, I would be seriously pissed off."

Silverman leapt to his feet and almost leapt across the table at Art. "I'm protecting no one, and you'll find that out when I get to court." He was gushing and spluttering his words so much that he had a trail of saliva dribbling down his chin. "We'll see who gets the longer sentence then. I'm not the spent force you believe me to be." Art decided on one last push. "When I interviewed your fellow conspirator Sharpe, he told me quite openly that he only took his orders from you, and it was you who organised and planned the murders so that you could get your hands on young Ben's inheritance. And you must realise that even though you didn't murder anyone yourself, you will probably end up with the longer sentence." Silverman slumped back into his chair, looking like a spent force. Art knew he had him where he wanted him. "There's something you need to consider urgently,

Joshua, under our current law there is a level of flexibility afforded to judges when they consider leniency or compassion against the level of culpability and eventual sentencing. Especially so when a culprit is found guilty of the more serious crime of homicide, so if you continue with your present stance that you're the one responsible for organising what's been going on, then neither I nor the D A will make any recommendation to the court for leniency. In fact we will be strongly recommending the maximum punishment available, three, possibly four life sentences that will run concurrently without parole."

He put a hand under Silverman's chin and turned his face head on. "I don't believe you ran this shindig, Joshua, not on your own anyway, but I can't do anything to help you unless you open up and tell me who it is that's giving the orders." Once again Silverman was about to say something but like last time he changed his mind at the last moment. "I'm feeling tired of this, I want to go back to my cell." Art believed he had enough to take to Delgado and called the guard in. "Take our friend here back to his cell, and make sure you see to his needs in terms of refreshments." He watched until the guard had Silverman on his way before heading off.

Delgado didn't even look up from what he was working on, he just waved Art in and pointed to a chair. "Should I be pleased to see you or am I being over ambitious?" he asked, a bit tongue in cheek. "That depends on where your ambitions lie, Marcus, but I have to tell you that I didn't get everything I hoped to get from Silverman, the guy can stop talking even when is mouth is open." Delgado looked over his glasses at him. "Does that mean you're giving up on the theory that someone else pulling the strings?" Art was as stubborn as ever and told him so. "No way, Marcus, I don't see Silverman as the prime mover in all this, he lacks the physical presence of someone in control, and the fact that we have him in a cell speaks volumes to me. Mind you, he did open up a little under pressure and say some revealing things that I'm convinced he regretted saying. I strongly advise you to listen to my interview tape and decide for yourself. I'm more convinced than ever that Mendelson is our man."

Delgado didn't share his enthusiasm. "You never bloody give up, do you. You're still toying with the idea that one of the best legal brains in Britain is a common criminal. It borders on absurdity, Art, just get over it for God's sake." Art leapt to his feet. "Are you telling me you're not interested in doing what I ask? Not even interested enough to run my interview tape through and listen to it before making a judgement." Art was beside himself with rage and Delgado sensed it. "Okay, okay, Art, if it pleases you I'll listen to your interview, just don't expect any miracles." Art turned on his heel and walked away, he'd had enough. He needed to think his way through what was bugging him, namely Delgado, and now wasn't the time to do it. He needed a clear head and not a flaming temper.

It didn't take him long catching up with Gina, in fact with their shift over she was hanging around her workstation waiting for him to take her home. "Hi, honey, how did you get on with Silverman, did he give up any state secrets?" She was in a light-hearted mood, while her man was simmering with rage as they headed downstairs to his car.

"Well," began Art, "I thought I got somewhere, but our illustrious boss doesn't see it that way, more to the point he didn't pay any attention to what I was asking of him. I almost begged him to come with me and listen to the recording of my interview with Silverman, but he shrugged it off and said he would listen to it later." Gina raised her eyebrows in sympathy. "Really, Art? I think that's a bit thoughtless, but don't let it get you down, lover. I have faith in your theory so just stick to your guns. I know you'll prove him wrong in the end." Gina had total faith in her man's ability to unearth seemingly insignificant little details and explore them beyond measure, sometimes to the embarrassment of others further up the chain of command. "I got the impression Marcus was warming to your theory about a mister-big the last time you discussed it with him. So what has changed?"

"I'll be able to tell you more about that after I see him in the morning, I've left him on a promise, so we'll see if he makes good on it." He chuckled quietly to himself. "All I'm thinking about now is food, I'm bloody starving. So let's get home and get our feet up and leave the job behind us for a while, okay?"

Gina prodded him in the ribs. "Suits me big boy," she said teasingly, "maybe we could have an early night as well?" Art reached for his flashing blue light and with his arm out through the open window he stuck it to the car roof. "This sounds like an emergency to me, so I guess we had better follow the drill."

Gina prodded him in the ribs again. "I see you've got your mind back on the job again."

Art's only reaction was to lean more heavily on the accelerator.

26

After a weary looking exit from the interview room Delgado had his serious face on, and it had nothing to do with the fact that he'd neglected to check Art's interview tape before going home the previous evening as promised, nor had it anything to do with the fact that he had to come in early in order to do so. No, his down in the mouth attitude had nothing to do with any of that, it had all to do with the content of Art's interview with Silverman, content that caused him, with much reluctance, to reappraise his opposition to Art's theory about the possibility of Mendelson being involved. He'd listened intently to Silverman getting pretty close to implicating Mendelson in his plot, certainly there was enough circumstantial evidence to prompt him to allow Art to investigate it further. A thought that was very much on his mind as he made his way back to his office deep in thought, mostly because he found himself being forced to concede that he had probably been wrong about Art's theory, and he hated having to admit it, even to himself.

The rain was absolutely chucking down when Art and Gina got out of their car and bolted for the safety of the station house. "Bloody hell," moaned Art, "where in blue blazes did that come from?" Pulling off his jacket he gave it a good shake. Gina on the other hand, who was doing much the same thing with her own jacket, burst out laughing. "I'd say it was just lying in wait for us to get here." She was still laughing as Art dragged her up the stairs. When they reached the upper corridor he asked her if she wanted to come in with him to see

Marcus. I think it's better if you go and see him on your own, Art, I will only end up being a distraction as I don't have any reason to be there." Art patted her shoulder and headed off to catch up with Delgado, ever hopeful of a good outcome.

"Well, well," announced Delgado, "you had better come in and sit down, you make the place look untidy standing there." He looked genuinely concerned when he saw the state of Art's wet clothing. "I was about to say you look wet behind the ears, Art, but you look wet all over. Why don't you take that jacket off and hang it up somewhere to dry off, it's wet through for God's sake?" Art removed the offending article and sat down. "Now then," began Delgado, "without going overboard I believe I owe you an apology, so you can take that as read, but after listening to your interview with Silverman I agree with your suspicion that Mendelson might be involved, and I don't believe both of us could have misinterpreted what went on during that interview. That said, it's my suggestion, and only a suggestion, that you inform Inspector Stewart of our suspicions and seek his help in finding the evidence to prove it. With Mendelson outside our authority we have to rely on our British friends to take up the challenge. Is that okay with you?" Art held his hand up in a stopping motion. "Let me think about this for a minute, Marcus. There may be an easier way that we can get at him, but I will definitely warn Ian of our suspicions, although I'll also be asking him to hold back on overtly pursuing Mendelson until we get him over here. He's due here soon to represent Silverman on his court hearing, which means he'll then be on our territory, and since three of the murder's we're investigating took place here he is answerable to us as well as the Brits." He gave Delgado a reassuring wink, but his boss cut in on him. "They can have him for Hardwick's murder, Art, there's no issue with that, but we must have him for the other three. If our suspicions prove right of course."

He left his seat and went walk-about round the office looking deep in thought, and it took some time for him to re-join his conversation with Art. "I'm not totally in the picture visa vie the legal implication of such a move, but I'll check it out with our legal boys and see how we stand, we don't want any dispute over who has authority. If we're going after Mendelson then we have to do it in the way the law demands. Okay?" Art shrugged his shoulders. "There's no other way to get it done, Marcus. Just try and get a decision from the D A before Mendelson gets here to defend Silverman." Delgado smiled. "I reckon he still feels he owes you one for his last little debacle, so I don't see him deliberately holding back on it, and you have my word that I'll be pressing him all the way, I can't be fairer than that now, can I?"

"That's all I'm asking of you, Marcus," agreed Art, "I'm not looking for you to break any rules. I don't want us blind-sided by some trumped-up legal get-out. We both know how devious these bloody legal eagles can be when they feel someone is getting the better of them."

It didn't look like it, but Art was enjoying a very satisfying moment of success. He had a distinct feeling that the tide was turning in his favour regarding Mendelson, leaving him to enjoy a moment of professional one-upmanship, although this was tempered a little when he realised Delgado had more to say on the matter. "We don't have any proof that Mendelson has done anything wrong mark you, all we have is a suspicion, and we need much more than that to get him in front of a judge so let's not get carried away."

"I'm aware of that, Marcus, and I admit I'm jumping the gun a bit, but I have Gina digging into his background and that of his family.

There might be something lurking there to help us, and we both know how good she is at that sort of thing, she's like a bloodhound when the mood takes her. If there is something there to be found I'm sure she'll find it." Delgado shook his head. "You're a crafty bastard and no mistake, Gardiner. Always ahead of the game like you said, but it's good thinking and I'll be interested to see what she comes up with."

"Why don't you tackle your friend Matheson on the subject. You seem to get on well with him, and now that he knows you a little better he might open up and have more to tell us."

"Funny you should say that, Art, because I was thinking exactly the same thing after I listened to your interview with Silverman. I'll give him a bell later and see if he knows anything useful." Art gave a big sigh in return. "I'm off to give Ian Stewart a bell so we can compare notes later, unless you have something else in mind." Delgado shook his head. "Suits me, Art, catch you later." Art headed off to let Gina know how he got on, but when he got there she was busy on the phone, so he decided to leave her be. "If it's inconvenient right now I can come back when you're not so busy I just wanted to know if you turned anything up on Mendelson."

"It would be help if you did come back later, Art, I'm up to my eyes in the Mendelson's family history and I don't want to lose the thread as there are a lot of sites to link up. I'd rather not stop unless it's urgent?" Art shook his head. "It's nothing that can't wait, Gina, you stick with what you're doing" He turned away without waiting for an answer and went off to phone Inspector Stewart, but as he approached his office he heard his desk phone sounding off, forcing his leisurely approach to turn into a sprint although he still got there too late as his caller was had rung off. But when he checked his missed calls he discovered it was the very person he was about to phone, so he hit the re-dial button and waited. "Hi, Art," Inspector Stewart sounded quite up-beat, "thanks for getting back to me. I only want to touch base and see how thing are panning out." Art gave a sigh of relief. "I think we're getting on top of things over here, Ian, we have two suspects under lock and key, one charged with multiple homicide and the other with conspiracy, and of course like the nice people we are we're doing our very best to make them as uncomfortable as possible."

Inspector Stewart gave a little chuckle. "Have you come you with anything else that's new?"

"A couple of little teasers, Ian, that have us on our toes. Marcus and I are seriously considering Mendelson as a suspect for orchestrating this shindig. We suspect him of being the mastermind behind the whole thing and it's our advice that you do the same, although I would ask that you keep any action at your end covert and well away from Mendelson prying eyes. We have something in mind for him and we don't want him knowing he's the centre of attention, not until we spring the trap. Can you do that for us, Ian?" There was a bit of low-level murmuring at the other end before the Inspector came back online. "I'm a bit surprised you're fingering Mendelson, although I don't doubt you have your reasons. It can often be the most unlikely candidate who turn out to be the villain. We'll take another look at him from a distance, and we'll do as you ask about keeping everything under cover. I won't ask any more about it, Art, as I'd rather not know what you're up to until you feel like telling me." He gave a little knowing cough. "Just protecting myself against accusations of unlawful release of police information and all that nonsense, you know how it is."

"I don't blame you, Ian. It's a wise man who covers his back in this job, but can I ask how you're getting on with the suspect you lifted for Hardwick's murder, any news on that would be helpful" The was a little chuckle from Ian's end. "The guy we lifted held his hands up to it right away once he realised we had enough evidence to clinch the case, he was just looking for some brownie points, but he won't get any from me, I can promise you that."

"Well done, Ian, you boys were quick off the mark, but tell me something, did he cough up to who hired him?" Ian came straight back. "No, he didn't, he reckons it was all done via third party phone calls and cash dumps for payment. Not sure I swallow everything he's told us, but it's all we've got for now." Art was disappointed with this; he'd been hoping to get the name of the person who hired him. "That's a real a downer, Ian. Maybe you should drop Mendelson's name into the conversation the next time you grill him. You know, just drop it into the conversation without making an issue of it and see if you get a reaction."

"I'll give it a try, Art, but don't hold your breath, he can be a stubborn bastard when he wants to be." Art decided it was time to cheer Ian up with some good news. "I have some news to cheer you up. We've identified the mystery claimant from Nevada, and surprise, surprise, it's none other than young Ben Silverman's girlfriend Claire Mathews, and that's something else I wouldn't want Mendelson knowing about."

"He won't hear it from me, I can assure you of that," there was a slight pause, "if you have nothing else for me, Art, I need to go, I have someone outside waiting to see me, but it's great chatting with you again and I hope we get the chance to meet up in person sometime. Bye for now." That was how the call ended, and now that he was free again Art went off to update Gina on the news that Mendelson was now a prime suspect by agreement with Marcus.

"Backing you on Mendelson is a serious change of direction for Marcus. So how on earth did you manage to get him on side?" She was impressed that he had stuck to his guns, but Art just shrugged it off like it wasn't important. "I got a little hint of something useful from Silverman during our last interview, and it turned out that Marcus read it the same way I did, nothing more than that really, but we still need evidence to prove our point, something tangible that proves Mendelson and Silverman conspired before this murdering campaign even began. Whatever comes of it, Gina, I'm locking the scumbag up as soon as he arrives here for Silverman's court appearance. He has questions to answer, it's as simple as that."

Gina nodded. "We both know nothing in our professional world is ever simple, but that doesn't mean we shouldn't keep on trying. I hope I find something to connect them in a meaningful way for you, and I'll keep searching in the hope that I do." Art gave a little frown. "How are you getting on with that, have you uncovered anything tasty yet?" Gina gave a knowing wink. "Strangely enough, I have found something that's interesting, but no more than that, as yet, nothing of any use on its own. It was a little newspaper article on his divorce that caught my eye. It turns out that Mendelson's father was divorced by his first wife, who headed off with one of their siblings in search of greener pastures."

Art rubbed his nose. "Nothing strange in that, I reckon it's an everyday occurrence around here, some people just don't get along. But what are you following up on now?" he asked, feeling a little tempted by her last comment. "I'm concentrating my effort on Mendelson's ex-wife just now, because when she divorced him she literally disappeared from the social scene rather hurriedly, and apparently remarried just as quickly according to media reports. Strangely though, this second marriage was kept very hush, hush and well under the radar, so I'm guessing they must have taken out a restraining order of some sort. Maybe they just wanted a little privacy, anyway, that's where I'm at and I'm afraid you'll just have to wait and see where it takes me, if anywhere?." Art gave her a big grin. "Wherever it's taking you, sweetheart, I hope you get there in a hurry. We need something tangible to prove Mendelson and Silverman are in this thing together, I can't wait to make a move on Mendelson when he gets here." Gina gave him a furtive sideways glance. "I am doing my best, lover. The problem is I don't even know what I'm meant to be looking for. I'm just groping in the dark."

Art gave a muted little giggle. "I've had experience of you groping in the dark, so I know how effective that can be," he gave another feisty little giggle, "just keep looking, Gina, if there's anything there you'll know it when you see it, I'll bet on it."

"I'm afraid I won't be looking for it tomorrow, I've got other things to get on with. The world doesn't come to a halt just because you have something that needs doing." Art gave her his little boy look. "Just work on it for me when you have some free time, and in case you're worrying about Delgado I've already told him what you're doing so he won't be bothering you."

Thirty minutes later they were back home with Gina pouring the wine and Art still thinking about the case. "I find it a bit odd that a newly married couple would keep their marriage a secret in the way you say Mendelson's ex did, don't you?" Gina set her glass down on the worktop and turned away from what she was doing. "I can't give you an answer to that," she admitted, "except to say that some people do weird things for no apparent reasons, although if I'm honest I do find it a rather odd too, but I guess that's just part of life's rich tapestry."

She went back to preparing dinner, but Art wasn't ready to give up on it. "Come on, sweetheart, you're a woman, would you want to get married and then keep your husband's name a secret?" She spun round with a glint in her eye. "Between you and me, lover, I'd just like to get married no matter what his name was, wouldn't you? Or shouldn't I ask?" Art gave her a guilty smile. "By God I asked for that," he admitted, "when will I ever learn to keep my big mouth shut?" She patted him on the cheek. "I'm only kidding, buddy, so don't go getting yourself all worked up about it." Art threw his arms round her and nuzzled her neck. "You set the date and I'll see if I can get there, okay?" She stepped back a pace or two and gave him a wide eyed look. "Are you serious?" she asked. Never been more serious," said Art assuredly, "although I think it might be more in line with tradition if we got engaged first, do you not think so?"

"Is that a proposal I just heard?" Asked Gina, her eyes were wide open with expectation and Art didn't shy away from giving her an answer. "It most definitely is, I think we should go out this weekend and get you a ring. What do you say?" Gina launched herself at him, grabbing him round the neck with both arms. "Not much of a proposal, lover, but I'll take it anyway. I always knew you would get round to it one day. Art eased her gently to one side. "Weren't you supposed to be making dinner or something? I'm positively starving and I'm sure you'll want to keep me alive long enough to get engaged." She cocked her head and gave him a coy smile. "You never change, Gardiner. I imagine I'll just have to learn to put up with you as you are." She spun away looking unconcerned and went back to preparing dinner, although she was so excited that she could hardly contain herself, but knowing the weekend was only two days away she wouldn't have long to wait to get a ring on her finger.

As long as tomorrow did nothing to spoil it.

27

Art only had his ass on the seat a matter of seconds before his desk phone interrupted his thoughts. He snatched it up a little grudgingly. "Gardiner." he announced dryly. "Good morning, Art," came the reply, "it's Ian Stewart again. I thought it only right to let you know that having discussed Mendelson with you yesterday he now appears to have gone walk abouts. I had a genuine reason to speak with him on an administrative matter to do with Hardwick's murder, but he was unavailable at his workplace, and nobody there seems to know where he is or when he will he'll be back. I even rang his home number and got his wife who said that she hadn't seen him since he left for work yesterday morning, and by the sounds of it she's a little worried about his well-being."

There was a momentary pause while Art got to grips with the issue. "What's your take on it, Ian. Should *we* be worried about his well-being too, or do you think he's done a runner?"

Ian wasn't very quick to answer. "If I'm honest, Art, I haven't a bloody clue what to think. When I spoke with his wife she admitted that he doesn't always tell her what he's doing or where he's off to, but she did say that he usually let's her know if he's going to be away overnight. So I guess there is a slight cause for concern. I've launched an all-out check on the airports and ferries to see if we can track his movements, but he doesn't appear to be using his phone so that's a dead end for tracing purposes, it could be that our best course of action is to leave things as they are for twenty-four hours and see how things pan out."

He stopped talking momentarily to think things over. "On the other hand, Art, we may be making a mountain out of a mole hill. There's always the possibility that the guy just decided to take a break and didn't bother telling anyone about it. Time will tell, Art, it always does."

"I go along with that sentiment, Ian, but it muddies the waters at this end because we're feeling a bit cut off with the ocean between us, but I know you'll keep us updated and thanks for the call, it's much appreciated. Speak again soon, Ian." With the call was over Art buried his head in his hands and muttered a stream of unmentionable obscenities. The news that Mendelson had gone missing had a nasty smell to it. Why would a guy like him take off when he had nothing to run from? Could he have found out they were on to him? He refused to accept that as the cause for his disappearance, it just didn't compute, but it left him nursing all sorts of other non-case connected possibilities for a while longer. Then another dreaded possibility hit him like a slap in the face and he vented his anger in a raging voice. "Fuck it," he yelled, he couldn't have, could he?" His anger wouldn't have made sense to anyone else as he leapt from his chair and went off in search of the custody sergeant, and he was in a furious mood and out of breath when he got to him. "Do we still keep a record of the prisoners phone calls?" he demanded. The sergeant looked confused by the question. "Of course we do, Lieutenant, prisoners on remand have a right to speak with their lawyers for limited periods and all calls are logged, but why do you ask?"

"I need to know if Silverman made a call to a company called Mendelson and Ackermann, and if so, when did he make the call?" The sergeant looked bemused. "I don't need to check the log to answer that. He made a very lengthy call to the company you mentioned just after you finished interviewing him yesterday. I thought

251

the bugger would never get off the damned phone."

Art cursed his luck openly and went off with an angry shake of the head. "It as clear as bloody day now." He muttered to himself as he climbed the stairs. "I'll be seeing you again very soon Silverman because you and I are about to fall out."

When he got back to his office he dived straight into his drawer and pulled out a bottle of Irish, unscrewed the top and took a swig, then capped it and went off to tell Delgado about Ian's update and his own latest discovery.

When he'd finished briefing him Delgado hardly turned a hair, much to Art's surprise. "Let's not get too worked up over something we can't control, Art," he advised, "let's see what materialises over the next couple of days before we go diving in at the deep end. It's always possible that Mendelson just took off on some business trip or other, so let's wait this one out for a while and see what transpires. I accept your point that Silverman may have passed on a warning to Mendelson since he has legitimate access to the phone. It's even possible he was setting you up by displaying a make-believe dislike for Mendelson, and it could be that was just to get you hooked. Let's bide our time for a day or two and see what turns up, we need to keep in mind that Mendelson is only a suspect as far as our investigation goes, and he'll probably stay that way until he crosses the pond, and we get our hands on him." Art couldn't hide his feelings. "I'm so keen to get my hands on him it's driving me crazy, I can't shake off the feeling that he's up to his eyes in this whole bloody mess, and in conjunction with Silverman too." Delgado rounded his desk and gave him a pat on the shoulder. "We should be happy with the way things are going, Art, don't lose sight of the fact that we have two culprits locked up and waiting to face trial, and they're going there on irrefutable evidence.

252

That's sound policing in my book." Art shoved his hands into his pockets. "You know me, Marcus, I can't let go of something I know is unfinished, and I don't think our case will ever be finished until we find out who was giving the orders and organising things."

"Okay, okay, Art, I get the message," said Delgado, "but you need to give it a rest for now, we have other things to be getting on with, and as far as I'm concerned it's the Brit police who should be checking on Mendelson, not us." Art gave him a surly look but accepted the criticism without argument and walked off, he was more interested in having another go at Silverman, although circumstance dictated that it was another twenty minutes before he could have his prisoner in front of him. Feeling a bit put out with the delay he wasn't best pleased when he eventually got a look at Silverman and noticed that he didn't look at all nervous or concerned. Art found this a bit disconcerting but didn't let it stop him. "I have a couple of questions for you, Joshua," he began, "firstly, I want to know what you discussed with your friend Mendelson after our last conversation."

Silverman's expression changed in a flash. "What the hell has my use of the phone got to do with you? I made a call to my lawyer, which I'm perfectly at liberty to do since he can't be here in person to give me advice." Art glared at him, his anger seething. "That may be so, but why has he suddenly gone walkabouts for no reason right after you had you little chin-wag with him? Silverman smiled knowingly. "Wouldn't you like to know, Gardiner? It must really upset you that communication between a prisoner and his lawyer are confidential. Even you can't change that, in fact I'm the only one who can, and only if I'm minded to." Art decided to tread water. "I was simply looking after your interest, Joshua. I was minded to think you might need someone else to give you council if Mendelson has disappeared and is no longer capable of representing you." Silverman shifted uneasily. "That's never going to happen, Gardiner, but if it helps put you inquisitive little mind at rest I will tell you that Alex has taken a little trip to Brazil, which he's perfectly within his rights to do. He's certainly not answerable to you if he wishes to travel."

Art got up from his chair and wandered round the room with both hands buried deep in his pockets, and he only stopped wandering when he was directly behind Silverman. "It might be in your interests to have him close down your business while he's out there, Joshua, it won't be any use to you after you're sentenced." Silverman smirked annoyingly without Art seeing it. "I appreciate your concern, Lieutenant, but that is exactly why Alex is visiting Brazil. I asked him to wrap up my affairs there. I'm not stupid enough to think that I will be back there any time soon to do it myself."

Art closed his eyes behind Silverman's back and offered up a silent prayer. "I see, so that's why he suddenly disappeared is it? Some of his staff are worried by his sudden and unscheduled vanishing act but thank you for bringing me up to date. None of us would want you facing trial without access to sound legal advice, Joshua, now would we?" He studied his prisoner more closely, looking for any obvious change in his body language or facial expression, but found no evidence of either. Silverman gave him a sarcastic smirk in reply. "I know my well-being must be at the very forefront of your mind, Lieutenant, but you may rest assured that such concerns are unfounded, and unnecessary. I will be well looked after, in more ways than you can ever imagine."

Art raised both eyebrows in a sham attempt to look interested. "I'm glad to hear that, Joshua, but let me offer you a friendly word of warning before we end this interview. It's not in your best interests to depend so heavily on your friend Mendelson being available to support you when you go to court. The poor man has his own court appearance to deal with, and it could well clash with yours. Who knows?" He leaned across the table to get closer to his prisoner. "There's a distinct possibility he might even be struck off, so where will you be then, Joshua? I hate to be the bearer of bad news but I'm afraid he's been charged with dipping his hand into a client's kitty, which is bit naughty really for a man of his standing. Don't you think?" Art witnessed a definite change in his prisoner's demeanour, so he pressed on. "More importantly for you, Joshua, he's in the process of dipping his hands into your step-dad's kitty too and there's a lot more money there for him to plunder."

This devastating piece of advice left Silverman lost for words, and it was clear to anyone watching that he was so devastated by Art's accusation and the way it had been sprung on him so unexpectedly, that he was unable hide its effect on him.

Art was in his element, especially so when he saw his prisoners state of unease. "I'm sure you have lots to think about now, Joshua, so you can go back to you cell and dream about your own lack lustre retirement, I'm talking about the one up in in Sing-Sing of course, not your little dream home in Brazil." He got up and walked away, leaving Silverman for the guard to deal with.

28

Gina's eyes were glued like limpets to her computer screen when Art crept up behind her. "Are you still working on that Mendelson thing?" he asked, hoping to catch her out. She swung round on her chair. "I was, until you interrupted me, well almost, I'm actually working on Silverman at the moment as I'm finding him much more interesting, very interesting in fact if truth be known." Art peered over her shoulder again, but he didn't see anything of interest and turned away as if to leave. "I take it you're not interested in Silverman then?" queried Gina, surprised by his lack of interest.

"Only if you've got something juicy for me." He confessed, sniggering quietly at his salacious remark. Gina turned to face him. "Oh I've got something juicy alright, but I can see you have better things to do."

She sounded all sweetness and light, but it had the desired effect and had Art turning back again like he'd just been jabbed in the ass. He crouched over her shoulder for a second time. "Come on, girl, out with it, what have you got?"

"Would you not like to know why Silverman is only a step-son?" Art dropped his hands from her shoulders and shoved them into his pockets. "I take it old boy Silverman remarried and inherited an additional sibling, but I'm sure you're about to enlighten me anyway."

"You're quite right, Art, he did remarry, but I bet you can't guess who it was he chose as his bride." Art was getting impatient. "For God's sake, Gina, just get on with it please."

She swung her chair round to face him again. "The woman Benjamin Silverman married after his first wife died was none other than Alexander Mendelson's mother, which means that Mendelson is a full blood brother to Joshua Silverman since they share the same parents. From all the reports that I can find the new Missus Silverman was a delightful lady who divorced their father when both of their boys were quite young. According to media reports Alexander remained with his father to complete his education while young Joshua went off with his mother and joined her new family, adopting the Silverman name in the process, and why wouldn't he when his step-father was so monumentally rich, but adopting the family name doesn't change the fact that he and Mendelson are brothers."

She stopped talking for a moment and being aware that she had unearthed some vital information she intended to tease Art a little with it. "So what do you think about that, Lieutenant Gardiner? Do I bring you good news, or do I bring you good news?" She sat back in her chair with a big grin on her face, leaving Art standing open mouthed, and his eyes staring wide with astonishment.

"Are you serious about this or are you making it up?" he asked, "are you asking me to believe that Joshua Silverman and Alexander Mendelson are biological brothers? Is that what you meant to say, Gina?" He couldn't believe what she'd just said. It seemed too far-fetched to be true, but if it did turn out to be true it would answer an awful lot of questions, not to mention giving credence to his long held theory that Mendelson was his main suspect and the mastermind behind the killing spree, but what on earth was his motive? Could a share of such a huge legacy really be tempting enough to entice a well-heeled lawyer like him to break the rules? It didn't seem so incredible when he thought of him in that role now, not when he knew so much more about his family connection.

His mind was so flushed with possibilities that he could hardly talk, but he knew how important it was to keep this seriously important break-through under wraps until they got their hands on Mendelson, it needed to be kept absolutely hush-hush until they got him over to Manhattan to defend the man who they now knew to be his brother, otherwise he would disappear like the slimy rat he is.

This new slant on the family history was way beyond anything Art ever expected or even dreamed Gina would unearth as it would have an enormous effect on their investigation, and on Art too. More importantly, it brought the whole scenario surrounding the killings and the claims for the legacy together in a much more meaningful way.

"Have you forgotten I'm here," asked Gina," or have I become invisible again?" Art shook his head like he was emerging from a deep sleep. "Sorry, sweetheart, I wasn't ignoring you. I was miles away and caught up in the excitement of what you've just dropped in my lap. This is one serious piece of investigative work that opens up all kind of possibilities for us. I'm so excited I don't even know what to say anymore. This priceless little gem puts a completely different slant on our investigation, we're no longer pointing fingers aimlessly at potential suspects, we know exactly who they are and where they are, so we can rope them in whenever we've a mind to."

He stopped talking and kissed her on both cheeks, but he had more to say. "I don't think you realise what a fantastic piece of work you've done today, Gina, but I do, and Delgado will too very shortly, but not until we're ready to tell him. This is undoubtedly the most important piece of incriminating evidence we've unearthed to date. I can't stress how important it is. A blood relationship between Mendelson and Silverman that's been kept secret throughout the years is going to be their undoing and no mistake."

"If that's the case why don't we go break the news to Delgado right away." Art waved her suggestion aside. "I know we're both up in the clouds over this, sweetheart, and rightly too, but I want to hold off for a just little while longer. I want you and me to enjoy the pleasure of facing Silverman and seeing his reaction when we reveal what we know. Let's get him into the interview room and watch him squirm. What do you say, are you up for it before we brief Delgado?

"You try and hold me back." Gushed Gina, rubbing her hands together excitedly

"Let's get hold of Silverman before they send him off to Rikers Island, he should be ready to go there anytime soon so we better get a move on?" Gina kissed him on the forehead. "Is this meant to be how we celebrate our engagement?" she asked, jokingly.

"Cheeky little madam," teased Art, "do you really think I'm so unromantic?" She giggled girlishly. "I don't mind how unromantic you are I still love you to bits." They embraced each other really tightly before heading off to interview Silverman, hitting the interview room in time to organise things before he was marched in, with Art thrilled to bits and ready for him like never before.

"Good afternoon, Joshua, I hope you're feeling well rested. I was a little worried about you earlier you know as I thought you looked a bit pale and out of sorts. You do realise that if you need medication for any purpose, any purpose at all, you only have to ask, you know what I mean, some heart medication, blood thinners, anything like that." Silverman looked fit to burst as he did his best to stare down his antagonist. "Stuff your medication, Gardiner. What do you want from me this time? Can you not understand that I'm not going to tell you anything you want to hear."

Art gave in a cheesy grin. "Don't be so mean, Joshua, I just want to know if you have any relatives we should get in touch with who might want to know about your current situation. You know, any former wives, any sisters, brothers, cats or dogs, any goldfish, anything like that. Surely there must be someone or something out there that cares enough about you to want to get in touch?" Silverman's face turned a bright crimson, yet he kept chewing on his thumb nail and spitting the bits across the table at Art, who had his mind set on remaining cool and not falling for any of his antics, he was enjoying himself too much to do otherwise. "That's not very sociable of you, Joshua, spitting bits of fingernail across the room at an old friend. What would your mother say if she caught you doing that?"

"I don't have a fuckin' mother and I certainly don't have anyone who would want to meet up with you." He was getting seriously riled. "No one, Joshua?" asked Art, "no one who cares enough to even come and visit you. You must lead a very solitary existence, but if there is someone out there that you think might be interested you only need to let me know and I'll invite them along; would you not enjoy having a visitor?"

"Fuck off, Gardiner, I'm not interested in your stupid ramblings and I'm saying nothing more until I'm in the company of my lawyer."

"Ah yes, your lawyer, the dear Mister Mendelson, but why do you always refer to him as your lawyer? Why don't you afford the poor man his proper status? I know you're not much of a family man but surely your dear and loving brother deserves a special place in your thoughts. After all, he is heading up this murderous campaign on your behalf, although I'm sure you plan to give him a little something for his efforts." He leaned closer to his prisoner. "But that's not likely to happen anymore because you won't be getting a red cent from your step-father's legacy. In fact, your step-brother Benjamin is recognised as the legitimate claimant, and he has already bequeathed all of his estate to his young lady friend. He did so just before you had him murdered, so it's all legally binding and legitimate, all signed, sealed, witnessed, and ready to be delivered. She is going to be one very wealthy young lady while you and your kind rot your miserable lives away in prison." Silverman turned the colour of dirty parchment; his bottom jaw dropped, and his mouth hung open, limp and drooling, he might have been having a heart attack judging by his expression.

Art prayed it was a heart attack as it would save the taxpayer an awful lot of wasted expense. Although he didn't want him dead just yet, not until he'd finished goading him, and he had only just begun to do that. "Let me tell you what's going to happen when your dearly beloved brother gets here, Joshua,. I'm going to throw him straight into the cell right next to you so you can both have loving conversations through the concrete wall and discuss the weather." He reached out and grabbed Silverman by his shirt front. "You thought you had us all fooled. You thought you were home and dry with a fortune in your back pocket, but that's *not* the end game, not anymore? I'm trying to figure out what sort of degenerate would murder his own step-brother for money? It can only be one as deranged as you I guess, but you won't be murdering anyone else, your time is up, so you can go back to your dingy cell and cry yourself to sleep thinking about all that lovely wealth you've missed out on, and you can take with you with the knowledge that we know all about you and your brother. We know what you've done and what you were planning to do, but it has all been a miserable failure, so much so that you will never even know if your step-father thought enough about you to bequeath you anything at all, and I intend to ensure that when his final instructions are fulfilled you will never get to hear a single word of it." He gave him an exaggerated make-believe sigh. "So it turns out you only thought you were clever, but you should know by now that your kind are never clever enough to outwit the long arm of the law. We'll always get you in the end."

He swung round in is seat and called in the guard.

"Take this piece of garbage back to his cell and tell the duty sergeant that all of his remand privileges are withdrawn. Instruct him to make absolutely certain that phone calls, even those to his solicitor, are withdrawn immediately and indefinitely."

With Silverman safely dispatched he and Gina went off in search of Delgado, cheerful as a couple of schoolkids, and it would be an understatement to say they were looking forward to seeing their boss, they were absolutely ecstatic about it.

29

If there was ever going to be a day in Marcus Delgado's life when he could be said to be deliriously happy then this was about to be it, although he didn't know it yet, but he soon would as two of his senior detectives were on their way to make it happen. Although Delgado, being unawares, had other things on his mind when they got there and found him propped up against his office door discussing transport issues with a senior officer from traffic branch.

It was safe to say that conversation quickly became less important when he saw who was approaching, in fact he cringed inwardly at the thought of another set-to with his Lieutenant and when they were close enough to hear him he issued an early warning. "If you two are here to give me grief don't even think about it. I'm already suffering plenty without you adding to it."

Art gave him a mournful look. "That's a very cold-hearted way to greet your two most senior staff members, Captain, especially when our only aim in life is to help keep you happy."

Delgado's brow gathered above his glasses, and he cocked an eyebrow in a suspicious way. "I smell something underhand going on here, so get it off your chest and let me get back on the job, okay?"

Gina was smirking behind her raised hand and was seriously tempted to laugh but held it back long enough to say her piece. "Why don't we all go into your office, Captain, and sit down. Art and I have something important to tell you that you will definitely want to hear." Delgado gave a boorish sigh and pointed a guiding hand at his office door, even though his expression told the world that he did not want them anywhere near him.

"After you, Gina," he invited, "but this had better be quick because I've got a lot on my plate just now." Once they were all seated Art opened the conversation, and to his credit Delgado had already spotted the serious look on his face and took the hint to keep his mouth shut and pay attention.

"Not very long ago I made a suggestion that we should open an investigation into Alexander Mendelson and his involvement in our current case, and I believe I told you at the time that Gina was carrying out an in-depth search into him and his family background." Delgado leaned over the desk. "Is that what this is all about, raising that old hare again. I thought we had already put a plan in place to deal with that bloody ------" Art raised a hand to stop him going on. "Before you go off on one, Marcus, Gina has new evidence that nullifies any need for such an investigation."

Delgado relaxed visibility by folding his arms over his chest with a winning smirk on his face. He was overjoyed at what he was hearing, but he looked a bit too cocky considering he had yet to hear the whole story. "I see," he said, his eyes flitting from Art to Gina and back to Art again, "do I take it you're admitting defeat on the mister-big idea, Art, is that what this is all about?"

Art got up from his chair and leaned against the wall. "I'm not giving up on anything, Marcus, I'm simply suggesting that the investigation into Mendelson is no longer necessary as I believe we have all the evidence we need to take him into custody as soon as he sets foot in our territory."

Delgado jerked upright in his seat. "How the hell did we obtain any evidence to support something like that without an investigation or an interview even? Has Ian Stewart discovered something else that I don't know about?"

Art pushed himself away from the wall. "No he has not, well not to my knowledge anyway, but Gina has, would you like her to tell you about it?" Delgado threw his arms in the air. "I wish to God somebody would tell me something. Just get on with it please, Gina, you have my undivided attention, but not for long."

Gina shifted to the edge of her seat. "I think it would be wise to tell you the big story first and explain the detail later. It's like this, Captain, Joshua Silverman and Alexander Mendelson are biological brothers." Delgado looked like he'd been pole-axed, and it was some time before he found his voice and was capable of speech. "You can't be serious? Where the hell did this come from?"

"We have all the proof we need, Marcus, believe me." Art was in no mood to start arguing the point, he was looking for a more favourable reaction from their boss. "I thought you would be more pleased with this news and not so bloody determined to question what Gina just told you."

Delgado shook his head like he was trying to un-fog his brain. "To be perfectly honest I'm flabbergasted, Art,. I had no idea you two were going to spring this on me and at the minute I'm not sure what to think of it." He buried his face in his hands, and when he looked up again it was Gina who got his attention. "Of course I believe you if this is something you're standing over with supporting evidence, but if I'm totally honest I'm too ecstatic to describe how I feel. I need to let all this sink in for a minute or two. Why don't you get us some coffees, Gina, and let me get my head round things?" He was hoping for a quiet word with Art while she was away.

Gina squeezed past Art who was standing right behind her. "I take it that's a signal for me to act as housemaid again." She went through the door too quickly for the others to react.

"I'm not trying to be awkward about this, Art," Delgado assured him as soon as Gina was out of ear-shot, "but it isn't something we can just take for granted, but if it is true it will have a serious effect on our case and will pump life into your theory as well." Art felt he was still undecided. "Leave it until Gina gets back, Marcus," he suggested, "she did all the work to get this result so it's only fair she explains how and where she found her evidence, but I can assure you it's genuine." Delgado's resistance looked to be waning. "I can't wait to hear how she uncovered a scoop like this." He still looked hesitant, although he was inwardly praying that Gina could back her claim up.

Five minutes later, when they were all settled with their coffee, Art opened the session again by handing over to Gina. "I think you need to explain to Marcus how you came by your findings."

Gina was all geared up and ready to go and some five minutes later when she'd finished talking, Marcus was grinning from ear to ear. "I don't need to tell you how important this is, Gina. What you've uncovered is mind blowing in my book" Gina threw her an arm round Art's shoulder. "It was my old man here who told me what to do so you had better thank him as well." Delgado reached into his drawer and pulled out a bottle. "I know exactly how to thank him, and you too for that matter." He poured a large measure into each of their cups, then raised his own in the air. "Here's to you two for your hard work and determination." Art was in no mood to celebrate; he was still focussed on the job. "You know, Marcus, I'm wondering if it wouldn't be wise to contact Mendelson and inform him that Silverman's court case is imminent. Get the cheapskate over here before he gets wind that we're on to him. What do you think?"

"We can give it a try it, Art, but we need to be careful not to wave a red flag at him by mistake, if he finds out that we know his family status it could make him suspicious if we push too hard.

Art grunted impatiently. "He only needs to know that Silverman is demanding access to his legal representative and should be afforded proper support for his court appearance that is now eminent. Surely there's no reason for him not to react to such a request."

Delgado's eyes narrowed ominously, but he didn't knock the idea. "That's about it, Art, we confirm by official letter that he's been named as Silverman's legal aid on our court documents, and if he's not available to attend then we will have to appoint someone else from the court books. That might get his ass into gear and flush him out, but we must bear in mind that the evidence against him is only circumstantial, and not strong enough to justify an arrest, although it would probably be strong enough to have him brought in for questioning as a person of interest with questions to answer.

"Let's go for it, Marcus," prompted Art, "if we get him into an interview room and let Silverman get a whiff of him being there, without actually telling him of course, we can play one off against the other. Silverman doesn't seem very keen on his brother from what I've seen, so it could work, although we need to be careful not to leave ourselves open to accusations of entrapment."

Gina, who had been sitting in silence for most of this exchange, decided it was time to have her say. "Why are we even discussing this nonsense when all we're doing is what the law requires? Every accused person is entitled to legal representation of their choice, it's a requirement of the law for God's sake so all we need do is remind Mendelson of his duty to facilitate his client?"

"Okay, Gina," agreed Delgado, "I understand all that, but we'll need to keep our fingers crossed that Mendelson thinks more of his brother than his brother think of him and decides to come here in person to defend him, bearing in mind that he could easily send one of his underlings." Art was horrified by the thought. "There's no way I see Silverman settling for some underling standing beside him in court. I think Mendelson will be duty bound to take it as a personal responsibility to represent his brother. Whether he likes it or not."

"Okay," agreed Delgado, "let's take that as a plan and run with it.. I'll get whoever is responsible to send off an e-mail advising Mendelson of the details and his clients need for legal advice, and let's see what transpires. Are we all in favour?" With everyone in agreement and nothing else to discuss they finished their drinks and went about their business.

Art was full of praise for Gina when they got outside. "That went really well thanks to your brilliant piece of work, sweetheart, finding out at this late stage that Silverman and Mendelson are brothers was absolutely mind-blowing to say the least. It changes our whole approach to this investigation." Gina pulled him round to face her. "I only did what you told me to do, Art, so it's you who deserves the credit, not me." Art shook his head. "That's not how I see it, sweetheart, as far as I'm concerned the credit is all yours."

"Okay, so what's next on the agenda?" she asked.

"The next thing for us is to make contact with Claire Mathews and warn her to be on her guard. I don't imagine she knows anything about what's going on here, just dig out her phone number and give her a bell and warn her to upgrade her personal security. We wouldn't want anything untoward happening to her, would we?" Gina's face lit up. "How considerate of you to think about her safety, Art, it's good to know you care that much, I'll get right on it." Art patted her on the shoulder. "Thanks, honey, I'm off to phone Ian Stewart so I'll see you later."

Sadly for Art, it turned out that contacting Inspector Stewart didn't happen as he had a number of important meetings and was unlikely to be available for at least another two hours.

All Art could do was leave a message and hope for the best.

30

Art had drifted off into a rare mood of retrospective reflection as he sipped coffee from his battered old mug and having allowed his mind to wander onto the subject of young Silverman's death he was unable to cast the intrusive thought aside for something less depressing. Recent events insured that Silverman's claim to his father-in-law's legacy was a lost cause, a fact that gnawed at his upstanding inner-self that the young man's death had not achieved a single thing for those who plotted to make it happen. Such a thoughtless and fruitless killing angered him like no other, because there would be no profitable outcome for the perpetrators, making it senseless and totally immoral. He was still engrossed on the matter when his phone sounded off and brought him back to reality. "Gardiner." he said wearily. The caller picked up on his weariness. "You sound a bit pissed-off, Art, have I caught you at a bad time?" It was Ian Stewart.

Art shook his head to clear the fogginess. "Nothing serious, Ian, just dwelling on things I should be giving a by-ball, but how are you?"

"I'm fine, Art, but I believe you were looking for me."

"Yes, I was, I want to update you on the latest developments at this end that are more than enough to fine-tune our investigation."

"Sound interesting, Art, in what way does it change the focus?" He asked. Art thought for few moments before replying. "You already know of my theory about Mendelson, but things have moved on and

We're taking that line of enquiry much more seriously now. You probably won't believe what I'm about to tell you, Ian, but I can assure you that it's a God given fact." He took a deep breath. "We've just discovered that our dear friends Mendelson and Silverman are biologically related, in fact they are full biological brothers." He could hardly wait to get Ian's response. "Come on, Art, you have to be joking, how the hell can that suddenly come about?" Art gave a little chuckle. "It's not sudden at all, Ian, it's been that way since they were born, and believe me when I tell you it's a proven fact."

He waited for Ian to say something. "How on earth could they manage to keep something like this a secret for so long?" He was really shocked. Art decided to enlighten him. "It's all to do with divorces and second marriages, Ian, it's not that complicated really. We know that the Silverman we have languishing in our cells and Alexander Mendelson share the same mother and father, but that marriage broke up when their mother divorced their father and married old boy Silverman, taking one of her siblings with her. That sibling was a very young Joshua Mendelson, while their other son, Alexander, stayed with the father to complete his education, leaving Joshua to take the Silverman name after Silverman and his mother tied the knot.

"Bloody hell, Art, that's a serious game changer. It looks like you were right to suspect Mendelson, but a development of this magnitude gives us justifiable cause to suspect them of being in cahoots. Well, well, what next I wonder?" Art cut in on him again. "Anyway, Ian, I thought it right that you know the situation and ask you once again to keep it under wraps. It's vitally important that Mendelson doesn't get to know we're on to him, as I'm sure you understand."

"Of course, Art, it goes without saying, but what's the plan going forward?"

"We're contacting Mendelson formally to demand his presence for Silverman's court hearing. If he complies, and we know Silverman expects him to as he has made that perfectly clear, then we'll take him into custody and question him. I take it you have no objection?"

"I would expect anyone involved in multiple homicide to be taken into custody at the first opportunity. I have no qualms at all with that, I hope it all goes to plan. It sounds like it should." Art gave a little chuckle. "If it doesn't, Ian, yours truly will find himself looking for a new job." He gave another little chuckle. "By the way, I meant to ask you earlier, have you any idea who it is that's taken out a lawsuit against Mendelson? We're a bit curious about that."

"I'm afraid I can't help you there, Art, it just hasn't been top of our agenda, but if I do find out I'll let you know."

"Thanks, Ian. I've got to go now, but I'll stay in touch." He hung up, but as soon as the call was finished he went off to see if Marcus had managed to contact Matheson. It turned out the news was more interesting than he had expected. "We did have a chat, Art, in fact it was quite a lengthy conversation, and while he wasn't able to reveal much about Mendelson's family background he confirmed that the charge raised by his client has to do with misappropriation of funds from a family trust fund. It appears his reputation is on the line if the court rules against him."

Art grinned knowingly. "Looks like another nail in his coffin. What do you think, Marcus?" Delgado pursed his lips guiltily. "I guess I had better admit that I should have paid more attention to your theory from the start, you suspected Mendelson of being complicit, but he has a lot more on his plate now that this other business has come to light." Art piped in quickly. "Okay, I know he hasn't been found guilty of anything yet, but you and I both know he soon will be. I just hope the devil has an open door policy and has the fires well stoked-up for his arrival."

"You say the sweetest things, Art, but joking aside I've just finished e-mailing Mendelson with regards to the forthcoming court appearance, so it's a case of wait and see now, but before I finish, have we made contact with Claire Mathews yet?" Art curled his lip. "I haven't a clue, Marcus, I left Gina to get on with it, but I'll chase it up and get back to you. If you've nothing else I'll be on my way, things to do and all that." Delgado just waved him away impatiently. "Don't forget to check that last; we need to keep that young lady safe in case Mendelson has something in mind for her." Art waved a hand over his shoulder as he went through the door and having left his boss reasonably happy he went off to get an update on Claire Mathews. It was important they keep in touch with her for more reasons than Delgado stated as she would have a role to play when the case got to court.

Gina spotted him heading her way and got up to meet him, guiding him away from the others who were hard at work. "What's up?" she asked. "Nothing much, I'm only checking up on the Mathews situation, Marcus is keen to know things are going."

"It sounds as if she's coping okay as she was very eager to find out how our case is progressing. I suggested she come here for a face to face and she's okay with that. She's hoping to get here late tomorrow afternoon and would like us to pick her up at the airport. We didn't have time to discuss the issue of her inheritance, although I think we need to in case there are any more surprises crawling out of the woodwork."

Art stifled a yawn. "I couldn't agree more, her evidence will be vital when we get to court. She's certain to be called as a witness for the prosecution so she needs to be briefed on what to expect. It would help if she jotted down a few facts while they're still fresh in her mind to bolster her confidence. We don't want her groping for answers when the defence sets about her."

He stifled another yawn as Gina looked on sympathetically. "I can see you're still suffering from last night's celebrations, but back to Claire Mathews, I don't think we need worry about her, she's switched on and bright enough. I'd say she's more than capable of facing up to a trial, in fact I'm absolutely certain of it."

"Well, that should help keep Marcus happy, he's got a bee in his bonnet about her since you reminded him of his responsibilities." Something else suddenly came to mind. "Are you picking her up at the airport or do I have to sort something out?" Gina waved the question aside. "I have it in hand, and since she's only here for one or two nights I invited her to stay with us, are you okay with that?"

"That probably makes sense. I'll let Marcus know, in fact I'll do that now before we head off for a bite to eat."

I still have a lot to catch up with, Art, so I'll give lunch a miss and catch you later, if that's okay?" Art gave her a mock salute and wandered off, satisfied that everything was as it should be.

31

It was a later than expected when Gina got back from the airport as Claire's flight had arrived in late. On top of that the heavy traffic on the route home added to the problem, but when they finally got there Art met them at the door and carried Claire's bag inside. "It's good to see you here again, Claire." He said this with genuine feeling and got a smile for his troubles. "I'm really happy to be back as it will give me an opportunity to lay some flowers where Roger and Sam were murdered. I haven't managed to do that yet and it's been on my mind, so I need to do it."

She turned to Gina. "It will also give me the chance to explain some things that I'm sure you must want to hear about." Gina cut in on her. "Let's get you settled first, Claire, Art will show you up to your room while I get dinner ready. You must have lots to tell us and I can't wait to hear all about it. An awful lot has happened at this end since we last spoke, but we can talk about all that over dinner." She ushered their visitor away and Art led her from the room.

Later, with all three sat round the table enjoying their meal Gina directed the conversation to Claire's forthcoming inheritance. "How did you find out that Ben had named you as his sole heir?"

Claire finished eating what was in her mouth before answering. "I was with Roger when he composed his Will, he had insisted that I accompany him, although until we actually got to the solicitor's I had absolutely no idea what he was planning to do." She paused to gather

her thoughts. He'd been a bit edgy and fretful for a few of days prior to this and when I asked him why he was acting so strangely he just put it down to having important things on his mind that needed attention. I have to say I was a bit shocked when I found out he was making a Will, but that only because I couldn't understand why he was in such a hurry to do so at his young age."

She took a sip of wine before carrying on. "Quite honestly, I never thought he had anything valuable enough to justify a Will. I still don't know what he left me as he never discussed it. The Will itself, from the little I saw of it, was short and uncomplicated. Roger simply said that in the event of his demise or failure to think, act, or communicate clearly, he bequeathed all of his worldly goods, assets, and any other possessions that were his by legal right, to me, Claire Mathews, as named and witnessed by those present. He further declared that his solicitor was to be recognised as executer to his Will and should receive remuneration composite with that duty."

Gina was about to eat something, but the fork never got reached her mouth. "Are you telling us that you still don't know what's involved with your inheritance?"

"No, I don't, I have no idea, neither do Roger's solicitors. I'm told that the ongoing murder investigation has left everything in limbo. Although they did hint that it has the potential to be life changing for me." She buried her face in her hands and used them as a shield, sobbing quietly under their cover. Gina suddenly had her serious face on. "I would suggest it's time you stopped referring to your boyfriend as Roger when his real name is Benjamin, or Ben for short, which would be more acceptable in the circumstances, especially as he has most likely secured your financial status far in excess of anything you could ever have imagined or thought possible." Gina's comment didn't have much effect on their visitor, she appeared to have other things on her mind and seeing no reason to pursue it Gina just let it drop, although she felt a twinge of sadness at Claire's apparent lack of civility.

"It's rather surprising that Ben didn't discuss his father's vast wealth with you before making his Will." Claire shrugged the comment aside. "What can I say. I always found him to be a very private person, especially on family matters. It probably sounds a bit odd when I say that, but I didn't even know he had a family as he never brought them up in conversation. Anyway, it was Ben I was interested in, not his family." Gina smiled at her last remark. "I guess young love has its own focus."

Art, who had been sitting quietly just out of Claire's line of vision decided to make a point of his own. "Ben must have thought very highly of you to make you his sole beneficiary, especially as he had only known you for a couple of years. That was a big decision on his part when you consider what's involved."

Claire swung round to face him "I don't know what's involved, Lieutenant, nobody will tell me, not officially anyway." The fact that she had suddenly become quite formal in addressing him by his rank when she was staying under their roof took him by surprise. He couldn't figure out what had caused her to suddenly address him like that, and when he glanced over at Gina to check her reaction he saw a puzzled expression on her face as well. "You do know that our conversations here are completely informal, Claire, so there's absolutely no need to address Art by his rank." Claire's face took on a slight pinkish hue. "Sorry, Gina, I didn't mean to be rude. I'm just a little confused with everything that's going on in my life right now." She had the good grace to look embarrassed. Gina reached out and laid a gentle hand on top of hers. "We understand, Claire, just relax and be your own self. Art and I are only interested in your wellbeing as there are some very nasty people involved in what's going on with this inheritance." Claire got to her feet. "I know it's early, but do you mind if I go up to my room? It's been a very long day and I'm feeling quite tired." She actually looked like she wanted to be somewhere else.

Gina got to her feet as well. "Of course not, Claire, we know how tiring travel can be, but just so you know we normally have breakfast around seven and leave for the office around seven-thirty. Is that okay for you?" Claire nodded in agreement. "Of course, that's absolutely fine, but if it's okay I'll say goodnight and see you both at breakfast." She headed for the door with two pair of concerned eyes following her every inch of the way.

"What on earth did you make of that?" asked Gina, in a muted voice. Art had his serious face on as well. "To be honest I wasn't very impressed There's something a rather odd going on with that girl. It's almost as if she's adopted a different set of values since we last spoke with her. She sure has me confused." Gina looked even more uncomfortable. "Are you thinking what I'm thinking?" she asked. Art got out of his chair, closed the lounge door, and began pacing about the kitchen looking seriously deep in thought. It was only after a short spell of pacing that he got round to answering Gina's question. "Yes, I think I am, Gina. I'm thinking everything is not as it should be with her. She has me feeling uneasy, but the odd thing is that I can't figure out why."

"That's exactly how I feel; surely it's not asking too much to have her call her boyfriend by his proper name?" she asked. "Not the way I see it anyway," she said, answering her own question, "it shows a complete lack of respect for the man she professes to love."

"I think that's maybe what has me feeling uneasy. Something about her doesn't gel with me," he sounded really edgy, "surely there must be something amiss with her for both of us to feel the same way."

"Maybe we're just reading too much into things, Art, after all, we don't know her all that well and we could be seriously misreading the situation." Art nodded in agreement. "Yeah, I take your point, but that doesn't stop me feeling uneasy. Although I agree we don't know her very well, maybe we should make an effort to find out more about her? What do you think?" Gina was a little apprehensive. "I'm not sure, Art. Are we feeling uneasy because we don't trust her? Or is it just that she doesn't conform to our set of social rules?"

"You and I have been at this game a long while, Gina, we're not novices. We often follow our hunch when we sense somethings not right, even when we don't have a shred of evidence to support our hunch. Isn't that what we do? Isn't that what makes us good at our job?" Gina drew her feet up under her on the settee and reached for her glass. "Let's stick with what we do best, Art, let's follow our hunch. That's what we always do, so let's just stick with it. I'll start digging first thing tomorrow, if nothing else crops up before then." Art slipped onto the settee beside her. "Good girl, I think we're at our best when we trust our own judgement." She finished what was left in her glass and taking Art by the hand she dragged him off the settee. "Let's have an early night as well, Art, I'm feeling rather bushed and ready for some sleep."

They went upstairs hand in hand, but before they got there they heard Claire being quite agitated about something with a slightly raised voice, presumably on the phone and she was definitely giving someone seriously hard time. But as luck would have it her voice quickly dropped to a whisper, leaving them unable make out anything else she said. So with nothing better to do they climbed into bed, although it was one of those nights when sleep wouldn't come easily to either of them.

32

The following morning breakfast was dispensed with in record time, but with very little conversation of any consequence, apart from the usual morning ritual. Nor was it any livelier in the car, with Claire answering most of the questions asked of her in words of one syllable, and it wasn't long before their forced conversation dried up altogether and the atmosphere became a little strained.

There was a genuine look of relief on all three faces when they got to the Station House and had other things to keep them occupied. Art went straight off to see his boss, while Gina kept their visitor occupied until Marcus was free to see her. It had been agreed between them that he would take on the role of updating Mathews on the state of their investigation and keep her occupied in his office for as long as possible. He'd further agreed not to mention Mendelson or his relationship with Silverman in her presence, nor to make any mention of Sharpe, although he was free to advise her that they had two people in custody awaiting trial. Art went to some lengths to explain their unease with her general attitude and pointed out that it would be inadvisable to say anything in her presence that they wouldn't want Mendelson to know. All this was purely on the grounds of their growing doubts over her trustworthiness.

Having finished briefing Delgado he phoned Gina and had her bring Mathews up to their bosses office, he also asked her to meet up with him in the main interview room immediately afterwards as they needed time to conjure up a plan to either prove or disprove their suspicions about the young lady. Some of their suspicion stemmed from the fact that they knew very little about her past history, apart from what she had told them. So top of their agenda, if the opportunity arose, was to get hold of her cell phone after her angry little outburst the previous evening had alerted them to the possibility that she needed keeping an eye on.

These were the thoughts going through his mind when Gina walked in and interrupted them. "So how are we going to play this, Art?" she asked. Art scratched they back of his neck. "Well need to be a bit creative I think. It would help if we got our hands on her phone, I'm convinced it has a story to tell, like identifying who she was balling out last night. The problem is we don't have any evidence to support our concerns, in fact we don't even know what it was that raised them in the first place, so we have to be careful and not overstep the mark." He sat back in his chair and narrowed his eyes in an effort to figure out a way forward. "I wonder what would happen if we arranged for her and Silverman to bump into each other?" His question got a rude reply from Gina, along with a blunt warning. "There's absolutely no chance of us setting that up, Art, not if you want to keep your job and your pension."

"Well I did say we needed to be creative. I'm certain she doesn't know we have Silverman and Sharpe in custody, or she would have mentioned it by now. After all, she's been tucked away in Nevada since young Ben died, so it wouldn't be difficult to arrange for her and Silverman to trip over each other, accidently of course. Let me think about it for a while. In the meantime I'd like you to check out her background on your computer and see what you come up with. There might be something there that we can latch on to." Gina headed for the door. "I'm off to get started then, but what's happening with our guest once Marcus has finished with her?" Art gave her a blank look. "I haven't even thought about it. I'm going back to see how they're doing; I want to know what he thinks about her as well, maybe he'll pick up on something we've missed." Gina went about her business.

Marcus waved Art in as soon as he saw him at the door. "Come in, Art, I've already brought Miss Mathews up to date on where we are with the investigation, but I think she's ready for a change of scenery. She has indicated that she would like to do some shopping while she's here so maybe you or Gina could arrange that and keep her company?"

"I'll get something organised, Marcus." promised Art, before switching his attention to their visitor. "I'm sure you must be ready to see a friendlier face than old sourpuss here, Claire, so let's go find Gina and get your shopping trip organised, she knows all the best places to spend money, and you can believe it when I tell you that she's very well practiced at it." He gave Marcus a crafty wink by way of apology for the sourpuss remark and led their guest away.

Gina closed her monitor when as she saw them approaching. "I take it you survived trial by Marcus then." she joked. Mathews smiled readily. "I thought he was really helpful and friendly, although to be honest I had hoped to learn more about the people you have in custody, just out of curiosity really." Gina wagged a finger at her. "We aren't permitted to release the names of individuals in custody until they've entered a plea in court, anyway, their names don't matter, killers are killers and need to be dealt with accordingly."

She turned to Art. "We need a formal statement from Claire about the night her boyfriend died. Are you up for that or is it down to me?" She cocked a knowing eyebrow at him and got a cheeky grin for her trouble. "You can get on with it when you get back from your shopping trip. I have plenty to keep me busy for the next few hours and it's only a formality anyway."

He swung round to engage with their visitor. "Sorry we forgot to mention the statement last night, Claire, but it won't take very long. It's only a case of procedural belt and braces, you know what officialdom is like." She gave him a stunted smile before Gina took her by the arm and led her away, casting a parting warning to Art over her shoulder.. "We're off to spend some money, might even find a nice wedding gown somewhere, see you later, sweetheart." Art shuddered at the thought but gave her a wry smile with his mind on something else entirely, and that something else was Delgado, who wasn't expecting him back so soon when he walked in on him. "How did you find little Miss Goldilocks?" He asked, sounding a touch cynical. Delgado raised both shoulders and wriggled into a more comfortable position on his chair. "A bit cagey would be the best description I can offer, although if I'm honest about it she didn't strike me as being deliberately evasive." Art pinched his nose. "She's away shopping now and I'm hoping Gina manages to get a quick look at her phone. We still feel there's something not right about her, and we've already had enough surprises with this blasted investigation without any more crawling out of the woodwork."

Delgado looked slightly bemused. "I wish I knew what it is about her that has you feeling so uneasy. I didn't get any vibes like that at all, she seemed fairly straight forward to me." Art's eyes widened in surprise. "Really? Maybe I've gone off at half-cock then, maybe I'm just suspicious of everybody that is involved in this case, but it's a bit odd that Gina feels exactly the same way I do."

"Are you planning on doing anything about it?" he sked. Art grimaced uneasily. "We're taking a formal statement from her as a prosecution witness. We've yet to do that and it should be a good way to get her talking and see if she trips over herself. I'm hoping to arrange for her to have an accidental sighting of Silverman while she's here. I'm keen to see how she reacts when she sees him in cuffs and ankle chains." Delgado bolted upright in his chair. "Don't you go breaking any damned rules, Art, just keep it in mind that Silverman is meant to be held in isolation while he's in custody. I don't want any comebacks."

"Trust me, Marcus. I'll play it strictly by the book." Delgado looked anything but convinced. "So you say, but I'm worried about which book you're reading from." Art gave a quiet little chuckle. "I think I'll give her a guided tour of the premises while Silverman is being interviewed close by, that should do the trick." Delgado closed his eyes at the thought. "Please don't even tell me what you're up to, Art. I'd rather not know, just get it done and keep it clean." His warning didn't even register with Art who was already heading off to get things organised.

Gina didn't get back with their guest until late afternoon and she was loaded with shopping bags when she did, as was Claire, a disturbing sight that had Art wondering where Mathews got her money from when she was supposed to be unemployed and homeless? With that in mind he decided it was time to get started. "I think you deserve a guided tour of our illustrious establishment before we get down to taking your statement, Claire. What do you think?"

"I suppose I might as well while I'm here." Art pretended to have just thought of something. "I tell you what, I've just remembered that we have a line-up taking place shortly, I think that would be a good way to start your tour." He swung round to Gina. "Bring Claire along and keep her company, Gina." She gave him a thumbs-up and they set off with Art leading the way, eager as hell to see what happened next.

Silverman had been shocked when told he was taking part in a one-man line-up, although he wasn't unduly concerned as there was absolutely no reason for anyone to pick him out for something he couldn't have done.

While he was being shuffled into position Art thought it best to explain to their visitor what was going on. "The guy in the line-up is being held on a murder charge, but a new witness has turned up who needs to pick him out to back up the other witness, if he ever gets here that is as we're running out of time."

He led Claire round a corner to an observation window, which in reality was just an ordinary window, although she was unaware of this. And there was sound reasoning for her not knowing, as Art was planning to let her, and Silverman, get a clear view of each other while he kept an eye their reaction. His eyes were focussed on her face as she got her first sight of Silverman and was seriously disappointed when she showed absolutely no reaction at all; not so much as a raised eyebrow at seeing him stood upright against a blank wall. She clearly didn't know him from Adam, warning him that his plan had just gone belly up. He was left with no other option but to implement plan B, but just as he was about to lead the girls away to do this he spotted an odd look on Silverman's face, a curious, wide-eyed look that he couldn't ignore. Was it apprehension he saw there? Was it a sign that he recognised Mathews, or was it something else altogether? He simply didn't know, but he would do his best to find out, and he would do it now while it was on his mind, and having got the girls back to Gina's workstation he arranged for Silverman to be taken to an interview room and hurried off to join him, and when he did it was impossible to miss the haggard, drawn expression on his gaunt face, or his notably worried disposition.

"Well Joshua, here we go again, but you should be warned before we start that we've gained some new information from a young lady who is involved in our case. You need to know that she came forward of her own accord and volunteered to tell us her side of the story, which makes her out to be quite innocent of course, but I'm more interested in what her role was from your perspective."

Silverman was rubbing the back of one hand with the palm of the other. "I don't have to discuss anything with you until my solicitor gets here." He continued rubbing his hand, telling Art that something had him on edge. "I don't believe you have a legal representative any more or you would have met up with them before now. So you can pull the other one, Joshua, but don't go worrying about it, we can get some cheap legal aid for you if you need it. In the meantime you need to consider how difficult things might get if you don't co-operate. I'm sure you're aware that some prisons are less dangerous places to serve your time than others, and if you cooperate now it might determine where you serve your time, and you are going to serve a very long time, Joshua, so think on." Silverman stopped rubbing his hand and leaned on the table. "What's in it for me if I do co-operate?" he asked, his voice a little weaker than normal, so weak that it was almost a whisper, almost as if he feared the walls were listening. Art gave him a knowing wink. "What's in it for you will depend on what you have to offer." Silverman ran his fingers through his thinning hair. "What if I name someone whose involved that you're not yet aware of?"

"Which someone is that?" asked Art. Silverman looked at him like he owed him something "That's for you to find out, if we cut the right deal."

"You need to give us something useful, Joshua, something that can earn you a little clemency, not some meaningless hogwash that springs to mind.."

"I need more than a few brownie points, Gardiner," warned Silverman, "much more, so you need to come up with something a lot more generous than that." Art was weighing him up, and he sensed a definite change in his attitude, a very noticeable change, but what card could he play now to help get his prisoner on side?

"You do know that there's no big money coming your way anymore, don't you, Joshua? You've already blown that so you might as well come clean and wipe the slate, after all, what have you got to lose this late in the day?"

"You had better believe it when I tell you that I *will* have my money, I have no fears about that. You see, Gardiner, you only think you know what's going on, but I believe my people are well out of your league." Art had to gather his thoughts before challenging Silverman again, he needed to be careful. "Let me explain something to you, Joshua. We already have you and Sharpe locked up and your other hired killer, Hardwick, has kind of lost his head so to speak, and his killer is safely in the hands of the Met police in London, so just who is this *we* you speak of?" A worrying change of expression altered Silverman's whole appearance; it was an expression that warned Art that he remained convinced that his cronies were able to get him off with a light sentence. He needed to knock him off his pedestal. "What are you going to do when your pal Mendelson gets locked away for misappropriation of funds? If his case comes up before yours it's highly likely he won't even be free to represent you, or anyone else for that matter. What will you do then, Joshua?"

Silverman's jaw dropped and he slumped in his chair in stunned silence, his eyes wide, staring and unseeingly. Obviously he had no knowledge of what he was being told and he looked horrified at the possibility that it could be true. He was too worried to even think of hiding his concern behind some throw away remark. Art could see a mixture of indecision and dread on his gaunt features. "You've gone very quiet, Joshua, why is that? I know this isn't the first time you've been reminded of Mendelson's little problem, so why are you looking so worried now?" He gave Silverman a questioning look. "I find it totally irresponsible and unprofessional of him as your solicitor to find himself charged with misappropriation of funds when you need him most."

Silverman didn't have time to reply, he was too busy taking stock of his situation, while Art, who felt he had gained the upper hand, goaded him some more. "Maybe you should sue him for breach of contract, Joshua? What do you think?"

Silverman finally lost his composure. "I can't fuckin' think straight with you blabbering on non-stop. How do I know you're not trying to trick me? That's the sort of thing you lot resort to when things get tough. Anyway, I only need to phone Alex to find out." Art gave him a wry smile. "I'm afraid that's a no-goer, Joshua. Mendelson is awaiting trial for fraud, and we can't have one criminal conversing with another while both are awaiting trial for the same offence. I think it's time you turned turkey and started looking after your own interests." He stopped and pointed at his quarry. "I think you're trying to bluff me, Joshua, you don't have anything to offer that's worth listening to. I was hoping to convince you to help yourself, but on reflection I think I'll just have you shunted back to your cell where you belong." He got up as if to call the guard in. Silverman stopped him in his tracks. "Just be honest with me for a change, Gardiner. Swear you're telling me the truth about Alex? Swear to me that he really is facing a court appearance." Art crossed his heart. "I swear that what I told you is the absolute truth, Joshua. I'm not trying to pull any kind of stunt, believe me. Mendelson is awaiting trial on a charge of fraudulent use of a clients funds, apparently it has to do with a family trust fund."

Silverman started a nervous rocking motion that had him rolling backwards and forwards on his chair. A clear sign of agitation. "I need a coffee while I think things over?" Art went to the door and when he got back to his seat Silverman was still rocking. "Don't get yourself all worked up, Joshua, just relax and sort out in your own mind what it is you want to do. I can't be sitting here all day if you have nothing useful to say that I want to hear."

Silverman had the look of a man defeated, but he also looked to have made up his mind about something. "Believe me, Gardiner, you will definitely want to hear what I have to tell you, but it comes at a price, like, everything else in this life, so you had better be willing to cut a deal?"

"You can't get a deal from me," Art told him bluntly, "but if you have information that assists with our investigation then it will be made known to the judge at the time of your trial. Any leniency on sentence can only be granted by the Judge, but it must not be disputed by the D A."

Silverman screwed his face up; he had been hoping to cut a deal for a reduced sentence, but it wasn't happening, and he didn't know how to change things. "I know you think I'm the one responsible for everything that's happened, but I'm not, and I'm not saying who it is until you get me a deal, so go and speak to your boss or the D A and see what they say about it."

Art shook his head. "They won't listen to me unless I have something to give them. You have to realise what a lengthy sentence you're facing. I want to help you, Joshua, but you need to think very carefully about this." He called in the guard. "Take the prisoner back to his cell now." As the guard moved in on him Silverman raised both hands in the air with his palms facing Art. "Hold on, hold on, let's sit down again. I do have something to tell you." Art eyed him up and down for a moment or two before deciding it was worthy of another go and motioning the guard to leave he dropped back into his chair. "This had better be good, Joshua, because I'm running out of patience.

Silverman buried his face in his hands and stayed that way for about thirty seconds or so, but he got talking soon enough for Art, who had already been very patient.

"You once asked me how we knew exactly where young Benjamin would be in order for Hardwick and Sharpe to administer their drugged burgers. I told you a private detective had been hired to find and track him and his group, and that was true as far as it goes, but the detective wasn't able to tell us their exact movements or timings for everything to go without a hitch." He stopped talking and stared at Art who was stroking his chin and looking interested, and it was a while before he said anything, but when he did he put an end to Silverman's party. "I think your plan was sound enough, but that old adage that you should never trust a lady when it comes to crime is very true. How much did it cost your detective to bribe Claire Mathews into setting her boyfriend up?" Silverman almost choked on his coffee. "How the hell did you get to know about her?" he spluttered. "I'm not as daft as you or Miss Mathews seem to think. When a young lady who is living rough suddenly turns up in New York with enough money to go on a shopping spree, my nostrils start twitching." He folded his arms and leaned back in his chair with a satisfied grin. "There are some things that didn't work out for you as you planned, things that even you don't know about, Joshua." Silverman looked like his world was caving in. "You see, little miss goldilocks is the other claimant who has made a claim to your step-father's legacy, thanks to young Benjamin having the foresight to nominate her as his beneficiary in a Will he made before he was murdered. So by murdering young Benjamin you have actually made Miss Mathews a very rich young lady. It might come as a shock to you, but there was never any legacy coming your way, and you need to prepare yourself for that, because unless I miss my guess your friend Mendelson was young Benjamin's legal advisor as well as yours. It was he who advised your step-brother on how to secure his legacy and also advised him to make a Will. I'm also informed that he advised him to go somewhere like Nevada to do it in case you had someone on the inside of his business to tip you off."

He locked eyes with Silverman. "It puzzled me why he was advised young Benjamin to do something like that, and exactly who it was young Ben needed protecting from?" Silverman became so enraged that Art believed he might resort to violence; he was so angry that he looked fit to strangle himself, never mind Art. However his anger quickly hit breaking point and with his hands still cuffed he swiped his mug off the table in a fit of uncontrollable rage. Art recognised the signs, this wasn't simply a display of anger, or rage, it was much more than that, it was an admission of failure and a confession that he could do nothing to change anything that was happening to him.

Art had his eyes firmly locked on the man in front of him, waiting patiently for the right moment to intervene. His objective was to prove that Mendelson was part of Silverman's murderous scheme, and the only person who could provide him with the evidence to prove it was right there in front of him. The silence, that seemed to drag on with no end in sight was intentional on Art's part. He knew that the longer Silverman was left in isolation after the shock he had just suffered, the weaker his resistance would be. After about two minutes or so he decided it was time to play his trump card and unfolding his arms he edged his chair a little bit closer to the table. "Your family life wasn't all that it could have been, was it, Joshua?"

What?" snapped Silverman, "what the hell has my family got to do with you?" Art placed his elbows on the table and nestled his chin on his closed fists, he had all morning to make Silverman wait for an answer, if he wanted to, but he eventually opened up. "It must have been very difficult for you and your brother Alex to be torn apart the way you were."

Silverman almost fell from his chair. The colour drained from his face, leaving it a sickly, lifeless colour of turned milk. He looked lost and helpless, the bright glint that had kept his eyes alive and inquisitive had disappeared, they were now lifeless and unseeing as he suffered an even bigger shock than he had last time. Lowering his arms onto the table he buried his face in them and groaned like a dying man. Art was delighted with his mental collapse, he had Silverman exactly where he wanted him, lost, alone, and feeling abandoned. "Did you honestly believe you could hide your family history from us, Joshua? We're better than that, but I understand this must be a sad time for you. Sad that your own brother would throw you to the wolves with total disregard and leave you to rot in a prison cell while he, and the delightful Miss Mathews, live the high life on a legacy that he so cunningly arranged for them to share. A legacy that might so easily have been yours." Silverman raised his chin a fraction. "I need a drink." He said, his voice slurred and weak. "All in good time, Joshua, all in good time," repeated Art, "now get your head off that goddamned table and sit up and listen to what I'm about to tell you. All you have left to help ease your burden is revenge, and I'm about to offer you a way to get it."

Silverman forced himself upright on his chair just as the door behind Art opened and Gina motioned him to join her outside. When he got there she asked him in a muted voice. "What am I supposed to do with Miss Mathews? She wants to be on her way." Art waved her remark aside. "Keep her with you no matter how you do it. I need words with that young lady, and I haven't enough time right now to go into the why's and wherefores. Just keep her under your wing and don't let her out of your sight." He turned on his heel and rushed back inside.

Silverman looked lost and confused when he got to face him again. "I'm sure you know what I was about to suggest before we were interrupted, Joshua, so let's get back down to business." Silverman did exactly that. "What proof have you got to back up what you're telling me? I haven't seen or heard anything to support your claims. I think you're trying another bluff, Gardiner. I may not be in a very strong position, I accept that, but I'm not about to give up. I still intend to have Alex in my corner when I go to court, he has a brilliant legal mind and he'll do his damnedest to get me the best possible outcome."

"You really don't have a clue about what's going on, do you, Joshua. The truth is that my partner, who just interrupted us, did so to ask me what she should do with Miss Mathews, who has been residing with us at our home since yesterday evening. I told her that under no circumstances was she to let Mathews out of her sight, because when I leave this room my very next task is to arrest her as an accomplice to murder, double murder in fact. So how does that grab you?" Silverman sank into his chair, he was losing the argument at every turn, and every time he thought he had something to offer in his fight back he ran out of ammunition. His fate was written all over his face. He knew he couldn't rely on anyone else to fight his corner now that his stupid brother had folded his hand, it was up to him now, no one else but him. "What's on offer if I go down your revenge route?" he asked.

Art wasn't in any position to cut a deal, that was down to the D A and the judge, but he wasn't about to give up, not when he had his man on the ropes. The truth was that he wanted Mendelson so badly it was like a bad taste in his mouth, but he didn't want him arrested in England, he wanted him arrested here in New York and Silverman could help him do it. "I'm sure the DA will take it kindly if you open up and give us your brother as well. All you need to do is confirm that he is the organiser and get him over here to plead your case. The minute he arrives here we will arrest him on a charge of orchestrating multiple murder and one of serious financial fraud, and everything else that goes along with such a felony. You get your revenge for being so callously abandoned, and in return we harass the D A to plead leniency on your behalf, that's all I can offer. Now do we have a deal, Joshua?" Silverman looked lost, everything about him said he'd had enough.

"I'm still waiting for that drink." He reminded Art, who duly obliged and waited until his prisoner had finished drinking before pressing him for an answer. "Do we have a deal or not, Joshua. It's make your mind up time because I'm gone from here in exactly two minutes." Silverman rubbed his face with both hands before taking another gulp of water. "It breaks my heart to say it, but yes, we have a deal." The words almost stuck in his throat.

Art could hardly believe his luck; everything was falling into place at last. "That's a wise decision, Joshua. I'll have you taken away for something to eat, then my partner will meet up with you again in here and take your statement. A statement that must reflect what you just agreed and if it does then we can get things moving." Silverman only nodded; he could no longer trust himself to speak.

Art had him taken away, then he went off to find Gina and Claire Mathews.

When he caught up with them they were in reception and there appeared to be some kind of dispute in progress. "Is everything okay, Gina? he asked, looking unduly concerned. "No it's not," she replied, "Claire is voicing her opposition to staying here any longer as she's very keen to get back to Nevada."

Art turned to the lady concerned. "Is our hospitality not good enough for you, Miss Mathews?" he asked. Mathews ignored his remark and kept her attention focussed on Gina. "I think I'll just order a taxi and save you the bother of taking me to the airport." Art placed a hand on her shoulder. "You won't be needing a taxi, it's only a short walk to the cells." Mathews looked at him like he'd gone mad, as did Gina. "You can cut the crap, girl, I know all about your involvement in the murder of Sam Blackwell and Benjamin Silverman, and how you colluded with Alex Mendelson to scam old boy Silverman's legacy." He got up close and personal with her, right up in her face "I hope you enjoyed your little shopping spree because it might be your last for a very long time." He turned to Gina. "Read this one her rights, and have her locked up, preferably in the smallest cell we've got. I'll be back shortly to interview her." He wheeled away with a trickle of sweat running down between is shoulder blades, but he was satisfied that he had just pulled off the biggest bluff of his life with Silverman and Mathews and got away with it. If there was ever a time to celebrate, this was it.

33

Art was on a real high when he went to see his boss, but he had to temper his enthusiasm when he saw the D A there, although Delgado was eager to see him and waved him in. "Come in and grab a seat, Art. Your timing couldn't be better, we're just going through the Silverman case to see whether or not we're ready to go to court."

Art took a seat next to the D A. "Before you go any further, Captain, you need to know that the picture has changed dramatically since we last discussed it." The *hail fellow well met look* vanished from Delgado's face and was replaced with what can only be described as a *don't you dare let me down* expression. "Don't give me any unwelcome news on that front, Art, it's a bit late in the day for any fuck-ups."

Art had the biggest smile on his face Delgado had ever seen on him. "It's nothing like that, Chief, in fact I think we have the whole thing just about wrapped up. I have arrested Claire Mathews on a charge of conspiracy to murder, with a small question mark over it for now, and having re-interviewed Silverman I now have him eating out of my hand. He's about to make a fresh statement admitting his full involvement and giving us everything we need to get our hooks into Mendelson as well. I've blocked him from using the phone, so Mendelson won't get to know any of this, he'll simply receive a formal letter warning him of an urgent need to get his ass over here to support his client. When he gets here he'll be arrested and locked up along with the rest of his sorry bunch and charged with orchestrating murder and fraudulent financial irregularities." Delgado glanced at the

D A and then back to Art. "Has this been recorded, detailed and placed on record, because unless your report has *the end* written on the last page I don't want to know." Art was too pleased to get annoyed. "When I've finished here I'm going to interview Mathews, and that should be the last nail in their coffin. I just need her to tell us who bribed her into setting her boyfriend up to be murdered, and exactly what went on there. Everything points to the private eye Silverman hired to track the group, but I need an admission from her to prove his involvement. If she doesn't cough up I'll get it from Silverman."

Delgado leapt from his chair and rounded the desk and grabbing Art by the hand he worked it up and down like he was pumping oil. Then he stood back and gave Art a cautious look. "All this seems to have turned on its axis very quickly, Art, have we got the evidence we need to back it up?"

"Take my word for it, Marcus, as soon as we lay hands on Mendelson and finalise the charges against him there's nothing more to be done except a few final statements and getting them into court." He turned to the D A sitting next to him. "I'm afraid I'll be giving you some extra work very soon."

The D A got to his feet. "I'm off, Marcus," he said, but he laid a comforting hand on Art's shoulder as he squeezed past him, "and well done, Lieutenant, I'll be happy if you keep throwing the work my way as it means the public are a little bit safer." He carried on past Art with a wave in Delgado's direction.

No sooner was he gone before Delgado dived into his desk and pulled out a fresh bottle. "A good time to celebrate, Art." Art waved his invitation aside. "Much as I could do with a drink, Marcus, the celebrations will have to wait until I'm finished with Mathews. "Keep it in a cool place for me until I get back." He was up and gone before Delgado had any hope of stopping him.

When he caught up with her Gina was fully occupied with the custody sergeant having Mathews booked. With no hint of an apology Art pulled her to one side and whispered in her ear. "Take madam here straight to the interview room as soon as she's documented, Gina, and hang around because I want you in there with me." He took off again before she could challenge him, he needed to check everything was in order in the interview room and having done so he planted himself on a chair. He needed a few minutes on his own to get into the right frame of mind to tackle Mathews. She had a lot to answer for, but most of all he wanted the identity of the person who bribed her into setting up her boyfriend. He saw that as the last piece of evidence he needed to wrap the case up.

The door behind him opened and Mathews walked in with Gina's hand on the back of her neck guiding her to a chair. Art had his arms folded and a dour look on his face.

"You know what I want from you young lady so don't be bashful, just tell me who bribed you into setting your boyfriend up to be murdered?" Mathews was studying her lavishly painted fingernails and ignored his demand, which wasn't a wise thing to do because it invited Art to slam his fist down on the table with an almighty bang, scaring the hell out of Mathews, who almost fell from her chair.

When she'd righted herself Art banged his fist on the table again. "Don't even think of messing me about, just answer the question before I get nasty." He leaned over the table going face to face with her. "Who bribed you and how much did they pay?" Mathews face was the colour of chalk following Art's vicious onslaught. Her eyes had moistened noticeably, and she was wringing her hands in a nervous, twisting motion. "I don't know who he was, he just introduced himself as Nick and told me he'd been hired by Roger's family solicitor to find him and convince him to return to the family home. He offered me five thousand dollars to let him know Roger's whereabouts on any night that he could meet up with him away from the rest of the group. I was to phone him on the day in question and he would meet me and pay me the money. That was all there was to it." Her story didn't sit easily with Art, he needed a bit more convincing. "Are you seriously telling me that you had no idea you were setting your boyfriend up to be killed? Is that what I'm meant to believe?" He unfolded his arms and eased back in his chair. "You had better explain how you're going to prove it in court when you can't even tell me the name of the detective who was involved."

Mathews looked close to tears, but she managed to hold them back. "I'm telling you the truth, honestly. There's nothing more I can tell you; I don't know who he was?" Art was becoming impatient, and he didn't attempt to hide it. "You can stop calling your dead boyfriend Roger for a start and explain how you came to be the sole benefactor to his inheritance?"

Mathews studied her fingernails again before saying anything. When she looked up there was a hint of something close to embarrassment lodged on her face. "Benjamin, or Roger, as I knew him, gave me the impression he was stressed out about something, like he was in some sort of danger. It was just a feeling I had and nothing Roger said, but once we got to know each other better and became a permanent item he gave me his solicitor's details and told me to contact them immediately should anything happen to him." She gave a little sigh. "Knowing what I know now makes me believe he had a premonition that something nasty was about to happen." She gave a much louder sigh this time. "After he was murdered I contacted his solicitor and learned of his father's legacy and was instructed to contact Roger's family solicitor, but when I contacted them I learned there was a family member already making a claim to the legacy. I naturally assumed that put an end to mine as I wasn't a family member, but the man I was speaking with explained that he was in a position to have the other claimant disqualified on legal grounds."

Art had moved to the edge of his seat, enthralled by this last piece of news. "I take it the man you were speaking with was Alexander Mendelson?"

"Yes, that's him, but he had a condition attached to his offer that made it clear he would only assist me if I awarded him ten percent of any legacy that came my way." Art couldn't help but smile. "I take it you agreed to these terms?" She shook her head stubbornly. "No, I didn't, well, not right away, I only agreed after he told me about the potential value of the legacy, and I asked myself what would ten percent of that mean to me? Anyway, he had me in an awkward position as he knew all about my involvement with the detective who had contacted me, not that I *knowingly* did anything to endanger Roger, but we all know how it turned out." Art was on the edge of his seat soaking her story up like a sponge. "This detective you speak of, did he tell you he worked for the Silverman family?" She thought for a moment then shook her head. "No, not in those exact words, he said he was employed by their family solicitors on behalf of the family to find Roger and convince him to return to his family and not disappear again."

Art wriggled upright on his chair. "So this detective you speak of was employed by the same person who had offered to help with your claim, namely Alexander Mendelson. Is that a true reflection of events?" She nodded. "Yes, that seems to be what happened, although I wasn't aware of everything that was going on at the time."

"Did Mendelson give you the name of this other claimant or any hint as to where he lived?" Gina decided to enter the conversation. "No, he didn't," answered Mathews, "he just told me it was a family member, but I naturally assumed it nullified my claim."

Art was beginning to fall for her story. He sensed a ring of truth in the way she expressed herself. "There is only *one* member of that family alive now that young Benjamin is gone, and he's your boyfriend's step-brother Joshua Silverman, also known as Joshua Mendelson, a full blood brother to the man you've been dealing with, Alexander Mendelson. These guys sure know how to keep it in the family."

Mathews was too confused to say anything rational. "You've lost me I'm afraid, I can't keep up with all these family ins and outs." Art couldn't help but smile. "Yes, it does get a bit confusing," agreed Art, "but that's what criminals do, they cause as much confusion as possible to camouflage their activities.?" He stopped talking to take a closer look at his prisoner, he was tempted to believe her story since it offered a perfectly reasonable explanation of events, especially when he combined it with the possibility that she might have been totally unaware of what others had in mind. A good conman could easily have convinced her she was helping Benjamin's family to track him down. The one weakness in her story was the fact that she didn't discuss any of this with young Benjamin, or the police. Art couldn't sort out in his own mind how he felt about her now, but sooner or later he would have to make his mind up and either release her or keep her locked up. Had she been complicit in young Benjamin's murder, or was she just a naïve young lady who had been hoodwinked by a a clever and devious individual? He wasn't sure, but he needed to be sure, in fact he needed to be absolutely certain, and quickly too.

Gina needed the same reassurance. "Why did you not discuss this with your boyfriend before making a secret arrangement with a complete stranger?"

Mathews decided to engage with Gina. "I was swayed by the fact that Roger had never discussed his family with me, he always ducked the issue when I raised it, so I decided, rightly or wrongly, that if he knew his family had tracked him down he might take to the road again and disappear altogether and bring our relationship to an end. I thought it proper that he know how much his family wanted him back so that he could make his own mind up over what to do." Her story sounded so plausible that both Art and Gina were doubting their original suspicions.

Art felt it was time to discuss it with Gina and indicated to her to join him outside. "What's your take on her story, Gina? Do you think her explanation is plausible enough to absolve her of suspicion, or is she just playing a tune on our heart strings?"

Gina cringed at the thought, she was having the same difficulty making her mind up. "I'm not sure, Art; I'm trying to be hard-hearted about everything, but in answer to your question, I'm undecided, although I have a feeling that even a small show of remorse on her part wouldn't go amiss."

Art raised his eyebrow and nodded in agreement. "I'm feeling the same way, but we have to make a decision one way or the other because it's time to get this case in front of the District Attorney." He stopped talking to gather his thoughts. "We have Sharpe all wrapped up and ready to go, Silverman likewise, and the boys in London have arrested Hardwick's killer on sound evidence according to Inspector Stewart. We also have enough evidence to arrest Mendelson as soon as he sets foot on American soil, but Mathews is a difficult one to make a judgement on. She clearly has motive, but that's not intent. The only way to confirm her story is to question Mendelson or that elusive detective who bribed her. Mendelson is the key to all this; he knows who this mystery detective is and needs questioning without delay." Gina patted him on the shoulder by way of agreement. "That sums it up very neatly, Art, so why don't we take what we have to Marcus and see if he can exert more pressure to get Mendelson over here, and if he can't do it then the guys across the pond will have to do it for us."

Art squeezed his brow. "We're in a difficult position just now, Gina. We can't take that young lady's case any further with all these loose ends. The problem is that it's her word against ours and we don't have conclusive evidence of her guilt. Thankfully it's not our responsibility to get Mendelson over here, so Marcus and those above him had better get their fingers out. Let's get Mathews locked away again and see what Marcus thinks we should to do about it."

34

Having been already been tackled by Art the Mendelson affair, Delgado wasn't very affable. "At the risk of repeating myself, and I don't know why I should, I have already e-mailed Mendelson on your suggestion *and* emphasised his client's need for legal support, but we haven't heard diddly-squat from him or his company."

He threw his arms in the air out of frustration. "I can't make the guy contact us if his mind is made up not to, nor can I make him get his ass over just to please us, so what else am I expected to do?" Art was in no mood for puzzles. "Get on the goddamned phone and demand that his client be provided with proper legal representation. This isn't something he can choose to do; he is legally obliged to fulfil his duty under the terms of his charter, so he has no choice in the matter."

Delgado pointed and accusing finger at Art. "Just keep your ass in that damned chair and listen up." He grabbed his desk phone and hit on the pre-set number. "Alex Mendelson, how may I help you?"

Delgado took a deep breath and got straight to the point. "This is Captain Delgado from the NYPD, and to get straight to the point Mister Mendelson I must insist that you get yourself over to Manhattan and represent your client Joshua Silverman. He has named you as his legal counsel and as such he requires you to support him on his now imminent court appearance."

Art was eyeing Delgado's like a snake about to strike, although it was obvious from the tone of his voice that his boss was in no mood for taking prisoners but was perilously close to blowing his top, and it showed on his angry face set. "You sound rather agitated, Captain Delgado so I'll be as brief as I can." There was a gentle throat clearing before he went on. "I have not heard from Joshua for some time so I'm unsure about what is happening with him. Perhaps you would explain his situation since he's currently in your care." Delgado had to curb his temper, but he needed to be careful and not give too much away. What he needed was a carefully tailored response. "If you were fulfilling your duty for your client you would be aware that he has been charged with conspiracy to murder, and while this is a complicated and ongoing investigation, the fact remains that he is shortly to appear in court to make his plea. And while your client denies his involvement in any crime he still requires legal representation for his court appearance and has named you as his legal representative. It is therefore imperative that you make yourself available to brief him, and the court advisors, prior to his appearance before a judge. Need I say more?" There was a seriously long silence before Mendelson chose to reply.

"Thank you for your advice, Captain Delgado, but I am well aware of my responsibilities. Indeed I have it in mind to visit Joshua just as soon as I can. I had to make a short trip to Brazil on his behalf to do with his business interests there so I'm a little behind schedule with some other work, however you may expect me to be with you just as soon as I can free up my diary. I would estimate visiting him within the next three or four days. It would be helpful if I could speak with Joshua while we're waiting for that to happen." Delgado cringed and bared his teeth, but he managed to control himself and stay calm. "Your client has refused to behave as a remand prisoner is required to under our laws, as a result of this his actions have caused considerable unease and grief among our staff, and as a consequence of this surly and unreasonable behaviour his remand facilities have been suspended until further notice. This is not a debatable issue, Mister Mendelson, so please do not attempt to make it one."

"That being the case, Captain Delgado, I see no reason to prolong this conversation. I will see you sometime soon." The line died without Delgado having an opportunity to challenge what was said, he slammed the phone down in anger. "Supercilious bastard," he snapped, "that guy needs a good seeing to, and I'm personally going to do just that as soon as we get our hands on him." When he looked up he saw a big smile on Art's face with Gina looking every bit as happy, but it was Art who sang his praises. "I thought you handled that really well, Marcus. You gave the sleezy son-of-a bitch something to think about, and it's obvious from what he said that he doesn't suspect we're on to him." Delgado looked well pleased.. "Thanks, Art, I appreciate the sentiment, can't say I didn't enjoy it either. I never did like that stuck up bastard from I first spoke with him. If he's guilty of what we're accusing him of I hope he rots in hell" Gina got to her feet and clapped her hands with a big smile on her face. "Well done, Chief, that cheered me up no end."

"Okay, okay, enough of the brown nosing, "muttered Delgado, "I can't take any more of it, and it's way out of character for you two anyway as you're usually kicking my ass, not licking it." They all had a little chuckle before things settled down, and although Delgado was pleased with their reaction he would never make it known, not to them anyway, it wasn't in his make-up to do so.

"Do you trust Mendelson when he says he's coming here?" asked Gina. Delgado scratched his head. "That's a very debatable point, Gina. Everything we've learned from Silverman tells us he's up to his eyes in this swindle, and if that proves to be the case then what is there

to trust? I wouldn't trust him to see my Granny across the road."
Another few moments of light-hearted laughter greeted his remark and
there was more to come from Marcus.. "Of course if he doesn't follow
through with his intended visit then we'll have to convince Ian Stewart
to do the needful and arrest him, but that will mean a long and drawn
out extradition process which is in no one's interest. We need him
over here, and damn soon too."

Art couldn't wait to get involved. "Silverman needs to up the ante, it's
in his best interest to have Mendelson over here. I think I have him
where I want him just now, and I've him persuaded to put pressure on
his brother. I don't sense any great brotherly love between them, not
now that Silverman is nursing a massive grudge at being discarded by
his brother over his claim to his step-father's legacy. I have him
primed and ready for a taste of revenge if we offer him the chance to
get it." Delgado looked interested. "If you have him so primed up, Art,
why don't you make the idiot an offer he can't refuse, without actually
giving him anything of course, except maybe a promise or two that can
easily be forgotten with a short term lapse of memory."

Art got to his feet and tapped Gina on the arm. "I think I have him
primed enough already, but he might be more easily swayed by a pretty
female face like yours rather than my ugly mug, after all it's been a
while since he's seen one. I have him in the right frame of mind so I'm
sure you'll be able to clinch it" Gina gave him a surly look. "I like to
think I'm more than just a pretty face round here." Having said her
piece she got up and stormed from the office with Art in hot pursuit,
and Delgado shaking his head in silence.

Gina was already in the interview room with a guard for company
while waiting for Silverman to be brought in. Art was next door
watching through the viewing window in hopeful expectation, but

neither of them had long to wait as Silverman was marched in wearing an angry face. "What the hell do you people want from me now?" he snarled. Gina gave him a sympathetic look. "Let's not fall out before we've even got to know each other, Joshua. I'm only here for your statement and an informal chat, so you have nothing to worry about. The recorder isn't even switched on."

"What sort of informal chat are you talking about?" he asked.

"The sort that helps you get your revenge on your turncoat brother." she told him." Silverman frowned. "Why would I want to do that?" he asked.

"Let's not play games, Joshua, Lieutenant Gardiner has told you how your brother edged you out of your step-father's legacy and dragged Claire Mathews in to replace you. Your brother knows it will much easier to talk her out of her money than to try the same scam on you."

Silverman leaned across the table with an indication that he was interested, but his eyes remained downcast, almost like he was trying to hide from Gina's penetrating scrutiny. "What exactly are you after? And don't give me any crap, what's in this for you lot?"

"It's very simple, Joshua, we want you to get Mendelson over here to provide the legal representation you require for your trial, and we want him here like yesterday, not next bloody month. All I'm after is a straight yes or no answer from you. If the answer is yes, then we will get you the top available lawyer on our books to replace your brother. We will also make it known to the judiciary that you co-operated with our investigation and helped bring other conspirators to justice, which will earn you some brownie points. Now tell me, are you willing to do this or m I wasting my time?"

"What are you not telling me?" asked Silverman, "why are you so driven to have Alex over here?"

Gina knew she couldn't hold back any longer. "We want him here so we can arrest him for running this scam. We know he set this whole thing up, it's as simple as that, and this offer gives you the chance to enjoy the sweet taste of revenge and ensure that your brother gets a longer sentence than you do." She ran her fingers through her hair. "You have five minutes to make your mind up, Joshua, starting now." She rolled her shirt sleeve back and watched the second hand on her watch tick by. Silverman had no watch to look at, but he knew he had to respond quickly if he was going to accept her offer.

"I don't owe my scheming brother any favours, I believe he's trying to have me carry the can for everything he planned, but he doesn't know me as well as he thinks. Anyway, we've been apart too long to be called brothers." He cast his eyes down at his badly chewed fingernails while taking time to think. Gina was watching him like a hawk; her heart was beating fast with expectation. She thought she had him on board, but thinking wasn't knowing. What she did know however was how important Silverman's answer would be to their investigation, so she had her fingers crossed behind her back.

"I want more than just a good solicitor," announced Silverman, "I want a guarantee of a reduced sentence." If there was one thing Gina feared would happen, this was it, a demand for leniency that she could not meet. She decided to be up-front about it. "I can't give you any such guarantee, Joshua. That would be up to the judiciary, not the police, we can only make recommendations, but I would expect, since you are not guilty of actually murdering anyone yourself, that our recommendation would be taken very seriously by both the District

Attorney and the Judge." She waited in growing expectation for his reaction as Silverman tilted back on his chair and gazed up at the ceiling. He was waiting for her to say more but Gina had already made her mind up not to say another word until she got his answer, and she would let him stew for as long as it took to get it.

Observing this encounter from next door Art was enthralled by what was he was seeing, Gina was making all the right noises, but like her, he too was eagerly waiting for what came next.

Silverman righted himself in his chair and looked about to say something, but the expression on his face told his watchers that he was still undecided. Gina decided to prompt him a little and eased her shirt sleeve back and tapped the face of her watch with her finger. Silverman reacted immediately. "You people are always in a fuckin' hurry, but don't you try pressurising me because it won't work." Gina stood up. "In that case you might as well go back to your cell."

She turned to the guard, but before she could say anything, Silverman stopped her. "You're asking me to make a very big decision just like that," he snapped his fingers noisily, "but I need to think carefully before you people take advantage of my weak position." Gina gave a loud sigh. "Nobody here is trying to take advantage of you, Joshua, but this can't go on forever, I need your decision and I need it now, your time is up I'm afraid."

Silverman wriggled his ass on the seat. "Can you fix it for me to do my time in a softer prison. I don't want to be stuck inside with a bunch of lifers?" Gina rubbed her brow. She suddenly remembered what Marcus had said about a short term lapse of memory. "Okay, Joshua, I think that can be arranged, but your time is up, so speak up or shut up, I have more important things to do."

312

Silverman had his hands clasped in front of him pray-like, but he suddenly dropped them. "Okay, okay, we have a deal. When do you want me to contact my brother?" Gina, whose hands had been clasped tightly under the table released their tight grasp out of sheer relief. "That's very sensible, Joshua,. I think you've made a wise decision. We'll let you know when to phone you brother and we'll give you a scripted set of guidelines to stick to. All we have to do now is take your statement that records your decision, then it's back to your cell." She turned to the guard. "Get our prisoner whatever food he needs before you lock him up."

While Gina had been at logger-heads with Silverman the subject of their conversation, Alexander Mendelson, was making a very secretive phone call. It was so secret that even though his staff had knocked off the day he had left his office and gone to a public phone booth some four blocks away. When he got there he pulled a card from his pocket, dialled the number scrawled on the back and tapped his fingers impatiently against the side of the booth while waiting for a reply.

"Jack Benson, how can I help you?"

"It's me, Jack, Alex," Mendelson began, "we need to talk about our young lady friend." Benson came straight back at him. "I thought you said we were not to contact each other until everything for Claire's claim is completed. Your voice tells me there is something amiss, am I right?"

"Nothing I can't handle, Jack, I'm just a bit worried that I haven't heard anything from her for a while, that's all, and when I try contacting her she doesn't pick up. Have you heard from her lately?"

"No I haven't," retorted Benson, "but why should I when our

arrangement was to have no further contact unless it was absolutely necessary. To be perfectly honest I don't know what your gripe is or why you're phoning me like this, all you asked me to do was stay in contact with you over my client's welfare." Mendelson gave a nervous little cough. "No need to get upset, Jack, so stop rabbiting on, but to put your mind at rest I'm only phoning to find out if you've heard from her since we last spoke." There was short interval before Benson came back at him. "Why are you so up-tight about her anyway? I get the impression she's more than capable of looking after herself, are you telling me she needs a chaperone?"

"No, it's nothing like that. I'm just worried that she seems to have dropped off the radar, but I think your probably right, she's most likely just keeping her head down." Benson seconded the idea. "I agree, and I suggest we leave it like that until she has her inheritance, especially as I don't see any reason to be concerned about her."

"Point taken, Jack," conceded Mendelson, "you're probably right, just forget I said anything and get back to work, which is what I'm about to do. I can wait a few more days for her to get back in touch, but not much longer." He hung up and headed back to his office, his mind filled with doubts about Mathews and what she was up to.

35

Art had both hands buried deep in his trouser pockets and was wearing a look of grave concern as he propped himself up against Delgado's door frame. "I have a problem, Marcus, I don't know whether to accept Mathews explanation of events or not," he confessed, "there are moments when I'm convinced she's as innocent as a virgin, then along comes something in her explication that makes me doubt her recall of events all over again. She can be so plausible at times that she almost makes me feel sorry I arrested her. I'm not sure what to make of her, and neither is Gina."

Delgado looked every bit as concerned and was quick to voice it. "The way I see it she's either guilty of complicity or she's not, she can't be both. We have to go where the evidence takes us. I suggest you go through the evidence again with a fine tooth comb and see if there's anything we've missed."

Art pushed himself away from the door frame. "That's exactly the problem, Marcus. The evidence is such that she may be innocent, or she may be guilty. We know she provided vital information to a third party that led to the death of her boyfriend and his companion, she freely admits that, but she claims she did so in the belief that she was helping her boyfriend's family and not setting him up to be killed. Unfortunately, we know nothing about this bloody detective who got the information from her that was passed to the killers. We don't even know if *he* was aware of the eventual outcome of his actions. If I had to make a guess I would say Hardwick set the whole thing up on instructions from Mendelson, but Hardwick is dead, so if my theory proves to be right then Mendelson is the only one who can tell us what happened, and the only one who can absolve Mathews of complicity." He went back to leaning against the door post.

Delgado covered his lips behind curled fingers as he made his own effort at solving the issues besetting his Lieutenant, but even he couldn't come up with an answer. "So how the hell do we unravel this little conundrum, Art? We can't bring Mendelson in for questioning when he's not here, and we need to get this case to court without delay, but before we can do that we need to know if Mathews is a witness for the prosecution or on charges of complicity."

"I have a plan in mind that might give us what we need, Marcus. It involves Miss Mathews, so a lot depends on her willingness to participate, but why would she say no when it's designed to clear her name and at the same time give us more evidence to convict Mendelson?"

"Is there anything in this plan that I shouldn't know about? Or is it on the straight and level?" asked Delgado. The warning grimace on Art's face gave him his answer. "Let's put it this way, Marcus, you might want to put your ear-muffs on for a while as I'm not sure how it will end up, but I have to try something, or we'll never get this bloody case sorted."

"I don't think I want to hear any more, Art, just get out of here and do what you do best." Art threw him a mock salute and headed off, hoping against the odds that Gina wasn't caught up in something more important as he was about to have Mathews brought up for interview again and he needed another officer in attendance to keep it legal. It turned out Gina was otherwise involved, and he had to settle for Vince, which was a bit concerning as Vince wasn't fully up to date with the Mathews situation. "Just go with the flow, Vince," Art advised him, "I know you're not fully in the picture so just leave the patter to me, for the most part anyway." When they walked in on her Mathews looked like she'd been caught in a force ten gale, her hair was all over the place and she was in a general state of disarray. Art stopped just inside the door and stared at her wondering what had taken place. "Are you feeling okay, Claire?" he asked. "You look like you've just gone ten rounds with Mike Tyson." The door guard gave him the answer. "Nothing untoward, Lieutenant, Miss Mathews has just come in from the exercise yard and it's blowing a gale out there." Art waved him away. "You can wait outside for now." He turned back to face his prisoner. "Sorry about the weather, Claire, it caught me out the other day as well, so you have my sympathies." Vince reached out to switch on the recorder unit.

"Leave that, Vince, this is an informal interview." Art put a reassuring hand on his shoulder while addressing Mathews. "I'm here to try and help you, Claire. You have insisted since your arrest that you're not guilty of the charges laid against you, even though most of the evidence we have following a thorough investigation has the ability to countermand your story. Our problem is that you are unable to identify this so-called detective you claim approached you on the pretext of reuniting your boyfriend with his family. How are we to prove your claim when you can't tell us the name of this individual or where to find him? You do see our problem, don't you?" Mathews looked a forlorn figure, and she could think of nothing else to say to help prove her innocence. Everything she had to say had been said, and it hadn't changed a thing. "We've been through all this before, Lieutenant, and every time I've defended myself against your charges

317

you've just brushed my explanations aside. What more am I to do to convince you?"

"All you've offered is words, Claire, nothing concrete, no witnesses or anything to substantiate your claim."

Mathews buried her face in her hands and sobbed bitterly, sadly, when she raised her head again she had nothing else to offer in her defence, except tears. "Words are all I have; I can't offer you anything else, can you not see that?" She was close to crying again, but her emotionally charged words had little effect of Art, although her general demeanour did. What Art saw in her vigorous defence convinced him she wasn't lying. The time was right to get her onside. "I'm about to offer you a chance to prove your innocence, Claire. A chance to prove that you were not in cahoots with Mendelson to legitimise your claim to the old boys legacy at the expense of his step-son."

He stopped talking and locked eyes with his prisoner. "You won't get another chance, Claire. This is it, but you have to do things our way or it's no deal. So think about it for a moment or two and give me a straight answer, yes or no?"

Mathews covered her mouth with both hands and closed her eyes really tight, but she wasted no time in agreeing to Art's offer. "How can I say no to such offer when all I want to do is prove my innocence, just tell me what I have to do to help find the people who killed my boyfriend." Art gave her a sympathetic smile and a friendly pat on the hand. "I think that's a wise decision, Claire, and the fact that you've agreed so readily adds to my own conviction that you *are* innocent. That said, we need to prove it." He sat back and folded his arms. "What I need from you isn't very difficult. There are two distinct and important aspects to the plan. The first is to get Mendelson to

318

confess to his involvement in what has taken place, while the second is to get him over here so we can arrest him." He stopped talking to check her reaction, and what he saw there convinced him to carry on. "To achieve these aims you must convince him that you no longer need his assistance to legalise your claim to the legacy. You do this by telling him that you have been advised by a senior legal advisor that under all current circumstances you are the rightful claimant, and as such you require all documentation relating to the legacy to be handed over to your solicitor. If he argues the point, which I expect him to, you must tell him he can read all about it in the Financial Times as they are keen to publish your fairy-tale, rags to riches story. Drive your challenge home by asking him what he has done to justify his demand for ten percent of your legacy when there is no one else with a legal claim. We need him to confess to ordering the murder of your boyfriend and his companion as a means of justifying his demand."

Young Vince picked up on the theme more readily than Art thought he would and decided to have a say. "You will be more likely to succeed with someone like Mendelson if you come across as a hard-nosed money grabber, someone who will go to any lengths to get what they want. If he believes you're of a similar mind set to him he will feel more obliged to confess in order to secure his cut. There is no other way he can justify his demand, and if he believes you're taking advice from someone who specialises in legacy law he'll be more obliged to see you as a serious threat."

Art was happy with the way things were going but he wanted to get back into the conversation. "For the plan to work, Claire, Mendelson must suspect that if he presses you hard enough he'll get you to pay up, so you must insist that he sign a document laying out the terms agreed by you both to safeguard your interests from any further claims by him or his company, and you must ensure that he does this in front of you personally in a public place where you will feel safe. Somewhere like a hotel lounge where we will be able to control events." He stopped for a moment to reassure her. "Your conversation will be recorded, and we will have armed officers in attendance during your meeting with Mendelson, if it takes place and you will be protected and perfectly safe. In the event that Mendelson confesses during stage one, there will then be no need for any meeting as he will be arrested the minute he arrives here." He slumped back in his chair again. "Is this something you think you can handle, Claire, or are we asking too much of you?" Mathews wasted no time in agreeing. "I'm quite capable of handling a telephone conversation, Lieutenant, even a difficult one, and I can see that it's in everyone's interest to drag a confession out of Mendelson, so that's what I intend to do. I want my boyfriend's killers punished for their crimes, properly, and painfully punished." She paused for a few moments to find the right words to express herself. "I want proper justice delivered, meaningful justice, not just a slap on the wrist." Her tone of voice was nothing short of venomous, so much so that it came as a shock to Art, even more so as it revealed an irreducible element of her character that she had never openly displayed before. He wondered if she had deliberately kept it under wraps, although that thought was quickly dispensed with when he got back to the matter at hand. "You sound very determined, Claire, and that's a good thing, but you must remember to keep your composure when dealing with Mendelson as he'll be scrutinising every word you say very closely."

"I think you can rely on me to stay focussed, Lieutenant." Art sensed a slight element of over-confidence in her attitude that worried him. He decided to remedy it. "We need to get this absolutely right,

Claire, so to help prepare you for phoning Mendelson we will run a number of role-play exercises today, with Vince on an extension playing the role of Mendelson and you and Gina in another room with you making the calls. A few practice calls should highlight any issues that need ironing out. Is that okay?"

Mathews gathered her brow. "I'm not sure all that fuss is necessary but I suppose it can't do any harm, so why not, let's just get on with it." Art got to his feet. "Okay, Claire, I'll go and set it up while you and Vince have a coffee or something." He hurried off leaving Vince to deal with their prisoner.

Some two hours later Vince knocked on Art's door and breezed in looking very chirpy. Art pointed to a chair. "Sit down, Vince, and tell me how things went with the role play."

Vince pulled a chair out and dropped into it. "I did my best with the brief you gave me, Lieutenant, and while she did hesitate occasionally there were absolutely no serious issues. She is more than capable of overcoming the unexpected during a forced conversation and I really did try to be devious and underhand to catch her out, bearing in mind the objective, but she is very astute and very persistent, she's like a dog with a bone but very capable and confident."

Art was grinning ear to ear. "That's all I need, Vince. I think we should set up her call with Mendelson right away while she's still wired up with her role plays. What's your take on it?" Vince nodded his agreement. "If it was down to me that's exactly what I would do."

Art got to his feet. "Okay, Vince, let's go and get it done."

36

Gina was sitting beside Art on one side of his desk with Claire Mathews on the opposite side. Art handed Mathews her cell phone that had been prepared to enable the planned conversation to be recorded. "It's time to get busy, Claire, time to prove your innocence, but if for some reason you get stuck for something to say just pretend that the signal has dropped off and you can't hear him, that should give you time to think." Mathews didn't say anything, she just ran through her contacts for Mendelson's number and hit the dial button. They got connected almost immediately and from his quick response Mendelson's own phone had identified her as the caller. "I was beginning to think you had gone into hiding when you failed to respond to my calls. It's important that we stay connected, Claire, especially as we're getting close to the end game."

Mathews deliberately held back and didn't answer right away. "Did you hear what I said?" he prompted. Mathews raised the phone to her mouth. "Why do you think it's important we stay in touch?" she asked, pretending to be puzzled. "What the hell is wrong with you?" demanded Mendelson, "have you suddenly acquired an attitude or something? Do you not want to become rich? Are you not interested in your inheritance?"

"Of course I'm interested in my inheritance, very interested in fact. I just don't see what it has to do with you anymore, which is the purpose behind this call." A protracted silence followed her remark before Mendelson was fit to respond, but when he did he sounded up tight and aggressive. "You can ditch the attitude, Mathews, I'm in no mood for silly games. It has taken a major effort on my part to get us to where we are, and you know I'm the only one who can formalise your claim, you also know what it will cost since we already agreed to that deal.

"Well it's like this, Mister Mendelson," argued Mathews, "I sought advice from another source since we last spoke; a barrister who deals specifically in legacy law, and he tells me that my boyfriend's Will is perfectly legal and my claim to his estate is undeniable. So your so called deal with me is no longer necessary, nor does it stand up to scrutiny since you've done absolutely nothing to warrant such a hideously large payment. I accept that I must reimburse you for your services as the executer of the original Will lodged by Ben's father, but legally I'm not obliged to pay you a penny more." The tension between them was almost palpable, and the silence that ensued was in itself quite threatening. Against all expectation when he finally got round to speaking again his voice was surprisingly calm and controlled, but no less threatening. "Don't mess with me young lady, that's not something you should consider doing, and don't you dare attempt to renege on our deal or you will not enjoy the outcome, and that's a firm promise I can assure you." Mathews smiled across the desk at Art; she seemed to be enjoying the role she was playing. "I have no wish to fall out with you, Mister Mendelson, I know you've been quite useful at times but even you must see that it's preposterous to expect such a massive pay-out for having done so little to justify it. In all honesty, I don't see what you ever did to warrant such a large pay-off?" There was a little throat clearing cough from the other end before Mendelson got going. "You have absolutely no idea what I've done on your behalf. The things I have done to justify your position as the legal claimant could cost me dearly, but I'm not going into the detail of that right now, suffice to say that it would absolutely ruin me if it ever got out." Mathews got straight back at him. "I'm afraid that's your problem, not mine, as I see it you have done very little for me or my claim, in fact my own solicitor has been much more involved and deserves a lot more consideration than you do." Mendelson completely lost the plot and yelled into the phone with a fierce verbal assault. "You stupid fucking girl, who the hell do you think removed the opposition for you? Do you think they just walked away quite willingly and left you to inherit the Silverman empire? Do you believe that low-life idiot Benson organised it all for you? How bloody stupid are you? Benson only does what I ask of him, nothing more."

Mathews took a deep breath before replying. "I haven't a clue what you're rabbiting on about, but it's of no concern anyway. I think we're through here, Mister Mendelson. I don't see that we have anything else to discuss." Mendelson spluttered his rage at her. "Don't you dare hang up on me, young lady. Are you so stupid that you can't see that what happened to your boyfriend was planned beforehand to get him out of your way? Who do you think persuaded him to make a Will in the first place, and who do you think planned and organised his sudden departure from the scene to put you in line as a claimant? Who was it who took all the risks?" He paused for effect. "It was me you silly bloody girl, me, yours truly, and you must pay heavily for it, and you will do just that because if you don't I'll take every penny of your inheritance away from you by telling the police I was following your instructions." Although Mathews had been hoping to hear something like this, she was shocked to the core by the extent of Mendelson's admissions. It was only then that she remembered about having to force him into a meeting. "Did you really do all that just for me?" she asked, in a thankful, little girl voice. "All that just to help make little me rich?" She waited a few moments before going on. "I think I misjudged you, Mister Mendelson, but if it *was* you who got rid of my boyfriend, as you claim, then I do feel I'm indebted to you, but I'm not willing to agree to anything unless we meet face to face and discuss a more realistic level of reimbursement. And after what you just said I don't trust you, but I want to look into your eye when we agree terms, and I want a signed statement of the facts to legalise any agreement we come to so that neither you, nor your company, can come begging for more later on. And one final requirement, I want us to meet in a public place where I will feel safe. If we can't do that then I'm out of here to await my change of fortune in glorious sunshine?"

"Why the hell do you want to meet up? Meeting in public can be very dangerous in the current circumstances. You must understand that I did what I did to justify your claim, and I intend to get what I was promised without argument, or something close to it." Mathews cut in on him before he got finished. "I want to look you in the eye when we negotiate our settlement, and you must sign a document to legalise that agreement or you get absolutely nothing at all, end of conversation. I will be staying in the Artezan Hotel in Manhattan where I wish our meeting to take place. I will only be there for four nights starting tomorrow, after that I'm heading off to warmer climes. So you have until midday tomorrow to advise me of your arrival and get your ass into gear or I'm gone. You already know how to get in touch so take my advice and don't miss this chance as you won't get another. Goodbye, Mister Mendelson." She disconnected with a loud sigh of relief. "My God that was frightening." she confessed.

Art, who had been engrossed by the proceedings shook his head in wonderment, he was totally mesmerised by her performance. She had

Mendelson right where she wanted him and had very cleverly worked him into a corner, and a tight corner at that. All they had to do now was wait for him to take the bait. "That was a brilliant performance, Claire," he gushed excitedly, "I can't believe you haven't done this before?" She gave him a timid, nervy smile, but it was obvious from her slumped demeanour and her shaky hand that her performance had taken a heavy toll on her nerves. "I was so nervous that I wasn't sure I could see it through, especially when he admitted what he'd been up to. I found it so frightening to know I was talking with a man who openly confessed to ending my boyfriend's life. Talking with him like that made him so close it was very unnerving."

Art reached out and took her hand in his. "You did brilliantly, Claire, so just relax now and enjoy your moment of triumph, because that's exactly what it was, a total triumph. I have no doubt Mendelson will agree to meet up with you, and when he does we will be on hand to take him into custody, and we will prepare you for that little ordeal before it takes place. You will also be wearing a wire so we can hear everything that goes on and be ready to step in if needed, and you will have at least five undercover police officers within arm's reach." He was pleased to see the colour returning to her face, and she was beginning to look much more like her old self.

"We intend keeping you in custody for now, Claire, but it's a protective custody until this whole thing is finished with and we know you are safe. I hope you understand." She nodded quite briskly and didn't question it. Art reached out and patted her hand again. "I'm off to check the recording. I need to know exactly what Mendelson has confessed to that will stand up in court and check if there's anything else we need to do to guarantee a conviction." He patted her shoulder as he got up to leave. "Vince will take you to the canteen for some refreshments and arrange for Gina to accompany you for the

326

remainder of the day. If there's anything special you want to do, Claire, just say so, I'm sure Gina will be happy to oblige, within reason of course, and you may consider yourself to no longer be a suspect, Mendelson's admissions and your responses make that obvious to everyone here." He got up and walked away, eager to collect his boss and check the recording to see if there was for any way out for Mendelson.

By the time they finished they had both listened to the recording twice over, with Delgado almost euphoric over the result. "Your role-play sessions seem to have done the trick, Art, that was a very compelling and evidential conversation with your young lady sticking rigidly to the script." Art shook his head in denial. "I don't think the role plays had much to do with it, Marcus, young Mathews did it all by her sweet little self, she didn't need a script. Vince and I had nothing to do but just sit and listen." Delgado waved his remark aside. "This is all down to your foresight and planning, Art, and I can assure you there's enough evidence on that recording for a conviction in front of any jury, so well done, you can give yourself a pat on the back and don't be so bloody coy."

He stopped talking and got to his feet. "So what's the plan? Where do we go from here?"

"We wait, Marcus, we wait, we wait for Mendelson to make contact with Mathews and agree to meet her at the Artezan Hotel right here on our very doorstep in Manhattan. She's being booked in there as we speak for four nights starting midday tomorrow, after that we cross our fingers and hope for the best. Claire has agreed to go through with the meeting to see if we can learn any more about Benson's involvement and get another confession or two. She's a brave young lady."

Delgado headed for the door, but he turned back before he got there. "We have enough evidence on that recording to have Inspector Stewart lift him right now if he turns down the offer of a visit to our beloved city." Art shook his head. "I want him here, Marcus," he said empathetically. "I want to see his ugly mug when I put the cuffs on him, surly bastard that he is." Delgado looked a little bit mischievous. "I don't usually volunteer for street duty, Art, but I want to be part of this, so include me in the support team, okay." Art gave him the thumbs up. "Glad to have you on board, Marcus. If he turns up for the meeting you can read him his rights. If he doesn't, then it's down to Ian Stewart to do the needful."

Marcus was laughing all the way to the door. "Rights," he muttered, he won't have any goddamned rights if I get my hands on him."

37

Gina cast her eye over the hotel room with their personal security in mind and made a beeline for the bed directedly facing the door. It was a sensible precaution against the likelihood of any late night intruders. She was mindful of how ruthless Mendelson could be and how determined he was to get his own way and needed to be on her guard in case he hired someone to pay them a visit. The fact that Claire had told him where she was staying and how long she would be there added to her concerns, although she had been right to do so.

To back up their security Gina had instructed the hotel management not to release their room number to anyone and to warn her if anyone asked for it. Setting these precautions aside she felt safe in the knowledge that there were five armed detectives milling about in the downstairs foyer in readiness for the meeting with Mendelson to take place, the problem was that nobody knew if such a meeting would ever take place.

Mathews had just sat down by the window when she decided to question what they were doing. "Do you really think Mendelson will take the bait, or are we wasting our time?" Gina was in no position to foretell what would happen, nor was anyone else for that matter. The only person who could to that was Mendelson, and not wanting to dishearten Mathews with the atmosphere already tense she glided very neatly over the topic. "Let's not get worked up over something we can't control, Claire. You're here and ready to meet Mendelson if and when he calls, and we have five armed detectives in the foyer downstairs ready to keep an eye on us anytime we put in an appearance. All we can do for now is enjoy our little break and wait for the big bad wolf to call."

She pressed her hands against her stomach. "I don't know About you but I'm feeling quite hungry so why don't we go downstairs for a coffee and a sandwich, at least it will get us out of this stuffy room for a while." Mathews got to her feet and headed for the door. "Good idea, Gina, a sandwich wouldn't go amiss." Gina pointed to her phone that was laying on the bed. "I think you'd better take that with you." She added a light-hearted giggle in an effort to lighten the mood, the last thing she wanted was Claire getting up tight and fretful.

Claire went back and picked up her phone with a shake of her head and they headed for the elevator together.

Down in the foyer Art was strategically placed with the elevator in full view. He was responsible for warning the other detectives anytime Gina or Claire put in an appearance, and they needed to be on their toes in case Mendelson turned up without warning. They also had the arrivals lounge at JFK covered by a couple of officers who were tasked to watch for Mendelson's arrival, but he was to be afforded free passage to his meeting in the hope that Claire might drag more confessions from him.

As they left the elevator Gina spotted Art and gave him a slight nod before leading Claire to an out of the way two-seater table that Art was able to cover. Thankfully the foyer wasn't very busy, but Gina's eyes were constantly scanning the room for anything untoward.

They didn't stay there for long and were back in their room twenty minutes later. Both accepting that they were in for a very long and boring day, which for now at least seemed to be passing without incident. That was how it remained until seven o'clock that evening when Claire's phone came to life. Snatching it up she paled slightly when she saw Mendelson's name on the readout. But nodding to Gina she took a deep breath before accepting the call. "Mr Mendelson," she began, "how nice of you to call." She heard a throat clearing cough from the other end before Mendelson got down to business. "I'm in the main lounge of your hotel, Miss Mathews and would appreciate your agreement to have this meeting right away as I have a private flight back to England scheduled for this evening. Would you like me to come to your room or would you prefer to meet me in the bar?"

Claire had her phone on speaker and when she looked to Gina for help who mouthed the word foyer at her. "The main foyer would be preferable," she replied, "I feel much safer in a public place with others around me."

"So be it then," agreed Mendelson, "but this must be a private meeting between you and me and no one else, so don't try anything silly. Let's meet ten minutes from now in the foyer." Gina gave her the thumbs up, but Mathews had something else on her mind. "We have only met you once before so how am I supposed to recognise you?" she asked. "You can leave that to me, I know exactly what *you* look like." His admission sent a cold shiver through Claire's body making her feel jittery and vulnerable. "Ten minutes it is then." She agreed, before disconnecting and tossing her phone on the bed like it had just burnt her fingers. Gina noted the strained look on her face and realised she might be having second thoughts and might even renege at the last minute. She had already texted Art while Claire was on the phone and warned him that Mendelson was in the hotel and had made contact, but she needed to deal with Claire nerves and convince her that she was in no danger and must go ahead with the meeting. Added to this she needed to test her wire to confirm the signal was carrying.

While this was going on Art was eyeballing a tall, lean looking individual in a light grey suit who had just been on his mobile. He watched him as he made his way towards the receptionist and ambled over to stand within a few feet of him. He could hardly miss the strangers English accent when he asked for Claire Mathews room number, telling Art that he had his man. He was sorely tempted to grab he guy by the collar right then and wheel him out to the Paddy Wagon, but he pushed the temptation aside, he needed to let the meeting take place if they were to gain anything for their efforts.

A few metres away Delgado was conscious that Art was on his feet, and he kept him in sight as he drifted in the direction of a man in a grey suit who was talking with the receptionist. Experience told him what was happening, and he immediately checked that the other detectives were alert and aware of what was happening. He then left his seat and wandered over to the main entrance like he was looking to meet someone, taking up a suitable position to block any escape. The other two detectives took up similar positions, with one at the rear entrance leading to the car park, and the other loitering near the foot of the stairs close to the elevator. The receptionist had already informed the enquirer that it wasn't permitted to give out room numbers but agreed to pass a message on to their guest by phone. Mendelson waved her offer aside and told her he would catch up with his friend later and having spotted a table in a secluded corner he made a beeline for it.

Within a matter of seconds everyone involved had their eyes firmly glued on Claire Mathews as she stepped out from the elevator. She looked a little anxious as she surveyed the foyer, hopeful that

Mendelson would make his presence known with a wave of his hand or something. Which was exactly what happened, but it sent a cold shiver down her spine as she made her way towards him. To be fair to him Mendelson had the good manners to get to his feet when she joined him, offering her a friendly handshake in greeting.

"You didn't waste any time getting here, Mister Mendelson." Mendelson checked his surroundings before answering; he was clearly very wary. "I'm fortunate to have a private plane at my disposable but let's not be so formal, just call me Alex please." Mathews squared her shoulders. "Mister Mendelson rolls more easily off my tongue, thank you, but let's get down to business as I have other things to be doing." She leaned back in her chair and folded her arms. "I know you think our original agreement still stands, but my entitlement to Benjamin legacy is now beyond reproach, so your claim for such a huge payment no longer passes the litmus test. I will of course make a nominal payment to your company, that's only fair for the time and effort you have put in, but that's as far as I'm willing to go."

Mendelson's eyes narrowed menacingly. "Don't mess with me girl, that's a very dangerous thing to do. Now you listen up and listen well; you *will* make good on our original deal, or you will suffer the consequences." Mathews felt a cold chill run up her spine. "Don't threaten me, Mister Mendelson, you're a lawyer not a thug, and while you might act tough, you're still only a lawyer." Mendelson lips tightened into a threatening sneer and his breathing became noticeably laboured. "I don't make idle threats, Miss Mathews. You *will* make good on the ten percent we agreed, or you will never get to enjoy your ninety percent. Do you understand what I'm telling you?"

"You're threatening me again, Mister Mendelson. If you do that once more I will be forced to call the police." Mendelson moved his head from side to side. "You really are a silly little girl." He was grinning widely at the thought. "You have no idea what I've done to secure that damned legacy for you. You're just a naive little child who is out of her depth. Do you honestly believe that somebody murdered your boyfriend and his pal just by chance? Think on girl, you were complicit in both of those murders. It was you who set them up by telling my man Nick Clark where to find them. He in turn passed that information straight to Hardwick and Sharpe who gave your friends a little treat for their supper. The silly boys thought it was a gift from the burger bar manager." He stopped talking to widen his grin. "So it really was a good nights work all round, although probably not the one you wanted it to be I'm afraid."

Mathews looked at him like he'd gone mad. "Who the hell are Hardwick and Sharpe, and what have they got to do with your stupid demand for ten percent of my legacy?" Mendelson greeted her question with muted laughter. "They are a couple of hired killers, my dear. Killers who were meant to cost me a lot of money that you agreed to provide as part of our deal." He looked around to make sure no one was within earshot. "You need to realise that there's no way out for either of us now, you are as complicit in those murders as I am so we are indelibly linked in a way that creates a very tight bond between us, and always will, which is why you must honour our agreement." Mathews had been edging forward on her seat, but she eased back again and folded her arms over her chest. "I think you're making this up just to get your way. I didn't deliberately set out to help anyone murder my boyfriend, or our friend Sam." Mendelson sniggered at her. "*I* know that, and *you* know that, but nobody else who isn't already dead or in custody knows it. I've seen to that. So I have you over a proverbial barrel." He sat back with a superior look on his face that said he was in complete control.

While this verbal duelling was going on Captain Delgado had left his post at the hotel entrance and joined up with Art. They were only a dozen strides away from where Mathews and Mendelson were locked in conversation. "I don't see any reason to put Mathews through any more of this, Art," said Delgado, "the message from the control van tells us we have everything we need for a conviction. Just give the other's the nod that we're going in and let's lift that arrogant bastard and get out here." Art gave a little snigger. "I'll let you make the arrest, Marcus, you can think of it as an early birthday present. It's been a long time since you've had the pleasure, although if I'm honest, I hope to hell he puts up a struggle so I can put my boot through his wedding tackle." Marcus saw the funny side of his remark and gave a little chuckle. "Me too, Art, me too," he added, "now let's go ruin his day."

They split their direction of travel and approached Mendelson from either side, with Delgado taking the lead. He flashed his badge under Mendelson's nose. "On your feet, Mendelson, and put your hands behind your back. I'm Captain Delgado from the NYPD and you are under arrest on a charge of multiple homicide. Anything you say will be taken down and may be used in evidence against you in court." Mendelson was too shocked to say anything, but Delgado dragged him to his feet and cuffed his wrists behind his back. The other detectives had also rushed to the table and Delgado handed his prisoner over to them. "Read him his full rights and get him out of my sight before I do something I might regret. I'll lay the charges when we get back to base."

He gave Mendelson a hefty shove in the back for good measure before turning to Claire Mathews. "I'm sure that was a very harrowing experience for you, Claire, but you did brilliantly, and I'm told you got us more than we even hoped to get. According to our technical staff outside his confession also cleared you of any deliberate involvement, but we do need another statement from you now that your status has changed from defence to prosecution, and you will of course be called to give evidence at the trial, but we can got through all that back at base. Apart from that you're free to go wherever you want to and do whatever you want." He gave her a big grin. "And it won't be long before you can afford to do exactly that, and I wish you every success with it." Claire seemed disinterested somehow and was scanning the foyer for something or someone. "Can anyone tell me where Sergeant Garcia has gone?" she asked.

"She went to the control vehicle after you met up with Mendelson," Delgado explained, "but you can catch up with her back at the station house, if you want, and in case you're worried about it there was no one with Mendelson when he entered the hotel." Mathews looked relieved, "I was a bit worried about that, but I would like to thank Gina for her help and support over the last few days. I was very much in need of it as I was terribly nervous." With their plan executed without a hitch Delgado wrapped one arm round Art's shoulder and the other round Claire's before guiding them away from a gathering crowd of onlookers. "Let's get back to base and run the recording through. Right now we're taking someone else's assertion that we got what we wanted, and I'm sure we did with our guys being so experienced, but you and I need to check it out for ourselves to ensure Mendelson has no way out." They wandered off looking well pleased with their days work.

The whole team were in a hurry to get back to the precinct where Delgado went straight to the custody suite and laid the holding charges against Mendelson. Having dispensed with that he instructed the custody sergeant to have him ready for interview first thing the following morning.

Art was intrigued at the level of commitment shown by his boss who stayed involved at every level, but he was more than happy to take a back seat and let him get on with it.

For his part Delgado was aware that he might be getting *too* involved and could be seen to be undermining his lieutenant. "I hope I'm not ruffling your feathers by taking the lead when we interview Mendelson, Art, but this case has suffered from so many twists and turns that it has me seriously interested, in an unusual and absorbing way I must admit. I'm not trying to undermine you and I want you in with me when we face Mendelson tomorrow, if that's okay?" Art raised an eyebrows in an agreeable way. "You're the boss, Marcus, but I'll be right beside you if you need me. Now let's find out what the recording has to offer and if we have enough to sink Mendelson. I can't wait to educate him on where he went wrong in life."

Having listened to the recording with growing satisfaction Delgado announced his delighted with the outcome and made the point to the rest of the team who were gathered for his debrief. "There is no way out for that murdering sleaze-bag after what he has admitted to on both of the recording we have. He has personally hammered the last nail into his own coffin, and more importantly, he has given us the name of the mystery detective who was hired to find young Ben Silverman. Apparently he's a private eye by the name of Nick Clark, so we need him bought in for questioning asap to determine his level of involvement. Unfortunately, we don't know if he was hired over here or across the pond? But we will of get Inspector Stewart from the Met police to check him out and do the necessary, while we run our own check over here. We need him found as quickly as possible as he's the last person involved in this mess who has yet to be questioned." Art nodded his agreement. "I'll get Ian on to it before I head home tonight, Marcus."

"Good man, Art, but let him know we need him lifted with some urgency to help us get everything wrapped up." He turned back to the rest of his team. "Now then, all of you have heard both recordings so this is your last chance to say if you found anything that needs further investigation before we tackle Mendelson in the morning?" His question was aimed at the whole team, but Gina was the only one who responded. "I'll have a go at finding this guy Clark on Google. You never know, if he's a detective of any calibre we might strike lucky." Delgado gave her the thumbs up. "Good thinking, Gina, us oldies are better leaving that internet crap to you young ones." His comment brought a few knowing smirks from the team, with Vince looking to have enjoyed it most.

"Okay, people, we have this case in the wrapper and just need to tie the strings, barring the Clark business of course, so well done each and every one of you. I know some of you have spent your time on paperwork and phone calls, but it all adds up to a successful outcome. Now get yourselves off home and I'll see you in the morning bright and breezy, and those of you who still have paperwork to complete get it done by end of play tomorrow." He was looking at Art when he next spoke. "We go for Mendelson at nine o'clock, Art, okay?"

"Suits me boss." Art just nodded as he headed for the door with Gina in tow, both looking relieved that Delgado had stuck rigidly to the agenda and had not wasted anyone's time.

38

Mendelson was sitting in solitary isolation in the interview room, actively taxing his brain for what lay ahead. He hadn't spoken a word with anyone, nor had anyone spoken with him since his arrest, except to book him into custody. Yet he was sufficiently arrogant, due to his high level of experience in matters of law, to believe that he could outwit his interrogators and walk free. But he had a big shock waiting just around the corner as he had no knowledge of the fact that both of his damning conversation with Claire Mathews had been recorded and would be used against him.

As he massaged his over-rated ego his interrogators were enjoying a morning coffee upstairs in Delgado's office, both quietly excited at the prospect of what lay ahead. Although Delgado was of the opinion that there was little left to do, and made it known to Art. "We don't need to waste a lot of time with Mendelson, we already have him bang to rights, the only thing we need from him is the whereabouts of the private detective he hired to track down young Benjamin." Art drained what was left of his coffee and set his mug down. "Let's go keep him company, Marcus. I'm sure he must be feeling lonely." Delgado gifted him a smile as they stood up together and headed downstairs.

Contrary to expectations Mendelson looked totally at ease and pleased with himself when they got to him. "Good morning, Mister Mendelson, I'm Captain Delgado, you already know me from our recent telephone conversations and your arrest, and the officer I have with me is Lieutenant Gardiner. We're sorry to have kept you waiting but we were relaxing with a coffee upstairs and you know how time flies when you're enjoying yourself."

Mendelson didn't look interested in the greeting. "I could not be less interested, Delgado. I would hardly expect you to get the time right when you've made a complete ass of everything else, especially this unwarranted arrest." Art placed his elbows on the tabletop. "To be honest, Alex, we didn't think time would be all that important to you when you're going down for the rest of your miserable life. That will give you plenty of time to regret your criminal past."

Mendelson pursed his lips and rolled his head gently. "You people have charged me with orchestrating multiple homicide, but for the life of me I cannot understand how you concocted such a charge. A charge of that by nature indicates a level of conspiracy, so who exactly did I conspire with?" This last comment confirmed that he had no idea Mathews had been wired and their conversations recorded, which, for someone who's profession brought him into contact with a variety of serious criminals, gave those facing him the impression that he wasn't very street wise, a frailty that brought a smile to Art's face. Although it was Delgado who had a go first. "We know who you conspired with, and who you hired to take the lives of the four innocent individuals who got in your way, one of them your own employee Joe Hardwick, who along with Rodney Sharpe murdered Benjamin Silverman and Sam Blackwell. Sharpe was also responsible for the murder of James Magee, another of your company employees." He allowed himself a few moments to study Mendelson's reaction, but he was even more stony-faced than before and unresponsive, so Delgado carried on. "You even tried to implicate young Claire Mathews into your evil plan so you could con he out of ten percent of

340

her inheritance." A sudden change in Mendelson's posture stopped Delgado in his tracks. "You look surprised, Alex. Did it never enter you thick head that we know all about your greedy little arrangement with Miss Mathews?" He sat back and folded his arms. "You can take that surly look of your face because I'm going to let you in on a little secret, your fancy career as a top class attorney is over, you're going down for life my friend. Your last two very enlightening conversations with Miss Mathews were recorded by us and gave us with all the evidence we need to convict you, and it came out of your own mouth. You see Alex, once you ring the bell you can't un-ring it, and you definitely rang it loud and clear."

Art had been a silent partner up to now but when he saw the look of horror on Mendelson's face he couldn't keep quiet any longer. "To coin a phrase, you murderous creep, we have you by the proverbial nuts and we're not letting go, but there is only one thing we want from you " He didn't get finishing, thanks to Gina opening the door and walking in unexpectedly. She handed Art a slip of paper and left just as quietly as she'd come in.

Art read the note and handed it to Delgado with a big smile. The note read. *"Details for our missing detective, he's from the Clark Detective Agency in Chelsea, London. I have the details."* It was signed, *Gina*.

Having read the note Art leaned across the table to get closer to their prisoner. "I was about to ask you something, Alex, but we already have the answer. In fact we have everything we need now, so someone else will take your statement before we send you to Rikers Island to await your court appearance." He turned to his boss. "I think we're finished here, Marcus. This clown hasn't got anything to tell us that we don't already know, so let's just lock him up and get on with something more important."

Delgado turned to Mendelson again. "Do you have anything to say on your own behalf, or are you still denying orchestrating multiple homicide?" Mendelson, who had paled considerably wasn't fit to say anything, but he felt compelled to do so anyway. "I'm a highly respected lawyer running a high profile international company, not some cheap bum off the street to be treated in this embarrassing manner. So in answer to your question, you can go take a running jump, or in language more akin to your own bastardisation of the English language, you can kiss my butt as I'm saying absolutely nothing more until I see every detail on the charge sheets. And as I will be representing myself in court I am entitled to see copies of everything you have relating to the charge or charges laid against me, and that includes every bit of evidence you will be presenting to the court."

Delgado got to his feet and called in the guard. "Take the piece of crap back to its holding cell and warn the custody sergeant that his telephone rights have been withdrawn until further notice." He tapped Art on the shoulder. "Turns out I was right when I said we shouldn't waste time on him. He's not going to own up to anything, but it doesn't matter because he has no say in what happens to him from here on in, his goose is well and truly cooked. We have everything we need to send him and his co-conspirators away for a very long time."

Having said his piece Delgado wrapped an arm round Art's shoulders and led him away.

It might have been the murky weather that clogged their minds, certainly something had, because they had forgotten all about Jack Benson in their eagerness to bring Mendelson to book, but not Gina, she had it firmly in mind when she joined them for what was an unscheduled meeting. "Did Mendelson tell us anything about Jack

Benson's involvement in this rags to riches saga?"

Art, feeling partially responsible for the oversight, did nothing to hide his guilt. "Good question, Gina," he admitted, rather tamely, "but Mendelson wasn't in any mood for talking. In fact he didn't say very much at all, except to advise us that he will be defending himself at trial, but you're right to raise the issue of Benson as it had completely slipped my mind."

Delgado decided to join in. "Mendelson did say in conversation with Claire Mathews that Benson only does what he tells him, inviting us to question what he was told to do?" Delgado's zeroed in on Gina. "We need Claire Mathews to ask that same question of Jack Benson, she is his client so he's answerable to her for his actions."

"I'll get right on it," Gina assured him, "she's down in reception waiting for me." Delgado flicked his head towards the door, and she hurried off.

"We must be getting old, Marcus," admitted Art, "we both forgot all about Benson." He was still wearing a guilty expression, as was his boss who breezed over it very casually. "I don't think Benson is too heavily involved, at least I hope not, but I don't want us chasing our tails to catch a fringe conspirator, not when it's more important to have Inspector Stewart lift Clark now that we know he's somewhere in London. We need to find out what he has to say for himself. It's a loose end that must be put to bed before the trial."

Just then the office door opened, and Gina came in with Claire Mathews in tow. Both men got to their feet to greet their visitor while Gina explained the situation. "Claire has already told me that she had a long phone conversation with Benson right after her conversation

343

with Mendelson and demanded an explanation regarding his involvement. She has made the point that she accepts it was nothing more than one interested party conversing with another regarding a legacy issue that they were both involved with."

She offered Mathews a seat before going on. "I knew you want to discuss it with her as it's a contentious issue, so here she is, ready to answer anything you ask of her. I've already invited her to stay with Art and me for the rest of her stay here." There was a confused expression on the faces of both men, although more so with Delgado's, although he appeared quite relaxed when he found his voice again. "Everyone in this room agrees that there are good reasons for suspecting Jack Benson of involvement in these crimes, especially when Mendelson stressed that very point in conversation with you and bragged about controlling Benson, so why are you choosing to ignore what he said. I'm finding it difficult to come to terms with that, Claire."

Art was finding the conversation too important not to get involved. "It's confusing me as well, Claire. I'm confused that you're choosing to ignore what Mendelson told you. It's an issue that is much too serious to be brushed aside. I suggest you give it a bit more thought before making a decision we may all regret." Mathews did as she was told and gave the matter more thought before re-engaging. She was conscious of the possible consequences regarding her lawyer's possible involvement and set about justifying her stance in a much more succinct and meaningful way. "I know there were genuine reasons for Jack Benson to be in communication with Mendelson when both parties were sharing an interest in my claim." She paused to reset her focus. "And you're right, Captain Delgado, Mendelson did ask my lawyer to keep an eye on me and tell him of any odd behaviour on my part, or any lengthy periods of absence when I couldn't be contacted, but he put this request down to concerns over my safety, an excuse that Jack Benson considered to be reasonable enough in the circumstances. He also explained that Mendelson questioned why I had lost contact with him at one stage, but there was nothing sinister in it." She switched her attention from Art to Marcus then back to Art again. "I don't think there was anything underhand in what went on between them, not from Jack Benson's involvement anyway, I think Mendelson was just trying to put pressure on me when he brought Benson's name into the conversation." She folded her arms stubbornly and sat back, fully satisfied with her explanation.

Delgado twitched an eyebrow. "Thanks for that, Claire. I admit that we have no direct evidence of wrongdoing by your lawyer, so I have no reason to doubt what you tell me. Our only interest in your lawyer was aroused by Mendelson bringing him into his conversation with you, but if you are happy with the way Benson has dealt with you as his client, then so be it, and since we have no evidence to the contrary we will remove him from our list of suspects."

Mathews smiled and shrugged her shoulders offhandedly and turned to Gina. "Is there any chance I can stay with you for the next few days, Gina? I'm waiting to get a definitive answer on my claim which I'm assured shouldn't take long now." Gina slipped her arm round Claire's shoulder. "We've already agreed to that, Claire. So don't give it another thought, you can stay as long as you need to. You can even help with my wedding plans." Art suddenly wanted away. "Are we finished here, Marcus, I'd need to go and warn Ian Stewart about this Clark guy." Gina pulled a slip of paper from her pocket and slipped it into his hand. "That's everything your friend needs to know about our mysterious detective. It should be an easy job for them as it has his full address and phone number." Art gave her a wink and raised a farewell hand before taking off.

While his involvement with Jack Benson was being discussed by others Mendelson was in his cell rocking backwards and forwards on the edge of his bunk deliberating over his precarious future. He was suffering from a serious attack of mental anguish, a state of mind brought about by his own stupidity and his uncontrollable desire to garner greater wealth. Truth be known he was *already* considered to be seriously wealthy, and in terms of his bank balance and his bricks and mortar assets that could not be disputed, but it was *Silverman's* vast and assorted assets that he envied so much. The five star hotels and holiday destinations, the multi-level business and conference centres, the diamond mines, and the oil fields. Together, these were assets that would stand the test of time and ones that he begrudged his client. But there was no way out of his current situation, and he knew it. Even his own highly skilled legal brain would have no influence on the laws final reckoning, not with the level of evidence his accusers had, evidence that was all the more painful to behold since it came from his own mouth. He would be too old to do anything useful before being considered for parole, a frightening certainty that filled him with a new and horrifying outlook over his future.

While he cringed miserably in his cell he took comfort from the fact that he still had his wealth to fall back on, and he knew that money could buy him some measure of revenge, revenge against those who caused his downfall was now the only pleasure left to help sweeten his confinement, especially if he were one day to read of his captors painful demise. It was either that or suicide, as he could think of nothing to help ease the pain of his demise and confinement. He would have a long time to live with the ghosts of his victims.

346

39

The day following Inspector Stewart notification of Nick Clark's involvement he phoned Art to tell him they had hauled him in for questioning, and that he had freely admitted to being hired by Mendelson to track down young Benjamin, but only with the view to pinpointing his whereabouts for other members of Mendelson's staff to convince him to return home following the death of his father. He even produced a written contract to that effect, a contract that was signed by Mendelson's own hand, and with no evidence of any wrongdoing he had been released without charge, albeit with the proviso that he would be called as a prosecution witness when the case went before the Judiciary.

Art gave Ian Stewart's decision a big sigh of relief because it gave reliable support to Claire Mathews explanation of events. Which meant there were no more loose ends, and their case was ready to be written up and put before the District Attorney.

It was particularly pleasing that Mendelson's private detective had pointed the finger at him for what happened to Ben Silverman and his friend, driving another nail into the already tight fitting coffin lid. With that joyous thought in mind he arranged for what he hoped would be his last interview with Mendelson and invited Gina to join him for what he described to her as a bit of light entertainment. After all, their prisoner deserved to know how they had gathered so much evidence of his criminal activities, and Art was going to take great pleasure in telling him all about it. He went off to collect Gina with a cheerful smile on his face.

Gina was all alone yet she was laughing quite loudly, but it was only to let Mendelson know she was enjoying herself when he was marched in. She looked him up and down as he passed her. "I'm so glad you have enough free time to see us, Mister Mendelson. I know how busy you attorneys can be."

Mendelson looked her up and down as well, but with a dismissive sneer. "You can cut the crap lady. I don't know of anything that we have to say to each other. You're wasting my time and yours." He gave her the same up and down look again. "Who the hell are you anyway?" Gina waved her warrant card under his nose. "I'm detective Sergeant Garcia and my partner, Lieutenant Gardner will join us shortly, but is there anything you want to get off your chest before he gets here?" Mendelson sniggered noisily. "You're the one with the thirty eight boobs lady, maybe you need to get something off your chest." He sniggered at his own sick humour and was still sniggering when Gina reached out and gave him an almighty slap across the face. "Listen up you murderous pervert, if my partner had been here just now you'd be a hospital case, so watch your mouth or I'll slap you again."

Mendelson was about to have another go at her when the door opened and Art walked in, but the hate filled expression on Mendelson's face alerted him to the strained atmosphere. "You okay, Gina?" he asked. Gina folded her arms and nodded slowly. "I am now, but if that murdering pervert speaks to me again like he just did I won't just slap him I'll bend a chair over his head." Art had no idea what had taken place but that didn't stop him from reaching out and dragging Mendelson across the table until their faces were inches apart. Then he

348

reached up with his other hand and took a savage grip on Mendelson's nose, twisting it painfully from side to side as he glared into his watery eyes. "You seem to enjoy bullying the fairer sex, Mendelson, but you have me to deal with now, and I can assure you that I will happily kick your ass round this room if you step out of line again. You're only here to be told one thing so plant your ass on that chair and pay attention." He shoved Mendelson back into his chair. "The private detective you hired to find young Ben Silverman, Nick Clark, has admitted to being contracted by you for that purpose, so there are no loopholes in our case, and you can't shift the blame. Your goose is cooked." He turned to Gina. "Did he get physical with you?" She shook her head. "No he didn't, he just brought my boobs into the conversation for no reason, so I slapped his face." Art glared at Mendelson, but it was Gina he spoke to. "Do you want me to hold him while you slap him again?" He offered. Gina shook her head. "I wouldn't dirty my hands, Art, but thanks for the offer."

Mendelson eyes were firmly fixed on Gina, and it was apparent from his expression that his insides were churning with malicious anger. "I haven't finished with you yet, young lady, nor you." He switched his attention to Art. "Just because I'm in custody doesn't mean I'm powerless. You should both remember that."

Art grabbed him by the shirt front and hauled him over the table again. "Are you making threats, Mendelson? Is that what you're up to?" He shoved him back into his chair. Mendelson shrugged his shoulders in a way that told those present he couldn't care less. "Make of it what you will,. I'm saying no more."

Art called the guard in. "Take this perverted non-entity back where he belongs and keep him under lock and key. He has already made a declaration that he intends to represent himself in court, so he has no right to make any more phone calls." He turned back to re-engage with Mendelson, allowing himself to smile in the process. "You can't buy your way out of this one, you perverted misfit, but you can say goodbye to your high society lifestyle because you're going down for the rest of your natural life." Having had his moment of fun Art turned to the guard. "If this creep gives you any trouble, any trouble at all, just use your night stick."

He took Gina by the hand and led her away, feeling just a little concerned that Mendelson's final remark might have caused her to feel threatened, which was why he had taken the liberty of cancelling his access to a phone. "I wonder how Silverman will react when he learns we have his brother in custody?" He muttered, thinking aloud rather than asking a question.

"Why don't we go and ask him?" Suggested Gina, stopping Art dead in his tracks.

"That's not a bad idea," he screwed his face up, "why didn't I think of that?" His admission was accompanied by a knowing wink. "The situation has changed drastically since we last spoke with him, and we now have all the evidence we need to put Mendelson and his bunch of cronies away for a very long time. More to the point, we did it without any help from him, so we don't owe him any favours as all bets are off." Gina cocked an inviting eyebrow. "Let's go and have some more fun, Art, I think we deserve a bit of light entertainment for a change." Art gave her a big smile. "He's been moved to Rikers Island while waiting on his court appearance. Give them a bell and tell them we're on our way to interview him. I can't wait to see his ugly mug when he hears what we have to say."

40

The staff at Rikers Island Correction Facility had everything organised with Silverman ready and waiting at the appointed time for Art and Gina's arrival. Although Silverman was still of the belief that he had a few bonus points in his pocket from their last meeting, so he was in a fairly relaxed mood, sadly, he was about to find out that the deal he thought was in his pocket was dead and buried

"You look to be in a very amicable mood today, Joshua," began Art, "do I take it from your relaxed attitude that you're not aware of your new next door neighbour?" Silverman's eyes narrowed and he focussed his attention on Art's face, scrutinising it with an inquisitive arrogance, although he chose not to respond verbally.

"Nothing to say, Joshua.? Not even interested to hear about your new neighbour?" Silverman shook his head despairingly. "Why should I bother answering your stupid questions when I can see from your sanctimonious expression that you're just chomping at the bit to tell me anyway?" Art nodded in agreement. "You're quite right, Joshua, I am going to tell you. I feel it's only right that I make you aware that we have your dearly beloved brother in custody. You should also be aware that he has, inadvertently I admit, confessed to organising and paying others to carry out a number of murders on his and your behalf, while at the same time planning how best to block any claim you had to your step-father's legacy. A legacy that is now to be entrusted to your step-brother Benjamin's fiancé, Claire Mathews."

Silverman snorted like a mad bull; in fact he was so enraged that he couldn't find the words to express his feelings; words by themselves were insufficient to placate the anger boiling up inside him. His eyes were wide open and glaring with both hands gripped into tight fists as he smashed them down on the metal tabletop with every ounce of his strength. The noise broke Art's train of thought, but he was quick to recover, and he even smiled when he locked eyes with Silverman again. "You've probably worked it out for yourself by now, Joshua, but the arrival of your brother here under his own volition nullifies any deal we had for you to entice him here. In fact Claire Mathews kindly did that for us"

He leaned back in his seat with a sneer. "But you can take comfort from the fact that his confession absolves you from the charge of running the show." He folded his arms and waited for Silverman's reaction, but there wasn't one, well not right away, the guy was so wound-up he couldn't find the words to articulate his feelings, and it was some time before he got round to venting his spleen again. "Just where do you have that mealy-mouthed brother of mine incarcerated?"

His spiteful demand highlighted a total lack of respect for his brother, which was music to Art's ears, he could think of nothing better than to have them at each other's throats. The last thing he wanted was the pair of them meeting up and concocting some fictitious story to get themselves off the hook. More than that, he needed urgent advice to confirm he had the authority to prevent them from meeting together. Especially with Mendelson still listed on the court documents as Silverman's legal advisor, a thought that gave him serious concern. Could it be deemed lawful for a felon charged with murder to represent another felon charged in connection with the same offence?

When Art looked at Silverman again he saw a subtle change in his body language. He was no longer tense and up-tight looking but appeared more at ease with himself and more focussed on what was going on. "Thank you for the update, Lieutenant," he told Art, "It's good to know that my legal advisor has finally arrived here, but you must understand that I must now have an urgent meeting with him to plan and prepare for my forthcoming court appearance?"

Art looked like he'd swallowed a wasp. In his eagerness to gloat over Silverman's dilemma he had let the cat out of the bag by telling him of his brother's arrival and subsequent arrest, but he was determined, come hell or high water to block any family love-in between the two. "You can forget all about a family get together, Silverman, your brother is in solitary isolation and if I have anything to do with it he'll stay there for a very long time to come. Now listen up and pay attention, you need to take my advice and get someone else to represent you in court because your homicidal brother no longer fits the bill."

Silverman's composure went out the window in a flash. He got to his feet and back-kicked his chair across the room behind him. "Who the hell are you to advise me, Gardiner? I don't take advice from the likes of you. Just do what the law requires you to do and give me access to my attorney and make it soon because I'm getting very impatient." Art shot round the table like a man possessed and pinned Silverman against the wall in a throat-lock. "You take that attitude with me again and you'll be wearing your balls for ear-rings, understood?"

Tossing him aside like a wet rag he picked the chair up and slammed it into the back of his legs, forcing him to collapse into it. Then he shoved him and his chair up against the table. "I've had it with your sort, Silverman, you're a fucking low-life, an accomplice to murder and

I'm finished pussy-footing about with you. We will appoint an attorney to defend you in court and like it or lump it you will have no further say in the matter, but it won't change anything because your fate has already been decided. Silverman was having none of it and he made the point loudly enough. "If you cast your mind back, Lieutenant, I appointed my brother as my legal advisor and that has not changed, so unless the court tells me otherwise, or I personally decide to dispense with his services, he remains contracted to fulfil that duty." Folding his arms he stuck his skinny chest out and rambled on. "That being the case I am legally obliged to meet with him to discuss a joint plan for my defence." He stretched his legs under the table. "To coin your own phrase, Lieutenant, you can like it or lump it, but one thing you must do is arrange for me to meet with my brother in private as the law dictates. You don't have any choice in this matter." It wasn't obvious from Art's appearance, but his stomach was churning at the thought of Silverman and his brother joining hands in private. There were two serious issues bugging him, firstly, he was uncertain about Silverman's rights under the law as he'd never come across a case before where a felon charged with an offence was being represented by another who was charged with being a conspirator for the same offence. Secondly, he needed to check with the District Attorney that he had sufficient authority to stop such a meeting taking place, and he needed to do it in a hurry.

Turning his attention to the guard he pointed at his prisoner. "Get this low-life out of my sight and tell the custody sergeant that he is not allowed any visitors or any means of contact with the outside world until further notice, and make sure he understands that command." Silverman was about to argue the point, but he saw the angry expression on Art's face and thought better of it. In any case he had other things to think about with his guard forcefully ushering him from the room with a hefty shove in the back.

Gina, who had been watching the whole episode through the viewing window collared Art as soon as he came out.

"Did that bimbo under the impression that he'd be permitted to link up with his homicidal brother?" Art wheeled her away like he was in a hurry. "It's not going to happen, Gina, so don't even think about it. We have this case wrapped up so let's get back to Manhattan and finish the paperwork. If I know Marcus he'll be wanting everything collated and signed up before we're ready to give it to him. To be perfectly honest I just want this case over and done with. It has already dragged on too long." He wrapped his arm round her waist. "Let's go and see what Marcus has to say."

Art didn't have much liking for departmental get togethers, but he was more than happy to head for the conference room and the round table meeting that was called to finalise the documentation for their case. A last gasp meeting like this was normal practice prior to forwarding the charge sheets to the District Attorney. Although Art was quietly hoping it would act as a distraction to help take Gina's mind of Mendelson's cryptic threat. The meeting would probably be boring and tediously long, as they needed to ensure every little detail of evidence was cross checked to ensure there would be no come-backs or any legal loopholes for the defence to take issue with.

Everyone criminally involved in the case were safely in custody, suitably charged, and ready for prosecution. So today was all about the paperwork as far as Art was concerned and he was beyond pleased when the meeting came to an end as he was so keen to get away that he reluctantly turned down Delgado's offer of a drink. He had more important things on his mind and Gina was top of his list, especially so as they were both supposed to be on a day off, which was the main cause for his eagerness. But before he could rush off to deal with whatever was bugging him he needed a quick conversation with his boss, and after explaining about Silverman's demand for a little get together with his brother he found Delgado every bit as confused as he was on the matter.

"Christ, Art, I'm not at all sure where we stand with that, it's not something I've had to deal with before." He scratched his head." I'll have to get advice from our legal buffs, it's not a decision I can make without consultation."

Gina, whose patience was being seriously tested, cut in on their conversation. "Aren't we supposed to be on a day off, Art?" she asked, "so tell me what you've got planned?" He gave her a crafty little wink. "I thought I would treat you to lunch and a nice bottle of wine?"

Gina took a backward step and looked him up and down. "Well, well, Mister Gardiner, I suppose if that's the best you can come up with it will have to do," she followed this up with an enquiring look, "but why are you looking so devious? I get the distinct feeling you're up to something, but how can a girl refuse the offer of a free lunch?" She gave him another questioning look. "Are you sure you haven't been up to something that I don't know about?" Art threw his head back and laughed at the suggestion. "You are suspicious minded little madam, Miss Garcia. I don't know why I put up with you."

He grabbed her by the arm and dragged her away. "Let's get out of here, lunch sounds very inviting to me." They shot down the stairs like it was a pre-arranged escape plan, but contrary to Gina's expectations when they got outside she was bundled into a waiting taxi and driven off without having any idea where they were heading. Nor did it help

356

that Art back-handed all her frantic questions until the taxi pulled up by the side of the road and the driver got out and opened the door for her. "What in blue blazes are we doing here?" she snapped, "I thought you said we were going for lunch." Art cocked both eyebrows at her and pointed a finger at the shop window behind him. "Look in there, and tell me what you see?"

"What the hell am I meant to see?" she asked. Art began to panic that she might have changed her mind. "Engagement rings, sweetheart, engagement rings," he repeated excitedly, "lots of lovely engagement rings for you to choose from." He took her by the hand and led her inside. "Come on now, don't be shy, let's find something that takes your fancy." Gina threw her arms round his neck, but he just hoisted her up and carried her inside.

There were more surprises to come, because getting an engagement ring wasn't the only one in store for her. When they got back to the station house, Delgado, having been forewarned of Art's intentions, had arranged an impromptu party for their return. A party that went on longer than anyone expected and left Gina feeling relieved when it was over, and she could get back home to admire her engagement ring without everyone else looking on.

The only work in progress in the squad room the following morning was paperwork. Everyone in the squad, including the admin staff, were frantically punching keyboards in their determination to have every piece of documentation and every scrap of evidence for the case they referred to as the 'legacy case' completed and typed up by the end of the day. Captain Delgado had decreed it to be so, and everyone involved was determined to meet his very rigid deadline.

And while their evidence remained unchanged there were other matters to do with the case that needed urgent attention. Like Mendelson's claim to having a legal right of access to all of evidence to be used against him in court. Delgado wasn't sure how best to deal with it and had waited all morning for notification from their legal department. When he finally got his hands on it he was in a position to brief Mendelson on his rights, or lack of them, and was mad keen to get it over with, but at the last minute he decided to take Art with him and went off to find him, aware that his journey would take him past the vending machine, so he was armed with a couple of coffees when they met up.

Art was punching his keyboard like he'd fallen out with it when Delgado got to him. "Leave that for now, Art, we need to see Mendelson now that I know what I'm doing with his claim of his for legal access. Can you think of anything else that needs finalising before he goes for trial as I have no wish to be visiting Rikers again just to see the likes of him."

Art grabbed his coffee and thought things over. "If he isn't permitted access to the evidence, which is what I hope you're about to tell him, then I'm think he will ask for someone else to take up his defence so he or she can access the evidence for him in that way. It's what I would do if I were in his position."

Delgado scratched his head. "Jeez, man, I hadn't thought of that. Is this likely to be another issue?" Art screwed his face up. "I don't see why it should, unless he finds another attorney who's as bent as he is." They laughed at the suggestion and went back to drinking their coffee. "Let's finish up here and go spoil his day, Art, I can't wait to break the good news to him." They headed for the door together.

Mendelson waltzed into the interview room like he owned the place, but his attitude soon changed when Delgado broke the news to him, in fact he went absolutely ballistic when found out he would be denied access to the prosecution's evidence until the day of his trial, and he wasn't shy about venting his anger. "Who the hell do you lot think you are? I'm representing myself at trial, so I am legally entitled to see all of the evidence that's available to the prosecution."

Delgado was having none of it. "No you're not, Alex, and that's an end to it." Mendelson tried to get to his feet but the heavy manacles round his ankles stopped him dead in his tracks. He was so enraged words disserted him, and when he found his voice again it wasn't exactly classic English. "Fuck you, Delgado, you goddamned asshole. I *will* get to see that evidence and you won't stop me. If I don't I'll have your balls hacked off and shoved down your throat." His face was purple with rage, with every vein on his face and neck standing out like knotted rope.

"Where is all this anger coming from, Alex?" asked Delgado, "What's the matter, is it because you've run out of people to kill?" He reached out and hauled Mendelson over the table, dragging him up close and personal. "You ever threaten me again and I will personally make you a hospital case. Do you understand me, you murdering scumbag?" When Mendelson failed to answer he repeated the question. "I asked you if you understood, Mendelson?" He waited until he got an acknowledgement before shoving him back into his chair, although he certainly wasn't finished with him. "If you intend withdrawing your notification to represent yourself in court then you must advise the court accordingly and you must let them know who will be representing you." Mendelson smiled for the first time during their encounter. "You dimwits only think you're clever, but you see I suspected something like this from you bloody amateurs and have already thwarted your attempt to stifle me by appointing a renowned

London Barrister to fight my case." He grinned at Delgado again. "And just so you know, he will be arriving here this afternoon for our first meeting and there's absolutely nothing you can do to stop that meeting taking place, or him getting his hands on the evidence." He stuck his skinny chest out like he had just won a big point.

Delgado looked him up and down like he had just stood in something nasty. "A renowned Barrister you say, he'll need to be a bloody magician to have any effect on your trial. You're going down for the rest of your miserable life without any chance of parole, so you might as well get used to it."

He turned to the guard. "Take him away and there's no need to be gentle about it." He nudged Art in the back, and they headed off looking pleased with themselves. "So our mass killer has found someone stupid enough to represent him. You hit the nail on the head when you said anyone stupid enough to represent him would need to be as bent as he is." He scratched the back of his neck. "It might be an idea for us to stay put and take a look at this barrister guy, it's afternoon already so let's see if the Riker's staff will let us eyeball their meeting. We can't listen in on their conversation, but we can watch to see who it is and how they interact when they meet up, that should tell us how well they know each other."

Art nodded his agreement. "Let's go clear it with the commissioner and find out when this meeting is scheduled to take place." They headed off with a real spring in their step.

41

As soon as the plane touched down at JFK airport a tall individual in a light grey overcoat got to his feet and reclaimed his hand baggage from the locker above his head. There was a noticeable sense of urgency about him as he rushed to the front of the plane ahead of the other passengers, displaying what could only be described as a competitive eagerness to be the first in the queue to disembark. This sense of urgency was even more evident when he made his way through airport security, where after clearance he headed for the main exit and the first available taxi. Only then did he allow himself a long awaited sigh of relief, relief that his recently acquired set of forged identity documents had passed airport scrutiny, documents that identified him as James Bulford, a Barrister and member of the Bar in London.

Settling back in his seat he glanced at his wristwatch and saw that he was ahead of schedule, inviting a little smile of satisfaction to alter his otherwise dour features. He'd planned to be in Manhattan by mid-afternoon, so he had ample time to get something to eat before travelling on to Rikers Island.

About forty minutes later the same heavily built individual posing as James Bulford presented his fake documents at the security desk at Riker's and was escorted into the interview room where he waited for Mendelson to join him.

Mendelson, like his visitor, was eagerly anticipating their meeting, as he considered his visitor to be the best defence lawyer in England. But his gaunt features displayed a shocked, almost horrified expression when he failed to recognise the person who lay in wait for him, and from the look on his face he wasn't only shocked but was doing nothing to hide it. "Who the hell are you?" he demanded, "and where is Bulford?" His visitors determined expression and the slight side-to-side motion of his head warned Mendelson to be quiet, leaving him grappling with the fact that something other than what he expected was taking place. His visitor addressed him in a voice that was just above a whisper. "You need to keep your mouth shut and listen carefully to me, Alex, because I'm the only hope you have of saving your skin, and if you look closely enough you *will* recognise me." With no one able to hear their conversation Mendelson's panic subsided a little. Others could watch but could hear nothing that was being said. The man posing as James Bulford gave Mendelson a steely look that carried a warning. "You are never going to be free to live your life outside of prison unless you listen to me, Alex; I'm your only way out of this situation and we both know I can't do it legally. So keep your ass on your seat, keep your mouth shut, and for Christ's sake smile a little and try to act like you're pleased to see me."

Mendelson was too shocked not to obey. He hadn't expected anything like this and wasn't sure in his own mind how to react. This stranger was not the person he had hired to defend him, and while there was something strangely familiar about him he couldn't put his finger on it, but whoever he was, he had bragged that he had a plan in place to keep him out of prison, so Mendelson suddenly got the message and smiled, sticking his hand out in greeting as he did so. With their greeting over his visitor decided to enlighten him. "Try to imagine me as I used to be, Alex, with a thick beard and one of your employees."

narrowed his eyes and scrutinised his visitors face, then his eyes opened wide with shock. "I don't fucking believe it, it is you isn't it, you're Joe bloody Hardwick, but how in God's name can you be here when I saw you with your brains blasted all over your car boot? For Christ's sake man, it was me who identified you."

Hardwick wanted to get on with things, so he sat down and pulled some papers from his briefcase while issuing another warning to Mendelson. "Forget about that *and* this bloody paperwork, Alex, just show an interest in what I'm saying and listen very carefully because you have a very important decision to make regarding your future, and we haven't a lot of time to discuss it."

Mendelson's head movement indicated that he understood. "It's like this, Alex," warned his visitor, "you were kind enough to give me a well-paid job when I was hard up. A job that I was very grateful for, but you owe me money, Alex, and it's money I need very badly right now, so I'm going to get you out of here and give you the chance to repay me. Plus maybe a little extra for helping you escape. I need to take off for foreign lands and leave my past behind, it's the only way I can survive so you need to listen-up and pay attention." He waited for Mendelson's reaction and was satisfied with what he saw. "We haven't enough time for long drawn out explanations, Alex, but I'm about to offer you a chance to get out of this hateful place and in order to start the process you need to listen up and listen carefully. I am going to slip you a couple of tablets shortly, and you must swallow both tablets immediately after you have your evening meal tonight. Once you've taken them they will bring about a profound effect to your physical appearance, in fact they will cause you to display all the symptoms of suffering a heart attack."

He scrutinised Mendelson for a few seconds. "When the medics check your pulse, your blood pressure, and your other vitals, they too will believe you're suffering a heart attack and will rush you to the nearest hospital, which is a laid down procedure here at Rikers. These symptoms will last long enough for me to execute my plan while you're at the hospital. I have a highly positioned insider there who will arrange to transfer you to a private ambulance that will be waiting outside A&E the minute you get there."

He looked to Mendelson for a reaction and detected a slight hesitancy. "The rest of the plan is fairly straight forward, but you need to have complete faith and total commitment to make it work." He leaned back in his seat and waited for Mendelson to say something, which he was quick to do, although it wasn't what Hardwick expected. "How the hell did you manage to fake your own death?" he asked. Hardwick put a warning finger up to his lips. "We can discuss all that later, Alex, when I've succeeded in getting you away from this crap hole, this is not the time or place to do it. The only reason I'm helping you is to get the money you owe me, and you can't pay me off while you're locked up in this crap hole. I know you have money salted away and I need my share to make something of my life." He wriggled forward on his chair and placed his briefcase on the table. "You need to listen to what I say and do exactly what you're told if my plan is to work. In a couple of moments I'm going to come round to your side of the table on the pretence of getting your signature on some documents "While you pretend to go through the documents I will slip two tablets into your left hand. Now listen carefully, Alex, you must swallow both tablets together immediately after finishing your evening meal tonight, and it must be tonight. This will cause you to display all the symptoms

I've described; a condition that will last for at least an hour and a half and certainly long enough for you to be taken to the nearest hospital, which is a routine procedure for such emergencies here at Rikers. Do you understand everything I've said, Alex?"

Mendelson already looked like he was having a heart attack. "Are you serious about this bloody nonsense?" he asked, "are you asking me to pretend to have a heart attack so you can get me out of here?" Hardwick looked at his watch. "Time is running out, Alex, you need to do exactly what I've just told you to do if you want your freedom back, and I can assure you that this *will* work, and I can promise that absolutely no physical harm will come to you from ingesting the tablets. This is the only way I can organise your escape, otherwise you will spend the rest of your life behind bars without remission."

Mendelson looked like a lost soul. "How do I know these goddamned tablets won't give me a real heart attack?" Hardwick ignored him.

"That's hardly likely to get me my money, Alex, and I need it badly, plus maybe a little extra for my troubles, but my time is up in two minutes, so you need to make your mind up, freedom or a life behind bars, it's up to you now." He gave Mendelson a warning look. "I still have things to do to finalise this plan, so I need your answer right now, and remember, Alex, I'm still your security manager."

Mendelson closed his eyes, folded his arms, and leaned back in his chair, deep in thought. When he opened them again all he could see was freedom. "Okay, Joe, I know I can trust you. Let's get on with it." Hardwick pulled some documents from his briefcase and pretended to put them in order before passing them across the tables to Mendelson. Taking a pen from his pocket he moved round beside Mendelson, and he gave him the pen before pointing to where he should sign. By now he was bent down and peering over his shoulder, using the opportunity of their closeness to slip the tablets into his left hand. Having done what he planned to do he gathered up the documents and returned them to his briefcase and offering Mendelson a satisfied smile he shook hands with him again and knocked on the door to be let out.

Turning back one last time to face Mendelson he gave him a final reminder of his earlier warning. "Remember everything I told you, Alex."

He left the interview room feeling satisfied that everything had gone as planned, but his confidence took a speedy nose-dive when he saw how many observers were gathered at the viewing window. He tried to cover up this loss of confidence by making a joke. "If I'd known we had such an interested audience I would have jazzed things up a bit for your entertainment." Everybody around them seemed to know who he was, but Art didn't, and he decided to challenge him on his identity. "Who exactly are you?" he asked. Hardwick gave him an indignant look. "Haven't these people told you?" He waved at the small gathering of prison officers. "I'm James Bulford, Alexander Mendelson's legal advisor, although I'm not sure I can do much for him when he has already convinced himself he's getting a life sentence." Art looked him up and down and it wasn't very often he had to look up to another man, something he made note of. "Are you a member of staff at Mendelson and Ackerman's?" he asked.

Hardwick took a moment or two to think about what to say but when he replied it was accompanied by a broad grin.. "Thankfully no, and happily so since it doesn't look like he'll have a company much longer where he's going." There was something about the guys stance that didn't rest easy with Art whose only reason for being there was to see who was nominated to represent Mendelson in court, and he was intrigued to learn that Mendelson wasn't having someone from his own company to represent him. So why should he choose to go somewhere else at this late stage? Art didn't buy it; he had an uneasy feeling about the guy and needed time to delve into whatever it was that was bothering him. Time to look into Bulford's background. "I guess you're right," he agreed, not meaning a word of it, "but you'll need to go through the prosecutor's evidence if you're to defend your man properly, so I guess you might as well come back to base with us now and get it over with."

Hardwick hesitated noticeably allowing his antipathy to show, he'd been caught short and unprepared for what was being asked of him. "Tomorrow would suit me better," he suggested, "but who are you anyway?" Art introduced himself and continued to force the issue. "There won't be a tomorrow I'm afraid, you either check the evidence today or you go to court without the ammunition you need to defend your client. Your choice of course, although I don't see that there is a choice, not on such a critical issue." Hardwick felt trapped, if he refused their offer it was bound to raise their suspicions, leaving him with no other option but to capitulate. "I guess my other appointment will have to wait, and I'd be very grateful to take up your offer of a lift as I came here by taxi." He was dreading what he was being dragged into, but he knew he had to comply if he was to maintain his cover. Art sensed something about his general attitude that didn't fit. He couldn't put his finger on it, not right away, but something wasn't right about the guy, his general demeanour wasn't that of someone of a solicitor's exalted position. In fact he looked wound up tighter than a Swiss watch.

Delgado, who was quite close to Art, sensed his unease and knew his

Lieutenant well enough to spot the sudden change in his mood, and he rightly suspected, for no obvious reason, that his sudden mood change had to do with their new travelling companion. Art cut across his thoughts. "Come on, Marcus," he said, patting him on the shoulder," let's get back to base and help our friend here prepare to defend his client."

Delgado cocked a questioning eyebrow at him, but Art deliberately ignored it before turning on his heel to lead the way out through security to the car park.

Once outside Art asked his company to excuse him while he made a phone call and wandered some distance away so that he wouldn't be overheard. His call was to the reception sergeant back at the station house, and as soon as he picked up Art dived straight in. "Never mind the greeting Sergeant Sefton just listen up and do exactly what I tell you. I'll be back at base very shortly in company with a guy called Bulford. I want you to ask him for his identification documents when he books in and tell him they must be retained until he leaves the premises. You can explain it away as a new anti-terrorist regulation. Do not let me down on this, do you understand?" There was only a short pause. "Consider it done, Lieutenant." With his call ended he rushed back to the others who were already in the car an ready to go.

There was precious little conversation during their journey, mostly because Art was deep in thought pondering over Bulford's noticeable unease, while Delgado was likewise in deep thought wondering what was bugging his Lieutenant.

Hardwick didn't even ask why his documents were being retained, he just accepted it as part of the routine when the duty sergeant just shoved them into a safe behind his desk without even looking at them.

He just tailed along behind Art, while Delgado headed off to do other things. Art took his visitor to an interview room and left him there on the pretence of going to fetch the case file. But as he hurried along the corridor he bumped into Gina who had heard he was back and wanted to meet up, but when she got to him he seemed agitated and preoccupied. "What's getting up your nose, Art? I can see something's bothering you." Art waved her question aside. "Do me a favour, Gina, nip down to the duty sergeant and ask him for the documents belonging to Bulford." She gave him a puzzled look. "Who the hell is Bulford?" she asked. Art sighed heavily, but only because he was in such an all-fired hurry. "The guy is supposed to be a barrister representing Mendelson, but we need a closer look at him. I'm not sold on the idea that he's any sort of Attorney, he looks more like a nightclub bouncer to me, but be as quick as you can because I don't have a lot of time. You'll find me in with Marcus, and free yourself up because I'm going to need you." Gina sensed his urgency and hurried off.

When she caught up with him again he was in front of Delgado and in full flow. "Like I said when I came in, Marcus, there's something not right about this guy Bulford. I'm about to check his documentation and see what comes up. Maybe I'm on a bum steer but I'm going to do it anyway. It's too late in the game for any last minute hic-ups with this case." Delgado looked confused. "I'm not sure I understand what you're telling me, Art, but I can see you have a bee in your bonnet about something so deal with it and get back to me." Art turned away and grabbed Gina by the arm. "Let's go, honey, we have things to do, or should I say you have things to do." He hurried her off to her workstation where he pointed at her computer. "Boot that thing up and see what you can find out about the guy named on those documents and please be quick about it, I reckon we have ten minutes at most.

He sat down facing her, fearful that he was being over cautious and wasting everybody's time. He glanced down at his watch and when he looked up again he saw a strangely startled look on her face. "You must have a built in radar or something, Art, because that person downstairs is definitely not the person named on this passport." Art leapt from his seat.. "So who the hell is he then?" She swivelled round in her chair to face him. "I haven't a bloody clue, but he definitely isn't Bulford." Art raised both eyebrows. "You had better explain, sweetheart."

Gina got up and faced him. "The man he's pretending to be is at this very moment in time attending a hearing in London's Crown Court on behalf of a client." Art grabbed her desk phone and dialled the custody sergeant's number. "Get a couple of uniforms down to the interview room where our visitor is and place him under immediate arrest. I'll deal with the charges when I get there." Having finished his call he thought things through for a moment or two before explaining himself. "There aren't many men that I have to physically look up to, but I almost got a bloody crick in my neck looking at this guy. He really is very tall, so who have we linked to this case who is that tall?"

Gina shook her head. "Your guess is as good as mine, lover. Maybe Hardwick but he's dead" Art grabbed her hand and dragged her along with him. "We need to visit the tech department, so bring that passport with you, there's more work to be done." She pulled back a little. "What the hell are we going there for?" she asked. "Wait and see, Gina, wait and see."

It took another five minutes to get everything lined up and running, but as they watched the security camera video from the Hertz stall at

JFK airport Art suddenly pressed the pause button. "Can you send a copy of the guys in that picture to Gina's computer?" The technician shrugged. "No Problem, it should only take a few seconds."

Two minutes later they were back at Gina's workstation. "What exactly am I meant to be doing?" she asked. Art was grinning like a Cheshire cat. "You need to scan a copy of our visitor's passport photo, then enlarge it and give it thick a beard. Can you do that for me?" Gina gave a little girlish giggle. "You know me better than to ask a silly question like that." Art patted her on the shoulder "Go to it, sweetheart, amaze me, but do it quickly." He turned away, praying he was right, everything up to now told him he was, but he needed confirmation.

After a few minutes Gina suddenly gave a loud gasp. "Isn't that one of the suspects for our first two murders, or am I going nuts?" Art looked at the enlarged image on her screen. "Yes it is, it's none other than Joe Hardwick and guess what, the crafty bastard has come back from the dead."

Gina looked at him like he'd gone mad. "How on earth can that be, and how the hell did you ever begin to figure out he was a fraud?"

Art folded his arms and gave her a knowing smirk. "When I first set eyes on him up at Rikers his general demeanour raised my suspicions, he just didn't look confident enough to be an attorney, those guys are always cocky as hell and over-confident. Then there was the matter of his unusually broad forehead, I don't know if you noticed it, but I was certain I had seen it somewhere before at some stage during our investigation, and when I took his height into consideration I became even more suspicious. Some people in this organisation accuse me of jumping to conclusions too readily, but I'm glad I do. Let's go and interview our feckless fraudster and find out exactly what he was up to with Mendelson." He suddenly stopped in his tracks and turned back to Gina. "You don't think that idiot is crazy enough to try and break Mendelson out of Rikers do you?"

Gina shook her head. "Desperate people do desperate things in a crisis, Art, and I would say Mendelson is suffering from a serious crisis right now." Art grabbed her by the hand. "Let's go find and out."

42

The first thing Art noticed about Hardwick was how really tall and overpowering he was, more so with Art being sat down and having to crick his neck to engage with him, but he got straight to the point anyway. "Take a seat, Mister Hardwick, and listen up." He stared straight into Hardwick's eyes without blinking. "Yes, we do know who you are, and we have irrefutable evidence of your complicity in at least three murders, two here in Manhattan and one mocked up murder at Heathrow airport in London. But before I deal with all that I want to know why you risked your freedom by coming all the way over here from London to have a chin-wag with your former boss? What the hell was so important about that little chat for you to risk your freedom posing as his attorney?"

Hardwick gave him a look of concentrated intensity. "I didn't expect to be recognised quite so easily without my beard, but I guess I must have done something wrong to get caught like this."

Art folded his arms and sighed tiredly. "Answer the dammed question, Hardwick, why was it so important for you to have a chin wag with Mendelson?"

Hardwick crossed his legs and glanced at his wristwatch before leaning back in his chair. "Okay you've got me with no way out, but Mendelson completely ruined whatever life I have left by getting me involved in his shabby deal. My life is over because of him., and I know it. I'm going down for a long time with no likelihood of parole, so everything is finished for me, my life is over. I have nowhere to go and no money to go with. You see when you're my size and build it's hard to hide away from public scrutiny." He sighed and let his shoulders droop in resignation. "I know I can't hide away forever, so what else is there for me to do? I've got nothing to live for apart from my revenge on Mendelson for ruining my life."

Art gave Gina an enquiring look, but she looked every bit as puzzled as he was, so he turned back to Hardwick. "You don't really believe you can make him pay for messing up your life when we have him safely locked away, how the hell is that going to work?" Hardwick glanced down at his watch again and smiled for the first time. "He has already paid in full, believe me." Art was even more puzzled by this remark. "What the hell does that mean?" he asked. Hardwick folded his arms over his burly chest and gave a quite nasty little chuckle. "Mendelson was about to throw me to the wolves when I faked my own death and believe me that little cover-up took a lot of organising and cost me plenty, but he never realised it wasn't me who had his head blown off, even though he was the one who identified me, but he did that by identifying my possessions, my watch, my ring, my passport, my car and all the personal documentation that the dead man had in his possession."

He stopped briefly to gather his thoughts "Once it sunk in that I couldn't escape capture I decided the only thing left for me was to make him pay for ruining my life."

Art leaned across the desk to get closer to Hardwick. "I'm still waiting for you to tell me how the hell you think you can make him pay when he's going down for life behind bars?" Hardwick eased his shirt cuff back and looked at his watch again. "It has already been done, Lieutenant, and there's nothing you or anyone else can do about it now."

There was a stunned silence in the room as both detectives struggled to understand what he meant. "What has already been done, Hardwick?" demanded Art. Hardwick spread his arms submissively and shrugged his heavy shoulders, then he leaned back in his chair with a dead-pan look on his face. "Mendelson is already dead" He checked his watch one more time. "He died immediately after his evening meal which would have finished about an hour ago." A stunned silence fell over the room before Art jerked back to life and pulled out his phone. He ran through his list of contacts and hit the dial button.

"Captain Murdock here, please state your name and the purpose of your call?" Art shook his head at the long, formal greeting. "It's Lieutenant Gardiner from the NYPD, Captain Murdock. I have cause to ask that you check on the well-being of one of your inmates, a guy by the name of Mendelson, Alexander Mendelson. I need someone to check on him right away." A lengthy pause followed before Murdock responded. "Exactly why are you asking about this inmate, Lieutenant?" Art became even more frustrated and raised his voice. "Because he may be in physical danger, that's why." He snapped. "Well I'm afraid you're a bit late with your concerns, Lieutenant. Mendelson dropped dead on his way back to his cell this evening after his evening meal."

There was a much longer pause this time before anyone said anything else. "We did everything we could to revive him, but it was all over in a matter of minutes, he died before the paramedics got to him." Art slammed his phone down on the desk and glared at Hardwick. "How?" he asked, "how the fuck did you manage to murder Mendelson?"

Hardwick just yawned and stretched out like he hadn't a care in the world. "I've had my revenge, I spoofed him into thinking I was arranging his escape so he could pay what he owed me. I gave him a couple of tablets and told him to take them with his evening meal and convinced him they would bring about all the symptoms of heart attack without actually causing him any harm and he would be rushed to the nearest hospital, since is the laid down procedure at Rikers these days. I even convinced him I had a plan in place for his escape from the hospital and told him I had an insider there who would help me carry it out. Once he committed himself to the plan there was no way back. The minute after he swallowed those tablets he was done for, there was nothing anyone could do to save him." Art was lost for words, so it was Gina who rounded on Hardwick. "That makes it four murders now," she said accusingly, "you must be feeling well pleased with yourself."

Hardwick had his serious face on. "For revenge to be complete it must be all embracing. My revenge isn't just levied at Mendelson." He pointed a finger at Art and Gina, "It's for people like you as well." Gina jerked upright on her chair. "There is no way you're going to be murdering anyone around here, so you can forget that little fantasy." Hardwick smiled and focussed his attention to Art. "Revenge comes in many forms, Lieutenant. My revenge against you and your partner here," he pointed at Gina again, "is that you will live the rest of your miserable lives with my death on your conscience."

He yawned and put his hand up to his mouth and before Art or Gina could stop him he shoved two tablets into it and leaned back in his chair looking very calm and composed. "Don't bother rushing around like demented lunatics, Lieutenant, by the time anyone gets here it will all be over, two minutes from now I too will be dead. So I won't be standing in front of your miserable judge, nor will I spend a single day in your damned prison cell." He gave Art a mock salute. "Goodbye my friends I'm off to sleep and I won't be needing a morning call." He sounded very sad and retiring as he closed his eyes and lay back in his chair, ready and prepared to meet his chosen fate.

Art, who had already hit the panic button, shook his head in despair. "There'll be hell to pay for this." He was saying this as he scrambled to check Hardwick's pulse for the second time, but he shook his head at Gina before taking her by the hand and leading her from the room, but he left her well behind once they were outside and he bolted off to report the incident.

Delgado was pacing up and down like a caged bear when Art got to him, but he stopped dead in his tracks with his arms folded over his burly chest and turned to face him with a face as dark as thunder. "Don't say a bloody word, Art, I already know what happened, but how in the name of everything that's holy did a prisoner in our care, and in your presence I might add, manage to take his own life?" He looked like he was about to blow a gasket, while Art, the recipient of this verbal attack, had no plausible excuse to offer in his defence.

"No harm to you, Captain, but you might ask how the same thing happened to Mendelson at the Rikers facility while in *their* care." He shrugged and spread his arms in an act of submission. "It happened, Marcus, and there's absolutely nothing we can do to change it. Hardwick should have been searched at Riker's, but he wasn't, and the way things later transpired it was all totally unplanned and off the cuff due to time restraints. The whole thing only came about because I suspected him of not being the person he was pretending to be. I didn't recognise him as Hardwick right away, so I couldn't prove my concerns until we got back here and Gina worked her magic on the computer, but I knew he was no solicitor."

He raised his arms in the air in an admission of guilt. "Anyway, why are we getting all worked up about a low life like Hardwick committing suicide, the guy was thoughtful enough to save us taking him and Mendelson to court. Good riddance I say, I wish more of his kind would follow his lead. It would save the taxpayer a small fortune."

Delgado locked eyes with him. "Are you telling met Mendelson is dead as well?" He could hardly believe what he was hearing, it was too incredulous to even take in. "How the hell did he die?"

Art explained what had taken place and waited for the inevitable with Delgado pacing around like a caged animal. "If there are any serious come-backs from this they'll be heading your way, Art, not mine, you need to bear that in mind with your wedding so close." He dropped into his seat and shuffled his it forward a little. "Let's Park that ruckus for now and get back to more mundane things in life. We need to ask ourselves how all this carnage leaves us in terms of our investigation?" Art screwed his face up and took his time thinking the matter through before offering anything. "It means we have fewer court appearances to put up with, and that has to be welcomed. It also means we should update Inspector Stewart without delay. He needs to know that the guy they arrested for Hardwicks murder has lied through his teeth. The real sufferer in this whole fiasco, according to Hardwick's confession, was the unfortunate victim of that prearranged and callous murder." He shook his head with a weary sigh. "I don't envy Inspector Stewart his job with what he has ahead of him, Marcus, he doesn't know it yet, but we are about to hand him a load of very serious issues to deal with."

"Thank God it's their cock-up and not ours, because it's a monumental one and no mistake. It took some planning to set up a sham like that and bluff the officials into thinking the dead man was someone else. It will raise a number of serious questions for their forensic team, and their coroner as well, although neither of them may have made a judgement on it yet, those things don't happen overnight, as we both know. And issues like this are always mush more difficult to deal with in retrospect, but the London pathologist has certainly dived in at the deep end by naming Hardwick as the victim on the sole evidence of his personal belongings and a bloody flight ticket." He clasped his hands on top of his head and swayed backwards and forwards before going on. "I wish to hell I had stayed in bed this morning."

Art could think of nothing to placate him, but he still had a point to make. "It looks like Ian has his work cut out and no mistake. I just hope we don't get dragged into their investigation and end up getting called to give evidence."

Delgado waved the comment aside. "I don't see it happening, so let's not worry about it until it does. I'm certain they can resolve the matter without needing us." Art had already moved on. "Are we going ahead with our own case as planned?" he asked. Marcus gave him a surly look. "Of course we are," he seemed shocked to have been asked, "I want Silverman and Sharpe through the courts and behind bars without delay, this bloody case needs putting to bed and locked away before somebody else snuffs it. In any event, the sun must be shining out of your ass because your side of things is all wrapped up now that Mendelson and Hardwick have saved you court time." He gave Art a questioning look. "Would I be right in thinking you'll be taking time off now is all but over?"

The worried expression slipped away from Art's face to be replaced by a big grin. "Between you, me, and these four walls, Marcus, I'm hoping to confirm my commitment to Gina by getting married just as soon as

I can afford the time off to do it, not to mention finding enough money to do it." Delgado leapt from his seat and did a little foot tapping jig behind his desk. "Party time at last," he yelled, "and about bloody time too!" He was suddenly hit by an idea that caused him to be more serious. "Why don't you and Gina hold off on your celebration for a couple of days until we have everyone through the courts. I'm planning a bit of a shindig to celebrate wrapping the case up and it will save you having to put your hand in your pocket for a separate party when we can make it a double celebrations. There's no law to stop you having the reception before the main event if there?" Art raised his eyebrows in surprise. "That's a very generous offer, Marcus, I'll talk it over with Gina and see what she says.

She hasn't made mentioned of it yet, but I've caught her browsing through some very expensive wedding magazines. But buying her engagement ring knocked a big hole in my bank balance so it looks like I'm heading for a few years in debt to put that other ring on her finger."

His boss gave a rib tickling laugh. "That's your problem, lover boy, not mine. I've been there, done it, bought the tea shirt and even survived long enough to talk about it, but don't forget we're in court tomorrow with Silverman and Sharpe, apart from giving your evidence your free to take some time off as soon as that pair of misfits are sent down." Art gave him a thumbs-up and left the room smiling from ear to ear, but with serious thoughts rattling around inside his head over the likely cost of his forthcoming wedding. He didn't have a clue what that would be, so he decided to have a sit down with Gina and work out some sort of guesstimate, something accurate enough to take to his bank manager.

43

There was a lot more chat over dinner than there had been the last time Claire had stayed with Gina and Art, but of course the situation was completely different this time around with Claire no longer a suspect and free to discuss everything and anything that came up quite openly, including her inheritance.

"What do you plan to do with all this money and responsibility that's coming your way, Claire?" asked Gina. Claire pursed her lips and tweaked the end of her nose. "To be honest, Gina, I haven't a clue. I haven't really taken it all in yet, it's much too enormous for me comprehend right now. One thing I do know is that I haven't the experience required to be involved in any business capacity with such a huge organisation. I'll have to take proper advice on where I go from here. What I will probably do is sell up and get out."

Art topped up their wine glasses before breaking into the conversation. "Whatever you decide to do, Claire, you can take it for granted that you will never have to face another financial problem, you will be financially sound for the rest of your life."

Claire smiled and added a little pleasing giggle. "While you were having your meeting this afternoon I got in touch with Jack Benson who reckons there's hell to pay at Mendelson and Ackerman's. The Solicitors Regulatory Authority have moved in to investigate the company following Mendelson's arrest and the Financial Conducts Authority are also taking an interest since shares in the Silverman group have taken a hit because no one has been appointed to replace the Chairman yet. Of more importance, for me anyway, he has confirmed that I have been legally asserted by those in a position to do so as the rightful claimant to Ben's legacy and that everything will be made public within the next few days." She hunched her shoulders and shook her head in wonderment. "If what Jack says is true then I will find out exactly what Ben has left me very soon."

She finger tipped her forehead in a thoughtful manner before going on. "If I'm completely honest, the thought of what lies ahead scares the hell out of me. I'm not cut out to be an active participant in such a huge corporation, that's in no one's interest, least of all my own." She suddenly got up and raised her glass in the air.

"Let's change the subject, I'm lifting this glass in honour of your forthcoming wedding, since it's unlikely I'll be here to see it. I have a feeling I might be a bit busy for a while, but I hope you have a long and happy life together." She was about to sit down again when she remembered something else. "I almost forgot; I have a flight booked to go and see my solicitor early tomorrow morning to catch up with everything." She gave another little giggle. "You'll be pleased to know that I won't be needing a lift this time as I have a taxi ordered. It's comforting to know that I might even be able to afford one this time." A little group giggle followed her remark before she moved on. "One thing Jack was adamant about that almost floored me is that I now have immediate access to the Silverman family wealth, although the corporate side of things is much more complicated and will take a lot longer to sort out. Ben's father held a lot of shares in various companies within the group that I have no wish to retain. Jack Benson has agreed to off-load them for me, although he has advised me to hold on to them for now until the share price stabilises. Then there are dividends to shareholders and company directors to be agreed, but that's an internal responsibility for the corporation to deal with and nothing to do with me."

She sat back in her chair and folded her arms contentedly before wrapping up her little summary. "You two need to know that as from mid-day tomorrow I will be a very rich woman, and according to Jack Benson I'm talking somewhere in the region of a billion pounds Sterling, and possibly even more. The tragedy of all this is that my boyfriend isn't here to claim his father's legacy for himself, or to share our future together as we'd been planning."

She buried her face in her hands as her tears filled her eyes. Gina rounded the table and wrapped her arms round her, holding her in a tight embrace until she stopped shaking. "We can't do anything about the past, Claire, and I know how much it hurts when you think of Ben, but you're young and healthy with a money free life ahead of you so you must learn to enjoy it as Ben wanted you to when he named you in his Will." Claire just shook her head in response, she was to overcome to say anything. Gina topped up her glass and went back to her seat.

"Do you intend going home to your family, Claire?" asked Art. She shrugged non-committedly. "Not right away, Art. I have things to do that will only bring me back here if I don't do them now. I need to speak with the owners of the property near where Ben and Sam were murdered and get their permission to put a plaque on the wall to commemorate their deaths. It's something I feel driven to do before going home. I think it's important that this city is made aware that Ben and Sam were dedicated to helping underprivileged children from everywhere and anywhere in this world." She stopped to think for a few moments. "But let's change the subject, what about you two, have you set a date for your wedding yet?"

Gina turned round in her seat to face Art. "Have we? she asked.

Art puffed his cheeks like he was blowing up a balloon, when he'd let all the air out again he looked like he'd been caught short. "We need to sit down and work everything out, Claire, but it will be very soon, if my bank manager treats me kindly." He grinned at the thought. Gina reached out and touched his cheek affectionately. "It doesn't have to be a big affair, lover. As long as we get married, and I get the ring on my finger I'll be the happiest girl alive."

Art put his arm round her and drew her close. Claire got to her feet. "Clearly you two have things to discuss so I'll make myself scarce and get off to bed, and there's no need for you to get up early to see me off. But I do want to thank you for everything you've done for me. I feel seriously indebted to both of you, and the rest of your squad of course. Things might have been so very different but for your persistence and intervention. I'll leave you with that thought and go and get some sleep." She bent over and kissed Gina on the cheek, then turned and gave Art a big hug before leaving the room. Art waited until he heard her going up the stairs before commenting. "Her departure is a bit different to the last time she went up those stairs, but it looks like we made somebody very happy, sweetheart, and what a change in lifestyle that young lady has ahead of her, and her family too I shouldn't wonder. She hasn't a financial care in the world now. I just hope to God she has the wit to handle what lies ahead and doesn't let it go to her head."

Gina had much the same thought in mind but was bit more positive with her assessment. "She's a mature young lady who knows her own mind, Art. She'll be fine. I'm sure of it, and I like what she has in mind with this plaque idea, I fully understand why it's important to her."

Art nodded in agreement. "Enough said, Gina, let's have one more for the road before hitting the hay." Gina topped his glass up. "I hope things quieten down over the next few days now this legacy case is wrapped up. I think we could all do with a break. Apart from that you and I need to sit down and talk about our wedding plans, and listen up, buddy, I don't want you getting into debt over it, I have a little money put aside that we can put to good use."

Art didn't comment, so she finished what was left of her drink. "Time to hit the bedroom, Art, so let's go, tomorrow's another day after all, and at least we have our investigation wrapped up and thank God it's behind us."

As she reached out to take his hand Gina noted from his expression that something was bothering him, but she was too tired to question it and just headed up to the bedroom with her man in tow.

44

Something dragged Art from his slumbers before he was ready to open his eyes, and it took him a little while to recall Claire's warning about her early flight, and another few moments before he realised it had to be her getting ready to leave that had dragged him from his slumbers. A quick glance at the bedside clock, and another at his sleeping partner, told him to stay where he was and let Claire get on with it, time enough to get up when she was gone.

Some ten minutes later, after hearing her taxi arrive and the front door open and close he decided a coffee wouldn't go amiss and crept quietly from the bed and headed for the kitchen.

He was on his second coffee when he spotted a white envelope propped up against the bread bin. On closer inspection he saw that it was addressed to Gina, so he put it back where it came from and finished his coffee before deciding to have a shower.

With his shower over he got dressed and went back to the kitchen where he encountered a bleary eyed Gina, who greeted him none to sweetly. "Why can't you just stay in bed and enjoy a lie-in like everyone else? There isn't any law that says you have to leap into action just because you're awake, you make me to act as a co-conspirator when you drag me from my slumbers as well. For God's sake, Art, why don't you just enjoy the comfort of a warm bed and contemplate nature like other normal men do?" Art gave a little chuckle, then he remembered the envelope. "Forget about that, sweetheart, there's an envelope over there with your name on it." He pointed in the direction of the bread bin. "Looks like our visitor has left you a little farewell love note." He enjoyed another little chuckle before dropping into a chair. "She seems to have come to terms with her new status rather quickly."

Gina reached for the envelope and ripped it open, and when she saw what was inside she dropped into a seat with a stunned look on her face. "Bloody hell, I don't believe this." she stammered.

"What don't you believe?" queried Art, confused by her shocked expression. Gina didn't answer right away, she was too engrossed in what she was looking at to respond, and Art's lack of patience soon got the better of him. "For God's sake, Gina, don't keep staring at the bloody thing read it to out for me."

Gina waved the contents of the envelope at him. "You won't believe what this is." She announced with a shake of her head. "What I have here is a cheque for fifty thousand dollars made out in my name that Claire wishes to donate to our wedding fund. I don't believe it, why on earth would she do such a thing when she hardly knows us."

She stared blankly at the kitchen wall while she tried to tried to come to terms with it. "I'd better check and see that else she has to say." She was too excited to stay seated and began pacing about while she read the rest of Claire's note and having read it through she slumped back into her chair and stared at it and the cheque in absolute amazement. "She's added a little foot note on the back telling me not to bank the cheque until tomorrow when the first of her inheritance money is transferred into her account. She also says we can have our honeymoon at any of the corporation's holiday resorts that we find suitable." Art snatched the papers from her hand and went walk-abouts just like she had, reading as he went. "According to what she says here," he muttered, more to himself than Gina, "she feels indebted to us for stopping others falsely claiming her inheritance." He scratched his head, looking every bit as confused as Gina. "We weren't the only ones working on the bloody case, what about all the background staff? Why single us out for special treatment?"

He dropped into his chair again. "It's a really generous and thoughtful offer, Gina, but we can't accept something like this. Gifts of this nature could easily be thought of as a bribe. I understand that she feels indebted to us after we secured her legacy for her and it's rewarding to know that she does, but something like this needs to be put before the powers that be to find out how we stand."

He shook his head solemnly. "I'm getting close to pension time, sweetheart, and I'm not putting my hard earned pension at risk over a fifty grand back-hander." Gina burst out laughing. "Don't blame me for you getting old, matey, that's down to your mum and dad getting off the mark too quickly."

They both ended up in fits of laughter, especially Art, who was laughing so hard his ribs hurt. After they had calmed down he got back to being serious. "Maybe we should donate Claire's money to the Police Benevolent Fund. If we can't have it that would be a nice donation to a very good cause." Gina had no intention of giving up on their wedding gift and wasted no time in letting him know. "It was gifted to you and me, Art, not the bloody Benevolent Fund and we should use it as Claire intended it to be used?"

Art shook his head. "Sorry, honey, but it's not your pension that needs safeguarding. I intend to take advice just in case somebody raises a red flag and makes an issue of it. Let's wait and see how things pan out, and if we get the all-clear I'll be more than delighted to give you the big wedding you deserve. Okay?"

Gina was fit to continue putting up an argument but thought better of it in the end. "Nothing I say is going to make any difference, is it? You're going to leave it up to Marcus to decide what happens to Claire's gift, so what point is there in arguing with you? Just do what you think best, Art and let's not fall out over it."

Art could hardly miss the disappointment in her voice and did his best to make amends. "Don't get into a mood over it please, Gina, if it makes a difference I'll phone Marcus at home right now and see what he says." He snatched up the phone and made the call before Gina could say anything.

Marcus didn't exactly sound pleased when he answered Art's call. "This had better be important for you to be phoning at this crazy hour, and at home too. I've already had two calls this morning before I've even had my bloody breakfast?"

Art winched at the thought. "I'm sorry for calling so early, Marcus, but I'm on a break as you know, and I need your advice about something." He took a deep breath before going into the detail. "Claire Mathews has decided to make a very large contribution to our forthcoming wedding, and I need to know where we stand with it." He heard a little chuckle at the other end. "How much of a contribution, Art?"

Art took another deep breath. "Fifty grand would you believe?" There was a lengthy pause before Marcus came back to him. "She must have that figure stuck in her head. I had a call from the duty Sergeant thirty minutes ago telling me that she called in at the Station House on her way to the airport and left a donation of fifty grand to the Benevolent Fund. What it must be like to be rich." He gave a little false cough. "So what has you all up-tight about it? Don't you like having money?

389

didn't you tell me you needed your bank manager to be very helpful for you to afford to get married?" He gave another little cough. "I know how your mind works, Art, but forget it. Take what's gifted to you in the spirit it was given and stop being so bloody pedantic about it. I don't want to hear any more about this, just give Gina what she deserves and think yourself lucky you can afford to do it properly now, but whatever you do, Art, don't buy any bloody steak burgers, we don't want another international investigation on our hands."

Art tried to laugh off his joke, but he was too stunned by his bosses reaction to do so. What Marcus had just told him was the last thing he'd expected to hear from him, but it left him delighted beyond expectation to get such an instant all clear from him. "What can I say, Marcus, but thank you, and I'll take your advice in the way it's meant. By the way, you know that Gina and I are off for a few days, but I intend to put our free time to very good use this time."

He ended the call without giving Marcus a chance to question him further, he wanted away before he changed his mind. Feeling on top of the world he turned to Gina who was sat behind him. "Do me a favour, Gina," he said quietly, "go upstairs and pack a weekend bag, I think we should get away from here for a few days." Gina was stunned by his suggestion. "Away where?" she asked.

Art grabbed her round the waist and spun her round in a tight little circle. "We're off to the quickest place I know where two people can get married. We're off to LA. Let's stop talking about getting married and go and get it done. What do you say, are you willing to take me up on it?" Gina didn't need to even think about it but added her five cents worth. "Why don't we go the whole hog and make it three days in LA?" She flung her arms around his neck, her mind in turmoil at the thought of going back into work as Detective Sergeant Gardiner.

The end

Printed in Great Britain
by Amazon